About The Grrrl of Limberlost

It's freezing cold in Seattle. A computer security expert, a traumatized prodigal son, and a server manager for a porn farm each learns that when you have to go home again, it's a dangerous, complex place. And your family of origin is a big part of the problem.

The Grrrl of Limberlost follows three self-absorbed voices through the frenzy and terror in their daily lives, mired in family losses and betrayals, while weaponized malware threatens to ruin Christmas. The mystery is: which voice is the unreliable narrator?

> "Cinematic. As chillingly pure as *Doctor Zhivago*. As heart-warming and hilarious as *Seven Samurai*."
> — Nicky Peterson, *American Business 101 as Cinéma Vérité*

Real People Are Saying ...

> "Annie Pearson's characters and story line in *The Grrrl of Limberlost* are contemporary to the mystery novel just as Dashiell Hammett's Nick and Nora Charles were in his day. Pearson captures the ethos of people caught in the electric speed and electronic maneuvering of our times, where a murder is just a click away and every double cross comes with a backup. Don't miss this one—it's your new world and it's shifting under your feet as we speak."
> — Don McQuinn, *The Moondark Saga*

By Annie Pearson

Rain City Incidents:
Artemis in the Desert
Nine Volt Heart
The Grrrl of Limberlost
The Pirate King

The Accidental Heretics Adventure Series:
(as E.A. Stewart)
The Blue Door
Bone-mend and Salt
Trebuchets in the Garden
Crux Lunata
Song of Valerós
The Mad Woman of La Catalane

www.anniepearson.com

The Grrrl
of Limberlost

ANNIE PEARSON

JŪGUM PRESS

For Martha Emily,
who explained how stories work.
No surrender!

Contents

One:
Seattle

1. Sam Refactors Reality, sans Caffeine

CHRISTMAS EVE MORN, AS I traversed the ice sheet cascading down Madrona Drive, a dark-eyed junco flittered up from my blind spot and bashed itself against my car window.

I accelerated, unable to help the poor creature as its heart pounded four hundred panicked beats in the minute it would take to die. Yet I could have prevented a pointless death, if only I'd seen what was coming.

My name is Samsara Ada Byron. I'm a programmer, a good one, fairly well-known in certain circles. However, the magnetic poles of my professional life swapped six months ago, spinning me back to Seattle, not to rusticate but to do new work. Life here is mostly peaceful. However, the universe perpetrates senseless violence such as the junco's death at unpredictable intervals; on Christmas Eve my little brother Pete tripped the lever.

After being incommunicado since September, Pete dropped in from Europe, taxiing to my house through last night's sleet storm, then staying in my kitchen only long enough to recharge his phone, video camera, and laptop before disappearing into the frozen Seattle night. But what's a girl to do? Given how we were jerked up together as children, I can't hold a grudge when Pete fails me. Still, I wish I'd been home drinking cold-brewed coffee over breakfast with Pete instead of driving to work in the early iced-over dawn. Hence, one could say Pete had a degree of responsibility for that junco.

Then bad news on the radio: Cliff Mass described the large cold air mass headed for the Puget Sound Conversion Zone, ready to dump record snow. I switched to KEXP. With my house south of the Convergence Zone, record snow wouldn't be my problem. If I left work early, I'd only have to cope with paranoid, incompetent Seattle drivers who freak at every dusting of snow and skid into your lane. Or into a ditch or a hedge or a Metro bus.

In the thin winter dawn's light, I grabbed my laptop bag from the passenger seat, skidded across the unsalted, unswept sidewalk (made worse by my Doc Martens, which couldn't get a grip after last night's sleet storm), and took my habitual place in line at Soul Meets Body Espresso, an indie coffee bar till lunch time, a last-choice South Lake Union café till ten p.m. Among the positive results from the shift in the tectonic plates of my professional reality, now that I'm back in the Pacific Northwest there's espresso to my liking. In this case, Caffé Vita.

The customer ahead of me departed, not giving me enough time to remember her name to say hello—it's something Dragon, I know, because she scares me. Natasha? Natalia? She manages the network where I work. Just as I nodded and half-voiced a greeting, it was my turn to order a triple-espresso.

"*¡Hola, Maria! ¿Que tal?*"

Maria the barista—the first person I speak to each day—waved good-morning. "*Estoy bien. Un momento, por favor,*" she called, just as my cell phone played Pete's call tone: *Return of the Grievous Angel.*

"A junco died because of you," I said instead of hello.

"Hey, Sister Sam. Your laptop ended up in my bag last night."

"Hell, Pete. Bring it back. Pronto."

The satchel that dangled from my shoulder now felt like an impending national catastrophe. I had some new pseudocode on my laptop that should be only in my hands, even though another copy was safely locked in the cloud. I ran a quick mental loop: I have a secure second-factor authentication mechanism for logging onto my laptop. In no way could anyone break the crypto without both the laptop and me coexisting in the same space-time continuum.

My new partner Quinn loomed over me. I'm tall, but Quinn is six-four, and with his long hair, drooping sad face, and perpetual faded black t-shirt, he makes you think of Uriah Heep (the hair-metal band, not the Dickens creep). He's Microsoft old money who left early and became an angel investor.

I twitched and murmured a greeting, then clutched the phone to my ear, so the bad news about straying code wouldn't leak out.

"I figured it out when I put my thumb on the fingerprint reader and it wouldn't turn on." Pete copped a plea of innocence, which ticked me off. "You gotta help. I need a video clip from my laptop. A man's life is at stake."

"Again? Come to my office, Pete. Now." My brother runs a video production business in which I've invested bongo bucks. While playing international man of mystery, he loses a laptop with works-in-progress at least once a year and always adds a statement about imminent jeopardy in the insurance claim.

That's my little brother: imminent jeopardy.

"C'mon, Sam. Just upload the most recent video file from my laptop to my website," Pete pleaded. I'm still clamping my phone to my skull so that Quinn can't hear. *Hi, Quinn, this is your security-genius partner who let her brother walk off with her laptop.*

"I'm at work, Pete."

"You don't have a real job any more. But in my case, a man might die. Or maybe a little girl."

"You will die if—"

The cell connection dropped, delivering dead air as a dividend for investing in my flakey brother. Reflected in the café window, my hair seemed to have absorbed the 220-volt shock that my laptop had wandered off with my brother.

"Hey, it's Samurai Sam at sunrise."

Alec, the totally metro attorney who worked with me on patent applications all last week, stepped into line in front of me. Yeah, "metro" is passé, but so is Alec. He leered as I jammed my phone into my pocket. Decades of practice had tattooed that smirk onto his fading pretty-boy face. He nudged my shoulder with his.

Eww. No touching at work. Or in an espresso bar.

"How are you." I inched away, not wanting to imply that I cared to hear an answer. Unlike the programmers I'm used to working with, Alec wears a tailored suit and an early-millennium metrosexual haircut, but he has reached his pull-by shelf date: guys that much older want to recapture what they've lost. However, a guy in a suit doesn't even know why he wants a math geek in black jeans—I got caught in that dilemma once before. They are organically unable to understand the inviolable rules for Friends With Benefits. Not that Alec has ever had the chance of Benefits.

I turned to Quinn. "I have the final algorithm for intrusion detection."

Quinn's ecstasy upon hearing that appeared as a slight twitch at the corners of his mouth. "What's left?"

"A round of verification passes, as we discussed."

"What are you doing for Christmas, Sam?" Alec asked, ignoring Quinn who, in fact, pays Alec's exorbitant fee.

"Nothing special." Just the usual: throttling my little brother.

"Joining your family on Limberlost Island?" Alec said, since he'd been digging at details in my personal life the whole last week we worked together.

"No, small-town life gives me hives."

"Join me for Christmas," Alec said, "so you aren't alone."

I fiddled with my three dollars for espresso. "When hell—"

Maria the barista stepped into the walk-in freezer for more coffee beans and began screaming.

I leaped over the counter, satchel and all, as Maria's shrieks rose to hyperventilating hysteria. Her hands flailed wildly, so I took firm hold, repeating her name over and over to distract her.

"C'mon, take a deep breath, Maria."

So Christmas Eve morning, I cradled Maria and murmured gently in her ear while bossing Quinn with a series of firm commands.

"Call 911."

Quinn fumbled with his phone. Alec disappeared the moment that he might be useful.

"Take my cell if yours doesn't work." I pulled it from my pocket awkwardly and tossed it his way. Gangly, geeky Quinn dropped the catch, chased the phone across the freezer, and then repeatedly punched the wrong buttons, while more heads poked through the doorway.

"Keep everyone out of here."

I shooshed while Maria cried. And, of all things, I'm telling my partner Quinn: "Put your head between your knees so you don't faint."

Ice crystals twinkled across the body that lay amid the crashed litter of soup-in-a-bag and raw French fries in the freezer. The man's blue-grey face screamed silently through its cellophane wrapper, complaining bitterly about his death.

2. Matt Calls His Attorney

"I'LL WAIT IF YOU think Karl might be free soon. Tell him it's Matt Owens."

I'd been trying for two days to speak with my new attorney in Seattle—new attorney, but old friend from college. Neither Karl nor I had time for a live meeting before next week when I was scheduled for a deposition in a set of lawsuits against my insurance company and others, so we needed to talk.

While I listened to indie music on hold—riffs by Karl's entertainment clients like Jason Taylor and Stoneway—the treads of the stairs in my parent's house creaked under running footsteps. Then pocket doors were thrown open downstairs, banging out everyone's happiness. The odor of Christmas baking drifted from the kitchen to hang like strands of fog in the boughs of the Douglas-fir tree in the living room, decorated by a child too young and too enthusiastic to apply taste to the chore. A log clunked as my father fed the wood stove, and my mother called for Pippi to set the table for breakfast.

I waited on hold, rehearsing the story I'm condemned to live.

I'm Matt Owens. I'm seeking new employment. I don't choose to accept a workers' comp judgment of total disability. I am still capable of an honest day's work. All I want is a fair chance.

Thousands of dollars of rehab and counseling amidst months of grief.

I'm Matt Owens, and I've returned from the city to the simple, quiet life of Limberlost Island. It's a natural evolution. The scenes of one's childhood can provide the foundation of a balanced, healthy life as an adult.

It comes down to psycho-babble: I believe I can shape a new life.

I'm Matt Owens, and I was in a freak accident that no one, even God, will claim responsibility for. No one wants to pay for more than the doctor, and no one involved either can or will admit what happened.

If I just learn to accept my limitations.

Today, I really am Matt Owens. I'm washed up and disabled at thirty, trying to be a good father while living at home with my own parents because I have nowhere else to go, lifting weights and playing guitar in my bedroom to keep from flipping out.

Blessedly, the line clicked.

"Hey, Matt. It's me," Karl said. "I have time to talk now before shutting down for the weekend."

"Hope I'm not interfering with your holiday."

Karl laughed as if I meant to be funny. "My wife doesn't celebrate this one. Which leaves me with a little peace for cleaning up around this place. For that matter you called about, I drew up a list of what they'll probably ask in the deposition. Do you want me to fax or email to it you?"

"I don't have email or a fax machine here," I said. In fact, we didn't have anything that one becomes used to in the city. The house didn't even have cable or satellite TV.

"Hmm. I want to review possible questions before your deposition."

"Come on, Karl. Why? I have nothing to hide. I'll just tell the truth."

"It can be confusing when attorneys start in on you. Especially when their position is adversarial."

Irritated by his condescension, I said, "I've done this many times before. And I had two marriages end badly. I am overly familiar with hostile lawyers."

Karl said, "Humor me, OK? The important point is not to volunteer more than is asked. Here's the first query: 'Can you tell me your name, occupation, and address?'"

I recited what I'd said in the last deposition, since it was a three-way lawsuit. Everyone asks the same questions. "My name is Matthew Leif Owens. I am presently unemployed. I currently live at 23541 Lost Point Road—"

"Stop! The question requires a yes or no answer. Do not volunteer additional information."

"Cripes, Karl, this is stupid. They already know my name."

"As your attorney, I advise you to learn good habits."

"I already know how to do this."

"Then let me help you remember habits that you haven't practiced for a while. Here's a probable line of inquiry about that tape. 'Please describe the transcript that was provided earlier for your inspection.'"

Cripes, I hated going over this crap. Yet there was no way to avoid it. No one knew how this transcript had managed to fall into an opposing attorney's hands, but it was out there now and had to be dealt with. "It represents a telephone conversation taped from my late wife's residential phone line. We agreed to this tap because of another legal matter I am involved in."

"For crissakes, Matt. How did you make it through college with shit for brains? You volunteered information, so now the other attorney can go fishing with the bait you hung on his hook. Please just read the transcript and explain what was said."

"Right, I knew that." I had the transcript with me, in the expanding file that now overflowed with the paper output from my ongoing nightmare. "Speaker One says, 'Hello.' My voice is Speaker One. Speaker Two says, 'We know where you are.'"

I've read the words typed on cold white paper a dozen times. Yet I still hear that voice and feel my spine freeze again. I took a breath and rushed into it. "Speaker One says, 'Who is this please? I believe you have a wrong number.' Speaker Two says, 'Don't fuck with us. We know you and your friend were in it together. We're coming for you.'"

I pretended to smother a sneeze in order to stop stuttering, and then I tried to read again.

3. Sam and the Eternal Cycle

"YOU'RE THAT HACKER THE FBI brought into our training in Virginia."

The City of Seattle detective seemed surprised. I took the card he forgot to finish handing me.

"Anti-hacker," I said, correcting him reflexively. "Is it the Clash t-shirt that reminded you?"

"It's Samantha, right?" He motioned for me to take a seat at one of the café tables where he and his partners were interviewing people. "You were amazing that day."

"Samsara Ada Byron. But I'm called Sam."

"Hippie parents?"

I nodded. "It's Sanskrit: the eternal cycle of birth, suffering, death, and rebirth." The product was originally code-named Samuel, but the shipping version proved to be XX rather than XY, and my dharma-bum father won in the last-minute renaming effort.

"They just tagged me 'Jeremiah' and tried to make me a vegetarian." The detective tapped his business card where I'd set it on the table before us. "Though it's because of their strong values that I chose this job. To give back to society."

"Because of how I was raised—" I paused to think of a nice way to describe the Byronic melodrama that is my family. "I prefer the orderly world of mathematics. My job allows me to do good in an otherwise disordered world."

"You did well here, Ms. Byron." Jeremiah opened his notebook. "You're a first responder? The vibe in Virginia was computer nerd."

"I'm both." The EMTs and police crew plodded through their tasks behind us. "At my last job, they nominated me to train, because body fluids don't bother me much. Before this, I've only helped at traffic accidents."

"It's empathy and presence of mind that make a good responder." The detective clicked his pen. He had beautiful green eyes, great hips, and a wedding ring that he twisted while watching the scene around us. "I didn't think of computer programmers as civic protectors until that training session."

"Yeah, I'm a civil engineer, building the digital walls to keep out hackers and thieves."

"They told us at Quantico that your team—"

"—flushed some wicked intruders from their cyberlairs." I pretended to be casual about the "Lights Out in Estonia" win for our side. Truth is, my whole team—my old Z-Crypto team—was stoked when the feebs and the NSA gave us a plaque and a white-tablecloth lunch with a video appearance by the leader of the free world. "Most hackers aren't terrorists. Most are only village vandals."

"I usually see vandals instead of what's in that freezer. Will you answer some questions, Miss Bryon? It is 'miss,' isn't it?"

"Oh yeah."

I'm back in Seattle because I refused the sole offer ever tendered to interrupt my single life. After the detective took my vitals—address, et cetera—I told the story quickly, ending with, "Voilà, naked dead guy."

Then Detective Jeremiah took me back over it again, digging for what else I might have noticed. This felt like a method from police procedurals on TV: keep asking in hopes of different, better answers.

"A stack of frozen muffins had fallen and knocked over a pallet. The poor guy must have been buried under all that for a while, because frost was scattered everywhere." I pictured what we'd seen in the freezer. "He was blue with gray hair. I assume he was killed."

"Yes?"

"Well, you wouldn't stick your head in a plastic bag, wrap duct tape around your neck, cover yourself in muffins and veggie burgers, and then lie down naked in a freezer to die." I blurted this, and then stopped myself. "Sorry. A blip in my first-responder serenity. Do you know who it is yet?"

"He didn't have a wallet on him," he said. I detected snark.

Then the detective launched into detailed questions: Who else was in the café? What did I know about how things function in the building? How long have I been coming here?

I held up my hand to stop the barrage of questions. "I've been here nearly every morning since July, and I'm happy to share my amazing powers of observation, if I could just have a cup of coffee."

I was dangerously under-dosed.

4. Matt Has to Say 'Yes' or 'No'

"MATT, ARE YOU STILL there, buddy?" Karl interrupted the silence.

"Yeah, just getting a frog out of my throat."

"Keep reading."

"Speaker One says, 'I believe you have the wrong number. In fairness, I must tell you that this call is being recorded.' Speaker Two says, 'Fuck you. I'll make you eat your own dick.'"

I faked composure, having been over this so many times.

"'Do you know the identity of Speaker Two?'" Karl asked.

Reciting the answer from the last time I was asked, I said, "At that time, I assumed it was a former associate in California. At the present time, I do not know who called. I don't believe that I understand anything that happened."

Karl sighed. "OK, ass-bite, you volunteered information again. If I were the other attorney, I'd now ask about all the shit you just laid on the table. So my next question will be, 'Who authorized that wiretap?'"

Feeling tension rising up my spine, I couldn't make myself breathe deeply enough to keep calm. "I didn't use the word 'wiretap.' I specifically said 'recorded' in the transcript."

"Back up a few questions. Remember you volunteered the word 'tap' when you described the transcript."

"Cripes, I must be getting old and slow. OK, start again with that one."

"'Who authorized that tap?'"

"I can't answer that question."

"'Why not?'"

I sucked in enough air to recite the standard answer. "It's in relation to a criminal matter in U.S. District Court. The case has been sealed, so I cannot provide details."

"'What are you allowed to say?'"

"Cripes, Karl."

"You're the asshole who brought it up. If I were the opposing attorney, I'd ask, 'What are you allowed to say?'"

"My band was playing at a private party. My business partner, our bass player, walked in on certain criminal activity and was killed. I was injured while attempting to protect him."

"OK, let's go to the next potential question on the list."

I muffled the phone to hide my relief as he shuffled papers.

"Let's see," Karl said. "'Do you know Peter Gawain Byron?'"

"Yes."

"Good. You're restricting your answers. Next question: 'Is Peter Byron the friend referred to in that transcript?'"

"I have no way of knowing who the caller referred to."

"Excellent answer. Now, 'Was Peter Byron involved in the situation where your business partner was killed?'"

Paralyzed, knowing not to give the five-thousand-word answer, I couldn't make my voice produce sound.

"For crissakes, Matt, you can't breathe hard on a yes-or-no question. Answer immediately."

"No."

"'Please describe your injuries from that situation.'"

"You already know, Karl."

"We are rehearsing for the deposition. Any reasonable attorney is going to probe your physical condition."

"I lost sight in one eye and received puncture wounds in my right lung. But I don't agree with the rest of what my medical record says, because—"

"You just don't know when to shut up, do you?" Karl said, but gently, as if he were offering counseling in a failed love affair.

I had no reason to be pissed with Karl, since he was right. I'd lost control in a single heartbeat, and this was only rehearsal. Glumly, I acknowledged my own stupidity.

Karl said, "So, pretending I'm this attorney who's going to eat your kidneys for lunch, I'll just ask, 'What else do your health records show in relation to that event?'"

"I was diagnosed with acute post-traumatic stress disorder."

In that pretend-Inquisitor voice, Karl said, "'Do you still suffer from that stress disorder?'"

"No."

"Very good, Matt. Nice, crisp answers. I think you're getting it."

"They said it wasn't my fault. They said there was nothing I could have done. But I could have—I should have—"

"Oh, for fuck sakes, Matt. Stop crying. Dammit, there's no crying at depositions. Look, I'm sorry I pushed you. There was no call for me to be such an asshole. Shit. Do you see now why we rehearse?"

5. Nicky Rocks in the Bosom of His Family

CHRISTMAS EVE MORNING, NICKY arose from bed still an innocent.

"*Dobri ranok, Nikolai.*" His Aunt Avrora touched his shoulder with her usual warm greeting. The kitchen lights burnished her auburn hair to gold. "Tomorrow's the day that every boy longs for."

"I'm not a boy, *Cho-cha Avrora.*" Nicky had given up trying to persuade her to call him by his American name.

"Ah, but you don't have a wife yet, so you are still a boy to me."

The holiest time of year in Aunt Avrora's icon-laden house began with Christmas Eve breakfast, when she laid the table with the first of the sweet braided breads, fresh from the oven that would burn all day in service to the coming feast. A Balkan chorus sang *Boh Predvichny* from the CD player, a touch too loud for easy conversation. *Kolyadky* carols would play throughout the house from now till Epiphany. The fairy lights strung around every doorway and window twinkled day and night. His aunt stopped to retie a gold-and-red bow on the door knob before returning to tend the poached eggs and toast.

Uncle Dymtrus looked up from his newspaper and murmured, "That's what you make money for, Nicky, to give it to a beautiful woman to spend for you. You need a good wife."

The soul-quashing Old World music played as Nicky sat down with everyone at breakfast, his laptop open while he blogged.

⏮ ◀ | ▶ ⏭

Nick's American Business 101 as Cinéma Vérité

Entry #25: The 90-Second Manager: Details – December 25, 08:00 PST

The last online lecture session focused on diligence. This session is about the importance of attention to detail. In this case, as you watch, it is clear that the customer became impatient about the details.

Click here for the video. And enter your comments. Your comments keep this site going, since this is a labor of love for me. Bring it on!

Update: You know I'm a student of Pete Byron's video style. His My Life as a Chisinau Dog [link] was nominated for the Indies. Hope my luck runs in his wake!

Nick's Fan Forum | Permanent Link | 10 comments

Nicky, my man!
BruceRulz | 12.20 - 11:03 pm |
Your work is finally seeming like real American business. When you were first doing this cinema verite biz and you used that Russian gangster persona, it put me off. But I like where this is going.

I liked the part where
ponyboy | Homepage | 12.20 - 11:06 pm |
Your bad-boy turned and smiled. The customer seemed to finally get it. He did a really good job with his part. I like how he screamed.

You need to change the lighting
AuteurGrrrl | Homepage | 12.20 - 11:07 pm |
plus the position for the web cam. Maybe use more backlighting. It came off more like an Eighties snuff film than cinema verite. Though your friend did a real good job pretending to scream when your partner held the cigarette to his nipples.

gosh nicky
JustMike | 12.21 - 5:08 am |
this might be over the top

It seemed more European than American
AuteurGrrrl | Homepage | 12.21 - 5:10 am |
Especially in that bit where your 'victim' friend pissed himself.

Nah

ponyboy | Homepage | 12.21 - 5:11 am |

what makes it solidly American is the duct tape and the peeing. It makes you laugh instead of feeling intimidated. Please don't cut that part.

How did you talk your friend

AuteurGrrrl | Homepage | 12.21 - 5:12 am |

into peeing his pants? Or was it just a stage gimmick?

Your friend forgot to fake it.

JustMike | 12.21 - 11:08 pm |

Hey, dude. Those passwords and usernames really work. I just tried one on Amazon, and it recommended The Terra-Cotta Dog, the Steve Earle Songbook, and a thing about mathematics and God's fingerprints. Tell your friend to block his numbers, dude.

I think

AuteurGrrrl | Homepage | 12.21 - 11:10 pm |

I've heard of The Terra-Cotta Dog. Isn't it about an autistic guy who kills dogs? Has anyone read it?

Not me, man.

ponyboy | Homepage | 12.21 – 11:14 pm |

I never read books. I'm too busy living life large on the world wide web.

⏮ ◀ | ▶ ⏭

"Did you check the servers this morning?" his uncle Dymtrus asked from behind the *Wall Street Journal*.

"Yes, *Vuiko Dymtrus*."

With a sigh, Nicky switched windows on the laptop screen, turning from his passion to his duty. In the past few months, he'd grown bored with the tasks for his family job. He longed to shift the detail work from his plate and had painstakingly trained other cousins in basic duties.

Dymtrus said, "It's one catastrophe or another and then money lost out of our pockets. You need to check at least every twelve hours. No one else has your touch, Nicky."

Accepting his uncle's praise (while unsure why anyone could fail at such simple tasks), Nicky clicked through the remote-access screens to see whether his cousins had performed the prescribed maintenance tasks on the servers.

A cousin banged open the door to the backyard, stepping out to smoke. As Aunt Avrora scolded about careless boys, Nicky felt the chill and looked out to the cold dawn. A good day for the grey cashmere with a silk shirt. Unfortunately, he'd have to wear a parka while outside. The icy wind blew the opposite of nostalgia through the room. Too much like former times and former worlds, best forgotten.

"The event logs are clean," Nicky said to Dymtrus. "Visitors are up twenty percent over last year."

"You have a good bonus coming, my boy. I promised life here would be good to you, didn't I? You have a better future than you had in California."

"Yes, *Vuiko*. With our new plan, even better next year."

He closed out the session with the remote servers, happy about the promise of the bonus, which he would use to advance his art. Then, thinking about the new business plan, and because he'd gotten into the habit of eavesdropping on his cousin Olekzandr's business, Nicky clicked the link that allowed him to remote into Zandr's laptop. Stupid Zandr asked for help to remove a virus, accepted Nicky's invitation for remote debugging, and then forgot all about it when Nicky made his computer happy again. Which left Nicky able to watch everything Zandr did—in slow motion: Zandr just couldn't get the hang of using his computer.

Zandr> I got my own ID to get inside where Nky works. Had to go for it myself coz he's got no guts

Kostya> does his hackery make money?

Zandr> close to zero dimes - so smart & dumb as a door

Kostya> just like his father - but you? this is to your taste?

Zandr> it's a poker game & i'm all in - didn't come this far to be left holding nothing - i don't care if we sell to chechnyan rebels or the transfuckistan President For Life. euros are euros.

Kostya> we give our customers the whole package tonite?

Zandr> yes i need out of the dickwad biznes w/ nicky fast

Kostya> these white knights - this is harder than you've done before, I think

Zandr> i'm not pissing my shortz over siberian tattoos, if that's what you mean

Kostya> they're not from gulag but similar style. yr cousin nicky is pants-pissing person?

Zandr> ROFLMAO

So innocence fell by the way early Christmas Eve morn when Nicky first learned that Zandr—his rolling-on-the-floor-laughing-my-ass-off cousin—and his uncle Konstantin conspired to hijack a new business opportunity that Nicky had scoped.

Nicky's plan was to adapt a new code acquisition for his uncle's server business, because they needed every possible edge to battle the thieves who took data without a valid credit card, most of them using tricks purchased from the White Knights of the New Russian Revolution and similar thugs with tribal value systems. Rich from a million credit card thefts and intercepted wire transfers. *"Our business is bleeding green to those thieves."* Uncle Dymtrus observed as much when Nicky showed him the data and the new business proposal. He'd shown his uncle how the White Knights didn't just compete for a share of the server business; they cut the legs out from every competitor—literally, in some cases. After shoring up their own businesses, Nicky planned to expand as a consultant: do the work once, reap payment repeatedly with minimal effort.

True enough, Nicky had gained the code assets through industrial espionage, but that's the way American business works, isn't it? Further, he had a better business model for distributing safe computing than others trying to come to market; he could be faster to market, offer wider and deeper coverage. It wasn't like he was out peddling malware or disrupting governments. However, since it's a hide-and-seek, finders-keepers game, he shouldn't be surprised that his thieving relatives planned to steal what he had found and sell it to their White Knight enemies.

Worse, Zandr and Konstantin considered him an idiot.

With mortification, Nicky acknowledged that he didn't have a strong backup plan. He'd prepared to adapt the code in order to advance the family's server commerce—strengthen the core business and expand into new online opportunities with a strong partner—using Zandr only as a go-between. How could he guess that simple-minded Zandr would try to mount a coup with Uncle Konstantin?

Men died. Nicky had seen it happen. And the stories about Konstantin and his own father—

Nicky needed a countermove. No one in the family beat Nicky at chess, even his own father, from whom he'd learned strategy. Patrolling Zandr's hard disk, since he was still discretely connected, Nicky deleted certain files as an early move on a new, more aggressive business plan.

"More coffee, Nikolai?"

Aunt Avrora breathed in his ear as she poured. The smell of potpourri from her sweater and the yeasty hot-bread odors overwhelmed him for a moment: he worked hard, and he deserved to be safe and to lay his head on a soft bosom, too. He glanced guiltily at his uncle. However, Dymtrus had been allowed butter by his wife that morning, so his attention lay elsewhere.

That's when Uncle Konstantin rang the front doorbell.

6. Sam and the Byronic Anti-hero

OK, IT'S DECEPTIVE TO represent myself as involved in an exciting mystery that involves a gruesome death.

A mystery story involves sin and redemption. This isn't a mystery: my Frequent Sinner card didn't earn any points for the body in the freezer, and I haven't earned enough points on my own, so I can't turn it in for redemption. I am, in fact, in the business of rendering evil harmless, but that blue body presented only a distracting side adventure.

When I left Z-Crypto, my former employer required a six-month cooling-off period before I could work on the same technologies again. Gone were the daily thrills of major cybersecurity investigations. Serving as an expert witness in court. Writing revolutionary security solutions. I'd built algorithms to find both sophisticated grifters and the idiots who post graffiti on websites or clone well-known viruses, and who then get caught after bragging about it on MyDumbFace.com.

So in my first month back in Seattle, for every report on Reuters or Reddit about a stolen government laptop or a major corporate firewall breach, I heard a five-alarm siren calling every able-bodied responder to the fire, while I stood in the Northwest silicon forest, begging someone to hand me a low-pressure digital garden hose.

From the start of this exile, I acknowledged that I made the choices that sent me back here. I chose to go solo instead of selling myself into another corporate entity, while retaining my mother wit, my security clearance, and (it is hoped) my professional reputation. I buckled down, alone, to work on a legendary security problem and, although I want to be modest, within a month I'd figured it out and was dancing with myself in my living room to celebrate when Quinn called me.

We'd met over the years at security conferences. Quinn had taken his billions earned earlier and built several decent new businesses. The one he cares most about is his white-hat security venture, which focuses on security practices in power utilities. The day he called, I not only intrigued the angel-investor in him, but he wanted to work on the project himself as an active developer. I found my best working partner, ever.

Together Quinn and I built an iron-clad intrusion-prevention solution for malware that hasn't yet been invented; hence, the last week's work with Alec, who wasn't the smartest patent attorney I ever worked with, but he took dictation well. I've done so much patent work in the past ten years, I was better at it than that paid attorney.

You don't want to know the silicon chip design details. Or the math. Or even the pseudocode. Here's the deal: the "Lights Out in Estonia" experience made me think about the legendary possibility that unknown chip errors exist in commonly used computers—errors that could be exploited by malicious hackers, for example. Following my insight into the (formerly) unknown chip errors, Quinn and I focused on the chips used on most power utilities' computers—many of which run software from Z-Crypto. Now we had both the error discovery and the fix for not-yet-invented-malware, for which I'd signed the patent application the day before.

Also, my cooling-off period ended December 1. In the meantime, our team replicated common utility-service computer configurations in Quinn's offices, and part of our testing was against intrusion attempts that government and corporate servers experience every day. We had both the usual and unusual items in the test plan. I love the names of some of these approaches: passive exploits, penetration testing, target brute forcing.

One thing I want to know: does Shur-locke (my old company's security software) identify whether real-world bad actors are attempting to exploit the chip error I'd uncovered? Quinn had arranged with the local hydropower utility that serves the islands and peninsula west of Seattle, so that we have the daily intrusion logs that record hackers' attempts to access the computers. We'd mapped a lot of our testing against these kinds of attempts. From this year's logs, most attempted intrusions are by kiddie vandals, who get nowhere through the security gates, but leave a sweet signature and Internet address trail that's sent to the feebs, who then knock on the kiddie's front door to ask if mommy and daddy know what's going on in their basement.

Anyway, in reference to the ice-blue guy at Soul Meets Body Espresso, I'm merely a spectator to random violence. I have bigger disasters to avert in my life as a digital first responder: the opportunity to prevent weaponized malware on an international scale.

§

By nine a.m. the detectives finished with us. I grabbed a third cup of coffee from the Starbucks up the block, and then punched autodial to call Pete again as I headed across the frozen street.

Pete's phone switched instantly to voicemail.

"Sam! Wait up."

Quinn nudged my shoulder awkwardly, in a different way than Alec had. I've worked for a decade in a universe populated with terminal slobs, mathematicians with affect disorders, and Battlestar Galactica v. Firefly freaks. When Quinn nudges me like that, it's just comradely guy stuff.

"Did you see how terrified that old man was?" His fingers clutched air at his side, a familiar nervous gesture. This guy in a trucking-teddy-bear Deadhead t-shirt was scratching alongside me toward a brilliant future; he writes genius code with those nervous hands. "I can still hear the barista screaming."

"Put it out of your mind, Quinn. It doesn't apply to us." I used my first-responder voice as I opened the door for him. After freezing on the street, we entered the warmth of the building in South Lake Union where he has offices.

I jerked to a stop so fast I almost dumped my coffee. Another invasive species flew up from my blind-spot, manifesting itself in the lobby.

My father, the Byronic anti-hero, his wild frizz of Einsteinian hair now more white than grey, his fringed leather jacket flittering as he waved hello.

"Samsara, my heart's song."

S

Huck wheezed asthmatically as he spoke my name.

"Hello, Huck. You're looking well," I said, as one does when greeting others. In fact he's an emaciated, post-psychedelic shaman wannabee. Years of self-medicating with drug-store inhalers and ephedra tea left him stooped and shaky. Though he looked better than former years, when there was too much Ecstasy in his daily vitamin mix, Huck didn't look his best.

Quinn hovered nearby. Trapped between them—and hating myself for still being embarrassed about my father this late in life—I did the socially right thing, like they teach in Remedial Human Relations for Mathematicians. I introduced them.

"Huck, this is my business partner, Quinn. This is my father, Huck—" I almost said *Byron* before I caught myself. "Aureliason."

Huck had once been Bill Byron (the name on my birth certificate), then Red Fern (the official name on Pete's), and Ganesh in his Rajneeshi days, before he took the name of that great fictional American. ("Huckleberry Hound," Pete says; but then, he would. Despite Huck's name on Pete's birth records, in truth we share only half of the same DNA.) Huck took a new surname last year, using his mother's name as an honorific after she died.

Quinn stuck out his hand in greeting. "It's a pleasure to meet you, sir. Merry Christmas."

Huck wheezed, "Peace be on you," and offered the patented Seventies hippie handshake while holding up his other hand in a blessing he probably learned from a set of Bodhisattva trading cards. Then Huck bobbed his head dolefully. Which meant that he was about to do what always works: yank my guilt chain. "While time remains in the illusion of this material world."

"What's wrong, Huck?" I asked with the first-responder gentleness I'd practiced all morning. Quinn, with more social sensibility than I possess, motioned that he was taking the elevator up with some of our testing team, not waiting for me. "I paid your hospital bill. Collections people won't pester you anymore. Do you need help paying for the meds?" I've tried for years to get him to choose inhaled steroids instead of arjuna, garlic, and ephedra tea.

"Other necessity causes me to take my ancient abode on Limberlost Island to the marketplace." Huck owned a fishing shack down the hill from my aunt's house on Puget Sound.

"Selling it?" I was mildly shocked.

My father called that house 'The Valhalla to which we will all one day return, like gods of old.' In spite of all his ridiculousness, and however much I resent that I've spent a lifetime taking care of the person who should take care of me, selling that house meant something huge and ominous.

He hunched up like a green-backed night-heron. "It's a wrenching break with the past. It's where I met your beloved mother."

Indeed, it's famous in family history: Huck buying that shack from the two Veda sisters and then sharing neighborly cups of coffee and nickel-bags of weed. And retreating to a commune on the Canadian border after my mother died in an accident.

Huck said, "Because of the role that house played in our mutual mythos, I wonder if you would purchase it, Samsara."

I closed my eyes, wishing I had Detective Jeremiah's inspirationally hip parents, not a mismatched grab-bag of relatives who can be relied on only to present problems. Big ones.

"What's wrong, Huck? You know I'll always pay your medical bills."

He dismissed that with a feeble wave, sending the leather fringe of his Neil Young jacket aflutter. "Breathlessness is a mere karmic limitation in my own spiritual evolution. Samsara, our family is in jeopardy."

"What's Pete done? Or is it Uncle Bob this time?"

"We had a small problem with our import-export transfer facilities. My business partners hold me responsible for lack of security."

Hear the sigh of all sighs in the universe? That was me. I did not want to know about Huck's import-export business. "Does your business insurance cover the loss?"

"Needs be, I must conclude sale of my house with speed." Huck took my hand and rubbed my lifeline. "There is no greater purpose in giving than the deepening of spiritual awaking." Huck lost his breath in such a long sentence.

"Your house might be more than I can afford," I said, knowing I'd have to make that be not true, and ignoring the mangled quote from *The Prophet*, which Pete and I had to choke down with our granola at our childhood commune home. "Limberlost isn't a repeat destination for me in the eternal cycle of life and rebirth."

"You say that now. But you're twenty-eight this year." He touched my forehead in a too-familiar way—to remove the mote from my third eye, he always said. "You don't know where your Saturn return might lead you."

"I'm a mathematician, Huck. My natal Saturn return—like the rest of astrology—is a crock." Also, because I'm a mathematician, I am capable of measuring how much water needed to be bailed out of his perpetually leaky karmic boat.

"Your heart is so hard," he said, sighing for thousandth time over the misdirection of my life. "If words would soften the callous, I'd beg you to care for more than the mire of this material plane."

I pressed my palm against my brow to keep my entire head from exploding, and caught the Dragon network admin woman sneaking glances at us from across the lobby. My guess: she saw a white-haired old man being spurned by his child—though Huck just looks eighty; the extra damage to his sixty-two-year-old body was all self-inflicted.

Behind him, out on the street, Uncle Bob waved at me through the window: shaved head and grizzled, in perpetual plaid flannels, and just as cheerfully unaware of reality as ever.

I said, "I'll do the math after the holidays to see if—"

Just then, a knot of Seattle police passed on the sidewalk outside, including my detective friend Jeremiah. Uncle Bob and Huck left at first sight of uniformed officers, disappearing like ectoplasm from the astral plane.

7. Matt Chops Wood

"MATT, COME HELP ME put my bike up on blocks," Harley called.

I'd been out in the yard chopping wood since breakfast. For the exercise. To have something do. To stand in the yard with a two-hundred-seventy degree view of anyone approaching.

I joined my dad in the garage, where he pulled the cover off his side-banger BMW, the motorcycle he rode for relaxation when he was county sheriff. Now, he seems relaxed every day. He wore the ratty sheepskin coat he keeps for cold garage work, which seems to be the same coat as in my dad's honeymoon photos, backpacking in the Oregon Cascades.

"Roslyn took out the battery when we stopped riding at Thanksgiving. But it's been below freezing all week, and now it's coming on cold as a witch's hiney." Harley chatted while he laid out the plank he wanted under the bike wheels. The white streaks in his beard and once-brown hair flashed under the rude fluorescent light. When did he grow old? Was I looking the other way? He incarnated a Viking god to me when I was a kid. Now, he looked—

"Help me with this, son."

I pushed with him, and we secured the bike in place. He could have done this single-handed. He didn't need my help.

"That'll do her," Harley said, wiping his hands over a job well done. This was such a sad excuse for getting me to drop the ax and act human, it made me want to weep.

"You should have done that before you went running off to California." Roslyn, my mother, had come up behind us. She's tall, raw-boned like a Viking's wife should be. To my thinking, my mother is as graceful and watchful as a cat—a Great Cat: a puma.

"You're still jealous that I was free to hit the highway and fetch Matt home." Harley grinned. He tossed me the edge of the bike cover, which I caught and collaborated with him to drape over the bike. "If you'd quit that fool job of yours, you'd be as free as the wind, too."

Roz stood in flannel shirt sleeves, the north wind ruffling her hair, tied back as usual, but long enough to be caught in the breeze. I looked for grey in the honey strands and found the same alarming change as with Harley.

"Someone has to be the adult here," Roz said, the same claim she'd made a thousand times in this life.

I cringed, even though I recognized this as their continuing banter: she should give up her social work job now that Harley had retired.

"You could spend four hours in your shop every third Thursday and earn enough for pin money," Harley said. My mother had a hobby making artsy concrete stepping stones that brought an interesting price at local high-end garden shops. "Or we could keep chickens."

"My mother kept chickens for her pin money," Roz said. "I grew up allergic to chicken shit. I'll just keep slaving for Limberlost County."

"You'll sing a different tune come spring, when Matt and me hit the highway, while you're stuck at the nine-to-five."

"Nobody's stuck here," Roslyn said, crossing her arms, which always implied a stern warning.

My dad wanted to josh me into good humor, but he'd crossed the unacknowledged line. He forgot to pretend that I'll be getting a job, too. Really soon now.

The phone rang when we walked into the house. At precisely nine o-clock, as it had the day before and each day before that. I leaped to answer it.

"Matt Owens," I said instead of hello, since there's nowhere left to hide, and expecting the usual heavy breathing.

"You think you're smart guy, Mr. Guitar Man?"

Having heard the growl before, I could discern the lighter sounds of a Ukrainian rather than Russian accent. Or maybe I imagined it.

"We have a visit soon, eh, smart boy? Without the attorneys?"

8. Nicky Knows Style

"Dobri ranok, dobri ranok."

Uncle Konstantin stood grinning at the door, his breath a puff of white in the sub-freezing chill as he said hello. Behind him on the street, his nephew Danilov pulled boxes and cases from a cab, and in a few brief moments, Aunt Avrora and Uncle Dymtrus were swamped with gifts and greetings. Boney, bald, and reeking of money, Uncle Konstantin flashed his ultra-white veneered-enamel grin and towered over Dymtrus, who looked more like a bushy haired Kiev shopkeeper.

The brothers hadn't spoken for ten years. Myths about why ran rampant among the cousins, many of whom lingered in the kitchen at that moment, unsure how to behave or what to think, their curiosity palpable. Whatever had happened in the past, Konstantin's sudden appearance and bounding goodwill, plus the iron-clad rules of hospitality, meant that he couldn't be turned away. Aunt Avrora hovered, offering fresh bread and coffee—*some eggs perhaps?*—even when Uncle Konstantin lit a Kool menthol in the kitchen. The cousins glanced at each other, since they'd be crucified, upside down like Saint Peter, for a similar offense.

"It's not that I'm pressing you to pay back a debt," Uncle Konstantin was saying. "You can do that anytime. This is an easy collection task for you, since it's up here in the bunghole of the universe you call home."

"Why not use Danilov?" Dymtrus asked.

Danilov looked up when Dymtrus spoke his name, but Uncle Konstantin didn't even glance his way. Danilov was Uncle Yevgeny's son, who all the other cousins called a fruitcake, though Nicky could care less about the gay thing, unlike the rest of their barbarous cousins. However, Danny was now in Seattle, which was

Nicky's town, where neither of them had to put up with the hierarchical beatings and petty feuds his other cousins perpetrated at Konstantin's family compound. Nicky looked over, seeking to make a connection with this cousin, but Danny was lost in the daydream where he usually seemed to lived.

"Nah, that won't work. I got Danilov busy on something private," Konstantin said. "And the problem I have is outside his expertise."

"I don't know," Dymtrus said. "I'd put Olekzandr on it, but he's got so much on his hands right now."

"Tell me about too much work," Konstantin growled. "I got such a shitsack full of troubles."

Nicky tried to get Danilov's attention, to make sure Danny understood that it was Nicky who held sway in Dymtrus's house. The family fruitcake wouldn't look at him, though. That nervous avoidance gave Nicky a small, unfamiliar thrill. To Uncle Konstantin, however, Nicky seemed invisible from the moment he opened the front door, so transparent that his uncle trod on Nicky's toes when he stepped into Aunt Avrora's powder room, cell phone in his hand, dialing with his thumb.

Things will be different one day.

That's what Nicky said once before, standing by the freshly heaped mound of his much-maligned father's tomb before casting aside the Old World and coming to America. That's what he was ready for now, standing on the edge of world-shifting changes. And Konstantin was old now.

Coming out of the bathroom, the commode still roaring behind him, Uncle Konstantin pulled his suit jacket closed and buttoned it.

Christian Dior, Nicky thought. From five years ago. The double-breasted style worked well with Konstantin's thin frame, but the dark grey didn't flatter his complexion. Navy blue would have been better.

The toffee-colored Bianchi shoulder holster held a Glock 17. Quite professional looking.

|◀◀ ◀ | ▶ ▶▶|

Aunt Avrora fussed, serving coffee and brandy, setting out coasters alongside plates of little Christmas cookies, flitting back and forth between Dymtrus and Konstantin, with Konstantin murmuring appreciation and compliments as a counterpoint to the *Kolyadky* ululations echoing in the background.

"What about Nicky here?" Uncle Konstantin said.

Uncle Dymtrus raised his brushy brows, which meant that he saw a way out of the corner Konstantin was pushing him into. "There may be something in that idea. Let's think on it."

A ringing cell called Dymtrus from the room, while Nicky stayed buried in work on his laptop, feeling his heart push an ocean of blood through his veins. Konstantin sat on the sofa beside him, his light frame sinking amid the overstuffed comfort of his aunt's living room. Nicky slammed his computer shut and smiled at his uncle.

"Zandr says you want to be an enforcer now that you're grown up." Konstantin's smoky voice rumbled in his throat. "You want to do big deals."

"That's not accurate," Nicky said. His heart thumped. "I help Uncle Dymtrus with his business in special ways. New ways. Zandr doesn't understand the technical details."

"Yeah, I hear you got a new business model here that uses computers." Konstantin's voice tumbled like gravel in a grinder, polished slightly from years of filter Kools with menthol. "Your father never had the gorm for real business. May God keep my brother's soul warm in His hands."

"I'm not like my father." Nicky picked up his coffee cup, wanting to hide behind it with the mention of his father.

"But you look like him. Or you used to. Zandr says you're smart."

Nicky looked into his coffee cup, feeling the heat rise in his face.

Konstantin said, "You want to come back to work for me, smart boy? Now that you're all grown up? I hear you got ambitions."

"I like it here. Dymtrus needs me."

"I'm sure Dymtrus needs all the help he can get." Konstantin smiled and cracked his knuckles, gold eye-tooth and iced-out rings gleaming. Old-fashioned flash, to Nicky's way of thinking. Then Konstantin pulled a cell phone from the inner pocket of his jacket and dangled it before Nicky. "Still, if you change your mind, you call me. Any time."

"Nicky can do this one collection for you. But he needs to finish his work for me this year," Dymtrus stood in the doorway, his voice growling like a bear's, "before he chooses another career. He has new server setups to tend to."

"And I prefer Seattle to California," Nicky said, wishing he could dissolve and reappear in a safer dimension.

"I'm sure." Konstantin lit another Kool and leaned back, his arm draped on the sofa, hovering over Nicky's neck.

9. Sam Explains Moral Accountability

OUTSIDE MY OFFICE WINDOW, the leaden sky was squeezing the dim December light out of the day. Juvenile cedar trees in the building's courtyard hunched under the weight of ice from the sleet storm. It would snow, snarling holiday traffic.

What I needed most was to bury myself in work, yet if I sat still for a moment, I saw that poor man's blue face and heard the echoes of Huck's anxiety—the first of which presented a problem that I could never solve, the second of which I couldn't solve until after Christmas. Intent on staying busy, I shut a mental door to the outside world and flipped on my brother's effing laptop. Crappy fingerprint reader for speed-bump-level security. No password. All of his files stored in the root of his C drive. What a slob. I clicked the video file with the most recent date in the directory.

And found myself watching our former next-door neighbor from Limberlost Island in an *Ocean's Two* movie: Matt Owens in a well-tailored tuxedo, his hair sleeked into a ponytail, sipped cocktails and talked business with a Slavic-looking, super-cosmopolitan Euro guy amid racks of network servers, computer wires hanging all around. Euro Boy gestured theatrically, pointing first to the rack of blade servers behind him and then at an old-fashioned computer monitor. The camera shifted to show the screen, which flickered when the camera and screen refresh timings clashed. It took me a moment to determine the nature of the show-and-tell report that made Matt laugh.

Oh geez. One of those capitalistic enterprises that had multiplied in the Ukraine and other former post-Soviet-bloc locations: a porn farm.

Our friend Matt looks like Tommy Lee Jones—you know, acne and no girls in high school; testosterone overload and hence plenty of women after college. In his tux, Matt laughed at unfunny explanations of business practices. I thought Matt had been into shady business since he left the army, but this was lower than low.

If I find out that Pete is involved with some porn master, instead of documenting the aftermath of war in Bosnia as he claimed, he'll be joining the blue gentleman in the morgue. Multitudes of those server farmers are self-taught hackers, expanding their incomes by thieving identities and whatever else they can find in cyberspace that isn't nailed down.

Just the kind of data mafia that I have spent years of my professional life pursuing.

I tried to log onto the network in Quinn's offices so I could post Pete's stupid video, but his laptop had a virus, so the network wouldn't allow access.

Slob is too good a word for Pete.

So I copied the video file to a thumb drive, virus checked that, copied it to his website, and then finished by cleaning up his laptop. Done with Pete's laundry and mail service, I logged on to my desktop machine to check messages, hoping for word from Pete.

Instead: fresh hell.

A message popped up from my favorite cyberstalker pen pal.

YrBlueHatLvr> Saw new Shur-locke beta. Saw Shur-locke fail on your legacy code.

I should block him from my messaging list. He claimed to be a bug-test security good guy by signing himself as a Blue Hat. He said he'd met me at a conference and fallen in love while I lectured the black hats (the law-breaking hackers) about joining the light side of the Force. He claimed that I look like a sk8ter's wet dream and that my passion had convinced him to reform. When he began stalking me in early November, I pinged his address—sending a **ping** command to trace the server he used. The computer address returned is always some no-name cybercafé in Singapore or Barcelona or Mazatlán.

From wherever Gerard, my former CEO lover, is currently visiting.

So I leave him on my message list but never let him provoke me into a response. He's amped up since I emerged from the Z-Crypto cooling-off period, always implying that I can't emerge from the Shur-locke refrigerator without freezer-burn scars on my reputation. My silence will make him give up faster than confrontation would. I bet he's done needing to provoke me before the coming New Year.

> YrBlueHatLvr> Who was the architect of this upgrade? Do you think Z-Crypto will fail without you!!!

§

Leaving Z-Crypto had been my own decision. When Gerard Fox, the CEO of Z-Crypto, decided to bury the business deep in the bosom of the military-industrial complex, my strong objections led to my exile. He wanted me to switch my focus, to work closely with the NSA on decoding the secrets that criminal and terrorist enterprises pass using Internet blog posts. That, and I wouldn't either marry or go to bed with Gerard anymore.

You could say that I had slept my way to the bottom. Truthfully, I'd been morally accountable at each decision point. Gerard was the technical marketing lead who did show-and-tell at sales meetings— so it was *not* a workplace affair as he was not a member of my team. No one at work knew, so we wouldn't cause people to take sides when it ended. He professed to understand the boundaries between us as Friends With Benefits—so we limited what we shared about our personal lives; for example, he never knew that my father grows medical marijuana in a commune on the Canadian border; I never knew that Gerard had close family ties to Jennifer, the original Z-Crypto founder and managing director of our closely-held company. The whole team went into shock when, in the midst of a series of seminars with M.I.T., Jennifer was killed while jaywalking on Memorial Drive, just off the Longfellow Bridge in Cambridge. The whole Z-Crypto crew emerged from mourning to learn that Gerard was her nephew and designated heir, intent on taking the company deeper into the national security complex, steering us in wholly new directions.

"You'll be back," Gerard said when I put my resignation on his desk. I'd gone to the trouble of printing it out, instead of just sending email.

I'd begun the mandated cooling-off period, designed to prevent me from competing with Z-Crypto, thinking that I'd be so cooled off by winter, my blood would thicken, like a frog hibernating beneath the frozen mud. Here it was December, and Alec had just filed patent papers that would cause my professional reputation to rise. Like a phoenix from the ashes, not a frog from the thawing pond.

Never mind that I was the original architect of the current Z-Crypto upgrade.

10. Nicky Drives the Car

"I'LL HAVE MY HANDS full all day today and then all night."

That's what Nicky told Dymtrus as he'd started out the door. His uncle insisted that Nicky get busy with Konstantin's collections.

"Please just do it. Get my ass out of that crack. Forget that new scheme that you and Zandr are hatching. It's Christmas. I need you on this night of all nights," Dymtrus said. "Everything needs to be ship-shape in our core business. There's more server traffic tonight than any other all year. Like there are more drunks on the road tonight."

This night of all nights, Nicky told himself, he would seize the new business back from his cousin Zandr. He held his shirt cuffs while he pulled on a North Face storm parka—the weather had turned as frigid as in his former homeland—regretting how difficult it is to look good in weather like this; he hated dressing down to the level of so many men seen on the streets of Seattle.

Yet even in a parka, style came easily to him. Nicky had polished his method and manners, seeking a cosmopolitan flair, though Avrora and his other aunts teased him, saying Cary Grant only mattered in the last century. However, watching a few of his older cousins—Krystiyan, Andrij, and Osip—who had found success in California, Nicky learned that it wasn't style or manners that mattered most. At the bottom line, power governed how other people responded to a man and bought the attentions of the right kind of woman. Working for his older cousins last year in

California, Nicky realized that it was power he craved. It's what he wanted in both his art and business.

With that clarity of purpose, Nicky stopped partying with his younger cousins and the hangers-on they called their posse. He attended social occasions with Uncle Dymtrus in the role of his uncle's lieutenant, solely for the purpose of making connections. Nicky always attracted women at such events, but they were husband seekers, and Nicky had no intention of marrying as part of his strategy. When he was ready for marriage, it would be like his uncle's and it would be a woman like his aunt Avrora: exotically beautiful and worshipping her husband, taking the privilege of bearing his children as a gift from God.

And tonight at the family gathering for Christmas Eve—

A cell rang in his coat pocket.

Puzzled, he reached in and found the phone that Konstantin had offered him, vibrating as well as ringing.

"Do you know the roads out here in the Wild West?" his uncle's menthol voice queried over the cell phone's crackle.

"A little. Do you need directions, *Vuiko*?"

Nicky clicked to unlock his car's door.

Konstantin sat in the passenger's seat smoking a cigarette, his camel-tan woolen coat draped around his shoulders. He snapped his phone shut and smiled at Nicky.

"I need a ride," Konstantin said. "Your cousin Danilov can't help me with this job I gotta do."

"I have to go to work," Nicky said.

Konstantin seemed not to hear Nicky's reply, which wasn't the first or last time he ignored Nicky's requests that day. "Do you know how to get to Limberlost Island, Nick my boy?"

⏮ ◀ | ▶ ⏭

"Your uncle Dymtrus doesn't understand how capital works," Konstantin said as they pulled away from the ferry landing in a rented Escalade.

Uncle Konstantin had talked constantly on the ferry ride over, when they went up to the galley to get coffee, while they sat in the padded seats in the lounge or the stiffer chairs at the bow, regardless of who might be nearby to overhear. In that stream of admonition and old stories (or tall tales), he scolded Nicky about the best ways to do business,

Leaving the ferry, Nicky drove slowly through Limberlost village (he had a fear of small towns in America that balance their civic budgets with speed traps, which he'd read about on a blog), while Konstantin harangued him over his choice to live in the wilds of the Northwest. In the commercial area outside the village, portable reader-board signs advertised horse feed, lumber, and slate flagstones. Unsold Christmas trees dropped their needles in a grocery store parking lot, where a cracked electric readerboard offered Xmas Tunkey w/ All Trimings. As Nicky pulled onto the main highway, 4x4 pickups with extended cabs passed, their truck beds filled variously with dogs, Christmas trees, and household appliances shrouded in blankets.

The road wrapped around the edge of the island, curving in and out around little bays on the Sound, outsized new mansions clinging above the water on one side of the highway, doublewide prefab homes dotting the hills on the other. As they turned onto Lost Point Road, Konstantin spoke of what he and Olekzandr intended to do, without prompting from Nicky.

"As I told Zandr, doing it my way, we gain ten times the profit as your idea." Konstantin spoke with his usual, immense self-assurance.

"Zandr doesn't have all the pieces." Nicky hoped he didn't sound like a beggar. "He doesn't know how it works."

"That's why I want you to join me." Konstantin clapped a hand on Nicky's shoulder. Like an eagle claw on its prey. Nicky clutched the steering wheel, taking a 35-mph curve too fast. "I'm thinking you can do a better job. I'm worried that Zandr can't deliver the package. But you're the kind of boy who could do a big thing."

Nicky let the compliment wash over him, smart enough to differentiate flattery from manipulation.

"Where are you selling this resource I discovered?" Nicky asked. He listened as Konstantin described the White Knights' beach-head: a nation-state near his former homeland. Dumbfucksylvania, as that beautiful woman at his office called it (which gave him pause; Nicky had a crush, felt he might be in love for the first time, but didn't like foul language in a woman's mouth).

"You'd be surprised where easy money is found these days." Uncle Konstantin changed the subject abruptly. "Zandr says you're an artist."

Nicky very much wanted to be elsewhere.

"You want to make movies, eh?" Konstantin pointed with his ring finger, the diamonds flashing, where he wanted Nicky to park the car. "Be a Hollywood big shot?"

"Documentaries. Not Hollywood." He couldn't say *auteur film*, because there's no way Konstantin would know what that was. Anyway, Nicky didn't want the family in that part of his life.

"I got a good friend who does that. Peter Byron. Have you heard of him?"

"I met him once." Nicky swallowed hard.

"Park right here," Konstantin said. He pointed to the path where he wanted Nicky to follow him. Though he couldn't get to the island without Nicky, his uncle seemed to know exactly where to go once he arrived. "I like to help my family. I talk to my friend, and I promise, he'll get you an agent. That's what you need, isn't it? To make money in that field?"

"Yes." Nicky felt he might choke if he said more.

"You put in with me, then. You got more brains than Zandr. I'm betting you got more balls than that fruit Danilov. Come on board. We'll go far."

"I made other promises."

"Yeah. You want to be a good guy. Just like your papa always did. I'll call my friend Peter and he'll make you a star with your movies."

"I would be grateful, *Vuiko Kostya*."

No, Nicky thought: *I'd be indebted. With astronomical interest rates.*

"That's what your cousin Andrij said when I sent him up here to do a job." Konstantin scowled, which always frightened the nephews. "Now we gotta traipse around the woods looking for him. Don't be grateful. Just do the right thing when everyone else screws up."

Konstantin didn't speak to Nicky again for half an hour while absorbed with the business for which he'd come to Limberlost.

"You want to hand me the tape?" Konstantin said at last. "You can at least help with that."

When they started back up the path to the car, Konstantin said, "One of the jobs I got right now is too big for Danilov to handle. Even though Zandr came to me for help on his commerce idea, I'm not sure I can trust him."

"Zandr already betrayed Dymtrus. And me."

"Yeah. And I got so much business on my hands right now. Too many frogs in the shit pond. Don't you want to help your old uncle?"

"If I can figure how to keep my other promises, too," Nicky said. He glanced back at the man below, sleeping peacefully with the angels.

That's how they'd found his father. Or so the story goes.

"What time is that ferry back?" Konstantin said. "I bet your Aunt Avrora lays a nice lunch."

Damn, Nicky needed to get to his day job before noon, and he needed to dump this rental and find another vehicle. One session with CCTV at the ferry dock had been one too many. Now it would be two.

11. Sam Tussles with Instant Messaging

QUINN HAS THE BEST, most thoroughly vetted test team in this part of the universe. Through most of that week, I'd held seminars with the testers, to both educate and focus their efforts on what we're trying to do. They took it seriously—one of the testers had even made a video script that they were using for reference. However, most of them came late and left early, or took the whole day as a holiday. It's a tradition in the Pacific Northwest computing scene: Christmas Eve doesn't count as a work day.

I put on headphones, skipped lunch, and burrowed in, starting the verification tests to validate my intrusion-detection solution, following the scripts the testers had been building, and then deviating into some manual testing. Mid-afternoon, I sent the network admin away, insisting that she could do the network upgrade over the New Year's holiday.

"What the fuck am I supposed to tell Quinn?" she said.

Natalia! Natalia Dragon. I remembered her whole name while thinking that I don't use the F word with people unless I'm on a first-name basis with them.

"Tell him that I wouldn't let you."

"I sent the memo last week, to say we'd do the upgrade over the holiday," she sulked. She's taller than me, and had broad Slavic features, though maybe what scares me is that she looks like she belongs in a Soviet-era Bond movie. Also, she doesn't like me. Though lots of people don't if they don't know me.

"Things changed," I said. "So now you have Christmas Eve off!"

Although she acted like it hurt her feelings to be stopped from dinking with the network, I was perfectly nice while insisting.

Then again, instant messaging was hurting my feelings. My bluehat friend was giving me a terminal rash.

YrBlueHatLvr> This looks to be a mighty FAIL for Z-Crypto. So glad you have nothing to do with this bomb.

I was blaspheming vociferously just as my pestering patent attorney pal, Alec, opened my door.

"Merry Christmas," he said, entering without knocking, reeking of YSL Live Jazz. I hate cologne, period, and in my mood, an attorney was not a pleasing sight, even though he carried two cups of coffee. "I told everyone you were a hero this morning."

After the past two intense weeks of work, Alec and I no longer needed to live armpit-to-armpit each day. However, Alec thought that meant we could get personal. In such cases, I always dash toward the superficial.

"Did the detectives interview you?" I asked.

"Yeah, sure. Come out with me tonight, Sam."

"We have to work together," I said, invoking the platinum rule. The rule I bent with Gerard.

Alec persisted. "I love how you talk with your hands. Those long fingers—it's damn hypnotic."

"Give me a break." Every time he comes near me, a sticky white-blues voice sings *my my my* in my head and I start thinking about the spider and the fly.

"We had fun when we went out last week," he said.

"Yes, I always wanted to know how to count cards at blackjack." Curiosity was the sole reason that I went with him to a casino featuring a Seventies tribute band. It wasn't even a date. *No more older men*, I told myself. And certainly not men that act like they're doing me a favor. When I need sex, I'm perfectly capable of asking for it.

"Spend more time with me." Alec touched my hand as he spoke, and I retracted it. No touching at work.

"My brother Pete is in town," I said, disliking that I didn't just say no. "We have plans."

"He's the documentary film guy, right? Bring him along. The more the merrier in my family."

"Not for us," I said. "We have our own traditions."

"Country Christmas on Puget Sound? With the snow coming, it will be charming. Take me with you." Alec beamed with reprehensible confidence.

"It will be just me and my brother."

Alas, having misappropriated my family as an excuse, I was inconvenienced by a statistically improbable coincidence. A message from Pete popped on my computer screen, right where Alec could read it.

Repete> can't come tonite. need yr help way bad.

Yelping like a wounded animal, I banged the keyboard to answer before Pete could escape.

Samlam> What's wrong?

For reasons well-grounded in history, I worried. I make fun of his "a man's life depends on it" claims, but then again, last year he was beaten and robbed while filming in Chechnya. The year before, I had to persuade the American consulate to help him get out of a small town in Croatia. As I tipped the screen so Alec couldn't read it, Pete messaged back.

Repete> need my laptop

Samlam> I posted your video. Come here if you want yr laptop.

Repete> can't. have bridges to burn & miles to go before i
sleep.

After two more failed messaging attempts, I accepted that Pete
had departed into the ozone. Which demonstrates how the vortex in
Pete's wake both sucks and blows.

Alec hummed, apparently pleased by what caused me pain. "So,
you're free tonight. What luck for me."

Except instant messaging proved to be the worst of the day's
bêtes noir, for instantly appeared:

YrBlueHatLvr> Here's the error dump where Shur-locke beta
breaks.

Then followed a report from the exact portion of code I had been
testing to verify whether Shur-locke could resist a hack against the
newly discovered chip flaw. I'd learned from my tests before noon
that Shur-locke did not prevent such an intrusion.

Worse, if my BlueHatLvr isn't Gerard, then the Shur-locke beta
break meant that someone, somewhere, was attempting the very
intrusion we're working to protect against.

So I broke my own rule. I responded to my stalker.

Samlam> Where is this beta installation? Who's the security
director?

I poked Quinn—instant message, email, phone text, buzzing his
office phone. His email autoreply: *Beginning OOF early. Back Dec
28.* OOF is "out of office," which meant he'd departed to ski at
Whistler, so OOF really meant "out of country." Then I tapped
another message to BlueHatLvr. The Internet echoed back only
inhumane silence.

"I'll pick you up at eight," Alec said.

Distracted, I said. "Bye, Alec. I'm seriously busy. See you after
the holidays." But not if I can help it.

What I did see was a security hole in Z-Crypto code big enough
to drive a Metro bus through. A hole big enough, you'd think I'd
planned many months ago to open that hole myself.

12. Nicky Makes a Move

NICKY STEPPED OUT of his own car in the parking lot. The annoying cold flooded his mind with memories of home: icy, soul-sucking concrete walk-up flats where root vegetables and mutton of dubious origins bubbled on a hotplate. He shook his head to empty those images, doing a fast frame shift to focus on the reality around him: corporate landscaping, Accords, Jettas, and Lexus SUVs neatly aligned amid the gridlines in the parking lot, representing the earnest workers like himself who dutifully reported on Christmas Eve.

He was here at home in America, making himself into a hero.

Using the disposable phone from Uncle Konstantin, he crossed the lot like any business executive making calls, although those petty collections were scarcely worth his time. Standing straight, the way he'd direct the scene if he were filming, Nicky growled business into the phone. Ice crunched underfoot as he walked between cars, headed for his day job like any good American.

Hanging up, he checked his own phone for email and other messages, poking for the presence of a business acquaintance—one of Nicky's personal heroes. No gulag tattoos here: this entrepreneur had honed his genius while directing armored SUV traffic on the streets of Baghdad.

⏮ ◀ | ▶ ⏭

NickCarraway> Are you interested in more business with my firm?

BlackPawn> Aren't we your best customers? I've got men around the world, off-duty with nothing to do. Every penny we pay you is a morale booster. Your new online poker scheme is a great supplement.

NickCarraway> We have new business that you might appreciate.

BlackPawn> Try me.

Then Nicky took the biggest risk in his life so far.

NickCarraway> A member of our firm strayed from the fold and looks to sell dangerous malware to outlaws.

BlackPawn> Anyone I know?

NickCarraway> The White Knights of the New Russian Revolution.

BlackPawn> Whoa. You want to sell to us instead? It's not our line.

NickCarraway> No, I want you to disrupt the business. From what I read in the blogs, you need to deliver new heroism to retain your masters' trust. You could invest with me to advance your profile.

BlackPawn> We don't consider anyone our masters. But I'm intrigued. What's the degree of danger?

NickCarraway> For you, not so much for the intercept. For the free world, there's great danger if you fail.

BlackPawn> That's the right balance for our business model. And for you, a chance to kill the competition, huh?

⏮ ◀ | ▶ ⏭

Nicky nodded his head, smiling wryly, thinking how he'd direct the scene.

Kill the competition. Heh.

Who could do irony best? Kevin Spacey—but he's given up film. Robert Downey, Jr. would be perfect. Irony can be so difficult to communicate.

Nicky spurned killing as Old World powerless expressions of underclass rage, which wasn't how he wanted to achieve power. Yes, you could take power by threatening someone's life. However, what benefit did it serve if you actually offed someone, following Konstantin's old-style business model?

What Nicky had learned from Konstantin that morning: unpredictability hastens people's willingness to cede power to others. In that whole scene with Andrij on the island, Konstantin had started out in the same manner that Zandr and other cousins used to bully Nicky. Then Konstantin's capriciousness tilted the dramatic scene into a nightmare.

NickCarraway> I will require protection after we launch this business.

BlackPawn> Think our Uncle Sam will get you for this? Aren't you promising us both an inside track there?

NickCarraway> No, it's my uncle I'll need to dodge.

BlackPawn> That's the problem with you oligarchs. You carve up your own gene pool.

Nicky swiped his badge over the magnetic reader, coming into his day job, wondering where unpredictability could take him. Inside, he poured a cup of the company coffee—they were drinking Caffè Umbria now because the test team voted for that vendor—and then zipped up his parka and joined the huddled masses twenty-five legal feet from the doorway for a puff before starting work. He offered a flame from his Zippo lighter to the beautiful Natalia, glad that she too worked in South Lake Union. Her ragged leather jacket made him think of what Zandr had said the previous night about the object of Nicky's affections.

"She never learned to comb her hair, and she's too cheap to get a decent haircut. She slathers eyeliner like homeless punks begging in the U District. She finds clothes in a Salvation Army cast-off bin. No curves. Thin and hard—no, brittle would be the right word."

Nicky laughed with the others when Natalia joked that the new laws made their kind hardier than the sniveling anti-tobacco masses.

"What doesn't kill you makes you stronger," he said.

Good line. However, as brave as he felt about his Black Pawn move, Nicky couldn't give Robert Downey Jr. that line. Maybe Chris Cooper?

13. Sam Crosses a Bridge Before She Gets to It

IN THE BUILDING'S GARAGE, Natalia looked daggers back at me before she got into her car: a BMW 335, similar to mine. You'd think that a network admin job wouldn't pay that much, but what do I know? Quinn seems to be generous with his staff.

In the furthest reaches of the garage, where I park to protect against door-dings, Alec leaned against my car. He had now crossed over to unforgivable acts. With a car like mine, that constitutes one of the seven deadly sins. I own that car because of how it handles when I drive it, not because of how Clive Owen looks inside it. And I believe valuable assets should be treated with care.

"Let me help you," Alec said, turning cavalier as he tried to take the laptop bag from my shoulder. I resisted. Then he started up again. "I can't stand the idea of you being alone for Christmas."

"I'll be with a friend," I said, holding up my laptop bag as a shield (even though the PC inside was Pete's).

"That's a cold friend." He put his hand on my arm in what he must have assumed was a warm gesture, while I felt that I'd been slimed.

"You have to talk to people to make new friends, and I don't have time for it. I want to work tonight."

"Right," Alec said. "But you'll enjoy talking with me." He effing kissed me. On the lips. I pushed him back; the smug lines on his face deepened. "I'll pick you up at eight. You can practice making friends with my whole family."

"You'll drive across Seattle for nothing." I wiped my mouth free of cooties. "Don't create an existential crisis for yourself."

"The human soul thrives on hope, Sam. I promise, you'll like my cousins and uncles."

"I'm particularly allergic to uncles. Please get off my car."

I backed out of the lot without looking to see if I might hit him, since doing so would have been a great stress reliever amidst everything else. Running over at least his foot would have been especially gratifying since I appear to be attractive to guys who either: (a) lean on my car, or (b) steer my professional life sideways—the last category wholly owned by my former CEO Friend-with-No-More-Benefits.

§

My cell rang through the car's dashboard. Wishing for a callback from Quinn, I was a bit disappointed to see that the caller ID was my Aunt Lucky's cell, probably checking to see if I was coming to the island for Christmas, which she knows I've avoided for ten years. I touched the dash panel to pick up the call.

"Samsara, are you coming home?" Wheeze.

"Huck, are you with Aunt Lucky?"

"No, she lent me her phone. I need—"

"Please be patient, Huck. I promised to help you after Christmas. Right now I have my own problems to solve." What I didn't say: and you never bother to inquire about my problems.

Wheeze. A sixty-cycle hum over the line, sounding like he'd called me from a bathroom where the fan was running.

"I have to go. I'm expecting a call," I said. Usually I'd fold by this point and let him go on at length. There isn't anyone else he can call who will listen.

"I don't care about myself," he said, "but I hope Pete and your Uncle Bob aren't in danger, too."

Oh geez. *A man's life depends on it.* Wasn't that what Pete had said?

Before I could speak, he hung up.

"Call back," I ordered the phone genie in my car.

Only raised a busy signal. I tried Pete's cell number. No answer.

Now I was tempted to drive straight to the waterfront and catch the next ferry to Limberlost Island. Then I could hunt down my father and wring answers from him, furious with both Huck and Pete for teasing me with fear.

My freaky family is a study in chaos theory. After my mother died, we were shifted around for years. My brother and I finally ended up with my mother's sister Lucinda—Aunt Lucky—while my older half-sister, Eliot, stayed with her father's family. Pete and I traded unsupervised transience for stability with Aunt Lucky, a brittle, migraine-plagued woman who looked like our mother, but without the same warmth. Pete and I both fled Limberlost Island as soon as age and law allowed. My other relatives reappear at variable intervals, like a nightmare from which I cannot awake, always begging for my help, which I can never stop myself from giving.

The local NPR station on my car radio discussed the mystery man in the Soul Meets Body freezer, pleading for any family missing an older relation to come forward to help identify the victim. So I switched to KEXP, which doesn't plague you with current events. My cell rang again, but the ID said it was Alec the patent attorney, so I let it go to voice mail.

I jealously pictured that City of Seattle detective clocking out of a meaningful job and going home to a sane, mellow family that sends each other visualize-world-peace holiday cards and serves tofu turkey and dressing.

Meanwhile, as I crossed the series of hills between South Lake Union and Leschi, three times I had to swerve out of the way of drivers who were unable to control their economy cars on the iced-over roads. Once I got home, it would be hell getting out of my street with the ice and the coming snow. Fortunately, I could remote in to Quinn's servers from my house to continue working, since I'd be pretty much house-bound until the ice and promised snow cleared away.

Because the day had repeatedly gone as foul as it could, my garage door refused to open. I had to park on the street and drag my rear end out into the cold. Looking down the driveway, I realized it was just as well. The previous night's sleet storm created an icefall in my driveway, and I'd never get my car back up until a total thaw arrived.

14. Nicky Gets a 100-Level Tutorial

AFTER NICKY LEFT HIS day job, he had an appointment to do collections with Zandr, which Dymtrus had insisted upon, as if Zandr had anything of interest to teach Nicky. Zandr insisted on driving the rented Escalade, laughing at Nicky's desire to dump that car because of the morning's chores. It gave Nicki time to do a post, sans video.

THE GRRRL OF LIMBERLOST

Nick's American Business 101 as Cinéma Vérité
Entry #26: Open Thread – December 24, 06:30 PST

You know my gig: Capitalism as viewed through the aperture of a video auteur. My calendar is booked today while I work on issues related to how capitalists play on pagan impulses. So no video this morning. Here's an open thread.

Nick's Fan Forum | Permanent Link | 3 comments

I'm hungry for more video
JustMike | 12.24 – 6:32 am |
Don't starve us just to tease, nicky. What's in your bag of tricks?

If it takes an extra day
ponyboy | Homepage | 12.24 – 6:34 am |
to repeat your last success, I'm willing to wait. That last bit made me spit coffee on my keyboard. Russian gangsters fighting over the religious significance of turkey stuffing at Thanksgiving dinner? Where'd you get that idea for a business lesson?

where do you get the fake gangsters Nicky?
AuteurGrrrl | Homepage | 12.24 - 11:57 am |
The one who ate the turkey heart and scratched himself when the fake mother left the room – he's kinda hot.

⊲⊲ ⊲ | ▶ ▶▶

"I'll do one contact to show you how, and then hand this account over to you," Zandr said, condescending to provide instruction on effective phone collections. He thumbed a number as he drove. His eyebrows lifted when a voice answered.

"We put you on a payment plan, but you're still delinquent," Zandr said. He started out with that same bullying tone that all the cousins used.

As the party on the other end made whatever excuses, Zandr mimed to Nicky what a dumb-ass he had on the other end.

"I'm going to have to turn this matter over to the next level," Zandr said. "No, really. You need—"

Nicky took the phone from his cousin.

"By Monday noon," Nicky said to the delinquent client, looking at Zandr as he spoke. "Or I cut off your fucking balls and feed them to the fishes."

"I can't do what I can't do," the voice squeaked at the other end.

"That's your problem, not mine," Nicky said, again studying his cousin. He'd stolen that line from Konstantin, but hadn't yet figured how to build it into a scene.

15. Matt Has Visions

WITH HER USUAL SENSE of humor, Pippi insisted I put on pajamas, then she tucked me in, imitating the way I tuck her in every night. Then she sat by the bed, serious as hell, and proceeded to read to me.

"Nana says," Pippi refers to my mother as the authority for all things, "we must observe tradition. This is how it was done in this house for years."

"I'm supposed to read the story," I said. "If we're talking tradition."

"We're still figuring this out," she said, quoting me. "Now close your eyes. 'Twas the night before Christmas, when all through the house not a creature was stirring, not even a mouse.'"

"We don't have mice," I said. "Roslyn wouldn't stand for it."

"That's why they aren't stirring," Pippi said. I'd tried to evince a smile from her. She knew that and denied me. The game was on. "'The stockings were hung by the chimney with care, in hopes that St. Nicholas soon would be there.'"

"Yikes, I forgot to hang my stocking." I threw back the covers. She blocked me with her skinny, little-girl body.

"Back to bed. Nana and I took care of that. 'The children were nestled all snug in their beds, while visions of sugar plums danced in their heads.'"

"I'm troubled by the sugar plum visions. Is it the same plum that Jack Horner mauled in his Christmas pie?"

She studied me gravely. "Nana says that you have a great regard for tradition. We must proceed."

Seeing the twitches at the corner of her mouth, I pushed it, wanting to hear her laugh, because it's Lidocaine for my soul. I said, "OK, but in principle I'm against people sharing their plums across stories, like chewed-up gum peeled from the bottom of a desk."

As Pippi started to giggle, I reached over to tickle the back of her neck. She shrieked and threw up the book to block me, laughing now.

I pulled the covers over my head. "Please respect tradition. Continue with the story."

She started over from the top, laughing when I repeated the same lame jokes.

"We'll never get through this if you can't be serious," I said. More peals of laughter. She pulled the book close to her face.

"'Visions of sugar plums danced in their heads.'" She raced through that line. "And Mama in her kerchief—'"

She looked at me over the rim of the book, her eyes wide. And sad.

The phone rang, and I leaped over Pippi to get it before anyone else in the house picked up.

I listened to the heavy breathing on the other end.

"Danny? Danny, don't be an asshole. I know it's you. Stop it."

The click on the phone line could be considered a halt. However, based on the early morning call, I was pretty sure there'd be no withdrawal.

"Pippi!" Roslyn called. "Jamma time!"

After Roslyn had her tucked in, I coaxed Pippi into letting me be the reader. Traditions must be maintained.

She was softly snoring—dang, she's congested again—by the time I got to "Dash away, dash away all!"

16. Nicky Gets an Agent

NICKY MADE ZANDR PARK the rented Escalade way down the block, sure he had the correct address. Zandr raced on ahead, leaving Nicky to follow on his own. Cold wind scraped his hands and face when he emerged from the climate-controlled Cadillac cocoon. Bracing is what people said in books. He checked his camera and slung the glove-soft leather bag over his shoulder, never before more confident. Success lay not just within reach, but already cupped in his capable hands.

Then that cell phone rang again.

However, it was pointless to dodge or ignore his uncle.

"Hello."

"I'm calling for Nicky Peterson."

"Speaking."

"A friend of Pete Byron suggested I call. He says you have documentary work that I'd be interested in representing?"

"Auteur video," Nicky said automatically. "Not documentary."

While talking to this agent, Nicky wondered what Uncle Konstantin believed he was owed for this. Or how Konstantin would calculate the balance owed when Nicky moved his pawn and retrieved the code project that Zandr had stolen from him. Even if his uncle threatened him with the CCTV recording at the ferry dock, Konstantin would be putting himself in check. Besides, Nicky learned long ago how to avoid appearing on security cameras.

Smiling—Nicky would describe it as enigmatic on his blog— he turned to conduct the evening's business.

The sun had never once appeared that freezing day, and now it was evening, so Nicky couldn't tell if he still cast a shadow when he walked up the street.

Zandr stood under the street lamp. He definitely cast no shadow.

17. Sam Knows Futility

EVERYTHING HAPPENS ON THE kitchen counter in my house. Don't know why I bothered setting up a home office in another room. Maybe I should be progressive and just get rid of the kitchen. I only need the espresso maker and the refrigerator. Maybe keep the sink to rinse my coffee cup. If I turned the kitchen island into a server rack, I wouldn't have to heat the house.

Anyway, I plugged in Pete's laptop and waited for it to boot while I spooned two bites of peanut butter from the jar and chugged some O.J. Because I'd cleaned up the malware earlier, Pete's laptop came online immediately, but the servers at Quinn's office wouldn't let me online. I couldn't even get an error message with enough information to guess anything other than that the whole network must be offline.

The revenge of the frustrated network technician. Natalia must have returned to her task after I left the office.

Crap. I could have scarfed peanut butter and O.J. at the office, without driving all the way back to Leschi.

§

Unable to connect with my digital universe, I changed into silk long-johns and a second pair of socks, found my hip black skull cap, swung the strap of my bag over my shoulder, and dropped a Montalban story in the pocket of my pea-coat. As I started out, the front door window framed my stalker-attorney Alec coming up my walkway. I flipped the deadbolt and exited through the alley.

As I hiked across Madrona and the Madison valley, the buses never came and every radio taxi I called promised two hours' wait. Oh well. I needed a long walk to calm down. While crossing Seattle, I must have phoned, emailed, and sent texts to Gerard and Quinn a dozen times from my cell. Neither answered at work, at home, or on mobile, so I left them cryptic messages, sounding more like Chicken Little on hormones than a serious, competent professional.

Pete's and my aunt's cellphones both went immediately to voice mail. In spite of my multiple attempts, no one ever answered the landline at Aunt Lucky's house. I left half a dozen messages on her service and at my sister's house, suggesting that Pete should pick me up from the ferry in the morning. Then I could ask Pete about the nature of the handbasket that Huck had us riding to hell in this time.

§

Since email and instant messages weren't my friends, I did what people do who are alone and working late on Christmas Eve: I dialed an old lover's number. The private line that no one has except a former Friend With Benefits. It was four a.m. on the East Coast; no one answered. Since I seemed to have subscribed to the cell plan where no one ever answers your call, I left yet another message.

"It's Sam. When you hear bad news, please believe I tried hard to warn you."

I was thinking that was about as much as I could do. Then I remembered my manners from Remedial Socialization.

"Merry Christmas."

18. Nicky Uses His Zippo Lighter

"NO ONE HOME," ZANDR said. "I really wanted to wrap up this project tonight. Watch closely, Nicky. Here's how to do aggressive collections."

He stepped onto the porch, pushing past Nicky, who was ready to call it a night. He took the cashmere scarf from around Nicky's neck, wrapped his hand, and bashed the pane by the door, reached through the opening, and unlatched the door.

Thereby adding B&E to the pointless crimes his family had embroiled Nicky in that day. Zandr poked around for ten minutes, asking stupid questions.

"There's nothing in the fire safe but a passport and some weird dollars." Zandr held up his find.

"They're pound notes," Nicky said. "From England."

"Far out." Zandr stuck them in his pants with the passport, as if petty identity theft were worthwhile. "Did you get into any of the computers?"

"Why bother? There won't be anything on these computers worth the time it takes to break a password."

"Let's take them with us, to make sure." Zandr went through the medicine cabinet, exclaiming his extreme dismay that nothing had a prescription label and nothing was illegal. The whole sham started to feel like a public-school brat-boy lark.

"There are five computers," Nicky said. "None of them are worth anything for our service business."

"Service business? Nicky, you are such a fuckwit."

"We need a long-term business model, Zandr. We sell clean services. That's what makes us different. That's why we have a future."

"Business model? You talked Dymtrus into selling porn in bulk to mercenaries."

"We guarantee no viruses, so the customer never blocks access. That's our business advantage." Nicky spoke evenly, ignoring the scorn Zandr heaped on him. "With new, stronger security, we can take a piece of online gaming. It's legal, and we promise a service free of malware. That's a long, rich future."

"Did that girl you have a crush on make you think 'clean' was worth money to people? That twat is clouding your judgment. If you ever had any."

Zandr touched a Bic lighter to the kitchen curtains.

"Are you fucking nuts?" Nicky yelled. He grabbed the kitchen faucet and sprayed water to douse the fire. Zandr laughed at the mess.

Once Nicky made up his mind, it took only two minutes to orchestrate the position of powerlessness and the single-handed engagement of zip ties that Konstantin had taught him earlier that day.

⏮ ◀ | ▶ ⏭

"I admire America." Nicky widened the focus to capture the room's Prohibition-era architectural details. "You are selling to the bad guys."

"Nicky, you dumb fuck. We are the bad guys."

"You are a bad person, Zandr. I'm just a capitalist thriving in the margins of the rule of order. Nothing could be more American."

Olekzandr stuck out his chin in challenge. "You live in a fantasy world, Nicky. You're not even a good enforcer, much less an executive."

"OK, Zandr. We end this when you provide the contact name and where you're meeting to hand off my code. I hope you understand that the portion in your possession is unusable."

"If I tell you, you better kill me. Else, I tell the White Knights what you're doing. And you die."

"Too predictable, Zandr. Don't struggle that way. You keep moving out of the spotlight."

"You're too stupid to breathe, Nicky."

Nicky produced his Zippo lighter. "You've shown disrespect about everything I consider important. It's tiresome."

"So you're going to have a cigarette and think about it?" Zandr sneered, though he was the one tied to a chair.

"I'll only be two minutes or so."

Within those two minutes, Zandr had changed his mind. Nicky had phone numbers, names, and location for the handoff of the stolen code. Not that Nicky wanted a face-to-face meeting himself.

"Is this supposed to be a joke?" Zandr said, gasping from the smell of his own burned hair.

"No, Zandr, it's irony."

⏮ ◀ | ▶ ⏭

The woman he loved—Nicky decided that it was more than a schoolboy crush—wasn't home. He borrowed her car, leaving the tainted Escalade for Zandr. If he didn't hurry, he'd be late for Aunt Avrora's Christmas Eve feast, for which she wouldn't forgive him.

19. Matt Says Hello

"MATT, I HAVE TOWELS hot from the dryer and—oh!"

Cripes. I ran smack into my mother Roslyn as I walked out of the bathroom shirtless. She had a bundle of laundry in her arms, hurrying through her chores with something else on her mind, but even in the dim light of the hall I could see that she turned ash-white at the sight of those scars.

"Pippi is asleep," I said, diverting her attention as I pulled on a sweatshirt. "Let's stuff the stockings."

We worked side-by-side, only talking about which trinket or toy went into whose stocking.

"Oh my, Pippi will love these," Roslyn said of a handful of toys from the Archie McPhee joke shop, her voice too bright, ready to break at the edges.

I see my mom buzzing around, trying to make Christmas right, and I feel so guilty about what I put her through. All I can do is shut up and smile.

The phone rang, startling Roslyn. Guilt washed over me again.

I stopped her from answering it. "I'll get it. You can bet it's my sister saying she missed the plane and won't be here till morning."

Fumbling the phone off the hook, I said hello.

Again with the heavy breathing.

"Danny?" I walked to the hall with the phone, away from where my mother sat holding Christmas stockings on her knee. She was getting used to how I answer the phone. "Can't you take a holiday?"

"Who's Danny?" A woman's voice asked.

As I predicted, my sister Isabella wouldn't make it: SeaTac had let the last plane in and she wasn't on it. Her flight never left New York. Christmas on Limberlost Island wasn't happening for her. I gave the phone to Roslyn and let them talk.

20. Sam Pings and Pings

AS I SWIPED MY badge back at Quinn's offices on South Lake Union, Natalia Dragon came blasting out the door, an overly laden messenger bag in one hand and an REI backpack in the other. I barely stepped out of the way as she barged down the hall, not even gracing me with her daggers-to-the-heart look.

"Thanks for screwing my night!" I called. "Merry Christmas anyway!"

"*Z Rizdvom Khrystovym!*" she called back. Which meant either *Merry Christmas* in some post-Soviet Bond Girl language or was the verbal equivalent of flipping the bird.

No one else was left in the office. The coffee had burned to a crisp at the bottom of the pot. The pink cardboard bakery box that held cookies from an earlier holiday festivity now held nothing but finger swipes through the remaining frosting. Lights were out or dimmed through every hall, office, and cubicle, and any computers that rebooted after the network outage just showed splash screens. Since the network had been fully restored to operating condition, I sat down to work, which offset the burden of Byronic foreboding that I carried on my hike across Seattle. As my programming and test screens came up on the monitor, I felt my tension dissolve with the promise of a few good hours of work to carry me through the night.

Once I settled down, I got plenty of work done, meaning I gained a clear notion of exactly what the new malware attempts looked like and what the changes in Shur-locke code needed to be.

When I was in the middle of sending detailed technical notes to Quinn and his testing team, a message popped on my monitor, like toast from hell.

> YrBlueHatLvr> From all your messages you must have me confused with someone else. I worry about you.

Sigh. Gerard and stupid identity games were not on the list for my holiday cheer. I logged off.

21. Nicky Identifies with the Iconoclasts

NICKY CAME AWAY FROM his uncle Dymtrus's house, his vitals burning as much as his injured hand, angry with his uncle for the first time in this life. As much as he loved his aunt Avrora, he blamed her. She had raised Zandr, the coddled little shit. The clutter and extravagance of that house, the too-lush carpets and embroidered silk pillows showed her bad taste.

After he'd freed himself, Zandr had called Dymtrus to moan and lie, so Nicky found himself being dressed down in front of all the cousins. Danilov played with his cell phone like he couldn't care less.

"Nikolai," his uncle said, treating Nicky as if he were a little child. "Zandr called me. He says you hurt him."

He protested: Zandr and Uncle Konstantin were betraying the family to the White Knights. Nicky's pleas were met with scorn.

"Stop fooling with that stuff you call art," Dymtrus said. "It's distorting your good sense." He paused to wave Avrora from the room, annoyed with her attempts to sooth him with her over-spiced Christmas tea. "You've got so much ambition. Take care of those collections for Konstantin. I can't afford to have him on my ass."

When the interview was over, Dymtrus still denied the truth in what Nicky told him—that Zandr intended betrayal with the White Knights of the New Russian Revolution.

"You've tried too hard to make up for your father's failures," Dymtrus said. "Cheating is not the way, Nikolai."

Nicky bit his tongue, since it was futile to say it one more time. *It's Zandr who's cheating both you and me!*

He stopped in his basement room to change his clothes, wanting to shed his uncle's alarming criticisms like a skin. Armani. It had to be Armani, because he needed to feel better fast after that setback. He began to relax as the soft folds brushed across his skin.

Still angry, Nicky closed the door on the house that formerly served as his haven, but now felt shrill and stifling. Overly warm and overly decorated. Nicky had to endure humiliation in a room where the tranquility had already been destroyed by his aunt's new passion for collecting Greek icons, all those suffering faces gazing down on him while his uncle berated him.

Nicky cruised through the neighborhood streets, looking for an unsecured wireless signal, since he hadn't had time to log on and upload his files. When he found a signal outside a remodeled Craftsman bungalow, he sat in the car with the motor running because of the cold—he did deeply love the woman he borrowed the car from; Zandr could go blow himself. He polished the last of his work before publishing it to the web, fighting the whole time against replaying in his mind that bad scene with Dymtrus.

Dymtrus used him like an errand boy, not a trusted part of the family. Zandr's betrayal, selling to the White Knights, made his skin crawl. Uncle Konstantin had compromised Nicky's well-being, making him drive to and from that disgusting lesson in the wild woods. He shivered away bad thoughts and shifted the laptop in his hand as he finished the file upload.

⏮ ◀ | ▶ ⏭

Nick's American Business 101 as Cinéma Vérité
Entry #27: The 90-second Manager: Fiery Ambition –
December 24, 21:00 PST

The good manager has many ways to ignite workers'
enthusiasm, and knows which methods work best in particular
scenarios.

The lesson includes key principles:
1) Take quick, decisive action.
2) Make the most of resources at hand.
3) Stay focused!

Nick's Fan Forum | Permanent Link | 3 comments

ZIPPO as metaphor
JustMike | 12.24 - 9:12 pm |
That Zippo helped me see the pattern from previous vignettes.
The lighting worked really well here too, with the kitchen fire
making the shadows flicker.

You are brilliant
AuteurGrrrl | Homepage | 12.24 - 9:15 pm |
The look of absolute fear from the man in the suit! You always
get great performances. This one pushed all my buttons —
where I usually say "Over the top". In this case, too much is not
enough!

I bow to your risk-taking
ponyboy | Homepage | 12.24 - 9:29 pm |
How do you get production insurance, Nicky? The chances you
take, it must be as hard as it used to be when directors cast
Robert Downey, Jr.

Tony Stark...
AuteurGrrrl | Homepage | 12.24 - 9:35 pm |
...solved that problem for Robert, who needed a Super Hero to
effect that rescue. I like what you do to create drama without
resorting to superhero comics, Nicky. The reality element,
including the shaky camera, is what makes this scene zing.

◄◄ ◄ | ► ►►

Since it was too cold to go for a run, and his gym was closed, Nicky pondered how to throw off the toxic effects of that interview with Dymtrus.

He needed a woman.

A real woman.

Gaining the attentions of a woman was never a problem for Nicky. The face his father gave him brought luck. He'd improved on the original, and had learned the kind of good manners that guarantee success. Where on Christmas Eve could he find one that met his ever-rising standards? His tastes had refined in the past couple of years, so he no longer wanted to go below a certain level. It was like the first sensations of silk boxers or a cashmere sweater— a sensual pleasure once sampled prevents a return to the mundane.

The woman he needed had to have manners that wouldn't disgrace. She had to have a brain in her head. She had to be beautiful.

She had to appreciate being treated with gracious care.

22. Matt Plays Difficult Music

"HEY, MATT. THAT SONG is way beyond your ability."

Pete crawled through the window of my room a little after midnight, just like junior high, interrupting my attempt to learn the fingering for a Buddy Miller song.

"A man's reach should exceed his grasp," I said, glad to see him, glad not to be alone.

"Once you master the art of reaching, what's next?"

Pete first crawled through that window eighteen years ago when he moved next door. Now, on Christmas Eve, he had half a bottle of cheap brandy, swiped (once again) from his aunt's kitchen cabinet. We poured Yule greetings into paper Dixie cups from my folks' bathroom.

The brandy burned. Cheap can be fine on this kind of a night.

I didn't answer his question about reach. The discussion over Christmas Eve dinner involved what I could do for work on

Limberlost Island, similar to Pete's question: what's next? After falling apart while rehearsing a deposition with Karl, my opinion now is that I'm not yet fit for much.

Sitting with his back against my bedroom wall, as if he had to keep watch for who might come through the door, Pete shook his head at the first sip of the brandy, since it was pretty brutal stuff. His hair fell over his eyes, like bleached straw, hiding him from close examination. He's one of those guys that you can't remember whether he's tall, and he could be any age between twenty and forty—until you look in his eyes. Ever since Pete came back from that work he did in Chechnya, I am too aware that this fucker has *seen* things.

He held his brandy up to the light—the goosenecked student's lamp that's been on my desk since high school—as if to admire the amber color of a fine liquor. In a paper cup.

"I have a gig near the Black Sea this spring," he said, "and I'm tired of working alone. It's not steady income, but I need a partner. Come with me."

Once more Pete was calling me out to what he considers adventure and what my mother always called trouble.

"If you want a steady income, Pete, go into journalism. You crave adrenalin, and you're already crawling through the same sewers as those guys broadcasting from war zones. That's the perfect long-term gig for you."

"I don't do long term," Pete said, speaking into his cup of brandy, "especially just for money. I can't work where people are always jawing about the boundary conditions for integrity. You know me, if there's a boundary, I'll cross it. Even if I don't have a passport."

Yes, I know Pete, and he knows me better than anyone. The only divide between us is that I grew up the son of a cop and Pete grew up thinking rules are a curious artifact of an alternate universe. The rules that bind the rest of us don't apply for him. You might think this describes your common, garden-variety sociopath, especially since Pete behaves as if he has no conscience. Yet if shit goes down, he'll be there for me, like the brother I never had. I know this because shit did indeed go down.

"You have talent for reporting," I said. If I had half his talent, I wouldn't have made the choices that dead-ended my life. "Your camera work is brilliant. You get people to open up in amazing ways. You'd have a great career."

"I'm too young. You're asking a boy to throw himself to the wolves."

"More people would see your work." I provoked him on what I knew was a sore issue: the exclusivity of his viewing audience.

Of course, Pete shrugged it off. "I'm a Renaissance man who occasionally finds Medici-style benefactors. What do I need with a career?"

I tried not to laugh aloud, but failed.

"Come with me this spring," he said. "I'm dog-tired of working alone."

Having met his current benefactors, I could imagine what a job near the Black Sea might mean. "Damn, Pete. I can't take those kinds of risks any more. I've left that life."

"You're thirty, Matt. Not seventy. You've got years before it's time for the Barcalounger. Even your Dad hasn't gone to ground yet." Pete started on this theme when I announced my Limberlost plans, urging me to join his circus and run away to the next episode of chaos.

"I'm trying to get sane. I need to find some peace and comfort." As I spoke, I caught myself rubbing at my eye, which I tend to do when stressed.

"So what are you going to do, holed up here?" Pete poured brandy. "You'll need a lover, pronto."

"Ix-nay. Like everything else, I screwed romance up for the past decade. Time to give it a rest for a while."

"Not you, *compadre*." Pete swirled his drink, savoring the heady aroma of cheap brandy in a paper cup. "You're too much in love with being in love."

"I don't have good judgment."

"We can't argue that. You're a hopeless romantic, Matt." Pete started dinking with my guitar. He was never good with strings, which is why we made him play drums in the old days. "An ill-informed observer might think your ideal is blond and athletic. A spirited liberal arts major who saved the tassel from her college mortarboard, yet doesn't want to work for a living."

"Stuff it, Pete."

No one likes to be nailed by Pete. He doesn't pick on me often, but when he does, he hammers close to home.

He persevered. "Ponytail and Timberland boots when there's a scenic view. Halter top and jeweled sandals for a sunset at the beach."

"Stop, you're killing me."

"Skis. Jogs. Alice Waters fantasies and a glue-gun. Counts carbs. Bikini wax."

"You're an asshole."

"It's been said before. The problem is, you get tangled up with what stalks you, instead of hunting what you want. With all the nouveau-riche development on Limberlost, another one will find you quick enough."

"You think maybe I'm naïve about women?" I said.

"Certified. Grade A. Also, maybe you're too sensitive. Your mom trained you to put the seat down," Pete said.

"Sensitive hasn't taken me very far," I said. "You've never shown sterling judgment yourself."

"You marry women who are looking for a fixer-upper, when any smart woman should see that you're not a candidate for redecoration." Pete yawned and stretched, seeming more like a cat curled on the rug than the feral child he had once been, the one my mother warned me about over and over again. "You keep getting tangled up with the opposite of your true ideal."

"And what's my true ideal?"

"Your mom. Roslyn."

"Cripes, Pete. It's too late at night for my own personal Freud."

"No, I'm talking Platonic ideals. Look: Roslyn never lost herself in her husband and kids. She's always had a life of her own. Lack of a personal life was Problem Number One with your wives."

"Thanks for the analysis, Pete."

"Am I wrong? No, I am not. Roslyn married a guy who's professionally interested in danger, but she's wicked cool with it. There's Problem Number Two in your past choices: misaligned goals."

"Damn, why didn't I call you for advice instead of wasting money on marriage counseling?"

"Also, Roslyn is as smart as the guy she married, or maybe smarter. Not to be a prick about it, but there's your Problem Number

Three. Plus Roslyn is beautiful in a better kind of way than your post-grad Barbies."

I tried to keep any expression off my face throughout Pete's harangue. It didn't matter. He'd go on without encouragement.

"Better than beautiful," Pete said, "Roslyn doesn't give a flying fig what anyone thinks about her. So yeah, that's your ideal woman."

"She's a lousy cook and a terrible housekeeper," I said.

"Who cares?" Pete said. "You can cook. You don't need a live-in maid. You need a partner like your dad found."

"Do I order her from the Lands' End catalog?"

"No," Pete snorted in derision. "Go for the obvious. If you're going to hide out here, then marry my sister next."

"Eliot?"

"No, asshole. Sam."

"Have you finally flipped?"

"You've been in love with her since high school. Which was Problem Number Four. Or maybe the original cause."

"Sam hates my guts. After she left me that one night—" Even though it was Pete, who doesn't follow the usual rules, I couldn't talk to him about the sole time I was intimate with his sister.

Pete put down the guitar, mercifully ceasing his miserable twanging. "I saw you that night. You were drunk on your ass. She ditched you because she didn't want you hurling in her car. She's finicky that way."

"She hasn't spoken more than ten words to me since."

"Yeah, she always tested in the genius range."

I pondered my empty Dixie cup in the dim lamp light. "I humiliated myself that night."

"Yes, you did," Pete said, pouring out the last of the brandy, splitting it between us. "That's because being in love with Sam was a bad idea then. It's different now."

"Why?"

Pete shrugged. A characteristic movement that makes you want to pound him. "You might be man enough now. To hang with a woman who's tougher than you."

23. Nicky Takes off His Glasses

THE BEST PLACE TO start was the best place. The second hotel bar Nicky tried, a woman sat alone at a table. Acceptably attractive, through probably twenty years older than him, she was of an age that he had learned to appreciate, like a fine whiskey. Well-dressed, self-possessed, she read a book while nursing a balloon of brandy.

Nicky wore the window-pane glasses, which made him look Stanford Business. He casually took a seat nearby, but not too close, only briefly capturing her glance and nodding a civil hello before ordering scotch neat. He opened his laptop to lose himself in his work, concentrating on the contact he needed to make.

NickCarraway> I sent the intercept details in a text message.

BlackPawn> Got it. We're set. Protection coming in the morning.

Half way through the Islay malt, he looked up when the woman with the brandy balloon spoke.

"Not working on Christmas, are you? Or don't you celebrate?" Her voice was as rich as a fine port, her eyes bright and curious as she smiled at him. She ran her finger around the rim of her brandy glass.

Perfect: Nicky always let the woman make the first move. He took the glasses off, rubbing the bridge of his nose before he spoke.

"No," he said. He nudged his whisky glass away, to indicate that she interested him more than his drink. "I just came from work. I can't join my family until tomorrow, so I'm writing email to each of my nieces and nephews. I missed seeing them tonight."

"It's nice that you have family," she said. She held the glass by its stem, washing the tawny liquid around the bowl. "I'm an only child, as were my parents. It makes for solitary holidays."

"I have twenty-one cousins and fourteen nieces and nephews."

"My goodness. How many of your own?"

"None. I'm not married." Important to make that clear early on. He pushed back the bridge of his spectacles, like he'd seen Bill Gates do. "How about you?"

"Goodness no." She sipped gently at her brandy. "I decided years ago that I couldn't achieve what I wanted and have children, too."

"So you're alone for Christmas?" he said.

"I flew out to be with my parents for the holiday. They live in assisted care and go to bed at eight. So here I am, wide awake and nowhere to go."

Better than perfect. Nicky said, "You are fortunate to still have them. Perhaps I care so much for my nieces and nephews and cousins because I lost my parents years ago."

She moved closer, not just a slight movement, but shifting her whole body.

"I'm Susan," she said, holding her hand out for a business-like handshake, which he returned in the firm, professional manner he had practiced.

"I'm Nick," he said, offering his business card.

"Nikolai Petrenko. Investments," she said, reading it. "What a beautiful name. Greek?"

"From the Kingdom of Galicia and Lodomeria. It was also my grandfather's name."

He touched the tumbler of scotch, so that she saw his hand.

"Oh my goodness. What happened to you?"

"I was with my cousin earlier this evening. There was a kitchen accident." To be fair, he felt that with a beautiful woman it was essential to be honest.

"Did you see a doctor?"

"Of course not. It's only a minor burn."

She took his hand in hers and studied it. Nicky relaxed and let her touch him, not sure if he should consider this the second move on her part. His solid principle was to always allow the woman to make the first and second moves and then to decide the next action on her own, too.

"I'm a doctor," she said. "Come to my room so I can treat that for you."

He paid the tab for both of them, slightly exaggerating the awkwardness in using his hurt hand.

⏮ ◀ | ▶ ⏭

"What kind of doctor are you?" he said in the elevator.

63

"Not a very good one," she said. "I started in Internal Medicine and settled into hospital administration. I didn't like the blood and the tears and giving bad news day after day."

"You seem to have a kind heart," he said, daring to tuck a stray lock of hair behind her ear in an early gesture of intimacy. "I should have guessed such a story about you."

"Are we guessing about each other?" she said as she used the keycard to open her door.

Nicky followed her into the room, leaving the door ajar as if he expected to depart in a moment. She stepped behind him and closed it.

"About me," he said, "there's nothing to guess. I'm just a business man, too absorbed in my work to build a personal life."

He sat on the chair by the table, rather than on the bed, and offered his hand for her inspection, noticing for the first time that he needed a manicure as a result of that debacle with his cousin. It would be Monday before he could manage that. She bent her head over his hand, inspecting the burn closely and then tending to it from her first-aid kit. She didn't speak, and he admired that she wasn't at all nervous as she endeavored to make up her mind. The only move he made was to let his little finger trail down the side of her hand when she freed his from her ministrations.

He said, "The romantic in me sees a beautiful woman like you, alone tonight, of all nights. And I want to understand that. I see a woman dressed with exquisite taste, but I'm a business man and I recognize that in you too. So, yes, I began to guess about you."

It progressed in the slow way that he liked, and he didn't urge or plead for anything. Later, when she placed her hand on his shirt buttons, already extraordinarily flushed, he stopped her.

"No. We can't. I hadn't considered this a possibility tonight. I don't have protection for us."

Even though it was invariably effective, Nicky didn't consider it manipulative to bring her to the edge and then let her decide whether to continue.

Moving back to study him, she reached up and removed his glasses, using two hands the way a doctor would. She set them on the night table and walked to the servibar, which is always thoughtfully stocked in a truly good hotel.

24. Matt Ponders Problematic Past Proceedings

SAM WAS BARELY SIXTEEN when we were freshmen at the U, since she'd skipped the fifth and seventh grades and then spent her high school years earning more Running Start college credits than God. So by the time she turned eighteen, Sam had enough credits to graduate from college. Then she did the kind of self-destructive thing my mom said one could expect from a Byron: she left school to take a job in Virginia.

Her aunt was in my mother's kitchen moaning about it for six months. *"How could she do that? What will come of her now?"*

I rejoiced when Sam left, because eighteen is the jail-bait boundary line. In her long-limbed, simple way, Pete's sister Sam is beautiful. Raven tresses—well, if you think of the raven on the snag at the tip of Lost Loop Road, feathers ruffled, resenting the wind. Anyway, what always kept me on the hook was how the unexpected happens every moment you spend with her. To my good fortune, Sam shipped out the same week as her birthday, so I could stop obsessing.

Now, in this modern world, she doesn't like that I'm a proven asshole.

I hadn't seen her for two years when, drunk out of my mind, I did what I had only dreamed of. It seems, from what I remember, to have been physically intense. I categorize it as the best sex I've ever had, the divine mystic—if only I could remember. I think there were tears on my part and "please" said many times, with several different meanings.

Then I was standing alone at the side of the road. She graciously left my pants, but not my shoes and shirt. Tom Tremain, who was deputy then, drove me home and rolled me out of his car without a comment. That's why insurance rates are so high for guys who just reached drinking age. At that time of life, we don't have enough brains to blow our noses without personal injury.

Yes, I was an asshole for initiating sex while plastered. Worse, I didn't call her up after. Hell, I should have flown to Virginia and crawled across shards of glass to beg. But I didn't.

Here are my excuses.

First, a woman PO'd enough to toss a guy's pants in the ditch probably doesn't want a phone call the next day. Or the next decade.

Second, a drunken mistake while your pants are off isn't sufficient cause for crawling across broken glass. I mean, we weren't in love, making promises to each other.

Third—OK, I'm a coward.

Anyway, after eight years, there's nothing to do but laugh at Pete for suggesting I pursue his sister. Pete isn't a provocateur—my mother first called him that when we were in high school. He just gets people free associating, and pretty soon you decide to act out your own insane ideas. Or he does you a favor that you live to regret. He recommended my band—which we called Undercover because we only play covers—for a wedding in the Castro Valley. He'd be there as part of a video biography he was filming for a family he met while working in one of those post-Soviet countries. If you insist on being naïve, as people tend to do, then please understand that I mean "family" in The Godfather sense. But from much more northern climates. That's where he finds his twenty-first century Medici-style benefactors.

Pete put business my way a couple of times before, in similar circumstances. This last gig, at Pete's benefactor's compound in Alameda County, was particularly ill-fated. We agreed to play one-half Motown and one-half Eighties covers, and they made it clear that it was important to follow the contract to the letter. On a break—since we were signed up to play for a brutal four hours—we strolled the family grounds, which constituted a walled village of homes and guest houses, with the patriarch's mansion in the center, a tribute to Black Sea kitsch. A lovely day. The place was huge enough to genuinely get lost, not just pretending while snooping on other people's lives.

Then Sonny Green, who's been my partner since the army, walked in on a conversation that both U.S. Customs and the Bureau of Alcohol, Tobacco, and Firearms would love to hear. Sonny always came across as scary—a big guy at six-four and two-twenty, and very black. Maybe that's why the family felt they needed to have three goons hold him down while a fourth tried to persuade Sonny he had been looking for more than the john.

I didn't interrupt in time, and the appearance of the county sheriff's men behind me caused Pete's benefactors to leap to conclusions about who I was allied with that day.

❧

"Come with me this spring," Pete said, calling me back from reverie. "You need to get out of here."

"I need to calm down and get my life back," I said. "Call me chicken-shit, but I need some time."

"Suit yourself." Pete dribbled the last of the brandy into our Dixie cups and chucked the empty brandy bottle in the waste basket.

I took back my guitar and tried to finger a series of chords that surpassed my abilities, since I don't possess one iota of talent.

Pete said, "You got high-carbon tungsten balls, suing both the Alameda County Sheriff, the family, and your own insurance company."

"Everyone screwed up that day, and no one wants to pay." My dad, every attorney I've tried to hire, all of them tell me I'm nuts, that it will all just cascade back on me. "And I still need my old cover."

"They asked about you last week," Pete said. I didn't have to guess who he meant. "Just wanted to know if I'd seen you lately."

Even though it was Pete, who's almost my brother, I didn't want to show what I felt at that moment.

I said, "I think either Danny or Andy already found me."

He set his glass by mine on the night-table. "Yeah? Well, I told them that I have some video to show them. I made a piece with you together with some of their family, in a way that proves you're on their side.

"Please try not to make it worse."

"Oh ye of little faith. I'm probably the only person who can do anything to get you out of this."

"Thanks."

"You have nothing to thank me for yet," Pete said, his hair falling over his brow. He didn't flip it back out of his eyes, which he only does when he wants to look honest while lying.

"Don't I know it."

He headed for the window, leaving the way he came, as if Roslyn still patrolled our late-night excursions.

25. Nicky Eases toward the Edge

NICKY WROTE HIS PERSONAL email address on his business card, since he owed her as much honesty as she'd shown him. He tried to remember her name.

Susan. He wrote it neatly, in block letters, like on an architect's drawing, while he wished he was leaving a note for the woman he loved.

Saving the door from closing behind him, he fetched a hothouse flower from the bowl in the foyer, noting in the huge hallway mirror that he showed an attractive amount of beard growth, sensual rather than merely ungroomed. He laid the flower where his head had dented the pillow beside her. Passing through the deserted hotel lobby, he calculated how much comfort cost: two drinks, heavily marked up in a bar like that, for a few hours of absolute pleasure.

He walked a full city block to where he had parked his car near a Starbuck's. The freezing cold tore at the sense of consolation that he carried out of the hotel. He lit a cigarette to warm his hands while the car's engine heated, and then he peacefully smoked while waiting for the shop to open so he could have coffee. Just to test the possibility, he turned on his laptop, feeling a surge of delight to find an unsecured wireless signal, from either the coffee store or a nearby office.

The message he most wanted awaited.

BlackPawn> I checked the money with the suits. We can go with the high 7 figures you asked. If you can deliver.

NickCarraway> Oh, have no fear on that account.

Just as he logged onto the family servers to ensure that the Euro cousins had it under control, his phone beeped with a text message.

Zandr> they say my package isn't enough. they want u dum fuk so I tol thm wher to look lol

He flicked off his cell and uploaded more video to his website. No matter how busy he was, his uncle Dymtrus's voice plagued him, haranguing him for Zandr's errors.

"Olekzandr is my own son, Nikolai."

"But Vuiko, it's my work that Zandr is stealing. And your profits."

Out of respect for his uncle, Nicky couldn't tell Dymtrus what was true: that Zandr had just waved his dick and never used his head, believing that Konstantin would take care of business details.

In an unusual act of poor planning, Nicky sat too long in the warm cavern of the car, letting the pleasure of the available Internet connection interrupt his need for caffeine. A blinding migraine descended while Dymtrus's voice harangued him, making it difficult to see well enough to drive.

"Nicky, lad. You know better. Zandr is family."

Nicky could admit to scaring his cousin, but he didn't believe that Zandr had been hurt. Pondering it, wanting to prove that truth, waiting for his headache to subside, Nicky held the cigarette against the soft underside of his arm to see whether Zandr really had anything to complain about.

Two:
Limberlost Island

26. Sam Sails on the Inland Sea

BECAUSE OF THE FOG and ice, SeaTac was closed. I knew this because in the wee hours I pondered flying to where Gerard was likely ensconced for the holidays—his family had a compound on Barbados, which is easier to get to from Virginia than Seattle. With nothing else I could fix in any of the code on Christmas morn and no one answering my messages, I left just before dawn for the ferry terminal, thinking I could resolve things with Huck and Pete and get my laptop back.

Most downtown sidewalks were salted, but runoff along the curbs was frozen, so it took time to cross town from Mercer Street near Lake Union to the ferry terminal. The predicted snow hadn't arrived, yet I found the downtown streets deserted, even of patrolling taxis near the hotels. Everyone else across Washington State and British Columbia was hunkered down at home. It was the morning of a promised white Christmas, and likely many folks were on the Internet, replaying Cliff Mass's video and the National Weather Service simulation of the Puget Sound Convergence Zone in action. Checking the hour-by-hour forecast on my cell phone, I determined that, with even marginal luck, I could get to Limberlost Island, at the heart of the Convergence Zone, and be back to Seattle by noon, beating the snow.

While getting cozy in the prosaic plastic Brutalism of the floating bus station decor that the State of Washington selects for its ferries, I read my Montalban mystery to put my brain on hold. Near me, supplementing the bus station motif, was an older unshaven gent who carried his possessions in a faded, flowered pillowcase. With almost every seat on the ferry empty, he chose to sit right behind me on the benches, placing himself as close as possible, after first greeting me.

"*Dobroe utro.*"

"How are you?" was the only reply I could stutter, not knowing what he said. Then I felt embarrassed for myself, because I couldn't recognize the man's language.

Buried in my paperback, I didn't look up until the ferry's double-bass horn tooted for the landing. Most passengers scurried away when the voice over the loudspeaker called people to return to their vehicles. When the last *All passengers must disembark* message sounded, I pulled my skull cap down close over my ears, wrapped my coat tight, and headed for the gangway, where I collided with a tanned Adonis replete with gold chain, spendy watch, and expensive North Face jacket that signaled Californicated snowboarder who had taken a wrong turn on his way north to Whistler.

Casually excusing himself, he stepped aside to let me pass, but then grabbed my arm and spun me around, while sputtering, "I've been looking all over for you, fuck-face. I am totally fucked because of your fucking friends."

I shook my arm free. "You must be mistaken."

The guy blushed in embarrassment. "Hey, man! I thought you were this dude I know. I am like so sorry."

"It's alright. Think nothing of it." I projected all the first-responder calm I could, repressing the vague Byronic discomfort that surged through me.

The surfer back-pedaled away from me, apparently upset. "Like I said, apologies. God rest ye merry and all that. Hope the Big Guy is good to you."

§

I walked off the island ferry into the freezing, salt-crusted cold and trudged up the slippery streets, tapping my cell to reach Pete. As usual, no signal; God has decreed my relatives' side of Limberlost Island to be a cellular-free zone.

Josh Hart, who's paid to wave cars off the ferry, hailed me as I walked up the concrete portion of the loading ramp, his words freezing in a misty cloud and falling to the pavement. I mimed not being able to hear as the last car sped past, a gun-metal grey BMW 335 coupe, like the one I left sitting on ice in Leschi. The driver in a hooded jacket didn't glance my way and then nearly side-swiped a pedestrian at the top of the ramp, who in turn slammed his hand on the BMW's fender.

Josh shouted as the car noise died. Josh has shouted come-ons across the ferry landing since high school, but when I made a move on him years ago, it didn't turn out to be anything personal.

"Yo, Sam! Merry Christmas! That sweet ass of yours needs more than jeans in this cold! Will Santa leave you something nice?"

"Oh yeah," I lied. Santa didn't leave me a pony, just pony-poop wrapped in an error dump from Shur-locke beta code, sent over instant messaging.

27. Matt Takes a Call

"MATT! COME SEE! YOU must have been a very good boy!"

Pippi giggled downstairs.

Day Eight of my brand-new life back on the island, I got up as soon as I heard Pippi and Roz whispering in the living room. When they heard my feet hit the floor, they sang out together.

"Look what Santa brought you, Matt!"

More giggling. Everyone had tacitly agreed to pretend to believe in Santa, even Harley and Roslyn who never used fairy-tales when we were growing up. However, making Christmas nice for Pippi had become the purpose of life for everyone in my parents' house. Pippi giggled, as if on cue, when each member of the family tried to please her.

I got a nice bottle of Macallan 18 Year. Someone spent more than they should have, trying to please me.

By the third cup of coffee, I'd forgotten the night's bad dreams and almost believed the mantra I chant: *It's going to be OK. I can make it through this.*

My dad was out chopping wood when Tom Tremain dropped by to visit Lucinda, our next-door neighbor. So Harley brought them both in to join us. After that incredibly lonely house in California, our new home seemed almost surreal with these laughing people all warm and cozy together, and Pippi grew more excited each hour about the prospect of snow. I locked my smile in place: everyday life could be like this.

Safe. Happy.

The left-over romantic in me wants Pippi to have what I had, and coming back home seemed the only way to achieve that. Christmas morning, it looked like it worked, if my mom would calm down enough to sit still in a chair. Roslyn was way too happy, trying to make everything right for Pippi. I asked to help in the kitchen and then I had to convince Roslyn to just watch, since I'm a better cook and all she really wants is to be within ten feet of me, to know I'm OK.

Once again, the discussion at the breakfast table was about finding me a job, given my disability. Harley keeps pooh-poohing whether that matters; psychological disability is a gulf that he and I can't bridge to discuss. While they're all talking, I'm sure that we'll wear out our welcome with Roslyn and Harley, but I'm not tone-deaf to people's emotions, and the truth of it is, my mom needs us here right now. It's one more lead weight I have to carry: how much she worried for me and how badly everything hurt her. The payback is that I need to stay in this house until it's absolutely clear that Roslyn and Harley have had enough of us.

So early that the morning, after we'd unwrapped the treasures under the tree, the grownups began scarfing homemade Christmas waffles—my mother had been up an hour early to start the batter—while Pippi was still swamped by wrapping paper in the living room. The phone rang. I grabbed it before anyone else, having made a habit out of necessity.

"Hey, buddy. It's Karl. Listen, sorry to interrupt your holiday."

"Hi, guy." I did not have a good feeling about this. "Sorry to hear you're working this early on a weekend."

He took too long to answer. Karl is never at a loss for words.

"Look, Matt. I got a call this morning from someone looking for Pete. I get them all the time since I do his contracts, but this one was different."

By now, I already knew I didn't want to hear this. "Pete's around. You should try his cell."

"They asked for you, too."

"Yeah?" These were dots I didn't want to see connected in this lifetime. Harley was busy with his waffles, but Roslyn watched me, listening.

Karl said, "I was busy looking at that problem you gave me to work on, and when I put the two things together, it creeped me out."

Cripes, as if Karl couldn't add two and two.

He said, "Call me chicken, but I have to take a pass on this. In fact, I'm not sure why you came to me."

I stepped into the foyer, out of Roslyn's hearing. "I need an attorney, and I prefer to work with my friends."

"It's not an attorney you need, buddy, since you aren't capable of taking advice. Call Stephen Trowbridge. He can handle your issues."

"I know him. He's great at criminal law. But I'm not accused of any crime, Karl. Pete thought you'd be friendly to my situation."

"Yeah? Well, where is the little fucker? I want to tell him that I don't like his friends calling me. Please don't take this personally, Matt. Ordinarily, I'd love to help you. Call me the next time you need a divorce."

I said, "I understand. Can you tell me what the phone call was about?"

Karl stayed silent for so long, I thought the line had gone dead. Then he said, "Do the locals know about this? Maybe you should talk with your dad and his cop friends."

"I don't want them involved." Of this much I was certain.

"Maybe you should get some protection," Karl said.

"There is no protection." I had to say this so quietly that Roslyn couldn't possibly hear.

"That's what I thought."

"What did the caller say, Karl?"

"He said, 'Tell Mr. Owens that the kid gets off the bus at 3:45, and it's fifty yards from the road to his house.'"

28. Sam Drinks Coffee at Casa D

WALKING INTO LIMBERLOST VILLAGE is like passing through a time warp. I came up the alley behind the Billy Shears beauty shop (recently renamed Curl Up and Dye, which indicated that my aunt had a new tenant), the Hot Type printing shop (which hasn't seen hot type since 1982) and the Casa D Café (now owned by a friendly European gentleman, with free wireless Internet and restrooms For Customers Only). It came as no surprise to find Pete pushed up against the Hot Type backdoor, amid the litter of cigarette butts left from a dozen years of smokers' breaks in the alley, with someone preparing to beat the crap out of him.

Just like high school.

Except this time, it was my sister Eliot ready to pound Pete. She's big enough to do it, but he's squirmy and hard to get a hold of.

"You drew the short straw!" Eliot was in Pete's face as I came up the alley. "You're supposed to be with Aunt Lucky all day."

"I will be." Pete wiggled away from her.

Pete has a doe-eyed look that we both inherited from our mother and that we share with our Aunt Lucky. On Pete, it seems to bespeak innocence, which he always exploits to his benefit. This season Pete is super-blond and, I'm sorry to say, slightly pudgy. My sister Eliot looks like a normal person except for being taller than us and vaguely Amazonian. She was also furious.

"What are you doing here in town then?" She punched his shoulder. "You've been responsible for twelve hours, and you already can't handle it."

"I came to pick up Sam," he said.

Eliot whirled on me as if whatever pissed her off were my fault. I held up my empty hands in innocence.

"You left her all alone!" Eliot said to Pete, not bothering to greet me.

"Aunt Lucky is drinking coffee with Harley and Roslyn," he said. "She's perfectly safe, and we'll be home before she can get into trouble."

Eliot eased off her hold on Pete's jacket. "All right then. But keep Lucinda off camera. Do not include her in your video garbage. Documentary art, my sweet rear end."

Pete said, "I wouldn't think of—"

"Yes, you would," she said. "Give Aunt Lucky the same free ride Sam gets. No pictures."

"Merry Christmas," I said when she glared at me and headed up the alley.

"If he screws up, then it's on you, Sam. You never take responsibility for anything. Both of you should stay with her until I get off work."

That's a typical holiday interaction for my family.

Eliot, a year older than me, grew up with her father, a Four-Square-type preacher who also ran a filling station and took to drinking backsliders' wine after he lost our mother. Eliot inherited the filling station, which she refitted to live in, and she does handyman jobs. She won't be at any holiday party, because she works 911 emergency dispatch for the bonus pay, among a half-dozen ways she scrounges money. She's always refused anything from me.

S

By this time, I was freezing, so I pushed my way inside Casa D through the alley entrance, making the brilliant deduction that Pete had come from the café, since it was the only place open downtown. The café door slammed shut behind us as Pete and I found seats at the counter, my face and ears burning from the sudden warm air on half-frozen skin.

"Nice to see you," I said. "They say you're still an asshat."

,"You're still a geek," my brother said. "You wear it as a badge of courage. High school damaged you more than you'll ever admit."

"Can't admit it, because I hardly remember."

The Casa D owner came out of the kitchen and reached for the coffee pot to serve us. Severely under-dosed for the day, I gratefully took coffee from Yuri Pavlo, the gnomic businessman who had arrived in town at about the time Pete gave up juvenile crime for film school. I ordered fried eggs and toast, the only thing I ever felt safe eating at Casa D. However, since I last visited, Yuri had up-graded the coffee service: real coffee from Zoka, likely because they deliver through the U.S. mail.

Pete said, "Yuri, *amigo*, you're the owner. Why wait tables on Christmas? You just don't understand capitalism, *compadre*." Pete is everyone's friend (except Eliot's right now), though I don't know how he does it. I missed the sociability attribute when I took my swim through the gene pool.

Yuri said, "In my house, we don't know Christmas from any other day. Everyone who works here is Christian or related to one, so it's me and Nolan."

He jerked his thumb in the direction of the alcoholic cook who has worked the grill since Juan Cortes bought the Drift On Inn a dozen years ago and painted it in the pastel hues of his home town: marine blue, sunset pink, límon yellow. That incarnation lasted only a year, but the Mazatlán interior has mutated quite gradually. Waving a hand, Yuri said, "If I don't open my store, how can you escape your relatives on Christmas?"

Pete nodded. "I am obliged."

When Yuri turned away, I grabbed Pete's thumb and bent it backward, satisfied that I'd hurt him more than Eliot managed. "OK, Pete. What the hell?"

Pete said, "I needed to see my attorney, and Karl had some free time when I came through Seattle. Then I ran into Huck and—"

"Karl?" I said, always startled at the idea of any kind of lawyer other than fangless patent attorneys. "Will this cost me money?"

Although Pete is currently making a modicum of money in his documentary film work, he survives off my investments. Over the last ten years, I've earned too much for a single person with no particular vices, and investing in Pete offers the same adrenalin rush as high-stakes gambling. Though some of his ideas from our youth, like stealing cars and hopping freights, might not have been so great.

Pete took the laptop bag from me and turned on his crummy machine. "No. There's just a problem with the distribution on my last documentary."

"There's always a problem with distribution. Do I need to invest more to get my money back?"

"No, the distributor is upset about the subject matter." He was connecting to the café's wireless network, browsing the PC's directory, and then watching his Super Stud/Stupid Dude video with Matt, the one I'd uploaded for him.

"You didn't come to town looking for an attorney. Where's my laptop? And why did Huck insinuate that you might be in danger?"

"Beats me, Sam. Business drew me to Seattle, so I took the opportunity to visit here for a couple of days. Your laptop is at Aunt Lucky's house."

I was halfway through my scrambled eggs and toast when the front door opened, letting in a blast of arctic air. Pete looked past me with that special smile he gets when he knows I'm about to undergo psychological torture.

A shuffling shadow fell over us and I felt compelled to look up. It was Huck, his thin, shambling figure filling the door frame, the early-morning light behind him creating a halo out of his wiry, once-blond frizz of hair. Then Huck closed the door, extinguishing the illusion. Huck would be disappointed to have missed seeing his manifestation as a visiting angel.

"Samsara, my dove," he wheezed. "You are blue. With dark edges."

He brushed at the edges of my aura—removing smudges, I guess —but didn't embrace me. He's still on the path to removing himself from the bonds of this mortal incarnation, the same path as years ago when he removed himself from the bonds of child support and summer visits. Oh well.

"It's the eye liner," I said. "Looks can be deceiving."

"The truest of truths in this world," Huck said, lacking—as always—any sense of humor. He took my hand and kissed my palm. "I prayed that you would come, and here you are."

Taking back my hand, I asked, "Why have you beseeched the gods over a real estate deal?"

I will not dive into the raging river under the bridge that keeps me connected to my father. Huck's complicated theology did not build that bridge. I did it myself.

Huck lifted his skinny, asthmatic shoulders in a shrug. "The karma of the place seems to have gone bad. It requires prayer."

Casa D's owner hovered over us, delivering coffee.

"I'm sorry," Huck muttered. Huck never says he's sorry.

Yuri put his hand on Huck's shoulder. "That's the way life goes. Don't you agree, Miss Byron?"

Pete said, "Sam hasn't heard."

"My brother was renting Mr. Byron's house," Yuri said.

"Aureliason," Huck muttered, but Yuri missed the correction.

"But he died last month," Yuri said. "We have to remove his things so Mr. Byron can show his house for sale."

As Yuri spoke, I noticed the red light on Pete's camera. Stealing this for his private use. I should have let our sister Eliot pound him.

§

Leaving Huck with Pete, I followed Yuri as he returned to the kitchen. While pretending to be a big-time misanthrope, I can't take it when a person is hurting. In the kitchen, Nolan was serving up a plate of eggs to the old gent from the ferry, who still toted the faded pillowcase and who fell to eating as if he had missed a couple of square ones over the past few days. Yuri put more toast on the old man's plate, looking over his shoulder to talk to me.

"It's a sad story," he said. "However, it's for the best. My brother had been sick for many years."

"I'm so sorry for your loss," I said.

"It's good of you to say so, Miss Byron. The sad part is that he was alone, and then lay there for two days before your aunt found him."

Oh brother. I said what I could that offered comfort.

"Things are OK here now," Yuri said, though anyone could see that the sad wasn't gone. He followed me back out to the café, picking up the coffee pot as he passed, ready to pour for everyone again. "My cousin asked if I could find a place for her nephew to stay, so he took over my brother's lease."

"That Andrij guy?" Pete asked. He held up his cup for more coffee.

"Yes. My cousin wanted him out of the city," Yuri said. "She thought his other cousins, on his father's side, were leading him into bad things, sending him off on plane trips all the time. One week here, and Andrij stays locked in the cabin alone. I worry about him. If you have time today, will you please drop by and see him?"

When I returned to my own coffee cup, Huck was saying, "The presence of death dims the aura of that fine old place. My brother Bob and I exorcised it, but ghosts cling to that house."

Eleven or twelve years ago, a renter was found dead in that shack. The police never solved the murder, and my aunt spent eighteen months trying to find another renter. Population increase brought enough strangers to the island that she finally found someone to sign a lease, though it seems as if the tenant changes every year. Urban rumors remained rampant about that shack. Perhaps they do for any house with an unsolved murder.

Huck said, "Poor Lucinda. She didn't need that in her backyard at this time, any more than I need ghosts interceding between myself and honestly earned capital."

"What about Aunt Lucky?" I'm always the last to know what's happening on the island, and my Byronic trepidations had kept me from pondering the significance of that incident in the alley with Eliot.

"The ferry is here!" Nolan yelled from the kitchen.

Huck put down his coffee. "I must be off," he said, taking my hand again, gazing at my palm. "I predict you will be our great deliverance. But I sense you are in danger, Samsara."

Huck slipped a crystal on a leather string from around his neck and pressed it against my forehead. *No, not the crystal!* I wanted to cry out. Then he put the wretched thing around my neck.

"Be well," Huck said, making his hokey pseudo-Bodhisattva sign. Then he was gone before I could say a word. Or ask anything of him. As always.

29. Matt Hears the Bells on Christmas Morn

NINE O'CLOCK IN THE morning. This time the phone didn't ring.

I worried.

30. Sam Resists Byronic Despair

I SIPPED WHAT WAS now lukewarm coffee, since Yuri missed my cup when he was pouring for others.

"Turn off the damn camera, Pete. No wonder people want to pound you."

"People don't like cameras pointed at them, but they're always interested in seeing the results. I'm discrete."

"Yeah, sure. What's wrong with Aunt Lucky?"

"Her accident at Thanksgiving had side effects."

Aunt Lucky goes gambling with Grandma Flo, who isn't our grandmother at all, but the mother of one of Aunt Lucky's ex-husbands. Our aunt also married multiple times, though no children resulted. Perhaps that's why she's called 'Lucky,' because it certainly doesn't describe her skill at gambling. She's one of many who graduated from bingo to the casino when the reservations and the government started making money off the mathematically impaired. At Thanksgiving, a patch of black ice between home and the casino had landed Aunt Lucky and Grandma Flo in a ditch. They swear alcohol wasn't involved, though they've been known to party hearty; however, Sheriff Tom (Harley's successor) had been fetched and Breathalyzers were involved, so we have to believe that black ice was the true culprit.

"The doctor said she and Grandma Flo were both fine."

Pete sighed. "She suffered more trauma than they thought. Subdural hematoma. She's been having headaches, giddiness, attention deficit."

"Those aren't symptoms. Aunt Lucky is always that way."

"It took a while to differentiate her symptoms from her habits. Then there's the money."

Every time I come home, it costs me. "What about money?"

"Hers or Huck's?"

"Geez. She has problems, too?"

"Aunt Lucky gambles more than she should. She hasn't acted the same since the accident at Thanksgiving."

"That's why Eliot wants to punch you? For not being a good babysitter?"

Pete shrugged. "You're here, so you can judge for yourself."

"Is she in debt?"

"She never shares her personal business with me."

"So tell me," I said, "what are you involved in this time?"

Pete toyed with his coffee cup. "One of my clients did business with Huck and Uncle Bob, and now the Byron brothers owe them money."

Taking a breath, I asked, "Are you in danger?"

Pete shrugged. "Of course not."

"What about Huck?"

"He's focused on selling his property. But I don't know that he needs to."

I closed my eyes so Pete couldn't peer into my soul while I calculated. Huck's "house" is a two-room shack that causes more hassle than the rent is worth. However, the shack came with hundreds of feet of waterfront property. I'm good at math, and I came up with numbers close to my total net worth.

"How can anyone get into that much trouble?" I said, too loudly, then sat back embarrassed when Yuri appeared to deliver the check.

Pete stood to leave, pulling money out of his pockets to pay Yuri, and then motioning that he was going to make a call from the ancient payphone inside Casa D. "Don't worry about my problems, Sam. I have it under control."

I've heard that reassurance from Pete more than once in this particular cycle of rebirth. Reflecting on the past few cases, I quietly panicked.

S

Out on Main Street, Pete unlocked the Dodge Challenger we rebuilt together a few summers ago, but I insisted on driving.

That car remains a thrill to me, though the ride parked on the street at my house is more practical. I took private pleasure in firing up the Challenger after moving the seat back a notch (I'm taller than Pete). You can't get up enough speed on the island's curving country roads to experience the Challenger's engine, but you can feel the power under foot and in your hands. There's also the unique sound of that engine—every time I hear it, I remember when Pete and I first got it running and then learned the physics of thirty-degree turns in that monster, when to shift, when to accelerate again.

I rolled the window down to listen to the sound of the road.

"Roll up the damn window. We'll get hypothermia and die."

"It's always summer when I drive this beast," I said, though the teasel and curly dock in the ditches were black and hanging their heads in despair. "I killed a bird, and I saw a dead body yesterday because you ditched me."

"You've seen dead bodies before." Pete had his camera out again.

"Do not include me in a single frame," I said.

"I know the rules. Your face cannot appear in my work. Hands are OK, right? Toes?"

He already had the focus he wanted, past where my hands grasped the steering wheel, out the window to capture the island country-side.

We're from a small town with a view of salt water. Over to the west on the Kitsap Peninsula, it's harder to find small towns because they've been buried in the last two decades beneath name-brand franchises and complementary huge parking lots. However, the Limberlost settlers of the Eighties—the 1980s—had the foresight to imitate Bainbridge and so passed zoning laws that restricted national corporations, making Limberlost a Costco-free zone. Newcomers and natives alike have to drive to Silverdale to get their warehouse-store fixes.

Alas, the island's valleys are now crammed with fake chateaus for families whose breadwinners commute by ferry to Seattle. The stay-at-home parents joined the PTA and took over the soccer leagues, and they fill the narrow country roads with their upscale SUVs. You can tell the newcomers from the natives, like my sister, because the natives buy the five-year-old GMCs and eight-year-old RAV4s when the newcomers upgrade. The natives who drive Ford F150 pickups have genuine dirt and rust in their truck beds, fishing rods on the window rack, and minimal irony on their bumper stickers.

It's hard to be ironic when exurban sprawl ate your home town.

Also, the natives have rock formations in their landscape because our grandfathers dug up the rocks and left them in a pile to make room for raspberry patches and vegetable gardens. Grandma Flo about peed her pants when her new neighbors paid seven thousand dollars to haul rocks to their lot instead of having rocks hauled away.

I turned from the main highway onto Lost Point Road. Everything in the Northwest is named for imperialistic pioneers or their children or the boat they floated in on or their favorite president, or transliterated from a Native American word (hence Chimacum), or repeated from a former home town (hence Des Moines and Limberlost). Or after some astoundingly obvious characteristic (hence Beaver Valley, Four Corners, Lost Point Road). Lost Point Road is a loop, which really loses the point.

Even after leaving the main highway, there were too many vehicles on the road, when everyone should have been home in their bathrobes, cavorting amidst torn wrapping paper. I had to brake too often when I preferred only the gas and clutch. That BMW from the ferry, for example, caused me to brake and hump it over a good half mile where I couldn't see to pass.

You can get stuck in traffic on Limberlost Island in ways that never happened when I lived here. However, the mist still rises off the Sound and weaves through cedar branches as it always has.

31. Nicky Taps Callback

NICKY FUMBLED TO FIND that cell when it rang.

"Hello?"

"Hey, Nicky. I missed you last night."

"Sorry, Uncle Konstantin." Nicky mistakenly broke the cigarette he was dying to smoke. "I had to go to Aunt Avrora's dinner."

"You can't stiff Avrora. That's for sure. Though I always wanted to give her a stiff one."

"I promised her." He shifted the phone to the other ear so that he could fish for the lighter in his pocket, feeling a twinge in his burned hand.

"OK, then. You and me, we're in business together now, Nicky. Here's where you go to get my stuff done." Konstantin recited an easily memorized address. "You go kill two birds with one shot. Find that bum to finish that collection chore, and then do Danny's job for him."

"I haven't decided." Nicky struggled with the phone and the cigarette and the lighter as one too many things in his hands.

"So I hear Zandr disappeared, huh?" Konstantin asked, as if he didn't know what that weasel Zandr was up to.

"He didn't come home last night." Nicky spoke past the cigarette, which he'd managed to get to his mouth, but not light yet.

"You gonna disappear?"

"No, *Vuiko*."

Nicky tapped the End button, then thought better of it and tapped Call Back. The connection switched immediately to voice mail. Uncle Konstantin had turned off his phone.

Nicky flipped the Zippo lighter.

It spit sparks, but no flame.

Flint, but no fluid.

32. Sam Finds the Personal is Political

"IT ALL HAS TO be just so with you," Pete said. He yawned. "Everything lined up on your desk. You iron your t-shirts. You wear those jack-boots to look scary, but the bow is tied perfectly."

"These are ordinary Doc Martens. What's your point?"

I was irritated with more than just Pete. The BMW 335 guy was still in front of us. Besides being an incompetent driver, BMW guy was an off-islander looking for an address amid the maze of back-country roads first carved out by the pioneers and then overlaid with a gridwork by developers. And more traffic lights every time I visit, dammit.

"Don't be such a hater," Pete said.

"Me?"

"You'll never be able to get your Byronic forebears to change, Sam."

I shifted down and humped the Challenger up close behind the BMW, hoping the driver might get a clue that he was on an effing public highway with a 55-mph limit.

Pete continued his harangue. "Huck and Uncle Bob have good intentions. They don't drink or do meth. They're kind to women and children. In fact, they are romantics about the meaning of family."

"They do a piss-poor job of executing on the romance. And Uncle Bob is worse than Huck."

"It's time to get past it, Sam." He shot pictures out the window while turning philosophical.

"We have to get this straightened out," I said. "Huck eats muesli because he can't boil water for oatmeal. Uncle Bob dropped several screws on aisle J."

Pete shrugged. "Maybe there's nothing for you to straighten out. Maybe things will be fine without you taking control."

"Someone has to take care of things."

"Fourth grade is over, Sam. You don't have to fix things for everyone."

"Yeah? Exactly what are you doing here, Pete? You never come for holidays. Don't tell me you came because of Aunt Lucky."

Pete hissed a long sigh. "Don't pull an Eliot and say this is all on me."

"Just tell me what's going on." I eased back on the BMW because the driver wasn't using his rear-view mirror.

He said, "One of my clients, who's a very family oriented guy, liked my work, and his idea of gratitude was to reach out and do favors for my family."

"Oh crap, Pete. Did you—"

"No, of course I did not offer up the identity of my beloved and secretive sister. He just offered to expand Huck's business. Then when his lieutenants saw what Huck had, they commandeered it for their own private commerce. Then their uncle—"

"Geezus pieces. With the change in Washington law, what can a medical marijuana operation be worth to anyone?"

"Are you serious, Sam? It's not the grass, it's the tunnel that interested them. They took it over from Huck and Uncle Bob for stronger stuff. Then the Mounties found it and blasted the Canadian end. My clients hold Huck responsible and want him to pay for lost freight."

"What tunnel? Huck promised that he only—"

"In what universe do the words 'Huck promised' mean anything? I refer to the tunnel that Uncle Bob engineered back in the early Nineties, that the Byron brothers have used to move grass and high-velocity toilets across borders for the last two decades."

"No."

"Come on, Sister Sam. You don't believe Aunt Lucky paid for the part of school that our scholarships didn't cover. You aren't that naïve."

I guess I am. Or was until that moment. My turn to sigh.

Pete said, "I can see that you're trying to discern whether that taste in your mouth is disgust or guilt. I decided mine was guilt, which gives me more clear options for action. Oh rats, now you're going to cry."

"I never cry. So what was the lost freight?" I asked. "Heroin? Humans? I feel like throwing up right now."

"It's hardware. And it really was down to Huck, the Mounties appearing when they did. He got scared and tipped them to the tunnel. Which is saying something good about him, I guess." As Pete filmed, the keys jangled against the gear shift as we crossed a section of frost-heaved blacktop. "Fortunately, his unhappy partners don't know that Huck ratted on their shipment."

"Hardware? Like in the tunnels of Gaza? What's there to smuggle into the States besides cigarettes and toilets?" People have smuggled high-velocity toilets ever since the State of Washington banned them twenty years ago. Low-flush saves water; outlaws don't care.

"The other direction, Sam. Going out."

"What was it?"

"A portion of the launchers and mortars that went missing from McChord airbase last summer." He sat up, excited to film an inflated Santa hugging an inflated palm tree in front of a rundown double-wide. "Even the Mounties were surprised by how loud the bang was."

My stomach was now too tight to heave. "Will the cops find out Huck was involved? How much do those friends of yours think Huck owes them?"

"The street cost for that portion of the McChord haul is about the same as the value of his waterfront land. Too bad Uncle Bob has nothing to contribute."

I ran the calculations, this time seriously trying to match it against what I could raise, while knowing there was more at issue than money. "Huck's worried about you, Pete. He says the family is in danger."

"He's misguided. I'm arbitrating for him and keeping it all friendly. This isn't the catastrophe Huck thinks it is. As soon as he makes some kind of modest restitution, they'll stop riding him."

I mused on what was possible. "I could throw the renter out of my house in Virginia and sell it. I think the market has recovered. I can't sell the Z-Crypto stock for another twenty-four months. I could mortgage the Seattle house." Though I rather enjoyed owning it outright. I was also calculating whether I should approach Quinn for help.

Pete said, "Can't you ask your Z-Crypto boyfriend?"

"Never in this lifetime." I shifted and then accelerated to finally pass the BMW dipwad on a brief stretch of single-yellow-stripe roadway. "Do I need to protect my assets, Pete? Should I put my property in a blind trust and change my name?"

Pete laughed. "C'mon, Sam. Have I ever got you into trouble before?"

"Yes."

"Anyway, it will all be taken care of."

He clammed up, leaving me to talk to myself as he filmed the traffic jam at the Sanctuary of the New Disciples of Christ, where the committed congregation had flocked to the early-morning service. Easing the Challenger into the curves where the road wound close to the shoreline of the Sound, I drifted to other things that needed saying.

"What's your new work? You didn't turn political, did you?"

Pete laughed, a short sharp bark. "It's a family story."

"Everything you do is a family story. Filipino maids in Bahrain. Hmong cannery workers. Families working hard to build an empire across many generations."

"I have more to explore in the medieval states of the Kievan Rus."

"Oh god, more *russkaya mafiya*?"

"You know me, Sam. I like to play it safe."

"By the way, congrats on the Indie nom, Pete. It's about time."

Pete beat a tattoo on the dashboard with one hand, still filming Limberlost Island with the other. "Yeah. Congrats on getting free of your corporate easy rider. Your CEO is playing International Man of Mystery now. Did you see his TED talk on secure futures? Multiple bazillion viewings, top ratings of the video."

"No, I looked the other way." I didn't want to talk about Gerard.

Pete was now filming over the tops of his oxblood eight-eyelet 1460s, which were on the dashboard, where they shouldn't be. Those boots are at least a dozen years old. He said, "I wonder if there's a documentary opportunity for me. I'd swear on the grave of one of Huck's bodhisattvas that your boyfriend's trippy TED talk was verbatim of the rap you laid on me five years ago on that long flight out of Sinaloa."

"That trip was expensive." I shifted to handle that sudden 35-mph curve just before the turn onto Lost Point Road, gliding through without braking. "Trust you to tick off both *federales* and *sicarios*. And I didn't get a single margarita the entire trip."

"I suppose sixteen hours isn't enough to experience the real Mexico. I'll make it up to you one day, Sam."

§

OK, here's the Byronic translation of sibling shorthand:
Me: *I admire your work. It's worth all the trouble you cause.*
Pete: *Gerard ripped you off. Contemplating an exotic revenge.*

§

Pete changed the focal point as we pulled into the long driveway that Aunt Lucky shares with the Owens family, who had taken it upon themselves in years past to lead Pete and me out of the feral state that had resulted from the various series of communes my father inhabited.

He filmed the fence posts and potholes along the driveway that led from the highway to the two Gothic farmhouses standing on the bluff above the Sound. Several cars filled the Owens's gravel yard, but Aunt Lucky's side of the lot held only the baby-mustard used Mercedes I helped her buy last summer. The painful scratch down its passenger side must have come from the Thanksgiving adventure in the ditch.

90

33. Nicky Can't Trust iDrive

APPARENTLY SOME OF THE roads were too new to be reported to the GPS robot. Nicky drove around, trying to remember the route that he'd taken the day before with his uncle, finally recognizing the side road.

As he eased the car over the crappy gravel drive, the Ruger 6700 slid from the passenger seat where he'd tossed it, tumbling to the floor.

Nicky braked, slamming the steering wheel in frustration.

This was the last time he let Konstantin or Dymtrus or anyone else bully him into low-life tasks that should be assigned to idiots.

When he accelerated on the gravel, still braking, the Ruger slid under the passenger seat. His cell rang—finding reception at last!— and the onboard USB audio picked up automatically.

"The White Knights want me to find you, Nicky. You dumb fuck. Meet me at the house. Make it easier for both of us."

34. Matt Opens the Door

AT THE CRUNCHING SOUND of wheels on a frozen gravel road, I left the table. It's amazing what the ear can filter amid clinking china, banging cupboard doors, several generations of voices, and blood thundering in your head.

In the hall, I slipped the .357 Magnum from the upper hat shelf and tucked it into the back of my pants before opening the door.

Roz would kill me if she knew there were firearms in the house not under lock and key.

35. Sam Examines Her Personal Error Log

MY BROTHER HAD THE Owens's house in his camera's sights as their front door opened and a sorta, kinda good-looking man with a pirate patch over his right eye stepped onto the porch and watched us park. He waved us over.

At that point, I saw that there would be no quick resolution to Huck's problems, no afternoon solitude back in Seattle for advancing my secure-code problems. I stepped out of the Challenger and into another world, not the one I'd planned to visit.

"Matt had a bad accident a few months ago," Pete said. "I helped him move home."

Hell. I suppose I'll have to feel sorry for the bastard.

§

I experimented with the concept of "being in love" as a teenager, discarding it when I was twenty.

In junior high, I tried to impress a skater barney by learning to skateboard and play the guitar. As an autodidact, I gave myself lessons in punk and grunge grrrl rockers to impress a guy who commented that few women had balls sufficient to play rock-and-roll as God meant it to be played.

My entire venture into the mythical state of 'being in love' had one object: Matt. The skater was Matt, as was the misogynist rock critic. I'm embarrassed to have ripped all the skin off my knees doing a frontside one-eighty on a homemade vert ramp just to impress him, but not about the grunge grrrl thing: I made myself into an adequate guitar player.

Still, unrequited love's a bore. Anyway, he went into the army straight out of college and emerged two years later, changed from the super achiever of our adolescence into a professional slacker, playing guitar in bar bands while working as a longshoreman or a baggage handler at an airport, lost in post-college stagnation. Then all of the sudden Matt was engaged to marry a Barbie clone with enough money to support him in the lifestyle to which he apparently wanted to become accustomed. And One Bad Night, I made a final but abortive attempt to get Matt to fall in love with me. A metaphorical short, sharp knock to the head brought me back to reality.

That's the biggest mistake I ever made. Not Gerard.

§

Correction: Matt Owens didn't look like a pirate. With his sardonic smile and the deep sunburn from his California existence, he looked way, way masculine, but not exactly handsome. He'd shorn his hippie locks in favor of a #1-blade buzz, and he seemed extremely fit, but slackers have time for the gym while the rest of us are working.

36. Nicky Gets Stuck in Neutral

SCREW IT. IF THE idea was not to be forced to do Konstantin's work again, Nicky decided he might as well stop working for him right now.

He jammed the gears, forcing the car into reverse, and then peeled out. One thing he'd admired about the woman he loved was how she took no rubbish from anyone. He needed to borrow her attitude as well as her car.

And he'd seen the beautiful Natalia drive her automobile in this squirrelly fashion. She made it seem very American.

37. Sam Enters a Strange Land

AS WE APPROACHED THE porch, Matt said, "Sam Byron, as I live and breathe."

"Hello, Matt." I calculated that Pete wouldn't block me if I split for Aunt Lucky's house, but it would be awkward. Pete focused his camera on Matt.

Looking only at me, Matt smiled as he casually pushed Pete's hands down, so that my brother filmed our boot tops. "Lucinda said you never come home for Christmas. Come inside. She came over for coffee while we watched Pippi open her presents."

Matt held the door open as I walked in, conscious that he watched the tail end of me. I began peeling off my coat as soon as we stepped inside, since there was at least a fifty-degree difference between the indoor and outdoor air.

"Nice holiday clothes," Matt said, with the same acerbic tone he used in the old days, as he tried to take my coat.

"I can manage a coat hanger on my own," I mumbled. I bumped into Roslyn as I backed away from Matt. When Pete turned to film her, she shook her finger at him, but then laughed and didn't try to stop him.

"I'm so glad you could make it home." Roslyn seemed genuinely happy, though she has never approved of anything about me, so perhaps she mistook me for my sister, or else she was heavily medicated. Dressed as usual in a denim shirt, her honey hair pulled back in a barrette—or a Beretta, as Harley calls it—Roslyn was the picture of happy housewife on Christmas morning. Which is not the Roslyn we know. If I were to draw her picture, she'd appear as Rosie the Riveter from the WWII We Can Do It poster.

"Merry Christmas, Roz," I said, the words getting lost as she hugged me, squeezing me so hard she must have felt my shocked surprise. Over her shoulder, Matt was still smiling at me.

"This is such a good Christmas," Roslyn said, heading for the dining room. Holiday noise spilled out to the hallway as she opened the door. "We're all together for the first time in several blue moons."

"We're only missing my sister," Matt said, "because of the weather."

Pete straddled a chair and sat by Aunt Lucky. Harley held a young, café con leche black girl in his lap, while Roz patted the girl on the back, whispering to her. I guessed the little girl was Roz's Big-Sister project for the holidays. (I'm ashamed of that, but I should report my observations honestly.)

Pete filmed Harley, who is a big guy, muscles filling out his shirt sleeves. He's strong enough to jerk a 1200cc bike upright with one hand and always seemed scary in his cop clothes, but now in jeans and a flannel shirt with the grey-streaked Van Dyke he grew after retiring, he looks like one of his Viking ancestors at rest in the mead hall. He and the little girl were playing with the webcam on a laptop, watching themselves in their own movie.

Roslyn said, "Sam, meet our best girl. Pippi, this is our very good friend Samsara Byron."

By then, I was wondering if space invaders had indeed taken the real Roslyn Owens. *Very good friend?* This from the woman who turned on the yard lights and sent the dogs out to bark the sole time I sat talking with Matt in the backseat of a car our senior year?

Pippi looked up from Harley's computer and stopped giggling. She had braids and freckles, and it seemed like nothing could make her stop beaming with joy. She forced an earnest expression over her smile and stepped over to shake my hand.

"How do you do, Miss Byron. I'm pleased to meet you."

"Likewise," I said.

I bent to kiss Aunt Lucky hello, but she hardly turned her head to accept it. After all this time, I know better than to get too close.

"Damn, Sam! You're home!" Aunt Lucky isn't more than five-foot and a hundred pounds, but she has a big voice, so when she says *Sam*, it sounds like someone taking a ball-peen hammer to the fender of a Ford Fiesta. She took up a Loretta Lynn persona in the late Seventies, and her long hair is still dyed brown, though now it's too dark for her fading complexion. What has changed since last we met: the shaking of her hands doesn't allow the drawing of so firm a line around her lips or her eyes, which distracts from her chirpily cheery expression.

Harley crooked his finger, beckoning me to sit beside him.

"It's good to see you, Sam. I missed it last time you came around."

"Hi, Harley."

I'm still taken aback every time I run into him, at how much Harley seems to like me, given how often we tangled when I lived next door. As I pulled up the chair beside him, I was wishing that I had a father like Harley.

Tom Tremain came in from the kitchen with a pot of coffee, offering his usual aw-shucks grin and winking hello when he saw me. Tom is the deputy who became sheriff when Harley retired, and everything about him cries out "law enforcement." He seemed to have inherited the clean-cut Eagle Scout mantle that Matt discarded. Tom was the sole person there who knows what I really do. Last

September, I'd been called to testify at a trial over a child porn website. I appeared to bear witness to the quality of the feebs' data tracing methods. Tom, testifying about how the computers were seized in a house on Limberlost, was surprised to see me that day, but out in the marble-floored corridor of the courthouse he said only, *"You clean up good."*

"Hey, brother!" Tom slapped five with Pete, who then filmed Tom pouring coffee in my cup. It's disconcerting to see my brother fraternizing with the Law, but I suppose we all get over high school at some point.

"Everything's still top secret about your work?" Harley asked, but not probing me. It was just a friendly exchange.

"Yep," I said. "Most I can tell you is that I type at a keyboard all day long."

He chucked my chin, in about the same way he treated the little girl on his knee. "You keep your secrets well, girl. You always did."

§

So there I was, playing E.T., an alien on terra firma.

But I can't phone home: this was home, where I endured adolescence. However, the analog audio level for noise and gleeful conversation between the Owens family and my own seemed to have been dialed up. I again contemplated bolting for the door. Synapses flooded by the cacophony and the complexity of the social situation, I settled uneasily onto the chair beside Harley and sipped at the coffee from Tom, though I had already drowned in caffeine at Casa D. This time, it was Stumptown coffee, which tastes more like Portland than Seattle.

"Boy howdy." Aunt Lucky's voice crunched like tin foil. Her hand shook when Tom poured coffee; he deftly steadied her cup with his other hand. "We haven't all been together since Sam went off to school. Seems like she never does come home. It's just too bad your girl Isabella can't be here, Roz. She always cooked up a storm at Christmas."

"Oh! I almost forgot," Roslyn said. "Pippi, come help me finish the cinnamon rolls we started."

"I have to go," Pippi said, nodding to me as if this were farewell. "I am truly pleased to meet you." She skipped after Roslyn, with Tom tagging behind.

"See what Roz gave me?" Harley, proud of his Christmas present, tipped the screen of his laptop so that I could see it.

Struggling to repress indignation, I said, "Pete, that's the laptop I bought you last year."

My brother shrugged. "I needed a better webcam, so I sold that one to Roz. You told me I needed to marshal my assets better."

"Lucky for me," Harley said.

For half a heartbeat, I wanted to tell Harley my secrets; not the secrets worth having, like how hardware-level security code works in certain government agencies, and how to exploit weaknesses in personal and corporate computer systems. I wished I could voice my own secrets: my aunt gambled away a small fortune, my father grows pot for a living, and my brother is a jerk

Oh wait, everyone in the room knew all those secrets.

38. Matt's Thumb Hurts

THE DAY GOT COMPLICATED when Pete returned from town with his sister in tow, though he never told me Sam was coming. Enigmatic, that's Pete. No one ever accused him of being obvious.

Sam seemed the same, dressed just as when our old band last played the VFW hall. In a room with more than two people in it, she still twitched like a small mammal seeking cover.

You can see that as you watch Pete's video.

Deftly, she never let Pete film her face, so she's just a shadow among the rest of us. Her hands appear, letting Sheriff Tom pour coffee for her. There's me on the sideline, being an asshole.

"Is that a tattoo?" I asked. I touched a little Celtic knot inked just above the web between her thumb and index finger. "Must have hurt like hell."

Pippi called out, "Matt, you have to give us a quarter."

I'm supposed to pay up if I use a bad word around Roz and Pippi. Instead of reaching for my wallet, I still had my thumb over the webbing between Sam's fingers. I swear, it was like getting hold of an electric fence wire. You can't hang on, you can't let go. The mark at the base of her thumb caused me to remember similar ink, but more like a bird in flight. As I tried to remember where I saw that mark on her, she seemed to read my mind.

"The other one is Celtic, too," she said.

Pippi sought attention just then—she has a mystical ability to rescue me from my lesser self. Before I stepped over to help Pippi, Pete caught on video what everyone else missed: Sam clasped my hand and bit the fleshy part below my thumb. I'd believe I only imagined it if Pete hadn't caught half the movement on camera. Sam's face is missing, so you don't see her biting me.

Slow down the video stream and look closely; you'll see the indents of teeth marks edged in red on my palm.

I don't know what she was thinking. I never do.

39. Nicky Tends the Family Farm

NICKY USED THE WIRELESS in that Wild West café to access the family's business servers, to complete the thankless chores that Dymtrus required of him. He removed the bandage his friend at the hotel had so kindly applied. He didn't really need it, but had kept it for a few hours in remembrance of her.

Christmas carols—American ones—played faintly from a radio in the café kitchen. Capitalist nostalgia everywhere he turned. Yet his own melancholy was brought on by the cold weather and being out here in the country, causing him to remember how ten years before he would dial up the world through his dead grandma Guilletta's phone line. In truth, she wasn't his grandma, but she was dead, and had been then. With all the civic inefficiencies of his former hometown—they couldn't promise sewers or running water to everyone—the authorities had forgotten about the phone service to the cow-bier that Nana Guilletta once called home, backed up against the steel shed that later came to house the family server farm.

Nicky poked to find his new friend on line.

NickCarraway> How did the pickup go?

BlackPawn> We found the shite nites you fingered and passed them to the feds. But they weren't holding anything, so they're back on the street.

NickCarraway> WTF? The details were precise.

BlackPawn> I think we just got them royally pissed off. And my guys can't find you. Since everybody's missing pieces, my boss says we can't promise protection.

40. Sam Opens the Closet Door

TOM GOT A CALL on the radio and excused himself.

Feeling the cold and seeing the steel-grey day when Tom opened the door to leave, everyone murmured about the white Christmas coming our way. Then Aunt Lucky got a bright idea about a snowsuit she'd stashed away that would fit Pippi. I took the opportunity to get away and walked home with her, where I spied my laptop on the sofa. At least Pete had it plugged in, so it was charging. We pawed through overflowing closets filled with clothes and junk that once belonged to Pete and me. Aunt Lucky saves everything.

While we rummaged, her miniature Schnauzers jumped all over me, barking and nipping at the hem of my jeans as if I were an intruder.

"Gretchen! Dick!" Aunt Lucky called to them. "Give the girl a break. She's excited to see you too."

Not.

Aunt Lucky's animals bring out the worst in me and my siblings. I shifted junk in the closet, taking care not to let anything drop on the pesky dogs, however tempting it seemed.

"Why did you keep all my math books from high school?" I asked.

"You never know when you might want to check a fact or two," she said.

My first and last skateboards were piled on the floor of the hall closet. The top shelf held the illegal fireworks that Pete and I got at the Sk'komish reservation for the Fourth a few years ago, but couldn't set off because Harley was home. Pete, a man of discerning taste, likes the loud ones, which are great when you fire them across the water.

An M-80 fell from the shelf, and I had to wrestle the dogs two falls out of three for possession, while wondering what happens if a miniature monster eats a small explosive device.

Seeing Aunt Lucky sort through the treasures in her closet was like viewing a glitchy web video. The limited motion in her arms and shoulders made her I'll-do-it-myself efforts painful to watch. Worse, when she forgot what she was saying, her eyes drifted sideways and then looked around as if startled to find her thoughts missing. Then she bluffed her way through.

"Why don't you stay a few days?" Aunt Lucky said, a familiar setup for her sly coercions. Gretchen got hold of my boot lace, and I struggled to dislodge the beast while I answered.

"I have to get back to work. As soon as we decide what to do with Huck's house, I need to catch the next ferry."

She waved away that idea. "No business on Christmas. It's just not nice. Stick around for a few days. It's the perfect chance for you to get lucky." She laughed at her own joke.

"Chance for what?"

"Matt's here. And you're both free as birds." She raised her eyebrows suggestively. "Roz and I were just saying that it's time you two finally got it on."

"Have you taken leave of your senses?"

She wagged a finger at me. "If you married Matt, it would solve all his problems. That boy is too banged up to go back to work, and you make plenty of money, so—"

"Aunt Lucky, don't be ridiculous." I urged the collection of closet-floor flotsam back in with the toe of my boot, grasping the door frame to steady myself. Dick jumped up and nipped my little finger.

"Makes perfect sense to everyone else," she said.

"Let's just spend the morning here at home with Pete. We can talk over this business of Huck's and—"

"It's no use changing the subject," she said.

"Aunt Lucky—"

She flashed a smile. "Honey, we're all adults now. Call me by my name."

I relieved her of the clothes. Gretchen and Dick jumped in unison, catching hold of a dangling sleeve, so I lifted two dogs with the clothes. I lowered them back to the floor in hopes the demented creatures would let loose. I don't hate dogs. Really. I don't even hate these dogs. I just wished they lived somewhere else. Montana would be good. Or Tennessee.

"Why do we have to spend the morning with the sheriff?"

Aunt Lucky drew herself up, indignant. "Pete spends all his time there, to help Matt cheer up. You should, too. Gretchen and Dick don't want you hanging around here. You get bored and start playing that awful music of yours."

Gretchen and Dick had my boot laces again, helping to ensure that I wouldn't be tempted to hang around and get bored.

She said, "There's every reason for you to stay. Matt needs us. You don't want to let your friends down, do you, Sam?"

A blur of wings beat at the feeder out the window, a shadow of movement like the speedy blur my aunt creates across her own landscape, except half her movements were shaky rather than purposeful.

I said, "Shouldn't you stay home? Eliot says you're supposed to rest."

"It's Christmas, Sam! It's family. I don't want to miss anything."

She whipped out the door ahead of me and likely didn't hear my complaint: "It's the Owens family. Not our family."

Before I could pursue her to continue arguing, the phone rang. I stepped back inside to answer, believing it to be my sister Eliot or Grandma Flo.

"Hello, Aunt Lucky's Reform School for Wayward Girls."

"Let me to talk to Pete Byron." The voice had an accent. European, I think. Half the strangers I met that morning had accents.

"Sorry, he's not here at the moment."

"I know he's there. I need to talk to him."

"Try his cell," I said.

"Give him a message. We're talking with his father, and we need his help with the conversation. Pete should drop by as soon as he can."

"Who is this?"

"Just give Pete the message. Then no one gets hurt."

41. Nicky Appreciates Western Civilization

TRYING TO CENTER HIS thoughts, Nicky craved the soothing sounds and anonymous space of a Starbucks. Sitting in a backwoods café, he felt exposed every time that old man poured more coffee in his cup.

If he were in a civilized place, this early in the day there'd be smooth jazz, just loud enough to let you sink into peace, plus a monotony of pointless conversation, like a Gregorian chant to create a wall of white noise, making it easy to concentrate on work. He longed for the tinny hiss of an espresso machine and the key-clicking of half a dozen laptops. He felt safe in that world, logged on and exchanging news with those faithful to his web story, giving his everyday existence larger meaning.

He clicked to upload the last file.

"*Dobroe utro*, smart boy."

Nicky felt the tiny hairs on his neck raise at the sound of that voice. Here, in this ratshit café in Bumfuck, Washington.

He had mastered American idiom, while Uncle Konstantin had never even bothered to try.

◄◄ ◄ | ► ►►

Nick's American Business 101 as Cinéma Vérité
Entry #28: Recess Time! – December 25, 11:00 PST

People who become powerful at an early age do so by working every available hour. Real-world amusements are simply lost time. Achievers rely on the ethereal world for pleasure, hence this virtual classroom. Video plus open thread. Your choice of topics.

Nick's Fan Forum | Permanent Link | 6 comments

Did you check out
JustMike | 12.25 - 11:12 am |
the Norad Santa site this year? They haven't updated it since
the dinosaurs. Kids have more sophistication than that these
days.

Nicky doesn't do Santa.
AuteurGrrrl | Homepage | 12.25 - 11:15 am |
you're on the wrong site. Check the videos for crissakes.

I can't see more than
ponyboy | Homepage | 12.25 - 11:49 am |
the odometer and tach. As soon as the frame starts to move
away, the video loops back. Is this right? Is there a glitch?

I think the car is German.
AuteurGrrrl | Homepage | 12.25 - 11:52 am |
Am I right? Is this the globalization subtext?

I can't get the video right either.
BruceRulz | 12.25 - 11:53 am |
I want to see what's next, but I have family sh#t all day and
probably won't get to log on again until late.

I'm there too man.
ponyboy | Homepage | 12.26 - 12:11 pm |
Fambly time. Tis the season. LOL.

42. Sam Does the Math

BACK AT HARLEY'S HOUSE, I cornered Pete in the kitchen where the
little girl was frosting cinnamon rolls. I smiled at Pippi and then
ignored her, because there was no other place to talk without
involving the entire nosey Owens clan.

"Huck's bankers have him. Or business partners, or whatever
they are. They just called at Aunt Lucky's." Out of the corner of my

eye, I caught Pippi pausing to listen, and so I dropped my voice. "They threatened you."

Pete preserves an expression of innocence in the face of all adversity. You'd want to help Eliot pound him. "You shouldn't worry so much."

"Geezus pieces. I've been on the island two hours and I already have Byron family woes coming out my ears. Your mobsters have Huck. You're supposed to talk to them before someone gets hurt."

"It's just jive," he said.

"How do you know?"

"If they want Huck to pay them, he has to be healthy to get the money together. And everyone knows I don't have a dime."

"How did they know to call Aunt Lucky's house?"

He shrugged, for crissakes. "Maybe they want you. You're the only one in the family with any money."

This I did not want to hear. "How do you know where to find them?"

"I don't," Pete said.

"They said you should visit soon. That must mean—"

Matt came into the kitchen, which ended our private discussion.

"Stop worrying," Pete said. "Like Huck says, karma works itself out."

In a move calculated to piss me off so much that my head would explode, he wiggled his fingers to clean my aura and touched Huck's crystal necklace, which I still wore. Ticked beyond mortal endurance, I ripped it off and threw it in Roslyn's kitchen trash.

"Didn't you like your Christmas present?" Pippi said.

"She wasn't a good girl," Pete said. "Santa didn't bring what she wanted."

§

Burning with the peculiar rage that one can feel only for one's close relatives, I banged through the door into the Owens's dining room.

Pippi followed, carrying the hot cinnamon rolls.

By this time, I'd had enough caffeine. With the added buzz of frosted pastry, I felt as if I'd swallowed an illicit rave drug. The noise and commotion around me over the next half hour became surreal.

I asked Harley, "When did Roz start baking? That's new."

"She didn't have grandkids before," he said, grinning. "It changes women on a cellular level."

Aunt Lucky said, "You went off the deep end, too, Harley, ever since Matt brought his baby here."

Whoa. Current computation threw an exception.

Harley said, "I'm not denying it. The silence in this old house got to be deafening. Pippi is a sweet relief."

Aunt Lucky was still speaking, though I heard her words as if underwater. "Hard to believe she's only eight. Reminds me of what smart little whips Sam and Pete were at that age."

Matt smiled. I lost track of the conversation while counting. Subtract eight from right now. That means his little bird was hatching at the time of that One Bad Night. And Matt was almost married then to his first Barbie, and married another later, when Barbie #1 didn't work out.

I'm as open-minded as any aging riot-grrrl, but sheesh. Some Eagle Scout.

Meanwhile, Pete sucked up to Roslyn like he was Eddie Haskell. Worse, Roslyn fell for it: "Pete, I really admire your work. You offer insight into new worlds." This from the woman who turned the hose on him more than once when Pete urged Matt to sneak out his bedroom window. Roslyn and Aunt Lucky began reminiscing up the yin-yang.

I take it back: Pete wasn't chubby. He'd cut his hair and dressed in loose-fitting "business casual" clothes, apparently to make himself look innocent. Or maybe it was Seattle camouflage.

Worst of all: Harley and Matt. While I helped Harley organize files on his new laptop, he sought Matt's approval over how he's planning to investigate cold case files now that he's retired. Whenever Matt spoke, Harley overflowed with parental affection, happy that his prodigal boy had returned to the fold. He wanted to kill the fatted calf and invite the entire island to celebrate. What once was lost, et cetera.

Gag me with a big fat gravy spoon.

In the old days, Matt had an overachiever's desire for his father's approval. He could fix a flat in under five minutes, start a fire in the rain using flint and steel, or give mouth-to-mouth resuscitation without making French jokes. Now, he looked like Harley's acolyte: collared sports shirt and khakis, rubber-soled shoes, a manly watch, his head shaved to a Zidane-style nub. Just last year in San Francisco, I'd been out with Pete to see this prodigal son in a scummy East Bay post-punk rock club, playing in his stoopid cover band (called "Undercover" fergawdsake), exchanging dollars and bags with people Roslyn would not want at her dining-room table.

Yes, it's wonderful when parents give unconditional love like Harley does. However, Harley was the same authority figure who had us on tenterhooks in our formative years over slights no bigger than smashing pop bottles on the highway. Aren't parents supposed to offer moral guidance along with their affection? I'm not grousing out of jealousy or wishing that a father like Harley would think the sun rose and set on my rear end.

Unlike me, Matt moved smoothly through the room: one moment he's considerate and deferential with Aunt Lucky, then he's jocular with Pete, and wrapping his arms around Pippi in a hug when she wandered past, holding her lightly on his knee for a few minutes before she could escape into the kitchen. He chatted with Harley about the possibilities in the coming year: the volunteer fire department, mixed-league softball, fishing when the season comes. Whenever someone asked me a question, Matt watched my lips as I spoke, as if I were the most interesting person around. "That's an unusual way of thinking about it," he said, in response to some inanity I'd voiced.

Then a crash in the kitchen brought Matt to his feet in an instant and he bolted through the door to check on Pippi.

The Owens family's happy Christmas hurt my head. Then I conceived of a way to have a word with Pete, remembering my promise at Casa D.

"Where are you going?" Aunt Lucky asked as I headed for the foyer.

"I told Yuri I'd say Merry Christmas to Andrij." I reached for my coat. "Pete, come with me."

Aunt Lucky said, "I've been worried about that Andrij boy. He's too secretive, always skulking around, if he's here. There's a batch of biscotti over at my place. Why don't you take that to him, since it's Christmas?"

"Fine," I said. Aunt Lucky's biscotti was famously inedible. "Pete, come with me."

Pete didn't even glance in my direction. "No, I'm showing Harley how to work his new video camera."

Roslyn looked up from playing Chinese checkers with Lucinda. "Matt," she called. He poked his head back through the kitchen door. "You should go with Sam. You haven't been out of the house all day."

Aunt Lucky slapped the table. "Damn good idea. Why didn't I think of it?"

43. Matt Tucks in His Shirt

I HELD SAM'S COAT, using the manners my father taught me, though she ripped it away, muttering soft words that included "boy scout." Then, as if to confound me on purpose, she stumbled into me, catching herself with both hands on my chest, fingers raking down the front of my shirt.

Again, the flow of electrons between us. My chest burned where the tips of her fingers touched me. My hands shook. If not a jolt of electricity, then maybe pure adrenalin.

Outside, snow had begun to fall. I jammed on a watch cap; she let her dark hair flow free.

"We're all happy to see you," I said. "Especially since no one expected you to come."

"I'm happy to be here," Sam said, though she couldn't have been less convincing.

"Roslyn's dying to know why you surprised us. She couldn't get anything out of Pete in the kitchen. Want to tell me?"

"I came to see Pete and Huck about some family business." She apparently begrudged saying even that much.

"Oh, right. Huck is selling his cabin on the beach. Wish I could afford it."

I came into Lucinda's house behind Sam, so I couldn't see her face to understand whether she was angry with me or just didn't want to be anywhere near Limberlost Island, as she had declared repeatedly over the past decade. She remained silent while searching her aunt's kitchen for the biscotti. I leaned on the door frame, watching her open cupboards. How could I have forgotten how graceful she is, after all that time I'd spent watching her skate or play guitar?

"I missed hanging with you the last few years." *Once upon a time, I had this one trusted friend.*

Standing near the doorway, she turned to me, a surprised frown on her face. We were far too near each other and, in a movement as natural as helping her with her coat, I kissed her.

Lightly, but on the lips. It surprised me more than her, I think. I stepped back to get a grip, but she hooked her fingers in my belt-loops and pulled me toward her. Our hips touched as she kissed me.

She knows how to kiss.

My large motor muscles would not obey the commands I sent to move away. She ran her hands up under my shirt, tracing my spine and then brushing her thumbs over my nipples, which tightened as soon as she touched me. So then I kissed her back. A real kiss, far too hungry, too fast on my part. She kept moving against me. I tried to steady us, to keep balance, until we were in the living room at the edge of the sofa, and she pulled me down on top of her in the most graceful, athletic movement I've ever experienced. We could have gone on kissing until we both contracted a terminal case of chapped lips.

However, just as she reached between us, grasping the buckle of my belt, voices echoed across the yard.

It's snowing, Pippi! Come see!

In instinctive response, I stopped Sam's hand and managed to cease kissing her, though I was paralyzed. Her warm, panting breath tickled my lips as we hovered close for a moment. I forced myself to stand up and tuck in my shirt.

"I can't do this with Pippi around. I don't want her to get weird messages." I had never before been in a position quite like this. I felt like a jerk, towering over Sam, who remained on the sofa, looking up at me with an expression that, of course, I couldn't interpret.

"She's far too well-behaved to come in without knocking," she said. "Why don't we take her over to my sister Eliot's house? She can baby-sit while we do it in the Challenger."

"You're joking." A cold sweat prickled at the back of my neck.

"Of course I am. Eliot's working 911 dispatch." She rose from Lucinda's sofa in a poised movement that put me to shame, whether she intended that or not. "You are supposed to allow me a graceful come-back after rejection."

I rushed to answer. "It's not rejection. Even without Pippi, I need your friendship too much to risk screwing up. It's too soon after what happened."

"We're friends?" She sounded truly incredulous, which hurt worse than when she said mean things on purpose.

The phone rang, but Sam ignored it for half a dozen rings as she brushed past me to rummage in the kitchen, as if a tidal wave hadn't just rushed over us. I found the sound of the phone not only distracting, but unnerving.

"Do you want me to answer that?" I reached to pick up the phone, but she snatched it from my hand.

44. Sam Climbs Down the Cliff

"HELLO."

A faint wheeze came before any words were spoken. It was Huck.

"Samsara?"

"Yes. Are you alright, Huck?"

"Just working through my karma. The wheel turns. Can you please tell your brother to do whatever they ask?"

Background voices crowded into his last few words, and the connection broke before I could answer him.

Hanging up, I turned to find Matt close by, looking nosey.

"Bad news, Sam? You're pale."

"It's just my father," I said. "He called to say Merry Christmas, which is so odd. He must be ill."

Again, Matt was doing that thing: looking into my eyes as I spoke. I pushed past him to fetch the biscotti. Between Huck and the threats and being in the same room with Matt, I had about lost patience with mankind. Fear is a tiresome emotion.

I set my feelings aside as we crossed Lucinda's yard to where the steps lead to Huck's shack. Most all houses on this part of the island sit on the bluff above the water. A few fishing huts from the

Twenties were built down below, just above the tide line, sheltered by madrona trees leaning over the water. As with most of these shacks, you could only reach Huck's by clambering down approximately four stories' of wooden staircase, with peeling paint and lichens on the handrail. A horror to climb up, the stairs are not too bad for the trip down, except that Christmas morning the treads were sheeted in ice from the past night's freezing rain and slippery as hell. Good for concentration though, since the effort stifled conversation.

In trying to lower my overly elevated pulse rate, I considered what to do. First, I needed Pete to get serious about Huck's options. No, first, I needed to get away from Matt and the Owens family to find room to think. Or—

It occurred to me that I should seek advice from Harley. I began silently rehearsing how to ask for help. I couldn't think of a way that didn't begin with *"Do you remember where we lived with Huck, up near Canada?"*

What I did not want to do was ponder mistakes I'd made based on who I'd kissed in the last few months.

Kissing the FWB-turned-CEO seems to have been a simple twist of fate—the kind that forces you to kiss your past good-bye. As far as my ol' patent-attorney buddy Alec, that kiss was stolen from me when he didn't read the signals right.

But geezus pieces, kissing Matt?

Better to jam the pedal full speed amidst a torrential rain in the dead of night, headed the wrong direction down a freeway. I suppose I started it.

Though I did not mean to find myself supine, his full weight atop me, with enough heavy breathing to mistake the whole episode for passion.

Halfway down the cliff stairs, Matt said, "Do you know this guy we're bringing Christmas cookies to?"

"No. Do you know Yuri at Casa D?" Whew, a chance to be normal.

"I was initiated into the perpetual coffee-break club the day I returned."

"Yuri sublet the cabin to a nephew of some cousin. Have you met him? I think he's only been here a week."

"No, though I heard someone was staying in the cabin."

"Yuri says the guy keeps to himself. He thinks Andrij has other cousins leading him astray. They give Andrij free tickets to fly to Canada and Mexico, to party. So his aunt wants him out of that scene."

Matt said, "Sounds like he's being used as a drug mule."

"You'd know about that." I didn't do a good job of hiding my disgust, given what I'd witnessed about Matt and sleaze in San Francisco.

"Yep." He stopped on the steps. "Did you say his name was Andy?"

I shook my head, still lost in whether I could ask Harley for help.

"Matt, did Pete talk to you about being in trouble?"

"Pete's not in trouble. If he were, I'd know."

§

"Geezus pieces, here's the snow Cliff Mass promised," I said. There I was, stuck in the heart of the Conversion Zone, with record snow promised. Big fat snowflakes were coating the icy steps, sticking to my eyelashes, turning Matt's black watch cap white. At the bottom of the stairs to the shoreline, as we stepped around the corner and climbed onto the cabin doorstep, Pippi called from farther up the stairs.

"Daddy, it's snowing hard!"

While Matt turned around to answer Pippi, I saw a reflection of mobbing gulls in the cabin window and looked behind me. A naked body lay on the dock, hands clasped across its chest, head hanging over the dock's edge. Gulls everywhere. Crows complaining in the trees.

Matt slipped his hand over my eyes, wrapping his other arm around me to hold me steady. In my ear, he said, "Take Pippi back to the house. Call 911."

"Let loose. I'm a first responder. I can—"

"Just go. I know what to do here."

I ran for the stairs, doing as he asked. Just like the old days. "C'mon, Pippi!" I called. "Back upstairs. We have a challenge from Matt."

I hurried up the stairs, blocking her from coming down any further.

"What's the challenge? What's Matt doing?"

Even while asking, Pippi turned back up the stairs. Everybody always does just what Matt says.

"Race me to the top. I have a message for Harley, and I told Matt I could beat you up the stairs."

The "race me" command made Pippi forget her question—I do so like to see a competitive girl—and we burst through the Owens's back door, tied in a dead heat.

"Grandpa, you have a message!" Pippi shrieked, since kids don't seem to get out of breath. I was leaning over, gasping for air. *Dead blue guy. Dead Andrij. If it was Andrij.*

Harley came to the doorway, took one look at me, and sent Pippi to find Roslyn while he reached for the wall phone. He was punching 911 as I said quietly, "Andrij is lying on the dock. Dead. I think that's who it is."

Harley's call went through.

"Hi, Eliot. This is Harley Owens. We need an aid car and an officer over at my place. See if Tom is free to come." He gave her a code that probably means "dead body."

As Harley hung up, Matt was at the back door, calling to my aunt.

"Lucinda, do you have a key to Huck's house?"

"Sure do, baby. Are you thinking about buying the old place? That would be a kick in the pants."

Actually, it seemed that yet again someone had bought the farm at Huck's shack. Huck would have one more karmic inconvenience to bear.

45. Matt and Pete Take Pictures

GULLS PECKED AT THE plastic around the body. I waved and shouted, and the birds shrieked while taking flight and then landing again in the water, complaining as they waited for me to leave them to the treasure they'd found.

The long, muscled body on the dock reminded me of someone I'd met before: Andy Peterson.

I unlocked the shack, looking for anyone else, but both tiny rooms were empty. So I had to trace my footsteps back out and stand helpless while first Harley and then Pete joined me to wait for Tom and the 911 crew to arrive.

When Tom came, he was halfway through taking care of business when his camera malfunctioned, so he asked Pete to take pictures. You could tell that whatever else Pete might be familiar with in his work, he wasn't comfortable with dead bodies close up. Not like this, anyway. At one point, while Tom was directing close-ups, Pete handed him the camera, showed him how to work it, then went to stand on the deck with me, staring out over the Sound in silence.

There wasn't much more to film: an undisturbed scene, with no footprints but ours.

"It's Andy Peterson." I leaned on the deck railing, affecting as casual a posture as possible, given the sense of jeopardy boiling in my blood.

"Not necessarily," Pete said. He spit into the blackberry vines that crowded the deck. "You can't see anything through the plastic. I don't remember that body ink."

"Those are new tattoos," I said. "It's a message for me."

"You're too self-absorbed. Everything isn't about you," Pete said. Gulls croaked at Tom down on the dock, wanting him to get out of their way. "The guy lying there was supposed to get a message."

"I'll have to sell them my soul to make it through this."

"No way. I've got the fix in," Pete said. He called out directions to Tom about the camera, and then spoke confidentially to me. "I'll talk to the capo tonight. You'll see."

"I can see clearly from here," I said. "The next guy will be more determined."

46. Nicky's Heart Skips a Beat

"GOOD DAY, VUIKO KOSTYA."

Nicky hoped the waver in his voice sounded like surprise. He held out his hand in greeting as hope ran out of the day.

Uncle Konstantin stood beside the table, dressed as a street vagrant, looking emaciated in his costume. With his dusky complexion and dressed in clothes retrieved from the ashbin, Konstantin could pass for any derelict living by the train tunnels. It was a famous story among the cousins: Konstantin dressed down when doing handwork among his own family. Nicky's heart flipped: his uncle had learned of the Black Pawn move against Zandr's White Knight. Nicky would soon be singing with the angels, alongside Andrij.

Konstantin shook Nicky's hand in the way that men did in their family. He pointed to the other chair at the table where Nicky sat, his eyebrows raised in a request, as if Nicky could ever refuse anything Konstantin asked.

"Please join me, *Vuiko.*" He hoped to appear as calm as when they'd traveled together the day before. As Konstantin seated himself, familiar scents of Versace Pour Homme and Kool cigarettes wafted over Nicky. That scent of danger had long ago made Nicky jealous of Konstantin's place in the world.

"I'm surprised to be so far from home on this holy day," Konstantin rasped, as if air had to be tortured to pass from his throat. He had a Styrofoam cup of Starbucks coffee from the ferry's canteen, and he sipped at it as he set a vile, filthy pillowcase on the floor beside him. The folds of the cloth molded loosely around the contents.

"I'm surprised to see you here, Uncle Kostya. Back to the north woods again?" *Let's just get it over with*, he wanted to say. His American story was to be *Reservoir Dogs*, not *Gatsby.*

"A man should be as busy as his heart will stand," Konstantin said, his voice echoing in the empty café like whispers in a tomb. He stared out the window. "It's cold today."

"As cold as my grandfather's barn at Twelfth Night."

"Aye, where he used to chastise us, your father and I, when we were children. Dymtrus escaped the willow cane more often than not."

"Grandfather upbraided me on occasion, also."

Konstantin laughed, as if they shared a fond memory. "Then you learned early how to endure the wages of your sins."

Nicky tried to choke out an answer. "Sin is in the eye of the beholder."

Konstantin's eyes glinted with cold humor. "I'm glad to find you again so we can talk. My brother Dymtrus can't create a world big enough for your talents." He laid his cold, dry hand on Nicky's wrist, grasping it. "When we lost your father, I hoped you could be the son I never had."

"I feel the honor, *Vuiko Kostya*." Nicky's coffee sloshed in his cup, betraying how his hands shook.

"That's you big as life in the film Peter Byron made," Konstantin said. "Here, you let me blab on about getting you an agent, and you already know Peter Byron."

Nicky's mind ranged back over everywhere he'd been in the wide world, in the heartbeat after Konstantin spoke. Peter Byron had made training videos at the server farm operation. But Pete Byron didn't even know his name.

Nicky said, "We're not close. I'm just here on family business, to collect on that debt you asked us to take care of."

"So, is that why you're out here for Christmas, Nicky? For Pete Byron? I trust him, so I thought I'd invest in those backwoods idiots he's related to." Konstantin slapped his thigh, laughing silently.

"I didn't plan to involve Pete Byron," Nicky said, smiling in what he hoped was an enigmatic way, while his brain raced over the idea that Uncle Kostya wanted him to bully Pete Byron's family into paying a debt.

"You must be jerking on your old uncle's leg, am I right?"

"No, I'm just here to work your collections," Nicky said. He decided humility might pay for him at this moment. "I know you preferred Zandr for this business."

"You're not here to fetch that little girl Zandr is supposed to grab? Danny didn't trick you into doing his job?"

Nicky shook his head, not knowing what his uncle meant, but hoping he appeared wise. If he were directing this, the camera would zoom in on his coffee cup, rattling in its little white plate.

47. Sam Works a Puzzle

WHEN HARLEY LEFT TO join Matt on the beach, I looked around for Pete, my own family problems weighing on me as much as that poor guy at the bottom of the cliff. Two bodies in two days, and I wouldn't have been in either place if it wasn't for Pete. As I went into the kitchen, Pete was on his way out the back door, following the Owens men.

Roslyn got to the door before I could nab Pete, her Christmas-day smile worn thin. "Sam, please help divert Pippi," she said. Mind you, Roslyn has never asked me for a favor in her life.

"Sure," I said, uncertain how one goes about diverting children.

Roslyn's eyes brimmed with tears. "She lost her mother a couple of months ago after a long illness. Let's not upset her."

By Roslyn's definition, "helping" meant I did the diverting while she slipped out the back door with the rescue crew.

In movies and in detective stories, people find dead bodies and then after thirty second of horror, your attention is diverted to stage business or thoughtful clues. I should have had enough Byron family drama to drown out distressing thoughts. Yet each time I blinked my eyes, I'd replay the scene at the bottom of the cliff, and the only soundtrack was my own voice. However, my attention was redirected to the hyper-cheerful Stepford child of Lost Point Road. Sliding shut the door to the dining room and foyer, I joined Pippi where she sat quietly on the living room sofa, looking at books, surrounded by a mountain of Christmas wrappings. As I took off my coat, I tried to engage her in conversation.

"Pippi is an unusual name. Who did your mom name you for?"

"I chose it. In this new town, I needed a new name, to blend in."

I didn't comment on that impossibility. Limberlost isn't as white as it was when I went to school here, but this girl would not blend in. "So who did you name yourself for?"

"Pippi Longstocking, of course. Can't you see the resemblance?"

"That's who I wanted to be," I said. "But my father was only a hippie, not a pirate king. And I didn't want a horse. I just wanted the chest with all the drawers and treasures."

"I like the chest, too. It would be funny if you could keep a horse in your house like she does."

"I identified with Pippi," I said. "Though I got sent to the principal's office much more than she ever did."

Her scandalized look tweaked me, so I pressed it further.

"I was the kid your mother warned you about."

This sent a frisson through Pippi that I rather enjoyed.

At her suggestion, we started a jigsaw puzzle. The card table was folded into the same closet as in days of yore, and the same goosenecked lamps were at hand to light our work.

That's what you're supposed to do, right? A puzzle to idle away the long hours of Christmas day while they haul a body off your father's dock?

§

Blink. I could see the scene again. It wasn't because I'm afraid or shocked by death. I sat with my Grandma Byron last summer while she shrugged free of this mortal coil. We sat alone and talked, and it was a transcendent experience. Last year, I was in a three-way accident when a thirty-five-year-old man died of a coronary while driving. I had to comfort his wife through the eons it took for the state patrol to come. However, the body on the dock and the one in the freezer seemed like random assaults in parallel universes.

Blink. *Dead blue guy. Dead Andrij.*

Pippi tugged for attention, in the quietest, most polite way, of course.

48. Nicky Chooses Door #3

KONSTANTIN WIPED HIS LIPS with a napkin after he finished his coffee, the careful gesture at odds with his beggar's clothes, as was the Rolex he wore.

"I see you have a nicer auto than the one you drove yesterday." Konstantin nodded at the German car parked in the street. "It shows that you're not a foozle like your old man. Andrij and Danilov failed the family, but you got guts and dedication."

"I am humbled that you say so, Uncle Kostya." Nicky's ears burned in that familiar anger that rose when they insulted his father.

"Join me." Konstantin sighed as he shoved his cup and napkin aside. "I can't raise Zandr on the phone, and if you don't deliver what he promised, we're all—how did Andrij call it?—down shit river."

"I'm working on it," Nicky said. "I need to finish this project today."

Konstantin nodded as if satisfied, and then veered in another direction.

"You're a friend of this guy, the guitar player at the wedding, like Pete Byron says?"

Guessing wildly at what the right answer might be, Nicky chose the lesser option. "Not really."

Konstantin slapped his knee, gleeful. "That's what I thought when I heard about the film. I bet your Uncle Yevgeny a thousand Euros on it. I said I'd have to see it in real life to believe it."

Nicky relaxed just a mite, not yet understanding why he was off the hook.

Konstantin smiled, too, his thin lips stretched over very white teeth that had enjoyed extreme American orthodontics. The gleam of dental work and Konstantin's grave, erect posture further marked him as a gentleman of wealth, however he chose to dress down for his intended prey.

"I want you to come off the guitar player for me. Danilov has been working on it, but he isn't getting the job done any better than Andrij."

Nicky sipped the last of his coffee. He set it down, trying to see the coaster on the table through the wavering aura of an oncoming migraine.

"We'll ride together again, eh, Nikolai?" Konstantin's voice scraped over gravel. "This cold has inconvenienced me. And it's getting dark."

"Of course, *Vuiko*. I'm not yet ready to depart." As he said it, Nicky knew he didn't have the balls to mean it. He clutched the screen of his laptop.

"I'll wait for you," Konstantin said. He held out his hand.

Choking on desperate reluctance, Nicky handed over the keys.

⏮ ◀ | ▶ ⏭

Nick's American Business 101 as Cinéma Vérité

Entry #29: Open Thread – December 25, 12:30 PST

Gotta take care of family business.

Nick's Fan Forum | Permanent Link | 1 comments

Hello?

JustMike | 12.25 - 1:12 pm |
Is this thing on?

49. Sam Learns About the Pirate King

WHILE I PONDERED TWIN corpses straying into the periphery of my everyday experience, and still sniffing in dismay about the direction Matt chose for his life, I found a small handful of puzzle pieces that seemed to belong together and started making them fit.

Pippi said, "You can't start work on the middle until the border is done."

"I can do it however I want to."

"No, you can't." Pippi seemed both shocked and distressed. "We'll get done faster if we work together. We need the border first."

I said, "If we're doing a speed puzzle, then it's every woman for herself."

Pippi said, "It's important to cooperate."

I put down the pieces I'd been fiddling with. "This is too weird."

Pippi glanced up. "That's what the kids say about me at school."

"I'm sorry. I didn't mean it that way. What I mean—you're so quiet, and you seem to want to do what everyone else wants."

"People are supposed to cooperate."

"No, kids are supposed to keep adults from taking things for granted." I paused, "Especially your dad."

Pippi said, "Matt needs people to be nice to him."

I wrinkled my nose. "After high school, Matt started calling his dad and mom 'Harley and Roslyn.' Now you call your dad 'Matt.' Doesn't anyone call their parents 'mom and dad' anymore?" Like Huck never let us do.

She said, "I just forgot. I try to call him Daddy to make him happy. But he isn't my real father. So I forget."

"He's not your father?" Nerve endings fired as I reinterpreted events: Matt wasn't siring a café latte child while marrying a series of Barbies and banging me in the back of the Challenger. His moral score rose one point.

Pippi said, "My father—my real father—was a hero like Pippi Longstocking's. He was a spy who fought for truth and justice. He could speak Arabic and Russian and Spanish. Then he got shot in a war and died."

I couldn't help but pry. "So what's your real name?"

She suddenly turned as solemn as my sister Eliot's preacher-father at a funeral. "I can't say. I promised to keep it secret. Only Matt's family knows. So don't try to make me say."

"OK," I said. It wasn't her name that piqued my curiosity at this point. "I never try to make anyone tell their secrets. It's not fair to do that. Especially since I have secrets too. It's a mark of character if you know how to keep secrets. Especially other people's secrets."

Pippi said, "Can you say what's really happening? Or is that a secret you aren't supposed to tell?"

Voices murmured in the hall again, the words indistinct.

"What do you mean?" I said, stalling.

Pippi said, "You're hiding something. You should tell me."

She had discovered how to push my buttons: I'd spent years hearing adults murmur on the other side of the wall, with no one to say what's really happening, just what Pete and I could discover on our own.

"There was a bad accident," I said. "Your grandma and dad thought you shouldn't see."

Pippi jumped up. "Is Matt hurt?"

"No," I said, using my first-responder voice and reaching for her hand, as if I know how to reassure children. "Matt's fine. A neighbor got hurt."

"Hurt dead?"

"I think so, yes."

"But it's not Matt," Pippi said, sitting down, turning her attention back to the puzzle. "And you have the mark of character. So I won't worry."

50. Matt Fails His Driver's Test

MISERABLE IN THE COLD wind, we climbed the stairs back up the bluff.

Above me on the steps, Harley was talking to Tom, laughing.

"Some things change, and others stay the same. Sam's always hot as a pistol."

Tom said, "Yep. Matt should make a move. He can handle smart-but-pissy better than most."

I said, "I'm not interested," while wondering if indeed I could handle it.

Tom stepped back, laughing at me. "Do you have a choice? I hear Roslyn and Lucinda picked her for you."

While we stamped snow from our boots, Roslyn called to us. "Close the door! We can't heat the whole island with a wood stove."

Tom touched my shoulder as Harley and Pete passed into the kitchen. "Sam has more going on than you think."

"Not you, too? Trying to set me up?"

"I mean in the real world."

In the living room, Pippi jumped up, smiling but obviously needing reassurance. I sat and pulled her down beside me, and put an arm around her. She leaned her head against me, so I could smell baby shampoo and Christmas cookie frosting.

"How's my girl?"

In the background, Sam was asking Harley how things went down below. They seemed to like each other, now that he doesn't have to worry about keeping her out of reform school.

Roz called out, "Hey, Pippi! Why don't you come see what I have in the kitchen?" She held out her hand to Pippi, who came to her side and they disappeared behind the swinging door. That gesture filled me with joy and relief. *Everything might be OK.* Though it's more likely that I have over-developed my capacity for self-deception.

Sam stood looking at me, everything not OK.

I said, "I'm sorry you had to see that down there."

She blinked several times, but didn't answer.

Harley and Tom came into the dining room, so I couldn't say more. They rehashed what they knew about the scene, which was close to nothing.

"We'll guess it's Andrij until we know for sure," Tom said, "I wish I didn't have to tell Yuri he has to identify a body. It's not my favorite part of the job."

The radio at Tom's shoulder crackled and he stepped aside to exchange words with Eliot. After the call, he said, "There's a major accident up at that five-way stop on the north end."

I said, "Why don't I go talk with Yuri? He knows me well enough."

"I'm headed in the other direction," Tom said, "so I can't give you a ride."

"Pete can take him. Can't you, honey?" Roslyn said as she pushed open the swinging kitchen door, with Pete following behind her. The open door revealed Pippi at the kitchen table, up to her elbows in flour and cookie dough, a streak of green icing on her nose.

Sam muttered behind me. "Oh geez, now Pete is Roslyn's honey."

Pete said, "Sure, Roz. I'm headed that way. I need to catch the next ferry to take care of some business."

"Are you effing leaving me here?" Sam whispered, furious.

Pete looked pitiable, which he'd practiced for years. "I'm marshaling my resources. I have to go, and you need to stay with Aunt Lucky tonight."

"Who's driving the car back here?" Sam asked, her voice ringing with sarcasm.

"I'll take it with me."

"No, you will not. Use mine when you get to Seattle. I need wheels while I'm here. And you can't just leave Matt in the village."

"All right. Matt can take me and drive the car back."

"He's not driving my car," she said.

"It's mine too." Pete said. However, it was a silly argument: I had yet to try driving with one eye blind.

"I'll drive," she said. "Lucinda is fine here."

She pulled on her coat (I'd learned not to offer to help) and walked across the gravel lot to start her car. I followed, the sound of our boots scrunching on the ice and gravel, echoing across the field. While waiting for Pete to return from Lucinda's house with his bag, I slipped into the passenger seat beside her.

"Don't slam the door," she said. "It's an assault on the mechanism."

"Sorry." Silence reigned until I found something to say. "The sky is so low and leaden, it already looks like dusk."

She shrugged.

Trying again, I said, "This car was primer grey for years. I never pictured you driving a red car."

"A Challenger is supposed to be red," she said. "Or black. This is the original color. We took great pains to match it. I wanted to get it right."

"That sounds exactly like you."

Pete opened the passenger door, and I got out so he could climb into the back. He started filming immediately, keeping the camera focused on me.

Sam was pissed. Pete had stirred up some business with her, it seemed. All the warmth from those moments with Pippi had dissipated, and Roz wasn't around to float my spirits. I played the stoic, but inside, I was freaked. The scene at the bottom of the cliff could have been captioned "Man comes to a bad end" in a silent movie, and the inference would apply to me, too.

Plus: how could I consider touching any woman, given the jeopardy that makes up my life? Standing in Lucinda's kitchen earlier, I lost it. It sounds juvenile: I got within ten feet of a healthy, attractive woman for the first time in over a year and in thirty seconds we were rectilinear.

In the car, with Pete's camera hovering over my shoulder, I silently rehearsed what I should say to Sam when we were alone. *Sorry I'm an asshole. I'm screwed up, but I'm better now.*

Pete says maybe it isn't Andy dead on the dock.

He also says he didn't know Sam was coming.

But Pete is a known liar.

51. Nicky Gets the Message

NICKY NEEDED TO SEND a message before he joined Konstantin on the next Horsemen of the Apocalypse ride that his uncle insisted they take together.

NickCarraway> Signing off – maybe for the night.

BlackPawn> Where are you, dude? we got blowback with the fbi. They got questions I can't answer.

NickCarraway> Limited connectivity here. Will answer as I can.

BlackPawn> They're giving us till 10 in the morning to comply with their request. You need to help. We didn't sign up to get our nuts in a cracker with feds.

⏮ ◀ | ▶ ⏭

Nicky stared out the window, ruminating on what could have gone wrong. The old gnome in the coffee shop stood beside the table, coffee pot in one hand and the bill in the other.

"I gotta close now, sir. Cook's gone. It's long past our hours."

Out the window, a car screeched into the lot. The passenger door flew open. A tall guy got out, and another guy followed. They hugged in that distant way the young men do here in the northwest of America, keeping each other at arms' length and then slapping one another on the back. The second man pulled a knapsack from the backseat and stood in profile for a half second before starting down the ramp to the ferry.

Peter Byron. It couldn't be anyone else.

Nicky stood, slamming shut his laptop and shoving it into his camera bag. The chair fell to the floor as he bumped into the ancient gnome.

"You gotta pay, sir!"

52. Sam Practices Interpersonal Relations

IT COULD BE SAID that at one particular moment in time, Sam Byron had the power to manage her own fate: I could have driven onto the ferry and returned to Seattle. However, I had locked into the assignment that Eliot gave us, to watch out for Aunt Lucky. If Pete had to go to Seattle for Huck's sake, then I was left to tend our aunt.

Limberlost Island sits near the forty-seventh parallel, which meant that it was fully dark by five o'clock that night. We sat in the Challenger watching Pete walk down to the ferry, the mercury vapor lights turning his journey into a sepia-toned postcard. Curiosity got the better of me.

"Is Pippi yours, Matt?"

He smiled in that twisted way he has. "Emotionally and legally, yes."

"Biologically?"

He quit smiling and looked out the window, which was steaming up fast.

"No. I haven't had the pleasure of making babies with anyone. If Lucinda and my mother put me up as a candidate, I trust you can see how unfit I am."

He grabbed my hand, which always alarms me. Maybe I inherited stand-offishness from Aunt Lucky. He said, "You can't believe how hard it is to see everyone now. To feel pitied. Then I see you."

"I don't pity you," I said.

"No, you wouldn't, thank god. You were the only one besides Pete who knew I was faking it all morning."

Since I couldn't honestly claim that I knew, I didn't say anything. Which left us in silence, but Matt seemed comfortable with that. He stretched out, leaning back, staring at the ceiling of the Challenger.

He said, "Her mother was widowed and had been ill for a long time. I married her after my accident to take care of the two of them." He rubbed at his covered eye with his open palm. "She died a couple of months ago, just after Pippi's adoption went through."

OK, I had to surrender a portion of my resentment about the failed Eagle Scout. All right: A significant portion.

As if he knew the rising score and wanted to go for a three-point shot, he said, "I'm sorry we left things unresolved between us all this time."

"What do you mean?" I said, as if I didn't know.

"That night. You know what I mean. Afterwards, I thought how you must have drawn a straight line on the analogy test, connecting 'drunk' to 'asshole,' which is fine. I can live with that."

I agreed, but didn't say so. Just tallying my score.

Matt looked at the palm of his hand, like people do when they're trying to tell a difficult truth. "Then I realized that you couldn't have known that I broke up with Brandi the day before. So I'm guessing you thought I was two-timing her. It must have gone against your moral code."

"Matt, we'd already done the sweet thing by then." I failed to suppress a tone of derision. "If I had an appropriate moral code, I wouldn't have been in the back seat with you."

Although I declared that I had no morals, I do. That particular night, however, the feral child took over and set out to make him recognize True Love. It's unpleasant to ponder the kind of idiot one had been at age twenty.

"What happened, Sam? If we're going to spend time together now, I'd like to know what you think of me."

"We aren't spending time together. That was eight years ago."

"Tell." He had my hand in a thumb-lock, like he used to do to Pete in grade school to attain compliant behavior. However, he didn't apply pressure, smiling the whole time, like he's such a clever guy.

I said, "It's what you said after."

"Which was?"

"'That's the worst thing I ever did in my life.'"

He sat back as if stunned. "I said that? I am so sorry."

"Yeah, sure. Forget it, Matt."

"Look, I didn't know better then, not to drink my way through grief. It was bad of me to bring that on you."

"Also, if you hadn't been drunk, I wouldn't have had the pleasure of getting to know you in the back seat." I opened the car door. "Let's talk to Yuri."

Matt took my hand again. "Please let me handle it. Oh, don't look at me like that, Sam. Yuri is an old-world guy. He doesn't need a woman watching how he deals with bad news. Give me ten minutes, and then come in."

53. Nicky Explores Themes of Good and Evil

NICKY FELT THAT HE had to abandon Uncle Konstantin's collection task, since he had learned that Pete Byron was involved. His other choices seemed to be slim. He could agree to go along with Konstantin's deal with the Knights from Transfuckistan.

Except that deal was far too evil.

He could watch while Konstantin offed that dumb-fuck guitar player. That portended more evil than Nicky could stomach, having attended the Konstantin Master Class the day before.

Which meant he had to kill Uncle Konstantin.

He'd never done anything but watch, and then only by accident or coercion. In this circumstance, it was like being on a battlefield: kill or be killed. He rehearsed how he would do it: trick Konstantin to get him out of his car, and then move quickly to get possession of that Glock, regretting that he hadn't retrieved the Ruger from under the seat before now.

When Nicky reached the car, he could see his uncle's shape on the passenger side, but the frost on the glass occluded details of his uncle's face. The passenger door was locked, and Konstantin didn't respond when Nicky tapped the glass to be let in. Rubbing his freezing hands, Nicky walked around and rapped on the driver's window.

Still no response.

He tugged open the unlocked driver-side door.

Konstantin grinned, his white American teeth bared. He stared off through the rimed windshield. Hesitant, Nicky touched his uncle's shoulder.

No one was home.

54. Matt Determines How Much Size Matters

MATT, OLD BUDDY, YOU'RE *still man enough to know how to tell a good person that his family is in trouble.*

As I walked up the steps to Casa D, I couldn't in good faith repeat my personal *Everything's going to be OK* mantra, so I gave myself a lame pep talk. The front was locked, but I could see movement in the kitchen, so I circled around to the alley and rapped on the flimsy door as I opened it. The smell of burned grease and industrial cleaner wafted over me.

Yuri stood in the center of the kitchen, leveling a 9mm Sig Sauer at my head, and once more I felt how overly sufficient that caliber is at close range.

Three:
Nightfall

55. Nicky Uses Bad Language

"Himno. Sooka suna. Upizdysh. Sukin sin."

Nicky softly chanted the swear words that his grandfather used to shout. He put his hands in his pockets, trying to think what to do.

He didn't like to touch dead things. When Dymtrus showed him how to touch a steak on the barbecue to tell if it's done, Nicky felt repulsed at the squishy splutter as his finger sank into it.

Still, he had to do something, and he didn't have time to complain about the complete unfairness of it all. Zandr's greed and stupidity. Dymtrus's misplaced loyalty. In a just world he wouldn't have to tidy up after either betrayals or Acts of God.

The family ties between himself and the body in the car weren't strong enough for Nicky to indulge in philosophizing. He had only moments to ponder what to do before taking action. He loved his father's brother, in the way that family duty calls, but the man's soul was gone, and the remains had to go, too.

He had to touch the body. A portion of the task had to be done without gloves. Nicky had to fully embrace death for a moment, so closely that he could smell everything: Versace Pour Homme, Kool menthol, emptied bowels.

Nicky stopped himself, repressing his natural tendency to run an inventory. He held his breath and did what he had to do.

56. Sam Displays Byronic Misanthropy

I WATCHED MATT BOUND up the steps to Casa D, but the front door was locked. He pressed his face to the window, shielding his face with his hands to block the outside light, and then he went around the corner and up the alley toward the back door.

I leaned back in the dark of the early Pacific Northwest winter night, listening to the sound of the Challenger's engine and liking it too much to turn on the radio. Then I found myself staring at the ceiling of the car again.

Maybe the old Matt still existed.

Maybe the rescue of Pippi proved the Eagle Scout was still on patrol.

Maybe, in spite of my loss of faith in the One True Love scam, a deep limbic system response existed between us.

Yeah, sure.

Maybe I should quit wasting time and get back to exploring the security logs I'd saved early that morning. I had my laptop back at Aunt Lucky's. I could log onto the work network remotely, and—

"Hey, Missy."

I screamed when the passenger door opened and someone piled in beside me.

"Shhh, it's just me." Byronic turmoil filled the air: Uncle Bob, twice the size of his brother, shouting hello at twice human volume, dressed in the same greasy sheepskin coat he'd worn for a decade. He plunked his duct-tape–repaired cowboy boots on the dashboard as soon as he sat down. I swatted at them; he ignored the gesture.

"You scared the bejeezus out of me, Uncle Bob." Once again, trepidation flooded my veins like a bad drug.

"Shit, yeah! I'm feeling the same. I came for Pete, but I missed him."

"He's on the ferry that's loading now," I said. "Pete says you're in the same deep doo-doo as Huck."

"I'm doing my best to help." His voice hummed and whined with the same tone of miserable excuse as each of the four thousand times he failed to pick us up after school twenty years ago.

"Then catch the ferry with Pete. Get out of my car."

"The thing is, I can't," Bob said. "There's a dude watching the ferries. I think it's one of them that's looking for us. So I'm stuck here."

"Jiminy goddamn Christmas. Aren't you supposed to be a tough survival guy who knows how to fight? And you let Pete walk down there alone?"

"Only American style fighting," he said. I hate it when manly men whine. "These guys—no missy, you don't need the details. I don't want to scare you."

"You already have, Uncle Bob. What do you aim to do?"

"I'll sneak on the ferry in the morning," he said. "But I'm about to freeze. Could you maybe take me home with you? I'm sure your Aunt Lucinda wouldn't mind, and—"

"No, not possible," I said, stopping any idea about going to Lucinda's before it went any farther. "Yuri is in the café. Even though it's closed, he'll let you wait there. Then you can sneak on another ferry."

"Can't do that. One of the gangsters is in there with Yuri."

"Oh geez. Out of the car. You hear me? Now!"

57. Matt Sets the Safety Catch

"HEY, YURI. IT'S ME. Matt Owens." I spoke softly without moving an eyelash.

Yuri blinked, squinting, and it seemed to take eons for him to recognize me and lower his weapon, so long that I guessed he was near-sighted, further amping my heart rate, which had been revving at a high RPM all day.

"Hey, friend," I said again. As he lowered the gun, I gently took it from him. He's such a little guy, it had to be a weight for him.

He sank, as if holding that gun had been keeping him upright, sitting on a stack of cardboard grocery boxes.

"You know, I come here to get away from those criminals," Yuri said, anger wrapped like an over-wound spring in his voice. "OK, yes, I paid a bribe to get here. But since I stepped on this shore, not once did I break a law or bow to anyone. Last year, I became a citizen. I won't have it in my store."

I sat beside him and quietly made sure the firing chamber was empty and set the safety.

"What happened?" I said, hoping that if I could keep him talking it would help him calm down. I tucked his pistol into the open drawer under the counter, recognizing that as its home.

"That fellow sits in my café all afternoon with his computer, using my network, and he doesn't buy more than a ham sandwich. When I want to close the store, he stops me, says he's looking for Huck Aureliason. I tell him Mr. Huck went away on the ferry this morning, and that his son Mr. Peter Byron just left. I point to the ferry that's leaving, and then this fellow goes nuts. He curses and then goes away."

"Did he come back?"

"No, but then when I'm locking the door, another one of those Mafioso bums knocks on the door, won't go away until I answer. He wants Andrij, so I figure he's one of those bad cousins."

"What did you tell him?"

"I tell him nothing," Yuri said. "Then he asked for you, Mr. Owens."

Oh Christ.

"I decided I don't like him. He does that thing—standing over me, getting too close. I know how those criminals do it, how they make you afraid. When I say I don't know you, he curses me. I see he has a gun."

"Yuri, I'm sorry—"

He worked through his story, not hearing me. He said, "So then I have my pistol and I tell him my store is closed." Yuri looked up, actually seeing me for the first time. "I got to call Andrij and tell him what trouble his bad friends are getting him into."

"Yuri," I put a hand on his shoulder. "We found a man dead on the dock by the cabin. We think it's Andrij. Tom will need you to identify the body."

The way Yuri looked at me, it was clear he had heard that kind of bad news before. When I held his gaze, I felt like I was looking back into many, many decades of terrible news.

Yuri broke the stare. He shrugged. "I didn't know him so well. I just did a favor for my cousin, giving her nephew a place to stay.

Maybe that punk who was in here killed him. Maybe that Andrij boy was a punk, too."

"We don't know at this point, but I don't think it happened today."

In cases like this, you just calmly repeat the facts of the situation. I mean, this is your basic Psych 101. You give comfort as the person works through denial and anger. Me, I was the one panicking. At least two people Yuri regarded as bad guys came to the island looking for Pete and me. One of the bad guys asked only for Pete, but undoubtedly I was the final prey.

"You want to call the sheriff for me, Mr. Owens? I need to describe that punk, so the police can find him."

It seemed to take forever, once I called dispatch, for Eliot to raise Tom, and then for Tom to listen to what I told him. At the start, I had my hand on Yuri's shoulder, but then he wiggled away to set out cups and pour coffee for the both of us. While I waited on the phone for Tom, Yuri signaled to ask whether I wanted sugar or cream. I suppose that's how one individual chose to deal with fear. I took the cup of coffee while telling Tom: "Yuri is concerned that his visitor caused the harm down on the dock."

Tom said, "Did you tell Yuri that body came to rest there no later than yesterday? Anyone looking for Andrij today didn't kill him yesterday."

"Right, Tom," I said. "Yuri says one fellow drove a sports car. The other one asked for Andrij." I left out that the dude also asked for me.

"So, you say you've got two unknown bad guys I'm supposed to look for?" Tom sounded testy. Yuri hung at my elbow.

"From Yuri's description, they were both dressed for cold weather," I said. What I wanted to say to Tom: *I don't know if there's two or a dozen—but they'll find me before you find them!*

Tom sighed. "I'm sorry. I've been fishing assholes out of ditches all afternoon. That poor guy dead on the dock didn't put me in a good mood."

I said, "Can Yuri give you a description over the phone? Or are you sending a man over?"

"Seriously? My whole goddamn force is out helping people who don't know how to drive. Half of those losers can't put on a decent pair of shoes before going out in the snow. I've got shit-all to send over there."

"Let me put Yuri on, so he can tell you what his visitor looked like."

Yuri took the phone and began to give the sheriff a detailed, succinct description of what sounded like Danny Peterson, the wise guy who ripped me out of that room where Sonny Green died. The wise-guy who had shouted in my ear, "*You didn't see that! You didn't see that! You didn't see that!*" all the while I was bleeding buckets into the palms of my hands.

The wise guy who calls me day after day, just to keep me on edge.

💣

I was dribbling coffee on my shirt like an unnerved idiot when Sam burst through the door, hyperventilating, a tire iron in her hand, the wildest look imaginable on her face.

Yuri hung up the phone.

"Miss Byron. Would you like some coffee?"

Her eyes darted around the room, and then she seemed to decide that whatever she expected wasn't in the kitchen. She nodded, dropping the tire iron to her side.

"What's up, Sam?" As I spoke, it felt like I needed to be as calm as I had with Yuri when I first came into the kitchen.

She leaned against the counter in an uncharacteristically awkward way, as if she wanted to seem casual, but she needed the counter to steady herself.

"I thought someone was here," she said as Yuri poured coffee. She started to pick up the cup, then set it rattling on the little plate as she turned and put her arms around Yuri. "I'm sorry, Yuri. I'm so sorry about Andrij."

"It's nothing, Miss Byron. He was practically a stranger to me. And the guy who asked for Andrij is gone now."

Then we all drank coffee, while Yuri once more told the story of his visitors and his certainty that his early visitor had brought the body on the dock to a bad end. Sam listened closely the whole time, her hand cupped over his. When Yuri finished his story, she clasped his hand in both of hers. She licked her lips and cleared her throat, getting ready to speak.

"It wasn't just Andrij he asked for, was it? He asked for Pete, didn't he?"

Cripes, I couldn't believe that Pete told her what I'd gotten us into.

"Yes, both men asked for Byrons," Yuri said.

We finished our coffee, and Sam hugged him good-bye—though I don't know why he rated that much empathy, just because some gangster got shirty in his café. The gangster wanted to kill me, but I wasn't getting any hugs. I'm the guy with enough awareness to retrieve her tire iron.

Walking back to her car—creepers, but it was cold—I asked what Pete had told her.

"Not a damn thing," she said. "It's my father and Uncle Bob they're looking for. Those guys must be some of Andrij's cousins." She brushed snow off the car's back window with her sleeve, then batted at her coat to clean it.

"Huck?" I asked.

"You remember my Uncle Bob?"

"Yeah, from that time when Lucinda chased him off with a shotgun." I thought for a second. "It was that super-hot summer when it seemed like it was a hundred degrees for a solid week."

"It's Huck and my Uncle Bob they want."

"What do Andrij's friends want with Huck?" I sounded more incredulous than I should have, but Danny Peterson could not possibly be acquainted with Sam's backwoods papa.

"He and Uncle Bob owe them money, of course. That's why Huck needs to sell his house."

As I opened the car door, I said, "Roz always said Byrons were trouble."

Of course, I regretted it as soon as it was out of my mouth. I tossed the tire iron on the floor behind my seat, and closed the passenger door gently, the way she likes.

"No shit," she said as she slipped behind the steering wheel. "I'd have them surgically removed if I had a choice, but I seem to be stuck with them."

58. Nicky Deals with Logical Consequences

AT THE SIDE OF THE road, Nicky used snow and a towel from the car's trunk to scrub the remaining odor from the leather seat. As he had after that kitchen fire, he'd have to discard these clothes to be rid of the smell.

He hated it. Hated it. Hated it.

"Himno. Sooka suna. Upizdysh. Sukin sin."

It was a crime—starting with Zandr's misappropriation of his new assets, and then on up to being out here in the goddamn woods, badgered by Konstantin when the FBI wanted to talk to him.

It pushed him near to tears.

One thing had led to another—and now, here he was, having to throw away what had been perfectly good Armani.

59. Sam Makes Boys Cry

"I'M SORRY, SAM. I didn't mean anything by what I said."

Matt sat so close to me in the car that I could feel heat coming off him. His voice vibrated at a lower register, outside the normal human auditory range, so I felt rather than heard him speak, like you feel a train before you hear the long, slow alarm of the train whistle in the night. I struggled to not think about the trouble Huck and Pete had gotten themselves into.

It took me a moment to realize he was apologizing for insulting Byrons, not for the biggest mistake he ever made.

"These past years were hell on earth," he said. "I couldn't have made it through without your family. Your sister is a rock, the best friend anyone could hope for—but you know that. If I didn't have Pete to talk to, I'd have crossed into the existential abyss long before this."

He paused where I was supposed to say, "Yeah, uh-huh," and then ignored my lack of response and kept talking, taking us to the Twilight Zone.

"You are so lucky to have them for family, Sam. "

It was freezing in the car, so I turned on the engine and let the windshield wipers clear off the snow that had accumulated while we were in the café.

Matt said, "I can tell you don't approve of what I do—or did. It leaks out of every pore whenever I run into you."

I had to clear my throat twice to speak.

"Sometimes I misapply my work ethic to others, Matt. It seemed back when I used to know you, that you had more to offer the world."

We waited in a kind of détente while the Challenger's wipers cleared the windshield, me feeling guilty for judging him and Matt looking at me for—what? Forgiveness? I strove to cease judging, to accept him as a nice guy, no longer the doper and slacker he had been. Yet I just had to ask.

"Matt, are you in recovery?"

"I think so. It's still day-to-day, but I'm on the way up." He made a rueful sound. "Truth is, I continue to blame God, but every day, I get closer to accepting that I've lost the life I had."

"Turning it over to a higher power?" I kept all feeling out of my voice.

"Hah! No, just coming home to Harley and Roslyn."

"It must be nice for you."

"C'mon, Sam. Don't bullshit me. You think it's a come-down, a grown man having to move home. I'm out of options. I'm on disability with a kid to support. My folks are happy to have us, so I'm trying to teach myself to be happy, too."

He put his hand on mine, where I had it on the gearshift, and in a feral response—because he was touching my car, because he was touching me—I flicked his hand away.

He clutched the armrest and burst into tears.

"I fucked up, Sam. I made mistakes that ruined people's lives."

He began shaking as he wept, then rocked himself, his face in his hands.

I don't do well with people's emotions, and I'd already exhausted what thin resources I had while we talked with Yuri. I don't know how to cluck and say *there-there*.

He sat up and turned to me again, still sniffing and shaking.

I slapped him.

Yes, it was a thoughtless impulse, but I didn't slap the injured side of his face.

He drew a breath, seized my hand, and kissed it.

"Thanks, Sam." He let me go and scrubbed his face with his sleeve. "I'm sick of self-pity, too. Cripes, don't tell Harley that I'm losing it. I don't want him to know what a mess I am."

"Your secret is safe with me."

I shifted into gear and ripped out of the lot, enjoying the swish of the Challenger fishtailing on the ice. Because of the ice and all the accidents from spin-outs, it was not the most satisfactory drive across island country roads. However, I savored the pleasure of making Matt cry.

Paybacks are sweet.

§

Back at the ranch, the cars belonging to Aunt Lucky and Harley were gone, leaving only the Owens's rackety 1970s Jeep in the driveway. As soon as I parked my car, Roslyn was out the front door, dressed in a parka and snow boots, a knapsack over her shoulder.

"Where is everyone? Where are you off to?" Matt said, giving her a peck on the cheek and a hug. Gag me. That family hugs every time you turn around.

"The power is out on the north end of the island. It'll be a couple of days before Puget Power can restore it." She ripped open the Jeep's rusty door and threw her pack across the seat. "I'm going to help move those folks from the assisted care home over to the Episcopal Church, where it's warm. They don't have sufficient backup power."

"Is Harley helping, too?"

"Later," Roslyn said. "He went out to help Tom's people with stranded motorists. Damn fools think an SUV is going to save them from stupidity."

"Do you have everything you need?" Matt asked, opening the car door for her. "Can I help?"

Roslyn shook her head. "I put chains on, and I've got blankets and the cots. Pippi helped me load the car while we waited for you."

Rickety as that old Jeep looks, it fired right up for Roslyn. Harley always keeps his cars in top running order. I like that about him.

Matt regarded me with that wry smile. "Come in and stay with us."

"Thanks, I have a few things to take care of."

Such as finding respite in solitude.

§

That's the biggest mistake I ever made.

I can still hear Matt saying that as he rose from my side that One Bad Night. No one has ever come close enough to hurt my feelings. Only Matt managed that.

60. Nicky Gets Smart

NICKY DROVE THE LENGTH of that god-forsaken island twice. The ferries weren't running, so he couldn't exit that way. When he came to the bridge to the peninsula, he found it barricaded. The police and tow trucks danced around each other, removing the remains of an accident.

It snowed ever harder, though the car's wipers seemed up to the task of keeping a clear window. He continued to curse both Konstantin and Zandr to the beat of the windshield wipers. His uncle had nearly frightened him to death. Then died and left Nicky to clean up the mess.

Nicky pounded the steering wheel, screaming—and then had to maneuver the car out of a skid. He opened his window and screamed into the night with sudden joy, snow slashing in fat globs on his face, his coat, the upholstery.

"I'm free!" he shouted into the torrential spunk of snow. Konstantin was no longer part of his story arc.

He closed the window and shook away the fat ice crystals, happy as he'd ever been. He let the car skid around yet another bend in the highway and then braked, so the car fishtailed along the country road in that goofy, fun way people drove in America.

Still, however, Zandr had ruined a good project, then betrayed him to the White Knights. And Black Pawn wanted Nicky to talk to the FBI, leaving him to—what next?

He pressed the button to open the car window and again screamed into the impending night.

Fuck Zandr. Fuck dead Konstantin. And fuck Dymtrus.

No more donkey's work.

61. Sam Secures the Premises

IN THE WISPY WINTER light, I walked around Aunt Lucky's house, making sure it was ready for this storm, given how big a weather event Cliff Mass promised on his blog. Everything seemed battened down for wind—there's always wind on the island—but one faucet in the back hadn't been wrapped in insulation. I applied the handy householder's trick, leaving it on at a small trickle, hoping that would keep the pipes from freezing.

On the kitchen counter, Aunt Lucky had scratched words on a notepad that had 'Veda Realty' printed across the top, but I misread it as 'Reality,' so it took a second to reset perception. She had scrawled:

> Gone to Grandma Flo's. That bastard she's dating dumped her on Xmas day!! So she's down at the mouth. Gretchen and Dick said they want to come too. Sorry to leave you lonely. Maybe Matt can help with that!!!!!!

Instead of worrying, I called Grandma Flo to make sure Aunt Lucky got there safely. I endured more lurid suggestions from both of them about Matt, and encouraged my aunt to bed down there for the night. Then I relaxed into the promise of a few hours of seclusion and went upstairs for a shower.

Aunt Lucky keeps her house at about the same temperature as the refrigerator, and there was no possibility that I could squeeze into any of her size-four clothing, however cold I got. I rummaged for clean clothes, hoping to have the same good fortune as Pippi to benefit from Aunt Lucky's predisposition to save everything. In a bottom drawer in my old room, I found a couple pairs of jeans, underwear with partially-sprung elastic, a ratty sweater, and a Violent Femmes t-shirt, dating from my adolescent obsession with emo rock. Best of all, I found a pair of silk long-johns with only a tiny tear.

Coming out of the shower, all minty from Dr. Bronner's soap, I was confronted by a ringing phone. Aunt Lucky's landline. I really didn't want to answer any more calls.

"Pete's not here!" I yelled instead of hello, at the same time seeing Eliot's number displayed on the caller ID.

"Good. Suits me fine. I just wanted to check on Aunt Lucky. She seemed down last night at dinner."

I said, "She went to Grandma Flo's."

"You let her drive in the snow?" Eliot shouted at me.

"She left while I was taking Pete to the ferry. When there was only a dusting of snow."

"A whole load of snow is forecast. There's ice everywhere. For heaven's sake, Sam. Can't you watch out for another person's well-being?"

"She's a grown woman," I said, repressing my resentment, since I felt like I'd been watching out for others all my life. "If the doctor didn't say she shouldn't drive, leave her alone."

"I'm calling Grandma Flo. She needs to keep Aunt Lucky at her house."

"Already did that. Especially since they'll probably drink too much. Grandma Flo has a broken heart again."

Eliot continued scolding me. "You should have stayed with Aunt Lucky."

"Dammit, Eliot. I stayed on the island for her sake when Pete took off. I can't help that she wiggled away. I actually have work to do. Since I'm not babysitting Aunt Lucky, I should just catch the next ferry."

"Can't," Eliot said. "They stopped running because of the weather. The bridge is closed, too."

She hung up.

Yes, I said bad words about being stuck in hell for no good purpose. I came here to see my father and brother, who went to Seattle to do business with Eastern European gangsters. My aunt is out in the snow with my promiscuous grandmother. Who isn't even related to me. And I found another dead body.

Home sweet home.

From which you can see through the kitchen window into Matt's bedroom. When he took off his shirt, I pulled the shades.

§

To calm down, I did what I dimly remember my mother doing one snowy Christmas—it must have been the last one with her. I made peanut butter and oatmeal suet, using up the last of Aunt Lucky's Jif peanut butter, which likely isn't the kind that's good for little birds. Rummaging in the pantry, I found sunflower seeds and loaded the covered feeders in her back yard and scattered suet under the bushes that birds seemed to prefer for cover.

Inside, I tried again to call Gerard and Quinn from Aunt Lucky's phone, because I like futility. Aunt Lucky gets TV and Internet from a dish network, which was a bit slower than I like. First, I sent messages to everyone from my old posse at Z-Crypto, since I hadn't found Gerard and the bad news needed to be known: Sam's old code lets bad guys in the back door. I added tips for closing the hole.

Then: again more messages to find Quinn and Gerard. I left Gerard a message so cryptic that only he would be able to interpret it.

While trying to focus, I seethed—mad because my Z-Crypto reputation had garbage dumped on it, and Matt had grown up to be weird, and because I'd been injected with Byron family DNA. I couldn't resolve all those metaphorical divide-by-zero errors, so I settled in to analyze the logs from the local electric utility, which I'd saved in Seattle before catching the ferry. When I connected to Quinn's remote servers in Seattle, the system forced an anti-virus update to my laptop as a condition of getting on the network (thanks, Natalia). I finally got some of the error logs copied from my desktop in Seattle over to my laptop. Then another infernal instant-message popped up.

YrBlueHatLvr> I'm worried about you.

SamIam> I'm going to bar you from my list. I distrust your bluehat handle.

YrBlueHatLvr> Don't do that. It would make it much harder to watch out for you.

Samlam> I don't need data pirates watching out for me.

YrBlueHatLvr> We need to keep you safe.

Samlam> Who are you?

Digital silence—which I seem to get only when I don't want it.

Turning back to family business, I tried to deposit money into Pete's account, to make sure he had at least some cash to maneuver, if he needed it. I couldn't get into any of my own accounts, because the connection kept dropping, which a satellite service isn't supposed to do. However, outer space is a long ways away. So I turned back to my own business, trying again to connect remotely to the servers at Quinn's offices, but failed. Maybe with the storm, the power had gone out in South Lake Union, though I thought Quinn's office building had backup generators. Maybe Natalia the Dragon had returned to create more upgrade havoc on the network.

The doors to Purgatory had been flung open on the last turn-off at the end of Lost Point Road. You can't find it on GPS because Limberlost Island appears to be analog only.

§

The snow had begun to accumulate in serious quantities. I switched on the yard light and went out to check around the house again. After a week below freezing, and even lower temperatures the last couple of days, the lawn behind Aunt Lucky's house, usually a swamp, was frozen solid, and the wind had swept the snow into drifts at the end of the tree line. I grinned with satisfaction as I pulled on my gloves, launched into a run, and then skated across the entire yard, stumbling blissfully into the snowbank at the far border of the ice lake.

"What are you doing?"

Pippi stood at the edge of the gravel yard looking down to where I was extricating myself from the snow, batting it off my pants.

"Freaking in the snow," I said. "Come on down."

Pippi wore Pete's navy-blue ski pants and had on my fuchsia parka, the snow clothes that Pete and I wore the first year we lived with Aunt Lucky. That Christmas must have been the last time I wore a color like fuchsia. Those clothes would have been forgotten, except it snowed that Christmas too, and Aunt Lucky preserved faded Polaroid photos on a shelf in her hallway, the kind of pictures that end up replacing actual memory. When you look closely at our faces as preserved in the photos, Pete and I weren't yet convinced we'd be happy here, so we had masks in place, looking at the camera as if expecting the presents in our hands would shortly be snatched away.

It didn't take more than a crook of my finger to lure Pippi over. She jumped down fearlessly and started exploring what her feet did. Maybe it was Pete's old navy ski pants that prompted the protective response, but I put my arm around her, taking her hand.

"May I have this dance?"

I waltzed the giggling Pippi out onto the backyard lake and held her close while she got the feel of the ice beneath her feet. I took a couple of exaggerated spills, as comical as possible, so she'd get the idea of falling, since it was inevitable. With my arm around her, I could feel her heart beating, like when you hold a small bird in your hand.

She threw herself into the snow bank three times, laughing so hard she got the hiccups. I demonstrated the applied science of certain skater-betty moves I had. Pippi got the basics immediately and began improvising.

"OK, crack the whip," I said. "To do this right, you have to scream as loud as you can."

Pippi said, "Daddy says I'm not supposed to scream unless there's something to scream about."

"No offense," I said, resenting again how stifled this kid seemed, "but that's B.S. Anyway, you'll be going so fast, there'll be plenty to scream about."

"I won't scream," Pippi said.

"We'll see about that."

We had slicked up the ice to a fine state by this time. She grabbed hold at my elbow, and I began twirling.

"Scream!" I shouted, screaming myself to get her started.

Pippi kept her mouth in a tight line.

"Scream, Pippi!" I whipped her around me, and we sped toward the snow bank, shrieking like banshees as we fell into the snow.

Struggling out of the cold stuff, Pippi gave me a tug and a shove, pushing me back out onto the ice on my butt while she screamed again. As I spun on the ice she fell silent. I stopped spinning to find

Matt on the path above us, dressed only in jeans, crouched in preparation for attack, clutching a huge gun. With his eye patch, the effect was chilling. I had never seen that look on a man's face before.

"Daddy, you'll catch cold," Pippi said.

"I heard you screaming," he said, only slowly letting up his battle stance. He had a California t-shirt tan, his bare chest pale in contrast—with a much better physique than I remembered—and he had two ghostly circles on his right side. Grey-white, puckered scars.

"We were falling," Pippi said.

"Please don't scream if you aren't in danger," he said, his voice a dead calm.

"Sam said we should."

"Just because Sam says so doesn't mean it's right."

Same thing I heard from Roslyn in the fourth grade. And the sixth and eighth grades.

"Daddy, you'll freeze," Pippi said, running to him.

"Let's go get supper." He had one hand resting on her shoulder, the other holding that gun up by his ear. "How does macaroni and cheese sound?"

"Yum," Pippi said.

She huddled against him like a tending tug nosing a ship into harbor.

"Daddy, your feet are turning blue."

"They'll warm up," he said. "As soon as my heart starts beating again."

They crossed the yard to the Owens house, leaving me with my butt frozen to Aunt Lucky's backyard lake, not quite sure how I turned into the bad guy. I didn't even have a gun.

The Owens's back door banged open again, and Pippi stuck her head out.

"Daddy says come to supper. Right now, before you freeze!"

62. Matt Cooks Supper

SAM NOISILY KICKED SNOW off her boots on the mud porch and came inside to hang her coat on the rack while I sat by the wood stove pulling on socks, rubbing my stinging, burning-cold feet and feeling like a case study from an Abnormal Psych text, shards of fear prickling my finger-tips from the sudden rush of adrenalin. True to the dynamics of dysfunctional families everywhere, no one said a word about my paranoid-psycho display.

I grabbed one of Harley's flannel shirts from the clothes dryer to put on, since I know from Roslyn's reaction that no one likes to look at my bare body. Pippi and Sam were setting the kitchen table with plates and forks for three. While Sam poured herself a cup of coffee, I recited at length the recipe I'd prepared for supper.

"Our family feasts on Christmas Eve and snacks on Christmas," I said, as if anyone gave a raving rat's ass about the menu.

"Yeah, I remember," Sam said, sounding even more matter-of-fact than I had managed. Since I'm a fool, I felt comforted that she remembered my family's Christmas practices.

Leaving the warmth of the wood stove took some doing, but I had to get the casserole out of the oven before it burned. I'd just started cleaning the kitchen when Pippi startled me, so the entire workspace was still destroyed from my efforts. Trying to see the Abnormal Psych 101 scene through Sam's eyes, I put too much meaning into ordinary things. The cheese-grater lay in a pile of cheddar curls. Whisks, flour sifter, and measuring utensils littered the counter. A mess betraying the disorder in my mind. I set the baking pan to cool for a moment and began shoving stuff into the dishwasher.

She said, "That's a lot of effort just for macaroni and cheese."

I couldn't turn to I answer. It had become way too important to attend to cleaning the kitchen.

"Back in San Francisco," I said, "our family counselor advised me to pay attention to basics. So I've been doing that, and looking for ways to celebrate the mundane."

I obsessively sorted onion skins into the compost pail, when I should have just chucked the whole mess into the trash.

"What is that?" Sam said. "There's no onions in mac-and-cheese."

"It's part of the recipe. Caramelized onions give it flavor."

"Welsh cheddar? 'Macaroni and cheese' does not mean pasta and buerre blanc. Kids hate that kind of stuff."

"When did you become an expert on child rearing?"

She dropped her voice. "I remember what it's like to be a kid around grown-ups who don't have a clue."

"You also believe you're always right."

"The comfort lies in consistently achieving certitude with a statistically negligible margin of error."

While resenting that she talked me into arguing, I couldn't stop myself. "I've made this for Pippi before, and she didn't complain."

Sam turned to Pippi. "Tell the truth. Macaroni and cheese is supposed to come out of a box, isn't it?"

Pippi said, "I don't want to hurt his feelings."

Cripes, I thought. Just shoot me and get it over with. "Don't worry about my feelings. Tell me the truth."

"Tastes like dog barf, doesn't it?" Sam said.

"It's not so bad," Pippi said. "Except the onions feel slimy in your mouth. Like stinging worms."

"Tastes like bad breath," Sam said. "Smells like old socks."

I pushed the pan to the back of the stove and threw down the oven mitts. Sam went for the cupboards, opening the door where Roslyn kept her stash of ready-to-eat wonders.

"Lo! The world remains as it should be," she said. "Roslyn always kept Kraft dinner around."

Pippi tore open the box while I ran water in a pan—the same copper-bottom boiler we used to cook after-school snacks fifteen years ago.

"It's OK, Daddy," Pippi said, stroking my arm.

After serving Pippi, I prepared to dish up food for Sam. "Do you want the kids' stuff or the grown-up kind that tastes like dog barf?"

"I'll have what you're having," Sam said politely.

"Don't try to be nice," I said.

63. Nicky Finds Shelter in a Storm

AMID ALL THE FALSE mansions and the country houses with bed-and-breakfast signs, Nicky found shelter from the storm where the standards of housewifery would have pleased even his aunt Avrora. He smiled at the thought of what a credit card could get you. The room's deep carpets had been raked so that no sign of foot traffic marred the surface, like that Japanese garden in San Francisco where one of his cousins took him for a walk. The walk had been with that cousin who was looking to grab a husband and had stalked Nicky solely for that purpose. Thank god his uncle Dymtrus had taken him in. If he hadn't seized that opportunity, there's no telling where he'd be right now. He thought of Uncle Konstantin and shrugged off that reminiscence.

After shivering through a reminder of winters in his childhood, Nicky felt grateful to find civilized shelter, where the hospitality and amenities included a long hot bath and thick towels hung over a warming rack, plus the sharp razor and decent toothbrush that one expects in fine establishments.

He stretched out on the bed, the kind with a plush pillow top, and pulled up the virgin-white down comforter, watching the snow fall through the grandiose picture window and loving the feel of the smooth cotton quilt on bare skin, still warm from the Jacuzzi bath. The sensation of Egyptian cotton gliding over his bare thighs felt provocative, but he resisted, determined to save that for later.

First, a call to Dymtrus from the room phone.

"Uncle Konstantin called off that collection errand," he told Uncle Dymtrus, after Avrora convinced him to come to the phone.

"Are you sure, Nicky?" Dymtrus didn't sound trusting.

"Absolutely. He doesn't care about that now. Or anything else related to Pete Byron," Nicky said. Or anything at all. He'd save the larger news for later, when he could deliver it personally and observe the look on every cousin's face.

The bar choices proved pleasing and the refrigerator revealed the depth of his host's exquisite taste. Nicky sipped scotch and watched the weather; then when he tired of the snowfall—nostalgia simply wasn't his style—he flicked on the television with the remote and watched the Bloomberg Report, flipping every five minutes to a History Channel special on how troops celebrated Christmas in each of the great wars.

Preposterous idea for entertainment, he realized, but he couldn't resist studying the methods used to capture viewers' attention.

Warm and contented with the local amenities—he had the heat up to eighty degrees Fahrenheit—Nicky tried different clothing choices, checking the mirror to determine what would prove both warm and flattering for the next day's work. His shirt off, soft light from the dresser highlighting his body in the mirror, he rubbed his hand over the pattern of hair across his chest and belly. Once again, he congratulated himself on leaving California for Seattle. Body-waxing had been one more mistake that told him California was the wrong place to build the kind of success he wanted.

64. Sam Dials "M" for Messages

AFTER HELPING PIPPI WASH dishes, I went back to Aunt Lucky's. I checked my aunt's message, hoping to hear from Pete or Huck. Then I called the message number for my cell, which had only one message: to call that cute (married) detective in Seattle.

Aunt Lucky's phone rang.

By now I felt more rage than trepidation.

"You can go blow yourself, assbite," I said as I picked up the receiver. "Pete's not here."

"That's because I'm here," Pete said. He seemed to be calling from a crowded room. Weird music echoed behind him.

"You're OK? Did you find Huck? Are they—"

"Yeah, we're both here. We're just hanging for the night, especially because of the weather. We've pretty much wrapped up that little problem. Except now I've got Harley's laptop. Can you bring mine over as soon as the ferry starts running tomorrow?"

"Are you staying at my house? How do I find you?"

"We'll head over to your place tomorrow. Our hosts asked us to bunk up here for the night."

"Hosts? Isn't Huck a hostage or something?"

"It was just a misunderstanding. Though it will be helpful if you'd buy Huck's house."

"I promised to figure it out after Christmas, Pete. Why does caller ID on this phone show my name and number?"

"I picked up your cell instead of mine when I got out of the car."

"Geezus pieces, Pete. How do you continue to make it through the world with so little nailed down?"

"Whatever. A policeman just called for you."

"I know. He left a message on my voice mail. He's working on the murder that I told you about."

"He's anxious to talk to you. Some dead guy they found called your cell number. Is it the same dead guy you found yesterday?"

"Of course not."

"Then if he calls again, I'll just say you don't know Alec Ramsey."

"What? No, that's another guy. I do know him."

"Not any more. He turned out to be dead."

Your heart really does jump into your throat. I strangled on the first attempt to speak.

"What did the detective say?"

"He was all like, 'Sir, your sister may have information related to a serious crime we are investigating.'"

"No way. You're the one involved in a bunch of crime." I told him about Yuri and the guy looking for Byron *père et fils*.

"I don't think anyone is there looking for us. Let me ask—" He muffled the phone. The sound of the party crackled again when he came back on. "No, that can't be about us. We're all sitting right here."

"Oh geez. If that detective calls my cell again, tell him I'm calling soon."

"He won't call. I told him you left town and I wasn't sure where you are."

"Pete, WTF? Why didn't you tell him I'm here?"

"Huck says it's a bad idea to help cops find people." Someone in the background called Pete's name. He yelled back without covering the phone.

"Pete, hang up before you make my head explode."

"You'll bring my laptop in the morning, right?"

I banged the phone down hard enough that my feelings about his laptop would be evident.

Then I dialed the detective's number, but I misremembered it, because I got a branch of the King County Libraries. This was like the dream where you keep trying to dial 911 but the numbers change while you dial. I dug through my bag and pockets to find Detective Jeremiah's card, which had several numbers listed. The first one I tried went to voice mail. After I dialed the second number, it rang twice and then the phone went silent.

Ma Bell and the decentralized inheritors of that legacy have had a century to work on the island's infrastructure, but the system still relies on wires hanging from telephone poles. The wind whistling through Aunt Lucky's ill-fitting windows meant that it would be tomorrow or later before I could call the detective.

Alec Ramsey dead.

Guy in the freezer and guy on the dock.

Alec was a deplorable work partner, but he should be alive. The universe wasn't functioning properly.

Banging my way up the stairs to my bedroom, I plugged in that ancient Stratocaster and had a Black Flag-style tantrum until I'd sweated through my t-shirt. I turned the volume up to distortion level and attempted to find one chord to play loud and long enough to exquisitely express my rage.

Until the lights went out.

Cursing my ill luck while stumbling in the dark, I searched for a flashlight and the fuse box, having to remove the junk that Aunt Lucky piled in front of it, barking my shin twice and bashing my hand against the sharp corner of a nearby table. I swore in disproportionate anger.

"Talking like that won't do you a lick of good, Missy."

I hiccupped in surprise, then heard whose voice it was.

"You didn't blow no fuse, Miss Ada."

65. Matt Finds the Answer Is Blowing in the Wind

I LISTENED TO THE storm wind, backed by the sound of her guitar. I interpreted the twang of her rage as a declaration of my idiocy.

Yes, I'm a freaking idiot.

There isn't medication to take for it. Or exercises to relieve the condition.

Thankfully, rural electrification failed, leaving us all in silence.

66. Sam Experiences Byronic Passion

UNCLE BOB SHONE A FLASHLIGHT in my eyes.

"The power is out all around the neighborhood."

"Where did you come from?" I quickly got over relief that it was someone I knew and moved on to resentment for who it was.

"I caught a ride as far as old Mrs. Waddington's house. Then I walked," he said. He had a Rastafarian cap pulled over his shaved head. "You sure play loud. That can't be good for your ears."

"You'd know about that," I said. "Don't sit down. You can't stay here."

"Missy, you'll be a lot safer if I stay. What with them guys on the island looking for Pete."

"Pete says there's no one looking for any of you."

As I said it, I began a series of selfish calculations. The bad guys knew to call Aunt Lucky's house looking for Pete. My phone number was unlisted, but they might have followed Pete to my house last Thursday night, when he stopped to charge his batteries and abscond with my laptop. Which would be the only way anyone could easily discover a connection between us. I wasn't worried that these people might hurt me—that seemed too farfetched—only how much it would cost me. In the last several hours, I'd come to accept that I'd end up spending money to rescue Pete and Huck, most likely by investing in Huck's house. Now Pete says not to worry.

"You can't stay here." I tried to sound my most adamant, but Uncle Bob's ability to hear nuance had been dampened long ago by lying between the speakers with Pink Floyd cranked up.

"You can't send me out in the snow," he said cheerily. It wasn't a challenge, just a statement of fact.

Rummaging through the pantry, Uncle Bob found the hurricane lamp and lit it. In the dim light, I recognized that he wore old clothes Pete and I had left behind after high school: a Mudhoney t-shirt, old skater flannels, and a hoodie that Pete had practiced mutilating.

"How long have you been here?" I asked.

"Since you went off with Sheriff Junior to his house," Bob said.

I tried to evaluate my feelings about seeing my uncle clothed in the equivalent of my high-school uniform. It wasn't a pretty sight. It's one thing to have to close your eyes when Grandma Flo wears an orange mini-skirt with high-heeled purple fuck-me boots. But a skinny, aging hippie in grunge and Goth put me on edge. At least there was no eyeliner involved.

While I stewed, Uncle Bob found a Coleman stove and a propane bottle.

"Huck's house is empty," I said. "You can stay there. Take some food from the pantry. I'll give you a ride to the ferry tomorrow."

Did I leap too far in making this decision? I think not. It was snowing, and he needed shelter, yet nothing on earth would induce me to sleep under the same roof with him. Sheriff Tom's team had finished their work. The house belonged to Huck.

"I was down there earlier," Bob said. "It's got police Do Not Cross tape around it. What happened?"

"A guy was found dead down there this afternoon."

"Oh lordy. We just finished a smudging to get rid of the old bad juju. You can't make me sleep where it's troubled by ghosts."

"The body wasn't in the house. It's not haunted," I said.

"You can't know that. The dead don't lie still most of the time."

"No one is home now, alive or dead. You can stay there. Or go knock on Sheriff Harley's door."

He shivered. "OK, but you got no need to be this uptight and mean."

"The trouble you and Huck got yourselves into is something that I have time or ability to solve. Work things out with Pete's help. He thinks it's not a big problem."

"You got no respect for family," he groused.

"My family has no respect for me. I need order and sanity, and you and Huck have nothing but chaos all around you."

"You were always so uptight." Uncle Bob said. "Everything has to be just so with you. I bet you have to step out of the shower to pee."

"Yeah, I do, as a matter of fact." I was done with this. "A lantern, the Coleman stove, food. If you can find one, grab a sleeping bag. Then leave."

"Well, Merry Christmas to you too, Missy."

67. Nicky and the Object Lesson

THE ACCOMMODATIONS HE FOUND for the night had one shortfall: slow Internet access over cable. It seemed to be metered, so that upload and download of files was painstakingly slow. Nicky sighed at first, but didn't complain, recognizing that he was so far removed from civilization that he should expect to forego some amenities.

After the shower and rest, he longed to work again. He had some programming he needed to do on his own website, since it was getting more traffic every day, and he had new material to upload. In the circumstance, there was nothing to do but tolerate the slow local connection to the European location of his service provider.

The warm room and the excessive comforts in these accommodations, however, left him feeling mellow in spite of the inconveniences. Scotch in a brandy snifter and a comfortable chair made up for the slow connection.

⏮ ◀ | ▶ ⏭

Nick's American Business 101 as Cinéma Vérité
Entry #30: The Object Lesson: Part 1 – December 25, 22:00 PST

I've been carrying this clip on my hard drive for a while, trying to determine where it belongs in this survey course. It is best presented as a demonstration of how old-fashioned ways of doing business quickly lose their place in the modern world.

Time once more for a video, class.

Nick's Fan Forum | Permanent Link | 5 comments

This is one of your best.
ponyboy | Homepage | 12.25 - 10:21 pm |
You've been holding out on us Nicky. It's like the Andalusia
Dog meets Century 21 capitalism. Unrelenting progress,
governed by a tragic amorality. And I think I get the symbolism
of the cellophane wrap and the ritualistic, repetitive
reassurances.

I like the meat locker setting
JustMike | 12.25 - 10:38 pm |
and how from Frame 1 you know the guy is doomed, yet you
watch because terror has its own hypnotic rhythm.

I didn't get the symbolism
ponyboy | Homepage | 12.25 - 10:42 pm |
of using the same actor as in the cigarette scene. Especially
when he turns to the camera and says, "You'd never have the
guts to do this yourself." He blew all his street cred when he
pissed himself in a previous chapter.

Where is everyone?
JustMike | 12.25 - 10:44 pm |
People should have been able to kiss the fambly scene good
bye and get back to reality by now. Anyhow, my question is
why Nicky titled this 'Object Lesson.'

I think it's ob-JECT
ponyboy | Homepage | 12.25 - 10:47 pm |
like in moral objection, not as in 'the object of my desire.'

⏮ ◀ | ▶ ⏭

As the night fell, he looked out the large window, trying to trace the
outlines of the territorial view across the island that he had glimpsed
when he arrived at the house in the dying afternoon light. The
snowfall grew heavier, so that only house lights shone, glowing red

and blue where people had hung lights, that New World tribute to the pagan roots of Christmas.

Then, as he watched the panoramic holiday show, lights blinked out in blocks across the valley and hillsides. He remained in a special holiday snow-globe, where electricity still flowed.

It tickled Nicky as funny how people living in nice houses spent a small fortune on fancy pavement for their driveways or hired working men to trim their bushes into unnatural shapes. Then, curiously, they put up fake signs to ward off common burglars. Or left the lights on, perhaps with a timer, to make it appear that an empty house was inhabited.

Out here in the wild woods of the West, down a long driveway, locks were as easily bypassed as in the city. Just the slip of a credit card.

68. Sam Comes in from the Cold

ALONE, I RETURNED TO my work, without the possibility of an Internet connection. Using the backlight on my laptop keyboard to see and feeling the house grow cold while I typed, I watched the laptop's battery meter dip as I tried to focus on details in the security logs I'd downloaded, which showed all the recent intrusion attempts against the local power utility's servers.

Quinn and I had identified seven theoretical lines of attack against the chipset error I'd discovered. The utility's security logs showed two methods of attack being tried between six o'clock and midnight on Christmas Eve.

I needed to get off this island at first opportunity come morning, find Quinn, contact the local utility. Thinking through what this could mean, there wasn't a dang thing I could do at that moment, unless I wanted to drive back to the village to see if the cop shop had phone lines. It could wait till morning. The logs showed the signs of attempt, not actual security trespasses.

The light from the laptop's display wasn't strong enough to prove it, but I believed that my fingers were turning blue. Aunt Lucky is not a home-maintenance sort of gal. The same rickety,

Depression-era wood-framed windows rattled in the wind as when we first lived there. Her house had the kind of insulation they put in walls when they built farmhouses in the Thirties: none. In the early Seventies, just before the energy crisis, the previous owner installed all-electric heat and appliances. With the power out, a storm like this made the place nearly unlivable. The cold front rolling down from the Yukon sucked the residual heat out of the house at such a rate that I could feel it running over my feet and knees, in search of the cracks in the doors.

As I worked through the logs to better understand how the new attacks were mounted, I began to identify with Napoleon's men, condemned to freeze on the road home from Moscow, but still thinking I'd give up my laptop when they pry it from my cold, dead fingers.

Then the warning light flashed for the battery level on my laptop.

Too wrapped up in examining the logs to curse my fate, I grabbed a blanket and the laptop and went out to the Challenger, turned it on, and plugged my laptop into the cigarette lighter, losing myself again to studying the security logs as the windows fogged, my toes warmed up, and the laptop battery recharged.

The Challenger generates the kind of white noise that they say puts colicky babies to sleep. It's a better white noise than any of those back-to-nature CDs featuring Texas rain and crashing ocean waves. Then at one point—battery recharged to eighty-five percent—I thought I heard more than the engine outside my car's frosted windows. The car rocked, suffering from the same wind that had shut down the ferries. For a moment, the wind let up. The only sound was the Challenger's comforting purr.

Crunching. Footsteps on the frozen gravel.

I stopped typing to listen. The sound stopped.

When I heard it again, I put my laptop to sleep to silence its fan. There. I heard it. Then it wasn't there.

Calling myself chicken-shit, I reached over to lock the passenger side.

Just as the door cracked open.

I didn't keep from shrieking like a banshee before I saw the intruder was Matt, though I did keep from bashing his head with my laptop.

"C'mon, Sam. It's just me. Come inside."

"Why?"

"Sweet Jesus. It's freezing. Roslyn called and said to invite you home. I told her you had enough sense to come over if you got cold. I guess I was wrong."

"I'm not cold."

"Come inside. You can have the guest room."

Reluctantly, I agreed to sleep in his house.

Then Matt played that same boy-scout routine with me as he did with Roslyn, holding the car door, steadying me with his arm around my waist when I slipped ever so slightly on the ice, his hand resting on the small of my back when he opened the front door. He took my coat with the grace of a maître d' and hung it in the hall closet.

The Owens family boy-scout troop was of course prepared for power outage: a fire ticked away in the wood stove, a Coleman lantern in the hallway provided light in the entry way and up the staircase. Matt switched off his flashlight and stowed it near the door. When he turned around, he stared at me quizzically for half a moment, and said, "Do you really want to hurt me?"

"I don't think so." I was irked, but revenge wasn't on my mind.

"Yes, it is. The quote on the back of your shirt. Violent Femmes. From 'Do You Really Want to Hurt Me,' right?"

"Yeah, right."

"We should play music together again."

"Um, sure."

"All those songs we got kicked out of the gym for playing—now they're on KTel compilations sold as golden oldies. Doesn't that make you feel old?"

"No," I said.

"I do. I feel way old."

Matt talked me into tea to warm my hands. The kitchen had its own small Coleman lamp, and Matt lit another kerosene lantern. The kitchen range ran on propane, so we quickly had hot water. As he set a teacup in front of me—Roz's blue-willow china, inherited from her mother—Matt turned that wry smile on me again.

"You're still mad about what I said that night, aren't you? After all this time."

With everything that happened that day, I had no compunction about saying what I thought. "Until that night, I believed only the best of you."

"What could you possibly expect of me in the circumstance?"

"Decency," I said.

"C'mon, Sam. I was handling it the best I could. Even a week later, I was still blaming myself. Pete dragged me back here because he was tired of hearing me say I should have been able to prevent it."

Puzzled, I couldn't answer because I didn't understand the emotional pitch in his voice, except he seemed to believe I was in the wrong.

He said, "God forbid you ever find out what it feels like when someone dies and it's your fault." He poured more tea, nonchalant as can be, as if that were a normal thing to say.

How to describe what happens inside your brain when it reshuffles data bits stored in memory—both images and other sensory input—to accommodate a massive realignment of reality? Perhaps it's the same as when the magnetic poles swap. You can hear the synapses colliding as they rearrange themselves, like the massive fall of dominos.

That's the worst thing I ever did in my life.

Reeling from the seismic shock of the realignment, I blinked once and said, "You think I reacted inappropriately."

He sipped his goddamn tea for a minute, and then went on. "It's long enough ago that I occasionally give myself credit for doing the best possible in the circumstance. It wasn't my fault the guy got hold of that cop's gun."

"I never heard you tell this story, Matt." I wasn't sure I wanted to hear it.

"It was pure coincidence that Pete and I were on that street corner with the cops trying to calm that kid down. I stood right beside that poor fucker, wondering how to help, when the kid grabbed the cop's revolver and shot himself."

"That was the worst thing that ever happened to you."

"Up until then." Matt nodded. "I wouldn't have felt safe with anyone but you that night."

69. Matt and the Night Visitor

WHEN I TURNED AROUND, Sam was nudging the kitchen door open with her hip, her hands full of cups and saucers. Hypersensitive, I began recording all the inputs: the mundane chatter of china in the sink, the whoomp of the swinging door, the tangy odor of the juniper-and-cedar fire as I banked it down for the night, the soft notes of Sam's voice as she said, "I'm going to bed," the squeak of the stairs as her foot pressed the bottom tread. I've heard footsteps on those stairs ten thousand times in the last twenty years, but the crescendo of that symphony swept over me. I caught her on the stairs, folded her in my arms, and kissed her.

The smell of mint in her hair and the taste of mint on her tongue piqued the hunger I felt—for comfort and safety. It wasn't about sex.

I just wanted to live. And be close to another human being.

Locked in a primordial embrace, we fit perfectly with me standing on the step below her. As we kissed, I felt that coiled tension release from her shoulders, and with it, all my worry and fear came unmoored.

It's going to be OK.

When I could make myself stop kissing her for a moment, I whispered, "The worst mistake I ever made was letting you leave that night."

She pushed away from me, stumbling on the stair tread. Then she steadied herself; all her tightly wound tension had returned. She backed up one more step above me, out of arm's reach.

"As you said, Matt, when you made the worst mistake ever, you put your body close to mine to assuage grief. Or guilt. Or whatever it was. Never again."

She stomped upstairs and shut the guest room door. Didn't slam it, just closed it tightly.

70. Nicky and Dickensian Moral Lessons

JUST AFTER THE GHOST of Christmas Yet to Come appeared in Mr. Magoo's Christmas Carol, it occurred to Nicky that some kinds of coincidences are highly unlikely.

His uncle's quest on Limberlost Island had to have a point in common with Nicky's own, because he'd assigned that collection task to Nicky.

He hadn't seen his uncle Konstantin for the past year. Konstantin and Dymtrus quarreled so frequently, they couldn't do business in the same town. Now both uncles were in Nicky's business.

Nicky searched out paper and pen, determined to practice what he'd learned that summer about mind-mapping. He drew cousins and uncles from Seattle in one circle, and those from the Castro Valley in another. He matched up those who had been at dinner Christmas Eve (his ears burned again with humiliation). When had any of them last crossed paths? Dymtrus went to the funeral in California when his aunt died. He took Zandr with him, but Avrora was ill, and he asked Nicky to stay in Seattle with her.

Several cousins from California came up north in May for the Sasquatch Festival, which they turned into a bacchanal. Then they were back again in November to ski at Crystal Mountain.

"There are no coincidences," Uncle Kostya always said, one of the first things he taught Nicky in the new world. So how had Konstantin ended up in the same café on Limberlost Island? Nicky drew where paths had crossed and knit themselves together.

First, when Nicky came to America, he had lived at Konstantin's compound in Castro Valley. At that wedding last year, it was Zandr who laughed at him. "You'll never get anywhere under Konstantin's thumb," he said. "Why do you think my father moved north?" Then Zandr turned around and linked himself with Konstantin.

Cousin Andrij in California wasn't useful for anything, being an unambitious donkey, too unimportant to have become Konstantin's target.

Where had Konstantin found any association with Limberlost Island or any of these people? The day before, Andrij had said,

"Everyone's calling today. Is it because it's Christmas, or are you looking for the wedding singer?"

Nicky tried to think. Who had sung at the wedding when Dymtrus's niece married that punk? To his memory, it had been that silly band Zandr had hired. They were all over fifty, played white blues, and were as grubby as that creep Oksana married. Konstantin hadn't come to that wedding. Uncle Kostya made it a point, he said, to go to weddings only if his own children—

The wedding debacle at Konstantin's house last year. That wedding singer. That's who Uncle Kostya wanted.

Or Danny, who was supposed to be on special assignment.

71. Matt Plays Prokofiev

I COULDN'T SLEEP.

That won't make the news of the day, since I seldom sleep. I tend to play scenes over and over again. These days, I can usually get myself into a space where my body is almost relaxed and my mind drifts away. To do this, I have to be alone, listening to music through headphones, somewhere other than in bed. What's more-or-less worked since I came back to Limberlost is to sit in the Mission oak chair I made for my dad years ago. The best music right now is Prokofiev, and Pippi gave me a Seattle Symphony recording of his First Symphony that I wanted to hear. I stretched out in the dark, dragged one of my grandmother's quilts over me, and let my mind drift away, staring through the wood stove's little window at the embers.

I drifted beyond the Caucasus to the vast grasslands of the Eurasian plains, thinking about generations of horsemen roaming free, thundering across the steppes. The nagging pain in my side eased away, taking my headache with it, and all I felt was my chest rising and falling as I breathed.

Being so far removed from my physical body, I'm not sure how I knew that someone was in the room with me. Once roused, my twitch muscles still react as rapidly as ever. I was across the room, my gun at the intruder's temple and his arm pulled into a painful lock before either of us recognized the other.

"Shit, Tom."

"Shit, your own self. You scared the hell out of me."

"What the fuck are you doing here in the dark?"

Tom stood in the dining room, shining a mag light, bent over the laptop on the sideboard. Bent, because I jerked him into a painful holding position. When I released him, he shook off pain like a dog shedding water.

"Pete asked me to fetch his laptop. He thought I could get it to him on the police launch when it leaves for Seattle at dawn."

"Why not just knock and ask for it?" We stepped apart; likely his heart was pounding as hard as mine.

"I did knock. You didn't answer," Tom said. "Harley gave me the key when he knew I was passing this way."

"This could have been a tragedy."

Tom stared at me, like he does when he thinks I'm being an asshole. "Why can't you let anyone help you? Pete said I need to do it for you."

"Do what?"

"Whatever is necessary, Matt. He called before you came back, to ask me to watch out for you."

The top of my head started burning. "I can take care of this myself."

"No, you can't. You're a good guy who ran into very bad trouble. You need to let your friends help. This is bigger than any man could manage."

"What do you suggest?"

"You need to tell Harley and Roslyn about your situation."

"I want to protect them from this."

I pointed to the kitchen, where we could talk without waking the house. Tom followed me and nodded when I motioned to put the kettle on. He said, "Your little girl needs to get away from this. Harley and Roz need to be able to protect themselves, don't you think?"

"Pippi and I need to be together." This was one thing I believed with every fiber of my being.

"Not until this is fixed. Send her to your sister in New York."

"I'll think about it."

"No, do it as soon as possible. The roads will still be ice-fucked tomorrow morning, but come the afternoon I'm driving you to SeaTac and you'll put her on a plane. You should send Roslyn along with her."

We faced each other in a stand-off. The most I could manage was a shrug. "I'll think about—"

"You know that guy down on the dock, don't you?"

I nodded. "I think it's Andy Peterson. He was supposed to testify next week for me, even though he's part of that family. The Alameda County sheriffs delivered a subpoena a week ago Wednesday."

"What was he doing down there?"

"I have no idea. I thought he was in California. Perhaps it was supposed to be a surprise for me. Not a happy one."

"Pippi needs to fly out to your sister as soon as the road thaws, Matt. You don't have other choices." Tom led us back out to the dining room, where he shrugged himself back into the County-issued parka. "Do Pete and his hippie father have anything to do with that dead guy on the dock?"

"No, nothing at all," I said, having decided long ago to stand alone in this hole I'd dug.

Tom opened the door, and the north wind blasted us. He turned on his flashlight to find his way off the porch.

"Drive carefully tonight." I started to close the door, but saw him turn back, shining his flashlight in my face.

"I'd walk through fire for Harley," Tom called from the yard. "And Roz. And you, too. Count me on your side."

72. Sam Sleeps Facing the Wall

THE SOUND OF THEIR voices drifted up through a grate in the floor designed to let the wood stove heat the upper story. Within a heartbeat after Matt yelled at Tom, Pippi hovered beside the bed where I lay eavesdropping.

"Roslyn said I could sleep on the floor in her room tonight," Pippi said.

"Did she?"

"Yes. She promised a slumber party."

"Why don't you sleep with me instead?"

The words were scarcely out of my mouth before the little girl was under the covers with me. I congratulated myself on having the foresight to crawl into bed in my t-shirt and the worn silk long-johns. She snuggled beside me, resting her head on my shoulder.

"I don't like shouting," Pippi said.

"Me either," I answered.

Then Pippi was asleep, almost before I finished speaking. So much for the slumber party.

I tried to eavesdrop, but I couldn't hear after the men's voiced drifted toward the kitchen. More Susie Homemaker stuff from Matt, I suppose. Little-girl breath tickled along my neck. Pippi squirmed into a new position, her head in the crook of my elbow while her sleeping fingers stroked my earlobe. Cozy as it was, two in a twin bed was not comfortable. I wiggled free and slid off the bottom of the bed. After covering her with the quilt again, I slipped into the other bed, the one against the wall.

Male voices wafted through the grate again.

I'd walk through fire.

Huh. That's strong testimony—the pieces of the Matt puzzle get more complex each hour. However, I had my own puzzles.

Matt said the guy on the dock had no connection with Huck. The guy in the freezer couldn't possibly be connected to Huck or Pete. The closest Alec had been to Pete was reading messages on my monitor. For all I know—Pete said so little—Alec was killed in a car wreck. Or a street mugging. Or a fire. Attempts to unite the three deaths seemed like catastrophic ideation.

My effort to connect the dots among three random events had to stop. Correlation with a single factor—me—did not represent causation. More likely, a new body-disposal fad was making the rounds with bad guys. My only responsibility was to unite that Seattle detective with Tom so they could talk it over, since it was outside my area of expertise. Tomorrow, I'd have to explain to Tom why I didn't mention the body from Christmas Eve morning.

I lay awake rationalizing long after Matt and Tom said good-night and long after Matt walked up the stairs and into the room next door. The clunk of his shoes hitting the floor echoed downstairs and back up through the heat grate. He must have thrown himself into bed, because it crashed against the wall where my pillow lay jammed. The springs creaked as he turned over.

§

Forcing my mind away from the body that lay so near, I listened to sleeping child sounds—Pippi seemed a little wheezy—as I considered the day's events, working backward from Tom's visit.

When you can't see a person's face, and their words are filtered through the floor, drifting up through the heat grate, you hear more music than meaning. Like, that Tom cared enough to do a favor for Pete that he'd trudge through a snowstorm. What folly.

Yet there I was, for example, having tossed aside the core concerns of my life to come rescue him, even though Pete ditched me on Limberlost while claiming the whole affair with Huck and the gangsters was a cosmic joke.

The bed with Matt's body in it creaked again, causing me to hold my breath. If my calculations are correct—and because I'm good at math, they usually are—I lay as close to Matt as ever in this life, while the snowstorm of the decade entombed us in the Owens's house.

As close as the space of a two-by-four stud wall and two layers of sheetrock. Let's say six inches, since the house was built when two-by-fours were really four inches. He slept as close by me as most married people do at night, right?

If he ever slept. He tossed and turned, rattling his bed.

I'm not an insomniac, which requires medical treatment. I just don't sleep. And I am not the sort of person to let my body or my mind run out of control. I'd never fall for a slacker's sob-story or clumsy attempts at intimacy. Whatever mix of pheromones made that man so attractive to women must have also flipped the polarity of his moral compass in past years. I myself have never been susceptible to such warped thinking.

I live a rational life.

73. Matt's Soul Comes Home

SINCE I COULDN'T SLEEP, I went to check on Pippi, after repeatedly resisting the temptation to look in on her every fifteen minutes.

She wasn't in her bed.

I opened door after door on the second floor, probably making enough noise to wake the dead, though apparently not enough to wake the two girls bunked down in the guest room, which was the last room I checked. By then, my heart was beating so hard, the pulse behind my eye left me nearly blind.

The dim light from the hall showed Pippi in one bed, her hair falling across the blanket.

Sam lay on her side in the other bed, clasping a pillow to her cheek, one arm stretched across to the other bed to rest on Pippi's shoulder. In the dim light, with all the intensity drained from her face, she didn't look much older than a girl herself, though her hair spread around her, as wild as she wore it in college when she hung with post-grunge ex-riot-grrrls. When she's not boring holes in you with those dark eyes, she looks fragile.

I went to bed, in my own room, knowing I'd never sleep. To calm down, I tried every trick I'd learned from the therapist I'd worked with in the last year, seeking something that could sufficiently divert my thoughts from the knowledge that the men who killed Sonny Green had found me. All I could dig up was the sound of Pete's voice saying, "If it's not one thing it's another."

Pete had hatched game plans to run interference. Forces of the universe had conjured Sam to my door, sweeping her into the vortex that surrounded me. That left nowhere to rest one's mind.

And then, oh god.

She came into my room and closed the door.

She got into bed with me, warm from sleep, wood smoke mixed with the mint scent of her hair. Her lips moved close by my ear, speaking without using words as she slipped her hand around my best attribute and tugged as if she owned it. When I groaned and tried to touch her, she kissed me as if neither of us knew about kissing before.

Because I felt that I had to move, urgently, I wrapped her in my arms, ready to turn us both over, but she locked her legs and paralyzed me.

"Comfort only," she whispered. "We don't trust each other enough for anything wild."

"Are you always in control?" I muttered.

"Yes," she whispered again. "Unless I'm in love. Which I never am."

As graceful as a dancer, she wrapped my thighs with hers, letting my hands have the freedom to explore the valleys and planes of her spine, and then coming to understand her breasts, my mind flying over continents through eons of time as we kissed, as lost as I had been with Prokofiev. Then she took me into her, and my soul slammed back into my body, awakened from the dream. As if I'd come home.

74. Nicky Searches the Stars

NICKY CHECKED THE ERROR logs on the family's servers, and satisfied himself that the business was serving up the sordid trash that every customer with a credit card or logon passcode requested. Midnight had passed, advancing to the best hours for old film noir. The best he could find was "Christmas Holiday" with Deanna Durbin and Gene Kelly, which was amusing while he worked over the piteously slow Internet connection.

He searched "Peter Byron + Huck Aureliason" and got nothing, though that old gnome had referred to Pete Byron as the other man's son.

Deanna Durbin was explaining her past as the obsessive wife of a gangster. Is any viewer able to believe that Gene Kelly could incarnate the (mild) evil implied? Nicky turned back to his search.

He tried "Peter Byron + Limberlost" in the search string.

Everything the search engine found was from the previous decade or older, which made sense. An international documentary artist would have a childhood, but "My Life as a Chisinau Dog" wasn't made on the shores of Puget Sound. Most of the biography links for Peter Byron listed Arizona as his birthplace. Anything that included "Limberlost" was an online article from the local paper. The articles had been posted as scanned images, nearly unreadable, with minimal metadata. Most were event entries for a dance band. One listed the local high school's graduates. Another called out the graduates' awards: Peter Byron won a scholarship from the Seattle International Film Festival for Best Documentary – New Artist.

Jealous, Nicky turned back to the movie. Deanna Durbin's bad-tempered husband escaped from prison, and of course confronted her with her new, kindly friend. Who could believe these nice people would find themselves in the throes of noir passion? No wonder this film was a rarity. The conflicting images kept one from relaxing into the comforts of true noir.

Nicky turned back to his own concerns, seeking the community response to his acts of art.

⏮ ◀ | ▶ ⏭

Nick's American Business 101 as Cinéma Vérité

Entry #31: The Object Lesson: Part 2 – December 26, 02:30 PST

Video that speaks for itself, as teaching videos should.

Nick's Fan Forum | Permanent Link | 4 comments

Nope nyet nada

AuteurGrrrl | Homepage | 12.26 - 2:09 am |
This doesn't rank among nicky's best. i'm sorry, nick, but i just don't like it when your material takes on the aesthetics of a snuff film. it makes me want to just take up needles and wool and knit until it's all over. how can any of you call it surreal when it's just brutal realism with gratuitous schlock-shock?

It's just the B-movie stuff

JustMike | 12.26 - 2:11 am |
that Nicky likes. He's good at it. It's how he bends it that makes it surreal.

or not.

AuteurGrrrl | Homepage | 12.26 - 2:14 am |
you've got 1) surprised subject, 2) binding of prisoner, 3)

inquisition, 4) gagging death behind cello-wrap. or maybe i'm being too hard and this object lesson is in fact a special "i object to this" lesson.

Nicky does good brave work.

ponyboy | Homepage | 12.26 - 3:12 am |

His grit makes you think, so you can't call it gratuitous. And I saw a real snuff film one time. The lighting was so bad, it was impossible to see anything.

⏮ ◀ | ▶ ⏭

In the night, or maybe it was just before dawn, Nicky woke, disturbed. He booted his laptop and, over the slow Internet connection, he retraced his search. He had missed one of the dots.

"Peter Byron will apply the scholarship grant at UCLA, focusing on film studies. His sister Samsara, who provided the video's music score, is in her final year at the University of Washington."

Nicky tried another search: that address Uncle Kostya had given him.

75. Sam Disregards Her Better Angel

"THAT'S WHY I KEEP getting married," he said.

"For sex?"

"No, for comfort."

"You don't move like a guy who wants comfort. You want to escape."

He sighed. "What do you mean?"

"Escape consciousness. Escape the bounds of weary existence."

"No," he said. "Just comfort. To get it. To give it." He brushed my cheek like a lover would.

Uh-oh.

This is what ruins good Friends With Benefits relationships: the guy wants to murmur things in your ear and cuddle and be all cozy afterwards, when he's supposed to just roll over and go to sleep as

God intended. Not lie there cooing about the cosmos and cutting off the circulation in my arm. Next thing, those dangerous three words will be uttered, and the FWB ideal will be tanked.

I couldn't make myself get up. I lay and listened to his heartbeat, the rumble in his chest when he spoke, the winter wind that rattled the windows and trees outside the window, sounds that drowned out the voice of my better angel, who shook a finger at me and scolded: *This is how a girl makes trouble for herself.*

"This feels so right." He pulled me close again. Not *that* way. "Nothing has ever felt so right."

Then he sighed himself to sleep (the universe functioning as it should for a moment). I had that brief sense of power that comes from overcoming a man's strength, as if a sexual encounter let me suck up his energy into mine. Yet I couldn't make myself get up. It felt too comfortable, though I never let comfort get in the way when there's work to be done. My mind raced, but what could I possibly get up and *do*?

Maybe the best thing would be to return to the slumber party with Pippi, for whom my heart bled because I'd lived that same life: no mother, braving along with whacked-out relatives and a mentally absent father. No, check that. Pippi had Harley and Roz, who previously had kept Pete and me out of the worst of the trouble we could put ourselves in. And Matt loved her. I couldn't fault him one squib for that. So why did he need a gun to show it?

No thinking about the gun. The Christmas holiday dead bodies appeared again. Blink. Add Alec. I needed to find a phone—though the telephone gods had not been smiling on me. I needed to get Tom and Detective Jeremiah talking to each other.

I really needed to reach someone who would care about what I found in the utility logs. Maybe I should drive over to the local utility offices at dawn?

I felt Matt's breath on my shoulder (it smelled of mint tea). When I moved, a little, not trying to get away, he pulled me closer, his leg crossed over to trap me in his arms. The snow-lit night cast silver shadows across the room. You could see how long Matt's eyelashes are. How handsome he is, in a rough, damaged sort of way. His guitar glinted where he'd leaned it against the wall. Hand weights littered the floor. Then I saw that we hadn't locked the door.

Should have thought of that, when there's a little girl in the house. I scolded myself about not getting up to lock it, or to leave. It was just one of those fake little push-button locks, where you can stick a nail in the hole to unlock it.

My office has a lock, too. It's an electronic combination lock, and no one can open it without me there. No one is ever in there without me, save a single moment a week ago when I chatted in the hall with Quinn while Alec sat waiting for me to finish our patent documentation. That's the closest there's ever been to a breach of my electronic moat at work. And Alec is too inept to break into his own mail if he mistypes his password.

Also, Alec was dead. Or so Pete says.

Someone had to have physical access to my office to see the detailed pseudocode that Quinn and I sketched about the seven possible vectors for attack on flawed chipsets. How the heck did anyone get that list to launch those attacks on the local power utility servers?

Four:
A Brave New World

76. Matt Carries the Weight

WHEN I WOKE, SHE was gone. The only surprise: that I'd been deeply asleep.

She'd slipped away so recently, the bed still held her warmth. My pillow smelled of peppermint. And us.

In my life as a serial monogamist, each object of my affection realized at some point that we weren't made for each other, that we had different values and life goals, et cetera, and then called the whole thing off. However, I always discovered the unsuitability first, and then stayed, intending to do my duty, since I'd made the "until you die" promise. That's why Pete says I'm an incurable romantic.

I pushed my way into a so-called marriage with Sonny's widow as duty. I promised Caroline that I'd make a life for her and Pippi that could be endured—but I failed: I couldn't convince her to stay alive. What hubris.

In spite of what Pete says, I had no more romance left in me.

Except with Sam, I'm more at home than with anyone. I can feel obsession beginning to pulse in my veins. Therefore, while I can still be rational, I have to decide: do I want to restore the great friendship we had years ago? Or do I want what I once dreamed of—a true partner in life, love, the whole enchilada?

While I'm still rational, I should also figure out how to convince her to like me again, in meaningful ways.

Which I can't figure out while someone's out to kill me.

77. Sam Finds a Checksum Error

OH GEEZ.

I slept with a guy who lives with his mother.

We did it in the same bed where he slept in high school.

The FWB integrity issues checked out. Except that I slept with someone who lives with his mother. And his mother is Roslyn.

78. Nicky Dresses for Success

NICKY DIDN'T LIKE WEARING another person's clothes but lacked choice at this point. He refused to count such a charade as identity theft, which always seemed like a scam of the lower classes. First, any child could do it. Second, Nicky's goal was self-actualization. You need your own (professional) name for that. So he didn't like peering at himself from inside another person's skin.

What he did like in the reflected image: the quality of the facework he'd had done. There had been an initial miscommunication with the surgeon ("Oh, you want to look less Slavic!") until he made it clear exactly how the eyes, the cheekbones, the nose needed to create an overall image. The dimple in his chin was a wise addition, if difficult to shave.

He turned from the mirror to a preferred view of himself: through his own video work. As a last task before leaving the night's accommodation, he uploaded the long video piece he'd worked on: a silent-movie stylization of identity invention, following the techniques he used when he left his old home, emphasizing the *what* without explaining the *how* or revealing the *who*. He launched the piece with a picture of his grandmother Guilletta and then ended with a manicured hand swiping a badge. It had taken him a couple of months to get the timing right. Now he had to trust that it was coming off as *Metropolis* and not *The Tramp*.

⏮ ◀ | ▶ ⏭

Nick's American Business 101 as Cinéma Vérité
Entry #32: Passport Expedited – December 26, 09:00 PST

The key learning for a growing executive is that he must establish himself as the end result of his life story. Telling a great story, coherent and compelling, is what makes a great leader.

I've been working on this a while. I'm interested in your views: Is the timing right? This has been tricky without a professional editor.

Nick's Fan Forum | Permanent Link | 3 comments

Call it "Coming to America"
JustMike | 12.26 - 11:12 am |
Slip in an image of Ellis Island somewhere. But you asked about timing: It needs about 15 seconds more focus at the key beats.

Memento without Meaning
AuteurGrrrl | Homepage | 12.26 - 11:15 am |
If you decide to run it backwards.

I don't get it
ponyboy | Homepage | 12.26 - 12:11 pm |
Is the old lady like symbolic? Is that who the William Holden character is running from?

79. Sam Questions the Scouts' Chore Wheel

"WHAT ARE YOU DOING up so early?" Matt asked. He slid his arm across the small of my back, as if he had FWB permission.

"You have the generator on and I have work to do."

I wanted to relax into his touch, but it was morning now. I don't know about how it is for you the next morning, but if I like a guy, I think about it afterwards all the time. Which seems undignified. Matt set a cup of coffee on the desk beside me, resting his other hand on my shoulder. Smelling the coffee, I looked up from my work.

"You have what every cell in my body has been screaming for," I said. "I will love you through all eternity out of gratitude."

I picked up the cup before I realized the double-entendre in that. Rats. There's no getting romantic when I'm at a keyboard. Matt took the coffee from my hand and tipped my chin up so he could kiss me.

"Hey! You're coming between me and caffeine. Not a good move." I tried to sound like it was a joke. I wasn't at all sure where we were going with this. "When do you think the roads will be plowed and the ferries will run?"

"Daddy!" Pippi shouted from upstairs, her voice muffled as it filtered into the dining room through the stove grate. "Are we having your special breakfast surprise, like you promised?"

"Yes," he called upstairs. "I always keep my promises."

He kissed me some more and then disappeared back into the kitchen. From the banging of cupboard doors and metal pots, he seemed to be in a cooking frenzy again. He popped back through the swinging door a minute later, wondering aloud.

"You're still dying to get off the island?"

"I have things I owe people that won't wait on the weather," I said. "I feel guilty just sitting here."

"So Harley and Roslyn succeeded on their mission, to instill a conscience in you." Matt smiled. "It's nice to see success, after all those years they made me watch out for you."

"What, were you assigned us like a chore? Feed the dog, clean your room and pretend to be friends with Pete and Sam?"

"Cripes, Sam, that was twenty years ago."

His voice vibrated liked a bassoon with a frayed reed as he rested his hand on my shoulder again. I wasn't sure how conscious he was that he kept touching me. The tense guy of yesterday was relaxed and happy this morning.

"Boy-scout duty? Is that why you never kissed me?" I didn't mean to say it, but it slipped out.

He wrinkled his nose. "I never kissed you for the obvious reasons. Even if you weren't jail-bait, my mother would have committed homicide if I ever touched you."

So. Except for that one Bad Night five years after high school, I was the Owens family morality project. Geezus pieces, had the scales of judgment tipped, or what? Who needed moral guidance now?

§

I didn't get my boots and coat on fast enough. Matt reappeared, that pot of coffee in his hand again.

"Where are you going?" He seemed startled, as if I were deserting him.

"I want to check on Aunt Lucky's house." I pulled on my skull cap, jerking it over my ears. "I'm checking Huck's house, too. Just to make sure there are no broken pipes."

"I'll come with."

"No. Stay here with Pippi. I need to find more clean clothes, too."

"That could be fun to watch." Again with the reedy bassoon voice.

"I'll be back."

It was a five-minute walk to the cabin on a nice day, but a ten-minute slog through the snow drifts—so who's laughing at my Doc Martens now? Alone for the first time in hours, I breathed in the cold air and squinted into the morning sun. Whatever had happened between Matt and me, we'd have to sort it out later. Hanging around and playing house in the winter wonderland didn't seem like the wisest way to start sorting.

He kissed like a man who loves women, as if he's drinking life from your lips. His hands move like he knows exactly what he's doing.

If we were alone, I'd love to make you scream, Matt said that morning. Then he attempted it anyway.

I shook off the thought.

Maybe by noon the ferries would be running, and the roads would be plowed, and I could go back to Seattle: find Huck and Pete, and then get back to my own work.

One sign that the universe was tilting in my favor: Uncle Bob was gone. He'd left cabin locked up, the police Do-Not-Cross tape in place. The only price I had to pay was the hike back up the icy stairs.

80. Matt Chops More Wood

WE WERE SNOWED IN. Mentally, I set about doing the be-prepared boy-scout things that Sam makes fun of.

Harley had topped off the fuel in the generator when the Channel 5 weather guy first showed the arctic front headed our way. We only used the power for the freezer, the fridge, and Sam's laptop, so we'd be good there for a long while. I used the hurricane lamp in the kitchen only when cooking; otherwise, we had the light from the windows. Harley maintained lamp fuel enough for a decade of power outages and a month's worth of propane for cooking. Plus enough firewood to keep us warm till spring. So this wasn't that kind of survival outpost.

But no phone.

I'd mused on this benefit while chopping wood: no phone calls to disrupt the peace. Ferry service had been out all night, and the bridge was out. So until ferry service was restored, we were safe. Whoever was plaguing me would need a boat, a snow plow, and an off-road monster truck to come here.

I had wood to chop, which helped work out other tensions. At least I can't think about her that way while swinging an ax. Sweating like a pig, I chopped and then hauled three armloads of kindling and firewood inside, dumping the loads into the woodbin.

Safe and snug.

"California never had a killer icicle like this, Pippi!" Sam's voice rang from the dining room as she called to Pippi when she came in the back door.

What the hell was I thinking, dipping into an ocean of comfort like a tourist, when a tsunami's about to roll over my world? The guys who were in Yuri's café might still be on the island. I refreshed the coffee pot, made more cocoa for Pippi, and then brought Sam another cup of coffee.

Her touch felt like ice.

"I want to go play in the snow," Pippi said. It was her fourth request of the morning.

I gazed at the door that led out into the wild and dangerous world. "Later," I said. "Not now."

Sam glanced up from where she'd buried her nose in her laptop as soon as she came inside.

"*Carpe* freakin' *diem*," she said.

81. Sam Hears a Note of Joy

MATT KEPT HANGING AT the edge of my chair, too close. When he wasn't hanging over me, he was fussing over Pippi. Fixing her a snack she didn't want, yet refusing her requests to play outside because of the cold. Pippi had been making calm, rational arguments for why she should dress and play in the snow, when it was way past time for whining.

"Matt, you've been away from here too long," I said. "You forget that snow melts so fast that it's absolutely critical to play in it as soon as possible."

"Thanks for the parenting advice," he said, pissed once again.

Tired of watching Matt play house, I put on my coat.

"Let's go, Pippi. There's a snowman out there, calling us to free him from the drifts."

"Or a snow-woman," Pippi said.

"Or a whole dysfunctional family of snow people," I said, helping her into snow clothes. "Lost in the snow and unable to pull themselves together."

We were rolling snow balls when the phone rang inside the Owens's house.

Oh joy. Service restored.

I could call Detective Jeremiah. I could call Quinn. I could call the security director at the local utility to tell them about the attempted intrusions. I could call Gerard at Z-Crypto and tell him—

82. Matt Makes the Ringing Stop

"Hello."

"It's all over. The final act."

The voice wasn't Danny. However, it had that tinge of Ukrainian rumble: therefore, one more voice that I didn't want to hear.

"There's nothing left for you to do." The voice growled in my ear.

I couldn't speak, but I swear it was from inchoate anger, not fear. By then, I was just sick of the Petrenko family thugs terrorizing me.

"So, my friend, there's nothing more for you to just keep your life, see? To keep your kid safe? I give you Konstantin's farewell. A fadeout shot for you."

83. Nicky Bears Glad Tidings

Nicky hung up, proud of himself for doing good.

First, he'd sought the phone number on Uncle Kostya's cell, and guessed which was the correct entry for the wedding singer. Then he found cell reception by leaning out an upstairs window.

Most of all, he enjoyed the pleasant feeling that the phone call gave him: Konstantin's demise would bring happiness to someone else's life, even though it was a stranger. That it was a friend of Pete Byron's merely salted the pleasure, giving him more to savor.

He rubbed his hands in anticipation of telling his cousins the good news.

Ding-dong! Kostya's dead!

84. Sam Goes Inside

PIPPI AND I RAN up the back steps, stomping snow from our boots before entering the house. As I pulled open the back door, Matt jerked the phone cord out of the kitchen wall, sending Christmas cards, utility bills, and Lands' End catalogs skittering across the sideboard and onto the floor. He bashed past us and crashed down the steps. I motioned for Pippi to stay inside, but I followed him. He sloshed through the snow into the backyard and hurled the phone into Roz's vegetable patch, where it rested amidst bolting Brussels sprouts that peeked through the snow.

Then he shot it. Twice.

After quelling my startle response, I came up behind him.

"I needed to make a call," I said.

Matt just stood there—wearing shoes this time, but shivering in his shirt sleeves, staring at the dead phone carcass.

I touched his arm, perhaps the first time I'd reached out to him since dawn. "You'll freeze out here. Let's go inside."

He didn't answer, but he came back up the trail he had beaten through the snow drifts, headed for the front of the house. I followed. Pippi watched through the living room window, so I waved, like this was really a lot of fun.

We turned the corner of the house and ran smack into the surfer guy from the ferry. Matt pointed his gun with a jerk, and the surfer held up his hands, but in that same instant Matt slammed the heel of his palm up under the guy's chin, and then slammed his other elbow hard on the man's breast bone. As the guy bent in pain, Matt dropped his gun and clasped both hands, ramming the poor guy's head back as he stomped down on the man's in-step. All the while Matt screamed, "Not my family! Not my fucking family!"

The man sprawled, prone, and Matt stood over him, seeming ready to kick him to death. Over his shoulder, Matt said, "Go inside with Pippi."

The guy struggled to sit up and turn his head, choking on the blood from his nose, which seemed to have been broken in one of Matt's blows to his head. Matt bent and grabbed the front of the man's shirt, jerking him up so that they were face to face, the man dripping blood onto Matt's shirt.

Pippi had come to the front porch—I guess to greet her freaky father. The two of us girls backed away from this manly business. The stranger spoke, but we couldn't hear. Matt grasped the guy's shirt and pulled him closer, and the man spoke again. Matt let go of his shirt and stepped back.

Then we heard what he was saying. "I'm looking for Pete. I didn't know you were here. Really, dude. I wouldn't lie to you. I'm not that stupid. I want to stay alive."

Matt spoke—and again we couldn't hear.

The surfer seemed to be denying something, shaking his head vigorously.

Matt put his hand up, commanding the man to be quiet with a gesture. Without turning around, he called to us.

"Girls, please go inside now."

He definitely meant me, too.

85. Matt Applies Excessive Force

"IT'S TRUE. THEY SENT me to hit you weeks ago. It was either that or get whacked myself."

Slamming him into the chair in Roslyn's potting shed, I grasped Danny's hand in a twist lock.

"My own father," Danny said. "Do you see? My own fucking father is so scared, he said it was down to you or me."

Duct tape seldom behaves when you're incautious, but the roll of tape seemed to accept pain compliance. I strapped Danny's forearms to the chair.

"Since I don't want to do it, I delayed. Now Konstantin says I'm taking too fucking much time. He'll do me anyway. Whatever else happens."

Hardly hearing him, I taped his legs to the chair, though if Danny weren't freaking out, he'd realize he could kick off his boots and be free.

"You got to help me."

He begged in that whiney way that makes you want to pop the beggar.

"OK, Danny."

"You'll help? I'll do anything. I'll tell everything."

"First, tell me something." I tried to get my blood to stop boiling.

"Anything, dude."

"What kind of surfer wears the same sheepskin boots as teeny-boppers do at the mall?"

He looked at the blood dripping on his shoes and parka, then at me.

"Wow, dude. Nobody says teeny-bopper anymore."

86. Sam Crystallizes Her Thinking

OH GEEZ.

I went to bed with a nut case.

87. Nicky Explores Mother Earth

PARKED OUTSIDE THE CAFÉ, Nicky picked up enough hot-spot signal to get driving directions from the onboard GPS. Then he stared at the results for a few moments before swinging the car around and heading back out to where Konstantin had taken them the day before.

The wild woods of the north.

88. Sam Knows Dysfunctional Family When She Sees It

WHEN I CLOSED THE door, Pippi said, "Girls never get to have fun."

"That wasn't fun," I said, more than appalled.

Pippi shrugged.

"So I guess we should—" I wasn't sure quite what to do.

She headed for the living room. "Don't worry. I know what to do."

"Do you—"

She put her finger to her lips, shushing me.

"Matt will take care of it," she said, "He always does. Look! I found that funny blue piece you wanted."

While I sat numbly trying to put pieces together in my mind, Pippi worked on the physical puzzle on the table in front of us.

Five minutes later, Matt came in and, without saying a word, took several of Roslyn's tea towels and then went out again. In another ten minutes he came back again. He ran hot water in the kitchen sink, washing his hands, bending to rinse his face. Then he seemed to notice the blood on his shirt and stripped it off, dropping it in the other side of the sink and running water.

"Always use cold water with bloodstains," I said.

"I know."

He destroyed another of Roslyn's tea towels in drying his face and then went upstairs. In a moment he came down in a clean t-shirt and jeans, pulling on a long-sleeve flannel shirt as he walked through the house. He went into the living room and sat by Pippi, murmuring as he stroked her back. She kissed him on the cheek.

§

In the kitchen again, Matt ran water in the tea kettle and set it on the stove, turning the gas flame on high. I followed, sitting at the kitchen table, trying not to ask The Obvious Questions. Taking ice from the refrigerator, he put it in a plastic sack, wrapped a towel around it, and sat by me at the kitchen table. As he swathed his right hand in the ice bag, I got lost in a thought: that bruised hand touched me before dawn and then battered a man half to death.

Matt touched my hand, his fingers cold from the ice.

"He wanted Pete," I said, stating it rather than asking, shivering from where he touched me.

"Sam, believe me, Pete wouldn't be involved if I had a choice. He stumbled onto what he considered a good idea and got in deep before he called me."

"Just like the old days, huh?"

"Stop it, Sam. I'm serious. Do you know what Pete does?"

"Yes, of course. I pay for half of it."

"I don't think you do know," Matt said.

"Pete makes documentaries about families in rough places, except not like a war correspondent. He stays in decent hotels, avoids battle zones. What makes me crazy is that he loses cameras and laptops everywhere he goes. Or gets his passport lifted."

Matt didn't answer at first, still staring where he touched my hand.

"Pete met this rich dude," he said at last. "He treated them like they were the effing medieval Medicis. He sold himself as a film auteur who makes American family stories."

"That's what Pete does," I said. "Make documentaries about families."

"Family," Matt said again. "Are you the only person in America who doesn't know what 'family' means?"

"Unfortunately, I have one."

"Sam, get a clue. Don't you go to the movies? Watch HBO?" He looked at me like I was an idiot. Then I realized I was.

"Oh."

"First, he filmed a wedding, and then a funeral. He got people talking about themselves on tape, reminiscing. You know how good Pete is at that."

Glum beyond words, I nodded.

"They liked his work—people feel flattered when the camera makes them look good. They wanted him to make a real family history." Matt didn't wait for me to answer. "That's when Pete got me involved. He suggested that my band play at a family wedding. Then bad things happened."

"Now gangsters want to off my brother?"

"No, don't worry about Pete. They still trust him. He finessed that just fine."

I sighed and sat back.

"It's me they want," Matt said. "I saw things I shouldn't have. They think they need to make me shut up."

"Oh geez."

Hence the gun when a little girl screams; hence the move to the hinterlands; hence Pippi choosing a new name.

Matt said, "It's OK. It's only Danny who found me. He wants out of the family business, so he came looking for help."

"From you?"

"Yeah. He wants me to help him disappear."

"Can you?"

"I'm sending him to friends who can protect him. Now, if you'll excuse me, I have to make a phone call."

"You killed the phone, remember? I still have to make some calls."

"You'll have to wait."

89. Matt Ponders Post-Soviet-Era Social Migration

I USED MY DAD'S OLD police radio to call Dispatch. As I hoped, Sam's sister was doing double shifts.

"Hi, Eliot. It's Matt."

"Hey, guy. I heard you're playing Jeremiah Johnson with my sister."

"Sam's not having fun." I said it quietly, though Sam could hear me. "Are the ferries running yet?"

"Bet she can't wait to get off island, as usual. The ferry left Seattle about twenty minutes ago."

"Eliot, will you do me a favor?"

"Always."

"I want you to dial this number. It doesn't matter who answers. Just say you have a message from me. You don't even have to say who you are."

"OK." Eliot took the number from me and then asked for the message, the radio crackling as if this were really police business.

"Tell them the Ukrainian surfer needs a new home. He'll be on the eleven-thirty ferry. Can you do that?"

"Yes. And throw away the number when I'm done?"

"Thanks, my friend."

"Bring Pippi over for New Year's Eve, Matt. We'll make popcorn and watch movies."

"I have to take a rain-check, Eliot. I think I'll be in Oakland."

"Ukrainian surfer?" Sam said when I turned off the radio.

"Can you please forget what you heard, like Eliot will?"

"Yuri and Andrij are Ukrainian."

By then, the kettle was screaming from the stove top. I used it to make a goddamn pot of tea, as if we were having a party. It felt awkward, pouring with my left hand, but the right one was still wrapped in ice.

"It's just a coincidence," I said. "Lots of people came to America when the Soviet Union broke up. Forget it. Let's help Pippi with the puzzle."

I didn't actually help. Pippi was faster, as much as I tried to concentrate.

"Your girl is better at pattern-recognition and small-muscle motor skills than you are, Matt." Sam wasn't even pretending to pay attention to the jigsaw pieces, just staring at me. I could feel her boring a hole into my skull, trying to stir things around. I went back to the kitchen.

She followed me, letting the door swing shut while Pippi worked the puzzle.

"Yuri was feeding a vagrant in the café kitchen. They were speaking the same language."

"It's just a coincidence, Sam." I didn't believe it, though I hadn't seen the old man. Danny said they'd sent an assassin after him.

"Yuri said it was one of Andrij's thug cousins who threatened him when asking for Pete."

"He was talking about Danny." I didn't want to explain more to Sam. I pictured Danny harassing Yuri. It didn't seem like Danny's style, but he was scared, so he could be capable of excesses.

"Where did he go?" Sam asked.

"Who?" My heartbeat had finally slowed, and I felt that fugue state calling to me. I needed to make sure Danny didn't slip into shock, but we hadn't been through enough of a tussle for it to have affected me. Yet my brain wanted to return to that half-sleep state I'd been stuck in for months. I could no longer afford to live that way.

"Your friend. The surfer dude."

"He's in Roz's workshop. I lit the stove and gave him a blanket."

I'd also duct-taped him to a chair. Although I wanted to believe Danny's story, I couldn't afford to be wrong.

It's all going to be OK. I can make it through this.

It's all going to be OK.

No, it's not. No chance.

Sam was saying something more that I couldn't hear as I let myself out the back door and slogged down the icy trail to the garden shed.

Danny twitched, startled when I banged the door open.

"Did you threaten Yuri?" I stood over him, as interrogator.

"I don't know Yuri."

"The café owner at Casa D."

"I just asked directions. I wouldn't be jiving strangers when my family is riding my tail."

"Who was the old hobo in the café talking in Ukrainian?"

Danny's face turned to chalk. He opened his mouth, but only stuttered.

"C'mon, Danny. No theatrics. Sam says an old man was eating in the cafe kitchen. They didn't speak English. Yuri says two different men threatened him."

Danny started crying. "Oh fuck me, I'm fried." He slurred his words. I'd hurt his mouth.

"Shut up, Danny. Tell me who the old man is."

"It's Konstantin. He's after me."

"Konstantin? Konstantin Petrenko?"

The Petrenko godfather had been captured on one of Pete's video streams, describing his departed mother as a saint. The same Konstantin who sold arms out of the Caucasus as a family business. Who brought illegals in to work for him, practically as slaves. Who sent his god-sons after every illicit scam imaginable. "Sam described a street bum. Unshaved. Badly dressed."

"He wants to show how he disrespects me." Danny started crying again.

"Oh cripes. Dude." I wiped at his eyes with the towel I'd brought. "If he's looking for Pete's help to find you, then Yuri told him that Pete left the island yesterday. He probably followed Pete back to Seattle."

"Geezus fuck I hope you're right."

"I'll bring you some toast and coffee," I said.

Danny looked up, seeming more pathetic than wrecked, snot dripping from his nose. "With milk and sugar, please."

As Pete would say, what a fucktard.

90. Nicky Uses His Sick Leave

OUTSIDE HIS IMPROVISED B&B atop the highest hill, Nicky used his cell phone to call in at his day job, to say he wouldn't be at work for quite a while.

Family business, he said. Though it was really an affair of the heart.

He brushed snow off the borrowed car, finding himself happy for the first time in—how long, really?

The day's challenge: how much heroism was he capable of?

91. Sam Helps with the Laundry

NOW I'D DONE IT. I'd gone from intimacy with a vain, vindictive CEO FWB to an everyday kind of guy who carries a gun and beats people with his bare hands.

Pippi came downstairs, having changed out of her snow clothes, and took up the jigsaw puzzle again. She apparently had better coping mechanisms than I did for cozy chaos.

Matt the-everyday-guy sat with us for a while, fidgeting. Then he tortured the wood stove with a poker. He sat down again, staring out the window, a couple of disjointed pieces of puzzle-sky in his left hand. Pippi glanced up at him, then took the pieces away, pretending like he offered them to her.

The only sound, besides the logs settling in the stove, came from Pippi expressing great satisfaction over the progress of the puzzle, which I had come to loathe with the fire of a thousand furies. I felt like taking the poker to Matt, to wake him from whatever bad dream he stared into. Each time he roused himself, he first rested his battered hand on Pippi's head, then reached for a puzzle piece, but his bruised hand wouldn't close properly, so then he leaped up from his chair and paced again.

Finally Matt went into the hall and put on a light jacket.

"Where are you going, Daddy?" Pippi asked. "You'll freeze if you don't put on a winter coat."

"I'm going to chop wood," he said.

I sighed, relieved when he carried that explosive energy away. Though it beats me how he could close his injured hand on an ax handle.

As soon as Matt closed the door, Pippi said, "I peed my pants."

This sentiment I could agree with. "I about did too. Geez."

"No, I really peed my pants. Can you help me wash them?"

I helped, but Pippi did most of the work herself, just needing assistance with wringing out excess water.

"Sometimes I pee the bed, and then I have to change the sheets. It's such a hassle." From the tone of Pippi's voice, it sounded like she was emulating an adult saying those words. "Roslyn promised she'd never tell. You won't either, will you?"

"Your secret is safe with me," I said. "You don't have to worry about peeing the bed until you get married. Most guys don't like to sleep with women who wet the bed. Until then, it's your own business."

Pippi lost her seriousness for a minute and laughed a little. "Is that what your husband said?"

"I'm not married. Never have been. I'm a sister, not a wife."

"Kids tease me. I peed my pants at my old school. What if I wet them at my new school?"

"Pippi, my friend, I'll let you in on a secret. Everyone in the whole wide world has wet their pants. Maybe it was yesterday, or maybe it was a while ago, but everyone has, and they all remember the last time they did it."

"Did you?"

"Of course. I was nine years old. My brother Pete dared me to drink a whole bottle of Mountain Dew without stopping. So I did. We were on a field trip, and the bus driver wouldn't stop for me. When we got off the bus, I peed my pants before I could get to the bathroom. Nobody saw but my brother, and he swore he'd never tell."

"I wish no one would ever tell about me."

"If anyone teases you, say this: 'I know you wet your pants one time and your mother had to tie your jacket on so no one would see.'"

"But I don't know that."

"Doesn't matter. It's true for anyone who teases you, so they will shut up. That's all we care about."

"Daddy says we aren't supposed to say 'shut up.'"

"You aren't going to say it. You're just going to make sure they do."

We hung her pants and underwear in the upstairs bath.

"So much for secrets," I said, closing the bathroom door.

She stood in the hall, hesitant. Then she said, "I have a big secret."

I said, "Don't tell secrets you shouldn't."

"It's my secret, and I want to tell you," Pippi said. "You have to promise to never, ever tell a soul. Stick a needle in your eye."

"I'm not sure this is a good idea," I said.

"Please?" Pippi said. "I have to tell someone. And you have the mark of character."

"OK, I promise."

She dragged me into her bedroom, which had been Harley's office. She made me sit on the bed, then stared at me for a while before she finally spoke.

"My mother killed herself."

Oh geez.

I took a big breath. "Matt said your mother was ill."

"That's what everyone told me," Pippi said. "I know better. Please don't tell Matt. He's so sad. I don't want him to feel worse." She patted my hand, as if reassuring me, wanting me to feel better too.

Like I'm supposed to know how to handle this? I'd been fed a raft load of bull at her age, and I didn't want to participate in that with Pippi. I scrambled for the right truth to speak.

"Matt must be very sad about losing your mother."

"Nope," Pippi said. "It's my father that he's sad about. Matt just took us—my mom and me—because he feels bad about my real father."

I took a breath, hoping I knew what to say. "Matt cares about you."

"Yes, but he lied about Mom dying. She wasn't sick and she probably isn't in heaven. If you kill yourself, you can't go to heaven."

Now I was thrashing in the deep end. Would you know what to say? "Your mother and father dying must be the worst bummer. I can't imagine how bad you feel. Roslyn said your mom was ill. You know Roz can't tell a lie."

"Matt lies to everyone about my mom," Pippi said with equanimity.

"Why do you think she killed herself?"

"She left me a tape," Pippi said. "I found it in my tape player. She said not to be sad and not to miss her, because she just had to leave."

"Oh Pippi."

"Do you want to hear it?" she asked. She tugged a cassette from her pocket. "I used to listen every night. Now I only listen on Sundays, so it's special."

She put it into the tape player on the table by her bed.

"Shhh," Pippi said as she pressed the play button. The saddest voice in the world began to speak, saying the saddest things I'd ever heard in this life.

When it ended, she rewound the tape and tucked it back into her pocket.

"I can't keep my promise," I said, when I could speak again. "You have to tell Matt. Or tell your grandma and grandpa that you know."

Pippi shook her head slowly, back and forth, back and forth. "Nope. Matt is already so sad because he thinks it's his fault my father got killed. It won't be any better if he knows."

I was boiling inside, so hot I felt my face burning. "I can't keep my promise."

"You have to. It's your mark of character," Pippi said. "It won't make Matt feel better. And my mother will still be dead."

92. Matt Goes to Town

PIPPI JUMPED WHEN I banged open the back door, which made me cringe. This is all my fault.

"Sam, do you have chains for your car?" I called.

"Yes, but I hate to use them." Sam had her head buried in Pippi's puzzle.

"I need to go in to town. Please lend me your car."

"No. I'll drive you."

"I'd prefer—" I stopped, bright enough to realize this would go nowhere. No way a one-eyed slacker would be allowed to drive her Challenger. Anyway, my hands hurt too much. "We'll have to bring Pippi."

It struck me that I couldn't leave either of them at the house alone.

93. Nicky Takes the Long View

NICKY FOUND A PULLOUT—the road running along those stubby chalk cliffs above the village—where he could get cell reception again.

He had freedom now, without Konstantin chasing him like the devil, yet he needed to preserve old relationships. At the same time, he recognized that he had new responsibilities for the woman he loved.

NickCarraway> I can't join you by ten this morning. There's a situation here. I need to provide cover.

BlackPawn> The feds let your White Knight buddies walk coz they had nothing to hold them.

NickCarraway> That is unfortunate. But perhaps they never received the package, and so all is well.

BlackPawn> My people followed them through town. They got on the first ferry running this morning. I'm waiting to hear from my guys where they ended up.

94. Sam Has the Mark of Character

AT THE STATE-POSTED THIRTY-FIVE miles per hour—if you have a heavy Detroit automobile and can attain that speed over ice—it takes eleven minutes to drive to the ferry landing from where Lost Point Road meets the main highway at Milepost Seven.

Right where the cedars crowded out the alders for a few hundred yards along the hillside, I decided that I could drive my car down the ferry ramp as soon as Matt got that surfer dude out of the backseat of my car.

Then I heard a sniff. I tilted the rear mirror to see Pippi staring back at me. No expression whatever on her face. She had a hand on Matt's parka, clutching it as tight as a hand that size could.

I couldn't leave her.

95. Nicky Practices Triangulation

NICKY LOOKED UP FROM his cell phone to watch two black Escalades and a black Suburban disembark from the ferry.

It was a tossup which had the darkest tint obscuring the windows.

BlackPawn> We got you whistleblower status. That's about as safe as you can get.

NickCarraway> Like Erin Brockovich?

BlackPawn> A little more drastic than that. The feds can cut warrants as soon as you testify.

NickCarraway> I gave you the details I had.

BlackPawn> They need more details for warrants. They want your cousins and all the other oligarchs you can deliver.

Nicky stared at the blank cell screen—the display had already timed out—and saw a movie replaying, where Konstantin betrayed his own family, offed his own nephew.

Nicky did not want to star in a noir remake of Uncle Kostya's life. What were the key tensions in the story? Neither Zandr's nor Nicky's life was at risk from the American government. Zandr interjected a new antagonist by leading Konstantin to the White Knights. Remaking *Criss-Cross* was never in any of Nicky's production plans. All betrayal of the family would be only on Konstantin's lost soul.

A headache started, and the aura made it hard to see as he punched succinct information on the text messaging screen.

NickCarraway> Attention to wrong detail. It's only Konstantin Petrenko they want. Others involved are only his victims.

BlackPawn> What more do I give them?

NickCarraway> They should check how Alec Ramsey moved code between these addresses.

He keyed in the Internet address for the Seattle servers, trying to see past the aura, trying to get past the headache to remember the destination address. Although likely as not the White Knights had already moved their servers.

BlackPawn> Who's Alec Ramsey?

NickCarraway> A dead man, thanks to Konstantin.

BlackPawn> How do they find Konstantin?

NickCarraway> Lost on Limberlost Island.

Never in his experience had a family disagreement about business choices gone so spectacularly awry. To change the plot, Nicky needed to direct himself in the heroic action segment.

96. Sam Checks the Rearview Mirror

PIPPI STAYED WITH ME while Matt walked that Danny guy to the miniscule passenger waiting area. A black Suburban pulled in behind them, blocking any view of Matt saying farewell to his surfer friend.

While we waited at the Stop-N-Go station that sits on a fingernail-sized area on the island where there's cell reception, I thumbed through my email. I sent a quick message to Quinn, warning about what I'd found in the security logs that I'd studied the night before, but my message was probably so cryptic he wouldn't be able to interpret it without hearing my earlier warnings. Then I checked my voice mail. Gerard had answered my message to his private line!

Honestly, Sam, I thought better of you. I blocked you on all my other accounts. Now you call with a threat? Why would you sink so—

No bars. No service.
Foobar with Gerard.
Back to normal.

I could only hope that the Z-Crypto crew would clue him in since I was being held incommunicado by the Fates.

Since my cell crapped out and Matt wasn't returning as rapidly as he left, I took Pippi with me and went in to the Stop-N-Go to prepay for some gasoline. And to ask to use their landline.

My phone request failed.

Root cause? I've angered the ancient gods of communications, like a woeful mythic Greek being pursued by Tragedy.

"I'd like to help," she said. "But I'd lose my job. I can make a 911 call for you."

The clerk was a very sweet high school girl, long dark hair, dark eyes as big as half-dollars (including mascara supplements), dressed in the casual work threads of our time: lacey skirt over leggings, Ugg boots, a shawl-collar beige sweater, a fake keffiyeh around her neck, and a wide, wide belt with fake peacock feathers. The usual wave of pity for her plight—*I'm sorry you're stuck in Limberlost; I feel your pain*—washed over me.

Finding that I had only two dollars in cash, I swiped a credit card for ten dollars of gas, then listened as the slow dialup system connected and started the check-and-approve steps for the transaction. The answer beep came at last. Then the clerk's eyes shift sideways. I could see her gearing up to watch me be embarrassed when she had to say, *"I'm sorry. It's not going through."*

This never embarrasses me. Pete uses one of my credit cards, and if he's in a jam, like that time in China or when he was robbed down to his shorts and shoes in Mexico, he abuses it. This time, I was ready to bet that he'd used my cards to go Huck's bail, metaphorically speaking.

I'm never stuck, because I have other cards that Pete can't touch. I was reaching into my wallet for another card when the clerk looked startled as she studied the read-out on the credit-card terminal. I couldn't tell whether it was dyslexia or simple illiteracy on her part, but she seemed to be mouthing the words as she studied the LED display.

She said, "I'm sorry. I have to call my manager. I'm new. I—"

Matt had come up behind me. "Never mind. We're in a hurry."

He snatched both my card and my cell phone off the counter and dragged Pippi and me out.

"Everyone in the car," he said. "Now."

That dude Danny was leaning on my car.

"Hey!" I said, coming up on them.

"The key!" Matt shouted to me. "Throw me the keys."

I tossed them over, and he began hustling Danny and Pippi into the back, shouting at her to buckle up and at Danny to lie on the floor. However, he must have pulled a wrong latch by the car door, because the trunk was ajar. I lifted it higher to get good leverage for closing it.

The old Slavic gentleman from the ferry was curled up in my trunk, his arms around his pillowcase.

In a fetal position.

Not breathing.

Blue.

Matt stretched from the passenger door to slam the trunk shut.

"Get in the car, Sam. Get us out of here."

He had that wretchedly ugly gun in his left hand, holding it close to his side. I slid into the driver's seat and fired up the Challenger, now recognizing the control I'd gained from extra weight in the trunk.

"Go back to Lost Point Road. Don't stop for anything till we get to the Episcopal Church."

"What happened?" I asked our commander-in-chief.

Danny said, "The SUV guy asked for directions to Matt's house."

"Maybe—"

"Drive," Matt said. "Don't talk. Pippi, pull up the hood of your coat. Duck your head down in case there's broken glass."

Every family has rules for the road.

Already ramming the Challenger into third gear, I passed two snail-like mini-vans on the right and turned onto the arterial that leads out of the village, checking my mirrors as much as the road in front of us. There was less snow in town than where we were, but the snow lay over ice on the roadbed. Like driving on Vaseline.

"Who are we running from?" I copied the overly calm voice Matt had used when Pippi screamed on the ice. It was similar to my first-responder voice. Except scared.

"I don't know," Matt said.

"Uncle Kostya sent someone to find Matt and me," Danny said. "We are so fucked."

"That's a bad word," Pippi said, muffled by her coat.

"Hell yeah," I said. "Who's Uncle Kostya?"

"Shut up," Matt said, as if that was a nice way to talk.

S

"Pull around back and stop as close to the door as you can," Matt commanded as we cruised up on St. Peter's By-the-Sea Episcopal Church. Roslyn's rust-bucket Jeep was parked out back.

I drove up on the sidewalk and stopped right at the back steps of the church's kitchen.

Matt jumped out and tipped the back seat forward. "Pippi, run inside. Tell Nana to lock all the doors, and not to let anyone in or out until Tom Tremain comes for you. Do you understand?'

"Yes, Daddy." She was out super-fast and up the steps. She stopped to wave, but Matt shook his head and pointed to the door, where she slipped in.

He slammed the car door. "Get us home. Danny, get down on the floor. Now."

I peeled out of the lot and jammed through the five-way stop, appreciating that I had better rear traction than God usually allowed for these road conditions.

"Why don't we go to the police station?" I asked.

That BMW from the ferry turned onto the arterial behind us.

"Shit." Matt saw the gun-metal grey car in the side mirror at the same moment I did. "Can you lose this guy?"

"I'd be embarrassed if I couldn't." As we accelerated, I took a long look in the rear mirror, trying to see what was wrong with that particular 335 that I couldn't place. "Tell me why I'm not going to the cop shop in the village."

"No one is there. It might only make it worse."

"The state patrol is at the ferry dock." I thought it was a sensible suggestion.

"Please drive. Lose this guy now."

"Who is he?" I persisted.

"He's one of Konstantin's hit guys," Danny said from the back.

"Shut up, Danny," Matt said. "We don't know that for a fact."

"Then why are we supposed to lose him?" I didn't think I was being unreasonable to ask.

"Drive, Sam. I'll explain later."

I accelerated, vaguely sure that I knew how fast to take the Lost Point curves. As the BMW 335 became history, now out of sight, I figured out what was wrong.

"That car is stolen," I said. "That BMW."

"What?" Matt wasn't paying attention to me, still craning around to find our pursuer.

"I own the same model. My license starts with AJJ. The plate on that car starts with 088. Those numbers are from several years ago. We should tell Tom to look for—"

"Just pay attention and drive. Faster."

I, however, didn't feel a need for silence, since I can drive and talk at the same time. So I asked the question at the top of my mind. "The old guy from the ferry—the one who was eating breakfast at Casa D yesterday—he's in the trunk of my car. Do you know who it is?"

Muscles worked at the side of Matt's jaw.

"A body," he said flatly. "In the trunk."

"Yeah. Didn't you see when I had the trunk open?"

"I'll look when we get home." Matt again peered behind us at the now-empty road.

Danny sat up, excited. "Maybe it's Konstantin."

Matt waved at him with his gun hand. "Get back down on the fucking floor, Danny."

"There's a tire iron here if anyone ever needs it."

97. Nicky Drives Fast

WHEN NICKY SAW THE wedding singer on the street in the village, the pieces of the plot began to cohere. The wedding singer, who was supposed to be Danilov's client, had Danilov in his car. Uncle Kostya made everyone worry that the guitar dweeb ratted to the feds after the debacle at his house in the Castro Valley. Yet there was Danilov, big as life itself.

The wedding singer was hustling other people into the car—the same red car he'd seen Pete Byron emerge from the night before.

Finally, Nicky saw the driver of that car.

It occurred to him, in a flash of the blindingly obvious, that she was in grave danger from the evil Zandr let loose on the world. He turned his car around, sliding on ice, so he could follow the woman he loved, to warn her.

Where were Black Pawn's people when he needed them? What's the use of collaborating with an armed militia if they aren't on the scene in the face of imminent threat to public safety?

98. Matt Repeats His Mantra

"IF YOU TAKE THIS CAR up the driveway, it might be days before you get out again." I commented further about Sam's low-slung Challenger, trying to be helpful about what snowplowing the highway might do to the driveway.

While she bitched about having to leave her car on the road— actually, on the generous gravel pull-in for Mrs. Waddington's mailbox, enough above the roadbed that it wouldn't get buried by the snowplow—I got Danny out of the backseat, and then once more yanked the release lever for the trunk. On purpose this time.

"Come here, Danny. Look quick."

When Danny saw the very blue body in the trunk of Sam's car, he cracked a huge grin.

"Fucking A. It's Uncle Kostya. Best Christmas ever!"

"Let's get inside. Sam, you too."

"I need to use Aunt Lucky's phone," she said. "And I'm calling the police."

Sam was driving me effing nuts, but I had Danny to attend to and couldn't grab her to stop the mutiny.

"Get back as soon as you can!" I shouted after her. "Five minutes max!"

Inside, Danny complained that I should uncuff him.

"I'm not out for you, dude," he said. "You need to calm down, buddy. At least let me take a piss. It's going to be all right. Kostya's dead. Ding dong."

So now Danny was repeating my mantra: *It's going to be all right.* Maybe we can cofound a new religion.

"No one will come after you anymore," Danny said. "Get over yourself."

99. Sam Leads an Interrogation

UNCLE BOB WAS IN Aunt Lucky's the living room eating Cap'n Crunch cereal out of a salad bowl, sitting by an open window, a shotgun at his side.

"Hey, missy. How's it hanging?"

"Nothing about me hangs," I said, immediately frosted by both the open window and the unwanted guest.

"We're ready for siege," Bob said. "I see your boyfriend is armed. Does he know both weaponry and tactics?"

"Geezus pieces, Uncle Bob. What are you doing here? I thought you were catching a ferry."

"I've been walking patrol all morning. You need a good man on point. Your boyfriend isn't a field-tested, proven ally who—"

"He's proven, Uncle Bob. And by the way, Pete says the bad guys aren't after you anymore."

"There's lots of things Pete's gotten wrong before, the little squirt. This might be one of them." Uncle Bob poured the other half of the box of cereal into his bowl and drowned it in milk. "What do you mean by proven? Looks like your cuddlebug spends a lot of time in the gym. Any foof can do that."

"Matt's ex-army. He was attached as intelligence to a Ranger unit." I remembered Pete telling me that years ago. Though maybe that was a lie, too.

"So you think the sheriff's spawn can shift for himself?" Uncle Bob talked with his mouthful. "We'll likely need every hand in the fight."

What could I say that was true? Matt goes into defense mode when little girls scream. He shot a telephone.

Since I was silent, Uncle Bob continued his ruminations. "OK, missy. Lock yourself in the bathroom. No direct hits, no ricochet there. That's the best place I found in this house. You aren't going to be much use." He tilted the bowl to drink the last of the cereal milk, then looked up, a milk mustache now painted in place. "Unless you plan to jaw them to death."

I reached for the phone, which sat on the sofa right near his cereal bowl.

"It's out again," Uncle Bob said. He was lining up shotgun shells on the window ledge, like a dozen toy soldiers at arm's reach.

"I'm going back to Matt's house," I said, since this house was uninhabitable, due to both human and inclement environment. When your moronic Byronic uncle leaves a window open and it's twenty degrees outside, you can't sit and argue with him.

§

I ripped open the back door into the kitchen, where Matt sat at the counter, coffee pot by one hand, his stupid gun trained on the door.

"Have any free time right now to tell me what's going on?" I fetched a mug from the cupboard and poured from the pot by him. His free hand twitched.

"When my accident happened, some bad guys decided that I was a problem for them. They promised to do me as soon as they could find me." Matt continued to watch out the windows, not really engaging with me. "Now they are coming for me."

"More guys like Danny the surfer? Pretty dangerous." I sipped the coffee. Matt had tossed in a triple measure of grounds, but I appreciated it, since there was no espresso. "Outside, your friend said the blue guy in my trunk means that you aren't in danger now."

"You didn't see the convoy departing the ferry."

I thought back to where we parked near the ferry ramp. "Yes, black Escalades. That Suburban. Like how gangbangers ride."

"Exactly," he said.

"Like you see when the FBI rolls out. Or BATF. Or freaking postal inspectors. We can call Eliot to ask if there's an action going on." I made for the police radio, which he'd used earlier.

He grabbed my hand as I passed. "No calls."

I took it back. "Have you flippin' lost your mind, Matt?"

"It might endanger them, and make it worse for us."

"Oh really? Now you're Superman?"

"Cut it, Sam." He finally looked at me while he spoke. "You've been judging me since you walked in the door yesterday."

"I just thought that your life would turn out differently."

"Yeah? So did I. Get past it. I have. So did Harley and Roslyn."

"Pippi." I said it so softly I wasn't sure he heard, but he must have.

"You haven't lived my life, Sam. You don't know."

"But I lived Pippi's life. I do know what it's like to be shifted around, not knowing if anyone will be there when I come home from school."

"We had to move. It's best for her." Matt folded his arms, defying me. His gun now pointed at the ceiling instead of the back door.

"I know what it's like for a kid to have to take care of the adults instead of the other way around." I thought of Uncle Bob across the driveway, and Huck, wherever he was in Seattle. "I can't respect that."

You can see when a body stops in his tracks, though Matt still puffed steam.

"Is this about the macaroni? I love her, Sam. I care for her, more than I've cared for anyone in my life."

"No." I drained my coffee. It was past time to show the mark of character. "Pippi knows."

"She knows what?"

"About her mother. That she wasn't ill. Pippi thinks her father was a spy and a great American hero. Now she's trying to take care of you."

"How could she know?" He grabbed my arm again, which was causing a severe number of demerits in his ongoing score. "Did you tell her?"

"Pippi told me." As I unpeeled his hand and gave it back to him, I watched horror wash over him as I told the secret I'd promised to keep. "Her mother left a tape, saying goodbye. Pippi keeps it in her pocket. She used to listen every night in bed, but now she only listens on Sundays. She played it for me last night. And made me promise not to tell you."

"Oh god. Oh god. Oh god." By the third appeal to a deity, he was kicking the wall. When his tantrum had nowhere else to go, Matt sat down, laid his stupid gun on the table. Head in hand, he shredded his hair in turmoil.

Then he told me a story as sad as the saddest voice in the world saying *goodbye, I love you.*

100. Matt Explains

SINCE THERE WAS NOTHING to do but wait, I told a foxhole story, the one that only my psych professional in California knows. Good practice for the deposition later this week.

"Pippi's father was military intelligence. That's where we met." I had to do something besides walk around the kitchen waiting for whoever was coming our way. We hadn't had food since breakfast, so I made sandwiches. "Sonny left the army when I did, because his wife Caroline was expecting and he didn't want them moving from post to post. We remained partners—he taught me most of what I know."

"Did I ever meet him?" Sam took the peanut butter jar from me, since I was having trouble opening it.

"No. As close as Sonny and I were, I didn't bring my friend up here to the island. Maybe I saw our friendship as part of my cover life."

"How did you end up with his wife and child?" She whacked the jar with the flat edge of Roz's chef knife, denting the rim, and then she twisted the jar open and handed it to me.

"Caroline severely derailed when Pippi was born. She was bipolar and meds weren't taking care of it. She tried ending it a couple of times with pills—before Sonny bit it. Years ago he made me promise to take care of them both if bad stuff happened."

"Your accident was the bad stuff?" She was looking at me and not the sandwich in front of her.

"Yes. After he was gone, marrying Caroline seemed like the best way to take care of them. Paige—did you ever meet her? My second wife?"

"No, I missed that one."

"Paige got an annulment the month before Sonny and I went up shit creek together. So I was free to take care of his family."

"I'm happy for Pippi," Sam said. "You adopted her?"

"Yes." I was finding it rough to revisit this. I couldn't eat my sandwich either. "Two days. Caroline waited two days after the adoption papers were final, biding her time. Then she was gone."

101. Sam Recompiles with Verbose Bit Turned On

NOW I WAS CHANTING *oh god, oh god*. My code compiled, but with heap corruption during execution, so to speak.

Matt was rocking himself. "How is she? Really?"

102. Matt Receives a Proposal

"PIPPI SAYS SHE ALWAYS knew her mother would go away." Sam had a tear leaking from the corner of her left eye, which I'd never seen before. I was about to lose it, too. She pushed aside her coffee and got up, sighing. She paced. "Pippi says, the important thing is that we all have to take care of you."

"Crap, no wonder you are so teed off at me." We were both like caged animals at this point. I was running out of inner resources. "What do I do?"

"Are you really asking me?"

"Yes."

"Tell her the truth, Matt. Free her from this secret."

"Also," she said, "I think you should marry me."

103. Nicky Takes a Hard Look

THINGS GOT DEPRESSING AND interesting simultaneously.

The driver of the red car was the woman he loved. And, like everything else she did, she could handle a car much better than he could.

Catching a glimpse of himself in the rearview mirror of his car, Nicky took a hard look, checking to see if the owner of those eyes had—as American men say—the balls to be a hero in someone else's scenario.

However, his borrowed car wasn't built for unplowed back-country roads. That caravan of Escalades from the ferry steamed passed him in the other lane. When he braked, his car skidded, and he mistakenly turned the wheels the wrong way, so that after spinning in a complete circle, the car landed not far from where Uncle Konstantin made him park on Christmas Eve.

Familiar territory, although that provided small comfort.

104. Sam Flips a Bit

MATT WENT UTTERLY STILL, though I know he heard me.

"Speak. You're freaking me out." I watched his eyes flitting left to right and then glancing out the window again. "This is me, Matt. You know me. You know I threw up in the hall in the fourth grade."

"Yeah, I was hall monitor. I had to clean it up."

"Exactly. If you can't trust me, who in the world can you trust?" I shrugged, uncomfortable. "Thanks for not laughing."

"I'd only laugh because Pete and my mom both suggested the same thing." Matt finally took a bite of the sandwich he'd made.

"See? I'm being practical, just like everyone else." I was thinking of the dowry I could offer: full health insurance for Pippi, a nice house to live in, a more-than-comfortable income.

Matt said, "Thanks for the offer, but I can barely take care of a kid on what I have. How could I take care of you, too?"

"Take care of me? I propose to take care of you. That's why I asked."

"Honestly, Sam, Pete says—"

"My brother the twerp says what?"

"He says you can't hold onto your money."

"Lord, this is rich." I laughed, up until I focused again on Matt, his gun, and how he still scanned the fields in front and beside the house. "The reason I don't have more money—and I have a suffi-ciency—is because Pete spends it on his documentaries. Talk about no visible means of support."

"He says you don't have a job."

"What job is it that he says I don't have?"

"Temp work. Odd jobs testing software."

"Um, I'm more of a programmer."

By then I was sure we all lived at a permanent address inside Pete's reality distortion field.

§

"I'm a bit overwhelmed right now." He was ruminating while staring out the kitchen window, gun at hand. "Harley says my sole mistake was working undercover too long."

"I'd agree with that," I said. Stupid cover band. Stupid band name. "Maybe you never should have started."

"That's what Roz says. Wrong personality type. I guess studies show that you're supposed to be damaged somehow to succeed." He paused, still musing. "Still, I never identified with perps or made friends with them."

I sat up.

Matt said, "The strain came from living a lie twenty-three hours out of every twenty-four, except back here on the island during down-time. Your sister and aunt could always get me laughing, as if I could live an honest civilian life."

I coughed, not able to speak.

"And effing Pete!" Matt exclaimed. "He used to crack me up, but last year I started resenting Pete's taunts about being a Lawman. He says I misplaced my sense of humor."

"You're a cop." Was I absent the day they sent the memo around?

"Yeah, but that's not an excuse," he said. "Pete says it's a character flaw, getting all my strokes from my captain and my handlers—and my dad, of course—telling me that I'm a damn good cop."

"Pete says?" I wasn't sure what planet I'd been living on, while everyone else drove off to an alternative universe in a U-Haul truck.

"Yes, but Harley says I stayed undercover too long, so the black and white turned to grey."

"Why didn't I see that?" Like, why Harley deferred to his not-flakey son.

"Well, that's just Harley's opinion, but I'm guessing that's why you also judge me harshly." Matt shook his head, as if to wake from a reverie. He walked between the windows to study the southern horizon and then the road up from the highway. I hadn't realized how much of the world you can see from Roz's kitchen windows. "Maybe you're like Harley. He learned everything he knows about undercover work by watching *Wise Guy*. He's never done it himself."

"Pete knows." And at the very next opportunity, it would be me beating the crap out of Pete in an alley.

Matt said, "Yeah. And Pete listens. Cripes, most of the time he's been the only person I could talk to. Though Pete leads his own deceptions."

"Pete is a lying little squib," I said, "who should be hung by his balls while having his molars extracted."

"Yeah, but he's our Pete," Matt said. His laughter betrayed more affection for Pete than I felt at that moment.

"How blind can a person be?" I said, a propos of myself, not Matt.

"You, however, always saw more than anyone else," he said, misunderstanding me. "Every unfortunate woman who ever got involved with me just couldn't understand that a morbidly conflicted peace officer makes a bad playmate. You figured it out long ago."

"I walked away." I saw the One Bad Night in yet another light.

Matt said. "Cripes, it took me months to realize you did the right thing, walking away. I came out of the bushes that night ready to say, 'Marry me.' You're too smart to get involved in a losing proposition."

At some moments, one must place one's head in one's hands, literally, not just figuratively. "There wasn't much wisdom in what I did," I said.

He laughed. "Pete said you just didn't want me hurling in your car."

"Pete doesn't know everything," I said. Back then, Pete said my whole idea of being in love was incestuous.

"You're so kind, and yet pretend otherwise," Matt said. He checked his gun again, like he'd done a half-dozen times that day. "I have preserved for years the fantasy that you picked me up out of the kindness of your heart, had your way with me, and then put me out when you were sure I couldn't hurt myself."

"Had my way—"

"Cripes, I was drunk that night," Matt said. "But I was sober last night. I don't want to repeat the mistake I made then. So why would you want to marry me now? Just pity again?"

"Why aren't we calling Tom?" I asked, needing to change the subject and increasingly uncomfortable with Matt's twitchiness.

"Local cops have a tendency to just make it worse with these people." He laughed without humor. "That's my experience. And also, I still need to keep my cover."

Cover? Like Pete might create? "Matt, did you ever visit a server farm in eastern Europe? In a tuxedo?"

"The only place I ever wore a tuxedo was at my own wedding. For the first two, anyway."

§

"They're here!" Danny called from upstairs.

105. Matt Decodes the Message

"IT'S NOT ANYONE I KNOW," Danny yelled.

"What do you mean?" By now I was watching the two black SUVs as they ambled over the frozen wheel-trenches of the driveway.

"Uncle Kostya must have let out the job to other professionals. These guys are strangers."

I moved into the position I'd thought through and motioned Sam to the back of the room. "Danny, play hostage. After I talk them into backing off, leave with them and keep a cover for yourself."

Danny whined. "I want out."

"Getting out now might be false heroism. Sam, call Tom on the police radio, and then grab the duct tape and pin Danny to a chair."

"Not a good idea," Danny said. "Those people have freaking neck tattoos."

Sam was as efficient as possible, carefully following my instructions for the radio. She quickly had her sister on the line. "Eliot, please tell Tom that we're being invaded by gangsters."

She began well, but she apparently wasn't convincing. The part I heard:

> *"No, I'm not kidding."*

> *"No, Aunt Lucky isn't here. It's just me and Matt."*

> *"No, Matt can't talk now. He's the only one who can shoot back."*

> *"Geezus pieces, Eliot. Just pass the message on. You'd do it if Matt called."*

Her request continued while I watched a half dozen men emerge from the vehicles. This was always how it was going to be.

"Stop where you are," I called. "Do not advance one more step."

"We want the girl." A growl emerged from one knot of these rats, the guttural call of Russian Mafioso, too familiar from my years skulking behind the lines of organized criminal intent.

I called, "You aren't touching my kid."

"Your kid? I don't want any kid."

"It's me you want," I said. "Let everyone else go. Forget about my little girl."

"It's that bitch with you we want. She's worth more than money."

I looked over at Sam, but she mimed bug-eyed cluelessness.

"She doesn't know you," I called out. "She's not joining your uncle's white slave business."

"Slave? No, we bought Miss NASA for her work. We paid for her."

Sam seemed startled by this. I muttered to her, "Space? What does he mean?"

She said, "I think he means NSA."

If the earth were flat, I'd have fallen off the edge. "What the hell, Sam?"

"In Virginia, NSA was one of our clients. I write anti-hacking code."

A man emerged from the rear of one of the SUVs and trudged through the snow to the front porch, while the rest of them stood where they had disembarked from their vehicles, guns at their sides, hulking in woolen overcoats like Russian mobsters. Well, hell, they *were* Russian mobsters.

"Alec!" Sam shouted, excited. She moved to get past me, but I blocked her. "I thought you were dead."

"He is," a voice called from the back, "if you don't come with us."

Since I prefer to be on top of things, I took a shot, aiming half way between the front door and where Alec stood on the first step. He ducked, raising an arm to cover his face as splinters flew.

"It's fourteen miles to the ferry," I called, directing my voice to the SUV, because front-porch Alec seemed to be a puppet, not a leader. "The county sheriff will stop you before you can leave the island."

"The bridge reopened," the Alec guy said. "We're off-island in five minutes. Come on, Sam. Existential choice is over."

Sam shouted out where he could stick his philosophy. I kept having to move to shield her.

The unmistakable sound of a shotgun pump echoed across the open field.

"Not so fast," a voice called from somewhere in the vicinity of Lucinda's house. "Missy, get your ass down Huck's trail."

"No," I half turned to Sam, while keeping that Alec person leveled in my sights, "Stay inside where you're safe."

She had already disappeared.

106. Nicky Ponders the Social Economy

NICKY ENDEAVORED TO FIGHT that migraine. He'd purchased aspirin and burnt coffee from the mini-market at that gas station, plus a multi-hour energy blast. The migraine had already progressed to where he couldn't eat, and he was down to the last two cigarettes, since they didn't have his brand in the mini-market rack.

And now he was a pedestrian.

He looked at the borrowed car, its passenger-side panel gouged by a boulder before the car had come to rest in the roadside snow bank. Behind the veil of a sick headache, his usual step-by-step planning had slowed.

He'd always worn gloves.

Only Uncle Kostya's prints might be found.

Since America is so generous with the form of socialism that is called insurance here, perhaps the vehicle should continue over the side of the road and down the cliffside.

107. Sam Bails from Her Longboard

WHILE MATT AND UNCLE BOB were covering those hoods, I tried to put the pieces of this puzzle together faster than I managed with Pippi's jigsaw. Dead Andrij and Danny. Matt's gangster nemesis shows up with Alec, who isn't dead.

Here I was running at Uncle Bob's command.

More than eight inches of snow lay on the open fields, but on the north side of the house, drifts had formed in the storm, now coated with a crust of ice, so a less-than-firm step meant sliding. Step in the wrong space, and find a surprising eighteen inches of snow swallowing your foot up to the knee.

Behind me, Alec called, "Come on, Sam. Use your genius. Don't run. There's too many of us."

It struck me—as fast as the brain can cogitate under stress—that if these people wanted me, then they weren't going to shoot me. Fleeing, as Uncle Bob commanded, seemed the imperative action. I stomped, slid, and ran, then slid again, headed for the stairs down to Huck's shack. Gunshots sounded in the driveway. The day had started with that racket (when Matt killed the phone), but I wasn't growing used to it.

"Trust me, Sam. Come back here." Alec was coming around the house, staying so close to its sides that Matt's gun couldn't cover him. Matt called out to him with multiple expletives. Alex called out again. "Stop there! Come with me, Sam."

I shouted back, "No more dates, Alec!"

A series of explosions rang from the front of the house, causing Alec to pause and look back. What I heard, though, wasn't Matt's gun. More like IEDs or mortars. Near the top of the stairs lay detritus from the closet where Pete's fireworks had been stored.

Another explosion.

Uncle Bob must have revived his tripwire career.

"Fucking A, Sam!" Alec called. "You'll only piss them off."

Bundled M80s and ashcan salutes drowned his voice.

I grabbed my ancient longboard from the closet trash pile, skipped up the two stone steps to the top of the stair rail, hoping the ice wouldn't betray me, and launched the sweet trick that got me grounded every time Aunt Lucky caught me at it. Too sketchy a move, even for her typically careless oversight.

Yet another explosion, and expletive language from both Matt and Alec. Pippi would be rich if she could collect the fines.

Whap! Board in place: at ninety degrees atop the stair handrail.

No wheels in contact with any surface.

Toes at the nose, heel at the tail.

Tweak, don't balance.

Doc Martens aren't Chuck Taylors, so my stance felt awkward, but I found my center of gravity; my backside barely touched the berry brambles and willow whips that crowded the stairs.

The trip down always rode like a vert ramp. In the winter ice, the ride gained plenty of speed; the frigid wind burned my ears and nose and sent my hair straight up. The bottom of the stair rail formed a modest launch ramp, so I was airborne at the end of the ride, and in spite of having become an aging riot grrrl, I remembered the exact point at which it was time to bail.

Too bad Pete missed seeing that we really got our money's worth out of the fireworks we bought on the Sk'komish reservation.

108. Matt Isn't the Hero

AT THE MOMENT WHEN the shotgun fired, multiple shots landed near the feet of our invaders. They each jumped—I hate to say it was comical—and tried to shelter behind car doors while keeping protective aim. There were six of them, including Sam's friend Alec, and they seemed trained. It wasn't Alec they looked to for direction.

"Samsara isn't here now," the shotgun-pumping voice called, now from further down the driveway, "and you won't find her. So you best be gone."

Another shotgun pump. The blast took out the first SUV's front tire; the ricocheting shot caused our visitors to dance. A large blast detonated on the other side of the idling SUVs. At that blast, our visitors piled into the remaining SUV and backed up the frozen tracks of the driveway and onto Lost Point Road.

As the SUV pulled away, two of the men leaned out the window to fire in the general direction of where the shotgun blast had come. The answering blast, which shattered the Escalade's back windshield, came from an angle twenty degrees off from where the goons aimed.

As I stepped out onto the porch, Danny was at my side.

Like the idiot he is, Danny took off running to the explosion sites, apparently without a thought that we might be standing in a tripwire mine field.

"Cool!" he cried, holding up the remains of a bundle of M-80s.

Up at the head of the driveway, a tall figure in jeans and a sheepskin jacket stood, watching in the direction of where the SUV had departed. After a moment, the fellow turned and saluted me and then, shotgun over his shoulder, he marched up the road toward town.

109. Sam Pushes It

"Nicky! What are you doing here?"

I was happy to see someone I knew and trusted. That sweet, cute tester from Quinn's team stood right there on Lost Point Road, thoughtfully studying a BMW 335 stuck in a bank at the edge of the road. He was far better dressed for the weather than I was.

"Is that your car, Nicky?" Everyone who worked for Quinn must have the same car.

He looked startled, of course. It's always jarring to meet people out of context, when you only know each other from meeting rooms, coffee breaks, and elevators. "No, Miss Byron. I'm wondering what to do about it, though."

"It's stolen," I said. "I've seen it around the island all weekend."

"Perhaps only borrowed."

"No, the plates have been swapped. You can tell by the year. Anyway, it's wrecked. The owner won't want it back like this."

"No," he said, more hesitant than I'd ever seen him. He was always willing to speak up with good ideas while we designed the testing plans last week. He had the idea to create a video to guide the testers.

However, I was beyond socializing.

"'Look," I said. "It's hard to explain but some bad people are after me and my friends. Would you help me turn this wreck into a defensive barrier?"

At that suggestion—which anyone but Pete would spurn as wild-assed insanity—Nicky's face split into a huge smile. He's really such a cute guy.

"I'd be honored to assist you," he said.

We went to work to push the car past the icy lip of the highway shoulder.

I've got stronger legs than shoulders, so I backed up against it, to use my thighs for power. Nicky has strong shoulders, so he pushed straight on. I didn't have gloves, so I pulled my coat sleeves down as a barrier against the cold metal.

As we sweated and strained ourselves, I asked, "Are you visiting friends?"

"No, I'm stuck here, protecting you," he said while pushing mightily, so I could hardly hear what he said.

"What did you say? Did you get stranded on the island?" I grunted while I pushed. Not at all lady-like. "Same here."

He said, "If this were a movie, this would be a great moment to share with the love of one's life."

"Hah!" I said. "It is. You know what, Nicky? I'm in love. He's back there, being a hero, trying to save me. No one ever tried to save me before."

We strained. One huge push got that car into the middle of the road.

"Well, Roz and Harley tried," I added. "But it's not the same thing. He loves me right back. Who could believe this would happen to me!"

"You are a lucky woman," he said, brushing his hands and soiled clothes. He always dressed well. "Myself, I failed in love. I've introduced chaos into the love of my life."

I assumed he meant Natalia the Dragon woman, since I see them on smoke breaks together and working in the server racks. "My heart goes out to you," I said. "I've been through that same hell."

We stood, surveying our work, and it was good.

"No retreat to the bridge for the marauding monsters," I said, rubbing my hands on my jeans to warm them. "Oh Nicky, you are my hero!"

I kissed him full on, like you'd kiss a hero. Due to the circumstances, it was not a workplace infringement.

"I'm sorry I took your code," Nicky said.

"What?"

"I wanted to prove a better business model to you. But my cousin Zandr stole your research and test plan. He sold it to the white nights."

"White nights?"

"The White Knights of the New Russian Revolution. They can't make the code work. That's why they came for you. With Olekzandr."

"Alec?"

"Yes, he lied and stole from you. But I was trying to help you. To make the world safe. There are important commercial models you didn't consider."

I shouted again, this time, not with joy.

"You nimrod!"

§

Hearing a vehicle approach before it rounded the corner, I leaped aside, headed for the ditch. Peeking from the brambles, I could see one of the black SUVs from hell as it slowed, stopped, then backed up.

The driver jammed on the gas, hit a corner of the 335 with a glancing blow that sent the smaller vehicle spinning sideways. Something flew from the SUV's back window and, before I could think or count, there was an explosion that knocked me further back into the ditch brambles.

Of course I chose the ditch with a running stream at the bottom, where even in this cold, the ice crust wasn't sufficient to keep me from plunging in. With cold water running out of my pockets, I pulled out Pete's cell phone, hoping to save it in case I ever came back to a world with reception.

Then, a second explosion. Flying metal—the license plate—knocked the phone from my hand, sending it into the icy creek flowing under the brambles.

Perhaps that was the most profound sign yet that I should give up and roll with whatever fate the gods decreed. Perhaps I should fetch my laptop and throw it in the creek, too, in hopes of propitiating those angry SOBs.

110. Nicky Would Like to Freeze That Frame

SHE KISSED HIM. SMACK on the mouth.

As he had dreamed, she tasted of coffee, the strong, bitter kind people drink in this part of the world. And he tasted salt, from the perspiration that shone on her face.

Or maybe he only smelled the coffee. She didn't kiss him for long.

Also, she loved another man. Wildly, she said. The man who was the hero trying to save her.

"Who could believe this would happen to me!" she shouted.

Then, when she shouted the last words at him, she was on the other side of the car, but he saw that she jumped off the road before the SUV came around the corner.

Surely it was Zandr who looked straight at him just as the grenade flew from the back window.

Five:
There, and Back Again

111. Sam Takes a Brave Survey of the Scene

LONG AFTER THE BLAST, when the ringing in my ears stopped so that I could hear again, I inched back up from among the brambles in the ditch to the edge of the road.

Besides the hole in the pavement, metal debris has scattered everywhere. The second blast—the gas tank, I assume—had been hot enough that little remained besides smoldering metal.

I'm brave enough to look, even when scared, but I didn't see anything in the wreckage that could be human. I assume Nicky jumped away when I did. There was a half-melted gun in the pit where the passenger cabin had been.

After calling Nicky's name for several minutes, I gave up.

What I most wanted to find was Matt. I started up Lost Point Road.

§

It was freaking cold. I wondered what it's like to be this cold and not have Matt and a woodstove as the destination.

Blink. The blue guys: Andrij on the dock. Man in my Challenger. Man in the freezer who wasn't Alec the betrayer.

It was so effing cold out, I felt myself about to be the fourth blue corpse.

112. Nicky Studies Detroit Design

THE LOVE OF HER LIFE had been her hero, not Nicky.

Nicky took some time to determine how to jimmy the trunk so he could remove Uncle Kostya. She deserved at least that degree of heroism from him, since he'd failed to be her ultimate savior from Zandr and the White Knights. Though he'd be the first to admit, taking action to deal with Konstantin's frozen remains would only remove an inconvenience, not a threat.

However, this time the trunk wasn't conveniently open. Nicky had never before confronted antique American engineering other than his Zippo lighter. It took all of his concentration and more patience than he knew he had to learn how to open the trunk without scratching her car.

That's why he missed hearing the man advance on him until there was a shotgun pressed against his backside.

113. Matt Follows a Cold Trail

"C'MON, MATT," DANNY GROUSED. "Can't I just stay by the fire?"

"No."

I dragged Danny with me on the way down to Huck's cabin, having to listen to him whine about ice, about treachery—though he swore he didn't recognize anyone who had been in that caravan of Slavic hit men.

"What about that Alec guy?" I asked. "Sam recognized him."

"He was on the porch. I couldn't see anything from upstairs but the back of him when they ran away."

I circled around the cabin, looking for Sam.

Who had apparently done what Lucinda always swore would get that girl killed: I found her old skateboard at the bottom of the cliff, its deck scratched all to hell. Sam's snow trail led to the shoreline, where she must have stepped down to the low tide line. It had only been, what, ten minutes? The tide was already coming in, and following the trail meant wading under the willows and madronas that hung over the water.

While I hesitated, wondering whether I should pursue along the shore, two explosions sounded. From the echo, the blasts weren't close to the water, but more likely up in the scrub forest farther north, inland.

I pressed Danny to climb back up the stairs—and yes, I threatened him with castration to get him to quit complaining. We walked north up the main road, guessing that Sam intended to retrieve the Challenger and hoping that those explosions had nothing to do with her.

Five minutes' hike along the highway, Sam appeared, walking toward me, coming from the opposite direction of the Challenger, hunched in the cold, dripping wet, and grinning.

"Uncle Bob came through for once!" she shouted.

I ran up to greet her, and together we trudged the fifty yards up the driveway to the house, crunching through the channels of crushed snow created by the SUVs. We reached the black hulk that our visitors had left behind at the same time that Tom and a second squad car screeched up Lost Point Road. They'd been stalled by a burned-out car on the highway.

"Part of this scene?" Tom asked, trying to bore a hole in me with his cop laser eyes, to which I'm immune.

Sam said, "We think so. But we've been here waiting for you."

I resisted looking at Sam, because it seemed like a gambler's tell—as if her wet clothes weren't some kind of giveaway. It took only a moment to describe for Tom what had happened at my house.

"They were looking for me," Sam said, which confused Tom, since he knew goons were looking for me. "They're Russian mobsters who stole my code and wanted me to make it work for them. The White Knights of the New Russian Revolution, to be exact. Can you contact people at the NSA for me? I haven't been able to get calls through."

Tom nodded, seeming to take in stride what Sam next told him about contacting certain people. Apparently, I was the only person in the conversation who didn't know what Sam does in the world.

Tom was on the radio with the license number and vehicle description of the second SUV, so both Kitsap County and the State Patrol had enough information to take action.

"There's another person you should look for," Sam said. "He works where I do, and he knows who those people are."

"How does he know?" Tom asked.

Sam seemed reluctant to answer. "It seems he's involved in stealing code from my business. I'm not sure how much yet."

As Sam gave him details, Tom repeated them over the radio. When he was done, Tom said, "We'll haul in the abandoned SUV to examine as soon as there's a free truck." He tugged me away so that Sam couldn't hear, though she and I no longer had secrets. "Harley left with Pippi for the airport. Roz refused to go."

"Of course she did. That's my mom."

I handed Danny off to Tom. The feds that I'd called to fetch Danny were waiting in Tom's cop shop.

"You were lucky this time," Tom said. "Next time—"

"There won't be a next time," I said. "I have been assured of that."

Tom's radio crackled. After he listened for a moment, he said, "We'll talk about this later tonight, if I get a moment. Else come by the station tomorrow morning so we can get a full statement from both of you." Then he and his deputy left to respond to a sighting of the Escalade.

As the red-and-blue lights trailed away in the fog, I turned to join Sam, who by now was shivering like a wet dog in her soaked clothes.

"Let's get you warm."

A horn sounded from up the road. The Challenger was at the head of our driveway. A man in a Rastafarian knit cap leaned out the window and shouted.

"I'm only borrowing it, Missy. Have it right back in a jiffy, I promise!"

Sam waved.

"Your Uncle Bob?" I asked. "You're letting him drive your car when you wouldn't let me?"

"He fended off those creeps," she said, chattering with cold. "Even though I was so mean to him that his Christmas was pretty much a feast of dirt in a bag. I need to do something nice."

The Challenger swayed and swerved down the highway.

💣

"I guess we didn't finish sharing secrets," I said as we reached the porch. Icicles hung from one gutter that I needed to repair after the thaw.

"We got as far as 'Pete's a liar.'"

"But NSA, Sam?"

"Those guys must have old information. I was only a contractor, and I left more than six months ago. Anything I knew then has been reconfigured."

"The effing NSA?"

"Actually, what I'm working on right now is more important. If those gangsters could get it to work, that would really be a problem."

"So tell me your secrets, Sam. You got all of mine out of me."

"That's as much as I can say. Ancient history doesn't matter now."

I slipped on the ice.

She almost caught me.

We both crashed into the ice-crusted field by the driveway. She was, of course, on top.

Staring into my eyes.

Then we skittered and grappled to stand.

"I forgot one secret again," she said. "I need to get Tom in touch with the detective who's investigating the other murder."

Putting my arm around her, hoping to get that move right, the one I failed to master in high school, I said, "Other murder? After the NSA, I hesitate to ask."

"It has nothing to do with me. I just happened to be standing nearby, same as with Andrij. But I have great powers of observation. I think the two cop shops need to share information."

She was shivering under my arm and I pulled her close, but Sam was too wet; that move did more to spread her chill than share my warmth. There was still too much adrenalin pumping for me to do anything with the idea that she'd seen another body done like Andrij.

"D—Do you think," she said through chattering teeth, "I could make a phone call? There's a security problem I need to report. Tom might not get through to the NSA fast enough."

We grabbed a handset from Lucinda's freezing cold house, where the landline still didn't work. I closed the windows that Sam's uncle had used to keep watch. We plugged that phone in at my house. She dialed a half dozen numbers, but never reached a live person. Most of the messages she left were the same: *I'm still trying to warn you. Follow my instructions to avoid catastrophe.*

Except the last call. I can quote her verbatim:

"Geezus pieces, Quinn. We are so screwed. Lock the code and keep everyone out. Call me before the shit falls."

It took considerable doing to get her warm. Her clothes needed to go into the dryer. Instead of borrowing some of mine, Sam insisted that we had to use boy-scout methods for warming someone with hypothermia.

I insisted that she didn't have hypothermia.

She persisted: warmth from a naked body was all that would work.

The related details are of interest only to me, personally. (Yes, I used a French raincoat, like my dad taught me.)

114. Nicky Produces the Evidence

The man apparently had military training, because he'd mastered the quick application of zip ties—better even that Uncle Kostya, who had been showing off when he tied up Andrij on Christmas Eve.

His captor demanded silence. Nicky chose to treat the capture as a momentary rescue, from which he need merely bide his time. Blessedly, her red car had a heater that worked well, even if the company of the driver wasn't to his taste.

"You're one of them," the driver kept saying. After the interminable ferry ride—when the engine couldn't be run to heat the car, and his captor refused all pleas to move to the upper deck—they stopped in Seattle and brought a second man onboard.

"He's one of them," the new passenger said, who was a good old fashioned hippie. What greater American icon was there in this age? Nicky longed for his camera, or even a microphone to tape such authentic dialog.

They explained their relationship. They explained why they believed Nicky was Uncle Kostya's agent, and meant harm for them and their kin.

Nicky repeated the news that would cheer every character who had a part in the story arc: "Konstantin is dead. The family isn't looking for you anymore."

The little one said to his brother, "Pete says we're safe."

"Except that squirt," the other man said, "is a known liar."

During this exchange, Nicky studied the little hippie and determined that God Himself would have to speak before Nicky could believe this creature was actually Sam Byron's or Peter Byron's father.

However, it was time to change the conversation. The pacing would not do for even the most patient audience, even for Bergman fans.

"Gentlemen, how can I assure you that I mean nothing but good for the welfare of Miss Byron? I admire her. I love her."

The smaller man, the hippie, shook his head. "Anyone can say he's in love. How can you show your love?"

"Yes," the big guy said. "Where's the body of evidence?"

Nicky thought for a moment.

"My uncle Kostya is in the trunk of this car. If I help you remove him, would that be proof of my affection?"

115. Sam Says Good Evening

THERE'S A PARTICULAR THRILL to be had, that I'd almost forgotten about, in spending close time with a man who loves women.

I don't mean a man who loves being in love. What I want to describe is the pleasure of intimacy with a man who finds the divine in a woman. He likes how my skin feels, that it's different from his, that I have hips (well, sort of), that God created such a different creature from Man.

I'd thought Matt was someone who loves being in love—all that marrying of those Barbie people is my prime example. Yet, when Matt touched me, it was with the awe of a man who loves women.

After an hour of the sublime, Matt entered into a Do/Until loop that might have continued infinitely, had I not inserted an interrupt. He said all the things I'd longed for years ago: you're beautiful, you have a gorgeous mind, I love to watch you move, no one makes love like you do, no one soothes my soul like you do, I love how wonderful you are with Pippi and my folks, I love how self-sufficient and strong you are, I want my life united with yours, et cetera.

Under the circumstances, lying in his arms, still warm from our extreme, mutual exertions, listening to his heartbeat, both of us still half shocked from fear, there could only be one possible answer.

"Are you nuts, Matt? I've rethought the pity thing. No one should marry you. You're utterly and completely screwed up."

"Cripes, Sam. I love you. I want to marry you so we're partners."

"C'mon, Matt. You're Looney Tunes. I need to get back to business in Seattle. Back to real life."

"Yeah? Admit that this is real life. We can't go back from here."

Then he shut up and plunged us back into the sublime.

The interruption was the sound of that rackety Owens family Jeep.

§

"Good evening, Roslyn," I said when I walked past her, as if I always walked out of her son's bedroom buttoning my jeans.

"Don't hurt him," she said. She was loaded down with more armloads of rescue blankets and headed back to her Jeep. "He's been through too much."

"I wouldn't," I said, aware that my clothes, while dry, still smelled of fear.

"Catastrophe has a way of finding him," Roz said.

"If it does, I promise you that I'll be suffering along with him."
As I said it, I could see that she believed me. "Anyway, I'm leaving
right now. I need to get back to Seattle."

"I thought you'd already gone. Where's your car?"

"It's parked over at Mrs. Waddington's, I hope." It did seem that
"have it back in a jiffy" would have meant *"by now."*

116. Matt Comes Fully Awake

THE ENGINE SOUND ECHOING across the field was from an SUV, not
Sam's Challenger. From my experience, distinctively Chevy
Suburban.

After pulling on my jeans and finding shoes, I grabbed my gun
and rushed down the stairs, nearly knocking over my mother
midway.

I couldn't hear what Roz was shouting at me.

117. Nicky Contemplates the Perfect Woman

THE YELLOW LINES ON the highway zipped past, leaving him in
reverie.

Nicky felt strongly that a woman should look like a woman. He
understood but regretted the historic and cultural forces that had
brought American women to a particular state in the early decades
of the twenty-first century. He wasn't backwards looking, but he
better understood the Marilyn phenomenon of three generations ago
than he could comprehend the purpose of tattoos on women, except
in bourgeois soft-core torture movies. Upper arm muscle definition
should not be considered attractive in a woman. Skinny was unap-
pealing to him, which he attributed to having spent his childhood in
a depressed agrarian community, where muscle definition meant
that a woman led the life of a beast of burden, and skinny indicated

deprivation, not discipline. He liked feeling a warm, soft body in the dark. He liked soft skin and fluid flesh under his hand. He liked mystery and beauty in a woman, and that softness made him feel closer to God, though his Aunt Avrora would call it blasphemy to say so.

Therefore, that crush he had nurtured for so long made no sense, except for one thing.

"I love Samsara Byron for her mind."

Saying it aloud elicited no response from the front seat, where the conversation focused on the merits of Phish over the Grateful Dead.

The big man, who favored Phish, said, "Next you're going to plead that Dave Matthews is a jam band, and not just a tape loop."

"Yes, yes I am," said the hippie person. "What's wrong with Dave Matthews?"

Nicky didn't like the country, even to pass through, preferring to fly over it if he had to travel. He certainly didn't like experiencing the weather of his youth, though he knew how to separate his mind from the physical sensation of bitter cold. Yet here he was.

Given everything else he had lost—time, comfort, money, his camera and laptop, the pleasure of driving her BMW—Nicky determined that the moment was appropriate to demand his rights.

"Gentlemen, I have a supreme need to void my bladder."

"What?" the big one asked. "Say it in English, dammit."

"He has to pee," said the little one.

118. Sam Turns the Corner

FROM SOMEONE LIKE ME, who lives at a keyboard, studies the Internet, and crouches over a cell phone all day, I'd been away so long that I needed at least a landline. Coffee and coitus weren't enough to block my digital need.

Downstairs, I pulled my skull cap over my ears, I hunched up against the cold and walked out the back door, headed for Aunt Lucky's house, closing the door quietly in the way Roz prefers, and then easily finding the too-familiar path in the dark and the fog, muttering to myself in the more-than-brisk winter evening as my boots bashed through the ice, thinking stern thoughts about Uncle Bob and my car, hoping not to have to ask Roz for a ride. Then I turned around, remembering that my laptop was at Matt's house.

When I came around the corner, the feds were waiting to arrest me.

119. Matt Knows

THIS WASN'T THE FIRST time I'd been picked up and kept in custody, and then had to wait for a handler to facilitate a release. But never fresh from bed with the accused, and never over a national security emergency.

Earlier, I had it all in my arms: the best thing that ever happened to me. Almost two hours of connected, passionate knowing of another person. For the first time, I understood that corny jive about two becoming one. Interrupted by that wakeup call from the FBI.

When you know a person intimately, you know what they're capable of. I don't mean people you run into in the course of everyday life. I mean those who are as close as family, who *are* family. Yes, they can surprise you, like Pete, but not out of all comprehension.

I know Sam. I will always believe her story over anyone else's.

This was not the worst thing that ever happened to me.

120. Sam Pleads the Fifth

IN A MERE TWO HOURS I went from being Sam the action hero to Samsara the world's best lover, and ended up being the Ms. Samsara Ada Byron named in a warrant for a whole sack of felonies.

"Don't resist!" Matt called as they hustled him into cuffs, since he'd burst through the front door with a gun in his hand, not knowing it was the FBI. Then, as they tucked his head down and pushed him into one of their cars, he yelled at Roz, "Call Stephen Trowbridge. Say Sam needs an attorney."

In the first silent moments of the tedious trip from the top of Lost Point Loop to the federal justice building in Seattle, I pondered what I'd put on hold while warming up with Matt after that debacle. If I understood what Nicky the cute tester told me, he stole the code Quinn and I made, to prove to me that other important commercial uses exist for our fix. Alec the attorney was Nicky's cousin, except he wasn't an attorney, and he sold the chipset error and attack vector details to those Russians, who couldn't make the code work. Who had therefore demanded my help, except Uncle Bob scared them off with fake IEDs.

When I repeated these insights to my companions on the trip to Seattle, they put out a call to find Nicky on Limberlost. I interrupted only to remind them that Tom Tremain already had details from me.

"Thank you for that information, Ms. Byron."

My new FBI friends had sufficient energy to stay up all night, asking me questions. Since I had to be my own superhero, I refused to answer without an attorney, but instead of name, rank, and serial number, I repeated what I'd been trying to communicate to Quinn and Gerard for two days: bad guys were attempting to hack their way through Z-Crypto software at the local utility, if not elsewhere.

"Thank you for that information, Ms. Byron."

121. Matt Tells What He Knows

WHEN THAT PARTICULAR TEAM of feds questioned me—both before they figured out who I am and then later, before they let me go—I explained how she behaved when everything went down. Nothing happened that indicated she was anything other than bewildered by the attack. It required some delicacy, explaining why I delayed getting law enforcement involved, why I initially thought the attack had been on me. I modulated my need to preserve my former cover in ways they understood, with contacts they could call for confirmation—including the other FBI team who now had Danny.

Then, having decided not to charge me with anything, they put me with Evan Mulasky, a first-year agent I'd met just before I mustered out.

"We're impressed with your priors," he said. "We think you can help if you know more about what we have on this case."

Everything his team had was retrieved from an unnamed informant, who was on the way to whistleblower status but had disappeared. The informant claimed that a major Russian network was involved, which made the evidence against Sam particularly heinous:

> Threatening phone calls to professional acquaintances.
> *(The conversations I'd heard sounded like a warning, not a threat.)*
>
> A fire at her house Christmas Eve that appeared to be arson.
>
> *(At Christmas breakfast, she didn't act like she just torched her own house.)*
>
> Multiple attempts to break into servers remotely on Christmas Day at her new company and at her old company.
>
> *(She was drinking coffee at our house and finding that body at the cabin.)*
>
> Hacks against public utilities on Christmas Eve and Christmas Day.
> *(Ditto for drinking coffee, with no free time for criminal hacking, at least on Christmas day.)*
>
> Her credit cards and passport used to secure air passage to Europe, early on the day after Christmas.
> *(I'm absolutely sure who was in my bed—and the phone service was out.)*
>
> Reckless endangerment with a vehicle; felony damage to a state highway.
> *(I forced her to drive fast; but they meant that stolen BMW.)*
>
> Felony association with a foreign crime syndicate, conspiring to commit acts of terror against U.S. infrastructure targets.
> *(She didn't know those Russian goons and ran from them.)*

Felony accessory to murder.

Whoa. If Evan had started with the last item, I could have declared from the start that nothing in his list was remotely true. In the story Evan wanted to build, Sam brought a lover into her company as a co-conspirator, disguising him as a patent attorney in order to fleece technical information to sell to Russian mobsters. Then she fled, either as a result of a lovers' tiff or to connect with a third party after cheating the first.

"In this alternate reality, who did she help murder?" I asked. Because of my professional training, I could ask without betraying any trace of humor, in spite of what I thought about the comic quality of their case.

Under Evan's theory: a real attorney had been murdered so that a false one could gain access to her company.

"That might make a great cyberthriller," I said, "but look at the obvious. Sam has no motivation. She could give her own stuff away or sell it to anyone without needing a third party."

The agent blinked, and didn't seem to take that in as he proceeded to describe the murder. Which was identical to how we'd found poor Andrij outside Huck's shack.

"That's a signature method of the Petrenko crime family," I said.

"You know this from your early work?" he asked.

I nodded, not willing to let Agent Mulasky into my own crime thriller story. "You have the details for a similar circumstance we found Christmas day. Sam informed the Seattle and Limberlost cop shops about what she observed at both scenes."

Evan frowned. "She's a witness at two identical murder scenes, and you believe that's just coincidence?"

"Stop inventing fictions, Agent Mulasky. Focus on the Petrenko family."

Yes, sure, Konstantin was frozen in the back of Sam's car, but given how ridiculous the rest of the feds' story proved, I felt disinclined to offer up that body or Pete's association, Huck's jeopardy, and my extensive paranoia over Konstantin's attacks. I hadn't yet figured out for myself how to draw a line between Pete, Petrenkos, and Sam; if Pete and Huck showed up on the feds' malfunctioning radar, things would only get worse.

"She appears too often in each of these scenarios, including that murder in your backyard," Evan insisted.

"For crissakes, why would Sam come to Limberlost at Christmas in the midst of an evil plot?"

"She threatened a software attack on the local utility. Perhaps she wanted to gain physical access. Perhaps she was fleeing the White Knights."

"Evan, you're just wrong. And, from my experience, what you have isn't sufficient to get a grand jury to indict. You are wasting time."

He faltered a bit—I saw it in his eyes—but he said, "The Petrenko branch here in Seattle is only involved with porn and used cars. And some drug trade that the DEA is trying to get a handle on. We'd like to pin a stolen arms event on them, but that's bigger than they are capable of managing. Our informant says that the White Knights of Russia are the principals in this scam. He mentioned Konstantin Petrenko, but we discounted that likelihood. The Petrenkos have feuded with the White Knights for years. They wouldn't collaborate without a third party like Samsara Byron bringing them together."

Sam told Tom that it was White Knights of the New Russian Revolution. I'd repeated it when Evan first started questioning me. Clearly, that was why Evan got overexcited: having bigger fish on his hook than crappy criminals like the Petrenko family.

"Who's your informant?" I asked. "The Petrenko family is as closed and tight as any we've studied. Where did you find someone to rat on them? It doesn't happen."

Evan hesitated. "The information came through an intermediary."

I didn't mask my feelings well. "For crissakes, the Petrenkos don't use intermediaries. That's why they've been impossible to infiltrate."

"We have good information. It came through a private security contractor who has business ties—"

"Mercenaries who buy porn from the Petrenkos? Go look again," I said. "Konstantin Petrenko has flipped his shit in unexpected ways in the past year."

Like what that evil bastard did to me, with slapshots of fear he sent my way on a daily basis. However, I didn't see it would help Sam if I offered up Konstantin as stone dead in the back of her

Challenger. Evan and his friends needed to untangle all their false leads before I could help.

Evan said, "We've been looking for him, but the last anyone saw of Konstantin Petrenko was in Alameda County."

"My bet is that any informer who felt safe to rat on Konstantin had to have killed him first, and didn't leave a trail for you to find him. You don't have anything without this mystery man, do you?" I didn't try to intimidate Evan, since it wouldn't be fair. There wasn't much more to be gained by arguing with him. "Are you letting me go now? I'm due in Oakland in a few hours."

"Go," the agent said. He wasn't happy.

My last words: "Look at everything again, Evan. There is no way on God's green earth that Sam is involved in a criminal conspiracy, unless as a target."

I know better than anyone. I've listen to her breathe beside me, as close as two people can be. I felt her true and bold heart beating under my hand.

122. Nicky Is Strategic

NICKY DIDN'T HAVE A CAMERA—it felt like being undressed in public—and so he couldn't capture action in real time. He had to replay it in his head to commit to memory the exact ways in which the scene unfolded, so he could recreate it to record and post as video later.

The two men were brothers, which Nicky had discerned moments after they picked up the smaller man in Seattle, before driving up the Interstate and over the Cascade Mountains. They were headed north on Highway 97 when Nicky finally asked for relief.

Then the two men quarreled, in an unending repetitive way that proved they were brothers if nothing else did.

"I'm not touching his dick," the bigger man said, the driver who had put Nicky in restraints and forced him into the car on Limberlost Island.

"No more shall I," said the other.

After much back and forth, silence descended. Nicky remained patient. And yet.

"I still have to relieve myself, gentlemen."

They determined a brief foray up a gravel side road was the answer. Then they couldn't settle on who would extract him from the backseat. Finally, the larger of the two brothers wrestled Nicky out, pulling painfully where the tie-wraps bound his wrists.

"You'll have to undo my ankles and not just my hands for this to work, gentlemen."

"C'mon, Huck. You do it." The larger one induced his little hippie brother to kneel in the snow and work loose the tie-wrap on Nicky's ankles. "I'm getting the shotgun, so don't go yanking your junk out of your pants yet."

While the soldierly brother opened the trunk and rummaged through its contents, Nicky began his overland passage. He regretted knocking the little man over. There'd be a headache when the man returned to consciousness, but surely Nicky had done no lasting damage. The echo of the shotgun was helpful: he could navigate better, knowing where his captors stood at each firing.

Nicky believed he had more resources than his captors: youth and therefore agility and good eyesight, a childhood spent amidst the outlying forests of his village, his North Face parka. And good, warm shoes.

One of the many points of wisdom he'd gained from the woman he had once loved: the value of Doc Martens for casual footwear.

123. Sam Ponders the Nature of Perception

The Federal holding cell had electricity, which was the sole improvement over Lost Point Road. They locked me up alone, which was better than juvenile detention fifteen years ago. But they took away my shoelaces and belt, and put me on suicide watch.

Standard operating procedure.

While my mind raced in unproductive ways (if it's never happened to you, imagine what you might think about while locked alone in a room for an unjust reason), I traced backwards over a set of delusions that I once had:

> My code and research are securely locked in Quinn's servers.

> Alec Ramsey is a trustworthy attorney, if also a playboy jerk.

> Nicky is a trustworthy team member and a really nice guy.

> Matt is a jerk-wad slacker, who betrayed his roots and his true self.

> Pete is a good but flakey artist, living in a dream world.

> Huck and Uncle Bob are selfish fools, incapable of taking care of themselves or anyone else in the real world.

> Limberlost Island is a wasteland, from which I had to escape to live.

> I'm alone and must face all dangers on my own.

Although not guilty of anything that the FBI was preparing for a grand jury, I had a whole wagon load of hubris and walking-around-blind issues that the feds couldn't adjudicate. I'd always avoided the dark, boggy areas in all my work related to national security technologies, but I've been too blithe, thinking I can just do my little work and not attract evil into my own world.

§

While I pondered the universe and tried to nap in that holding cell, Tom Tremain had connected with Detective Jeremiah in Seattle to chat about dead guys, which was when the body in the freezer came onto the FBI's radar. Tom also traced the vehicle ID from that wreck. It was mine.

One small piece of luck that came from being solo in a cell: the tantrum over my wrecked car went unobserved.

In the very early morning, the feebs gave me bad coffee, access to my attorney, and the news that the feds were accusing me of accessory to murder, when all I'd killed was my own BMW. And maybe my career.

One more delusion I had to face:

The blue guy in the Soul Meets Body freezer had nothing to do with me.

Therefore, I was living in a mystery story, but I still didn't know the nature of my real sin, or how I would be redeemed.

While I answered questions for the FBI guys, Stephen Trowbridge, whom Matt had suggested as my attorney, asked me only once to plead the Fifth Amendment. My chief interrogator, Evan Mulasky, was the same height and about the same age as me, but with much better posture and a ginger complexion. Ramrod posture. Military-short hair. He didn't seem comfortable wearing a suit as everyday attire. Although he looked straight at me when I spoke, it always seemed as if he was seeing someone else (say, the guilty person he believed I was).

I rallied every bit of my meager social skills, but I couldn't get us on the same page with Agent Mulasky. One of us would interrupt, thinking the other had finished speaking. We'd proceed at length, and then find that one of us held mistaken beliefs, so the questions had to be asked again. It made for a long humorless morning, punctuated frequently by him saying "No" and tapping the desk with the heel of his hand at any point when he disagreed with me.

I became distracted by a quirk the agent had: before he asked a new question, he'd line up his pen and yellow pad so they were at a ninety-degree angle from the table top, and he'd nudge the yellow pad so it was at a precise distance from the edge. Two inches, I think. Then he'd sit even more erect, bore a hole into me with his eyes, and ask the next question. Or ask the previous question all over again. Since I read somewhere that mirroring posture builds trust, I mirrored his movements: lining up my single sheet of paper and the pencil nub they'd allowed me. Except instead of sitting up straight to answer, I leaned toward him, opened both hands, and spoke as earnestly as I could, hoping my honesty was apparent in my open attitude. It didn't seem to contribute to my get-on-the-same-page goals.

At the end, Agent Mulasky gave me a transcript to sign as a sworn statement. You can see portions of the day's hassle in that transcript:

I have never met anyone named Konstantin Petrenko.

I've heard of the White Knights as a cybercrime syndicate, but I never met them until they appeared on Limberlost Island with guns.

Alec Ramsey was on Matt's porch with those creeps. He is not the body in the freezer. When we met, he presented his ID to the receptionist, who confirmed he was Alec Ramsey the attorney. You'll find all the email from his law firm on the servers. He was in my office for two weeks. You'll find papers from him all over my desk.

No, I did not wipe my e-mail store and I didn't destroy the hard copies in my office. There are rules against that. Haven't you found the backup mail stores on the server?

Why would I torch my own house? How could I do it when I wasn't even there? Why would I destroy my own car?

There really is a security crisis. I reported it when I first discovered the chipset error. I didn't create a second crisis. I'm not threatening anyone, and you need to call the people I named so we can prevent any damage.

As soon as Evan Mulasky got around to asking—rather late in the session—I gave them the crypto key for my laptop, which they'd taken from Matt's house. I was a tiny bit pleased that they hadn't otherwise found a way into my machine.

§

The night alone felt like an eternity, the question session felt like Eternity+n. Then, just before I was to be arraigned for the sack of extravagant charges, most of the insanity went away. The feds dropped all their charges, leaving only Washington State's vehicular endangerment claim (they wanted someone to pay for that hole in the road on Lost Point Loop).

After nearly twenty-four hours of fear and trepidation, I no longer was in dire jeopardy with the FBI. Physically free, I retained the heart-palpitating fear that foreign enemies were hacking the nation's infrastructure *at that very moment*, using intellectual assets I had created.

Only now I was being heard. My help was requested to understand the security situation. While we were in the middle of shifting gears (from adversarial to cooperative), Quinn showed up in response to an international call that interrupted his ski trip. He burned with a fire hotter than what burned my house. Or my car.

Quinn cleans up well. He came dressed as Fake Steve Jobs in jeans, black turtleneck, grey silk suit jacket, with his hair slicked down. His demeanor was a 180-degree-turn from the nervous Quinn who coded with me, though his fingers still twitched at his side in unguarded moments. He brought along his attorney and a mutual acquaintance from the NSA, a guy who worked with my old Z-Crypto team in the Lights Out in Estonia days—one of the people I'd suggested that the FBI call to help connect the dots in a better way than they had.

Evan Mulasky, the FBI guy who led the questioning earlier that day, shook hands with the NSA guy, who shall remain nameless. And in the Pacific Northwest, "guy" is a gender-neutral phrase, so I'm not even giving up that much detail about my friend.

"I'm late to the party," the NSA guy said. "I understand there's some confusion about the identity of the perpetrators in a series of events."

"We arrested Ms. Byron based on evidence provided by an informant," Evan said. "The tip came through a private security con- tractor, who gave us the Internet address of her computer where code was stolen."

"As if Ms. Byron conspired to steal her own software!" My NSA friend slapped the back of his FBI colleague and laughed, as if we all had come to see the cosmic joke.

Evan said, "No, we believed Ms. Byron conspired with foreign mobsters to create an artificial crisis, in order to accrue value for her work through cyberblackmail." This was the argument that Stephen and I battled earlier in the day.

"Yet now we know Ms. Byron tried to avert a national crisis." My NSA guy smiled. A palpable hostility existed between my NSA guy and Agent Mulasky.

While Stephen continued to make *shut up* signs, I said, "You wasted a day looking for me. If you guys—" by whom I indicated all the federal agents in the room "—had trusted the local law on Limberlost and let them know what you wanted, Tom Tremain would have told you exactly where I was."

"We were waiting for enough information to get a warrant," Evan said. "We had good evidence."

"You had good intentions," my NSA guy said, in a peace effort. "Everyone else in this room wants the same thing."

"Yes," I said, in spite of Stephen's raised index finger, which meant *shut up*, "to protect the public from bad guys."

"Who are now a day ahead of us," Quinn said, "since we were all comatose with Christmas pudding while Sam tried to raise an alarm."

§

By the time Quinn and I made it across downtown to his office, my ex-CEO Gerard and three of his Z-Crypto programmers were there, ready to go to work. Tackling the tasks with Gerard would have felt weird if I had mind space left to think about it. Intimacy had utterly ceased between us, so working together was merely ordinary, though I noted his serious suit and upscale haircut.

Also, I now had both NSA and FBI watchdogs; the former could follow the technical discussion; the latter, Evan Mulasky, slowed our work down by frequently interrupting: "Hey, are you guys talking in code?"

"Yes," the NSA guy said, "they are."

The Z-Crypto fix was straightforward—as I had predicted before various Acts of God and a weak cellular infrastructure disrupted communications. Quinn and I worked with Z-Crypto to get fixes to all possible targets for intrusion, starting with the power utilities. I will not provide technical details—and not just because my friendly NSA shadow reviews all my communications, written and verbal, cyber or postal.

Gerard's task was to convince the hyper-conservative Chief Technology Officers of public utilities and other institutions to deploy the fix without waiting the usual ten days for stabilization testing. The NSA guy put his crew to work in support of the Z-Crypto effort. Gerard seemed to revel in the high-level NSA attention. Me? Although my NSA friend is a good guy, I reconfirmed my decision six months ago: Do not get too tangled up with those guys.

"We'd have gotten this far faster if you'd answered my damn messages," I whispered to Gerard while the NSA guy was whiteboarding the structure of communications for the utilities and other possible targets.

"How was I supposed to tell the difference between real messages and all your stalker crap?" Gerard seemed as indignant as I felt.

"Stalker? Me?" I forgot to whisper. "You're the one who's been stalking me, Mister Blue Hat Lover."

"Ms. Byron, do you have details to share with us?" the NSA guy said. As if I were talking to Matt at the back of calculus class.

"We're discussing instant messages we received over the course of these events," Gerard said, as if he were innocent. "I misunderstood Sam's messages and missed the emergency."

Then Gerard added to the proposed messaging from NSA: the only Z-Crypto name in public messaging would be his. So I owe the preservation of my public reputation to Gerard. It seemed generous and chivalric of him.

"Thank you for keeping my name out of it," I said. "Even though that beta was my architecture."

"We changed the architecture," he whispered at the end of the conference table. "And we can't manage the PR correctly if we blame former employees."

Two more lessons for me: Don't second-guess Gérard. Write better email.

124. Matt Wins

PETE, USEFUL FOR ONCE, convinced Karl that it was safe for him to come back on board as my legal representation. When I flew Alaska Air to Oakland for the deposition, I dressed exactly as Karl had instructed: a closet-aged corduroy sports jacket, a blue shirt with frayed cuffs, and my dad's necktie.

Ahead of me in the TSA line, Danny got on the same flight and sat with a gentleman in a wool blazer and Dockers, whose cop shoes indicated a long-time law enforcement professional who wanted to be in the field again. He might as well have worn a name tag that read "Air Marshall." Danny kept his nose buried deep in the in-flight magazine, and I traded my aisle seat with a mother who needed to sit closer to her two children. We continued to ignore each other at the Oakland airport, when Danny walked away with his new best friend.

The goal for the day, I told myself on the cab ride into downtown Oakland, was merely to endure the questioning. I'd started this whole lawsuit just to make sure someone paid while still preserving the cover I'd created for myself and others, though that plan seemed to have devolved into self-torture. The elevator, as I remember it, rose more slowly than any in the world. I stared at the backs of businessmen's necks, counted the fake marble squares on the wall, watched as floor numbers lazily appeared on the LED display. People shuffled on and off, as I stepped farther and farther to the rear.

This attorney's office had the sink-knee-deep carpeting and glowing rich woodwork of an outfit whose second-year attorneys charge four-fifty an hour. Following the receptionist to the meeting room, I shook hands with Karl, who'd flown in earlier than I could, and shook hands with the County attorney, and then with our host for the day.

That attorney opened the door to a meeting room with a decent view across the Bay, leather chairs, and a rosewood conference table that probably cost my last year's salary.

At which sat Danny, his father Yevgeny Petrenko, and his uncle, whom I recognized from pictures as Dymtrus Petrenko. The brothers came across more as late-middle-aged Smothers Brothers than the newly crowned heirs of a modest-sized criminal empire. Dymtrus was the taller of the two, but Yevgeny did most of the talking and was the better dressed. Dymtrus looked like his wife still shopped Nordstrom Rack for his clothes. The less verbal of the two, he watched everything in the room, hyper-alert.

"Hey, dude!" Danny stood to shake my hand, almost tipping over his chair. The desperate Danny had disappeared and the over-eager surfer had returned. "How's it hanging?"

"Just fine, Danny. And you?"

"My son says you entertained him well at Christmas," Yevgeny said. "Our entire family thanks you for your hospitality.

"You're OK?" I asked. Danny's face was badly bruised. I assumed that the FBI was using Danny, handling him better than I had. "No hard feelings?"

"Of course not." Danny turned to their attorney. "I slipped on the ice at Matt's house. No blame."

We didn't do depositions that day. Instead, each and every one of the Petrenkos apologized: their brother Konstantin had let his anger lead him astray about me. Good friends had assured these brothers that I meant them no harm, and their attorney had prepared a proposed offer for a full settlement. It was their negligence that had led to my so-called accident. Although they'd hired security for the wedding, unsavory neighbors had spoiled the day by attacking my friend Sonny and turning on me when I tried to protect him.

Alameda County's attorney sat with his arms crossed, never saying one damn thing.

Karl held the cashier's check in his hands. I read a number that was sixty-five percent larger than the total we'd been seeking from both opposing parties. The related papers to sign as a condition of accepting that check were simple: they acknowledged liability and left it open for me to approach them again if I developed future health and welfare issues related to my unfortunate experiences that day. The statement on the page was too short for Karl to beg time to study it in detail.

"You are being too kind," I said. Karl kicked me under the table.

"The Petrenko family would like to conclude this," their attorney said.

"So we can all forget about it," Yevgeny said.

"And never speak of it again," his brother said.

We signed. We shook hands.

Effing Yevgeny Petrenko slapped me on the back and begged my forgiveness for this misunderstanding among gentlemen.

The County's attorney remained silent. This wouldn't cost them a damn thing—not a single admission for having blasted their way into a tense situation, and not a dollar spent by the County toward my well-being.

125. Sam Has a Cookie and Thinks About It

AT THE END OF THAT very long night, after Gerard and his team departed, Quinn invited our FBI and NSA friends to stay while he reviewed what his team had provided when the FBI came with their search warrant.

"Oh boy!" I said.

Still irked that I hadn't been sent to SuperMax, Evan said to Stephen, "Please remind your client that everything she says can and will be used against her if any new criminal activity is exposed."

"Can you advise that advisor to give it up already?" I asked Stephen, who ignored me.

"Actually," Natalia Dragon appeared in the conference room, her arms full of file folders, "I've reviewed the available data, and I believe I can show exactly where Sam Byron is culpable in what happened."

She really, really doesn't like me. Natalia Dragon took fifteen minutes to lay out the details she'd amassed, having been busy from the moment the FBI showed up at South Lake Union with a warrant. I kept wondering why Quinn put Natalia on the forensics task. As it turns out, there's no surprise that he had a superstar forensics person for his network administrator. It's a coincidence that she happens to look like she could take a role in a James Bond movie. She doesn't publish or speak at security conferences, so there's no way I'd recognize her. My former dismissive view of the role of network administrator is a different issue, for which I feel shame.

"If you'll examine my research, you'll see that Ms. Byron wasn't responsible for any code destruction or theft," she said, as she passed around folders with her research. "At least not directly."

"Not at all," I asserted.

Natalia's eyes flashed at me. "You're so much in love with having groupies hang on your every word, a pair of moon-eyed guys didn't flash on your radar."

She has tattooed eyeliner. I'm not brave enough to go there, but it must pay off in efficiency every day. Also, she still scares me. So I was defensive.

"I don't have groupies."

"Phffttt!" Her air-spit ruffled her Bond Girl bangs from where they'd been gelled into place. "The sole person in our office to pay attention to in this investigation—besides the fake attorney—is Nick Peterson. Your attorney friend couldn't quit staring at your ass, and Nick couldn't quit staring into your eyes."

"I've given details about Nicky to the FBI, Natalia—"

"At every blackhat or bluehat conference where you speak, there's two dozen fanboys hanging on your every word. That's where we recruited Nick, and he was gaga for you then."

"I thought Nicky was your lover," I said. "I chose to be discreet and look the other way."

"*Pul-eeze*," Natalia said. I swear you could hear *bitch* under her breath. "That doesn't pass any reality sniff test. Why would I doodle with a twit like Nicky? I've got two kids and a guy who cares about me. Anyway, Nicky had a crush on you from before you even came to Seattle. When he heard Quinn brought you on board, it was like he'd been sucked up to heaven."

While I added that to the multiple kinds of blindness I'd pondered in jail, Natalia continued. "If a Russian organized crime element is involved, Nicky Peterson is either the informant or the code thief."

"Nicky told me he stole the solution to prove he had a better business model," I said. "He said his cousin Alec stole the chipset details and the test plan for intrusion vectors. And Nicky isn't Russian. The creeps who came for me were Russian. Nicky looks— I don't know. French? Not Slavic."

"As if his actual ethnicity matters?" Natalia said. Her tattooed eyeliner heightened the challenge.

"Girls, let's all work together," Evan said.

"Girls?" Natalia focused her Slayer stare on Evan. "Did you just say 'girls'?"

Evan squirmed—we all knew he'd been trained better—and NSA guy smirked, and from there on, the hostility chilled between Natalia and me.

Sandwiches showed up for dinner and Evan asked for a bio break. Only Quinn and I seemed used to working long hours without a break. Oh, and Natalia who didn't drink coffee and probably received an iron bladder from the Bond Girl field equipment store. As we reconvened and chewed on cardboard sandwiches, potato chips, and oatmeal-raisin cookies prepared in the previous decade, Natalia restarted the conversation, distributing printouts to each of us.

"From what I can determine, all the code movement up to Christmas Eve was by Nick Peterson. He took tiny increments of your code over several weeks, which was why our algorithms for detecting code movement over the network didn't catch it."

My NSA buddy said, "The FBI's informant said to look for code theft on Christmas Eve and Christmas Day."

"Yeah," Evan said, grasping at the straw thrown his way, while chewing on one of the straw-flavored sandwiches from our box lunches. "That was the basis for our warrant. The records we seized showed the code was sent from Ms. Byron's computer. Are you saying it's this other guy who did it?"

Natalia said, "The Christmas Eve and Christmas Day activities were from Sam's desktop computer here, but sent by someone else, not through Nicky's accounts, like the other transfers were."

"So one guy stole the problem, and Nicky stole the answer?" Evan said. "Like Spy versus Spy?"

"Yeah," Quinn spoke up, having been silent through most of this discussion. "The Mad Magazine version."

I pushed further on this. "The logs I studied from the utility servers showed attacks on Christmas Eve, attempting two of the attack vectors we'd identified. So someone got our work then and was trying it out."

"Attack vectors?" code-illiterate Evan asked.

"The ways in which bad guys might exploit the chipset error that Sam found." Quinn patiently explained it to Evan, again.

"But it didn't work on Christmas Eve, right?" Evan asked.

NSA guy and I were looking at each other: we'd studied similar blackhat actions before. NSA guy said, "Power went out on Limberlost Christmas day."

"Yes, but thanks to crappy, aged infrastructure, it was because of the weather." I'd never thought it could be a blessing that a local utility hadn't hardened their infrastructure. "The utility power outage stopped our code thieves from repeated efforts."

"The White Knights' hackers weren't good enough," my NSA champion said. "That's why they came looking for Sam's help."

"Did you find Nicky's fingerprints in Sam's office?" Quinn asked Evan.

"We don't have matches for any fingerprints taken, except people documented in your Human Resources files," Evan said. "Also, no matches in Ms. Byron's office, except for her own prints."

Quinn praised Natalia. "You were right about the security protocol for our H.R. practices."

"Except," Evan said, "no prints matching your H.R. file for Nicky Peterson appear anywhere in your offices."

Quinn mused. "Half of this is industrial espionage, not national security."

Evan nodded, but my NSA guy shook his head. "Industrial espionage involves stealing trade secrets for a foreign concern. If this Nicky person stole your code to do business with a U.S. company, then it's only theft of trade secrets. So unless he's a foreign national—"

"Nicky is just an effing ghost." Natalia tossed her pen down. "We're getting nowhere."

Quinn said, "Our patent work should cover all issues if anyone else tries to use our fix."

"You mean all the work I did with the Fake Alec Ramsey?" I too tossed my pen. "Who stole all the patent work and details for all the attack vectors?"

§

They failed to find Nicky or other unaccounted individuals in any B&B on Limberlost. No one on the island except Yuri answered the posters and local newspaper articles seeking information. The owner of Casa D reminded Tom Tremain of his Christmas visitors. Based on the picture, Yuri avowed that Nicky had been in the café, using the Internet. Though he claimed that Nicky was a gangster, he couldn't remember exactly what Nicky had said or done. *"Too many gangsters that day."*

From all the information that Tom Tremain, the feds, and the state patrol gathered, it seems that after I shouted "Nimrod!" at Nicky and jumped in the ditch, he disappeared off the face of the earth.

126. Matt and the Brothers United

THE END HAPPENED SO much faster than the elevator ride up that it's a blur in my mind. Karl had to split for other work in the city, and I found myself alone in a cab and headed back to the airport. I checked in and begged for an earlier flight than I'd originally reserved, only to find that my seat had been upgraded to first class, so I could switch to the next flight north.

In the first-class lounge, Yevgeny and Dymtrus appeared, ushering me over to share drinks.

"The Macallan 18 Year, I believe?" Yevgeny asked.

They quickly cut through the greetings and we're-so-sorry claims.

"We're missing some relatives," Yevgeny said. The gold on his many finger rings flashed when he tipped his glass to drink. "Danny and your friend Pete Byron think you can help us sort out what happened and find our boys."

This was what they wanted in exchange for that cashier's check and the plane ride home. "I don't know how I could help," I said, swallowing harder than a sip of Macallan required.

"My brother Konstantin, the one who was being such a hard-ass with you, he's gone," Yevgeny said.

"The body of an elderly gentleman was found in a latrine in the mountains," Dymtrus said. "On Interstate 90."

"That other young man found near your house?" Yevgeny said, asking a rhetorical question to which I pretended not to know the answer.

Dymtrus said, "Danilov had the idea that we should report them missing, so the police would ask us to identify Konstantin and my nephew Andrij."

"So I did that," Yevgeny said. "It's understandable that Danilov didn't want to get involved while visiting you."

"We were so busy partying, we missed all that excitement," I said, finding that I could still tell lies on demand.

"You can cut the crap," Yevgeny said. "We know Konstantin sent Danny to off you. But my Danny bravely refused, even though he felt certain Konstantin had Andrij taken out for failing the same task."

"You know, after what happened at that wedding, I really don't want to get involved in your family affairs." I sipped at my drink, mustering the stock-in-trade bravado I'd plied in my trade over the past decade.

Dymtrus nodded. "It's understandable. I moved north because of Konstantin. He never could shake loose of his old-country ways."

"Let us tell you the puzzle we have," Yevgeny said. "Pete Byron thinks it will interest you."

"All right." As if I had a choice.

Yevgeny talked. Dymtrus put in a word only now and then, but they seemed thoroughly united in the story they spun.

"Let's start back when Konstantin went off his nutter about you," Yevgeny said. "He kept saying you were a cop and that we needed to prove it. Even when your lawyer went after the Alameda County cops."

"I never understood that," I said.

"I knew you weren't a fed. A government employee couldn't play guitar that well," Yevgeny said. "Did you maybe know your friend was a fed?"

"Pete Byron? How could anyone think that Pete—"

"No, smart boy. The black guy who ate it."

"Sonny. Nah. He was army for years. That's where I met him. But—"

"Yeah, yeah. You married his old lady. She's the one who told Konstantin the guy was fuzz."

I lowered my voice to offer a man-to-man confidence. "You know she took her own life? Her hold on reality had been weak for years. That's why Sonny asked me to look out for her if anything happened to him." Boy, did I fuck that up big time. Knowing now that Konstantin got to her, I added that to the long list of my failings.

Dymtrus sighed like a priest in a confessional. He turned to his brother. "I told Konstantin over and again that lady was a whack job. He got his balls in a wad over fuck all."

Yevgeny wiped the air with his hand, which I think meant Dymtrus was supposed to shut up. Yevgeny said, "No matter. Along the way, Konstantin got involved with new business, so his obsession with you got to be a distraction and he wanted it ended."

"I understood from Danny that Konstantin wanted me dead."

"My brother got involved with some very bad people," Dymtrus said. "We think he pulled my son Olekzandr into his web."

Yevgeny said, "Konstantin always had one thing or another on every one of our boys. There's no saying how he pulled Zandr into this business."

"Nikolai told me, and I didn't listen," Dymtrus said. "So that poor boy was left to battle Konstantin on his own."

Yevgeny nodded in agreement. "As near as we can put it together, when our Nicky uncovered Konstantin's plot, he killed Konstantin and then sent Zandr out of the way to protect him."

"Who is Nikolai?" I asked.

"He's involved with your girlfriend," Yevgeny said.

"He's in love with her," Dymtrus said.

Oh shit.

"She's not my girlfriend," I said.

"Yeah, sure. So now, Peter Byron committed to finding Nicky and Zandr," Yevgeny said, "so we offered to fund his efforts. He says he needs your help."

"I'm afraid we're back where the conversation started," I said. "I don't want to be involved in your family business. I know Pete Byron, but I'm not a close associate of his."

"And I'm the czar of all Russia," Yevgeny said.

Dymtrus said, "We heard that my son Zandr went home to the motherland. Peter Byron says he can find Zandr with your help."

"I have family here to worry about," I said.

"You'll talk to Pete, though, yes?" Yevgeny asked, but didn't wait for an answer. "We told him about the bad people Konstantin got involved with. Those people came to us, asking us to give up Nikolai and Zandr. We need to protect our boys."

"They're threatening your family? That's not fair!" I aped being astounded, and from the looks on both men's faces, they didn't miss the irony.

"We think of Pete as family," Dymtrus said. "He says all of this is like a threat to his own family."

My stomach fell into my shoes at that point.

To Pete, "like" means "is."

"That's Alaska Air calling my flight," I said as I rose to leave, unhappy about Pete's lifelong ability to get me involved where I don't want to be.

"We'll stay out of your way, Mr. Owens," Dymtrus said as he shook hands good-bye. "Call if you see trouble."

They left before I did. Besides over-tipping the wait staff in the lounge, they left a very thick pile of hundreds on the table.

127. Sam Just Asks a Simple Question

WE ALL WATCHED CCTV playback from inside and outside Quinn's office suite. You can see Fake Alec Ramsey coming in with Quinn and me on the days we worked together.

The NSA guy and Evan took a break together, which seemed to help Evan sharpen his toolset. When they returned, Evan said. "Based on the Seattle detectives' work, they think this guy killed the real Alec Ramsey. We assume he did it to steal the real attorney's identity."

"Fake Alec Ramsey wasn't smart enough to insert his badge correctly in the reader," Natalia asserted.

"He could have lifted others' cards," I said. "That would account for the nights when other people were logged in who weren't actually around." Based on Natalia's research, that included Nicky, Natalia, and Quinn himself. So I wasn't the only one who was conned by Fake Alec Ramsey.

"How'd he get into your office or the server room?" Natalia asked, genuinely curious. She'd stopped harassing me for being a groupie hound. "Those doors all have electronic keypad locks."

Indeed Alec wasn't the brightest pony in the harness while we worked. I closed my eyes to picture Alec in action, striving to re-member anything unusual. "He took me to a show at a casino one night. After the music, he tried to teach me how to count cards at blackjack, to show off."

Natalia nodded at this insight. "Yes, that's got to be it. You can see him watching on the CCTV footage."

"What are you implying?" Even asked.

"Fake Alec learned Sam's password and door lock-code by watching her key them in," Natalia said.

Since I don't let people watch me type PINs or passwords, it seems that the "attorney" metadata erroneously attached to Fake Alec Ramsey had caused me to lower my persistent-paranoia defenses. One more item on Sam's "walking around blind" list.

On the CCTV footage, Alec's hooded figure comes in and—thankfully—left again before I returned to the office on Christmas Eve night. Evan said that fingerprints for Fake Alec were everywhere (including on my keyboard) and in the freezer where the real Alec Ramsey was found. However, the feds couldn't correlate them to anyone on record, including people with known ties to Russian syndicate crime organizations.

After working through the night, we had two ghosts and two kinds of code transfer, but only one blue body accounted for. No one said aloud what chilled me: If I'd walked any faster over all those hills between Leschi and South Lake Union, Fake Alec and the White Knights wouldn't have had to come to Limberlost to snatch me.

128. Matt Is Called to Reserve Duty

WHEN I DISEMBARKED AT SeaTac, Pete met me with another boarding pass, a backpack, and my passport.

"One bag each," he said. "We travel on their expense account. To help Sam."

"We aren't going anywhere." I used the pain compliance move from early law enforcement training to steer him to the taxi stand on Level Three. "We're going to help Sam right here in Seattle."

"But my benefactors—"

"Can go screw themselves."

Our first stop was the FBI offices. I asked for a friend (who shall remain nameless) in the organized crime unit. Pete helped list all members of the entire Petrenko family by showing all the footage he had ever shot, including that stupid green-screen thing he made, combining shots from my second wedding with footage he'd shot at a porn farm in the Ukraine.

"That's the guy we're looking for!" The agent just about leaped over the table to grab Pete's laptop when he showed the fake porn king.

"Can we keep this in perspective?" I said. "Konstantin Petrenko dictated everything in North America. The power has switched to his brothers."

"They just play in stolen goods and porn." The agent laughed. "Several agencies are looking for this guy. He's a master-mind of coded messaging among the eastern Europe oligarchs.

"I don't think it's this guy," Pete said. "He was the fix-it guy on a server farm in the Ukraine. I think he slept there."

"But he's in the U.S." My agent friend was getting too excited.

"He was at the wedding in the Castro Valley last year," Pete said, glancing at me. "He's some orphan cousin that the rest of them treat like a tool. He followed me around that day, wanting to talk about video as art."

The agent shook his head. "He's the mastermind of a huge cybercrime network. Not just the porn-farm in your picture. He runs a blog that delivers coded instructions for partners in Russia and the Ukraine.

Pete disagreed. "He's a nice guy who's lettuce, meat, and mayo short of a full sandwich. I haven't seen him since that day."

"Let me show you what we have." The agent insisted.

We watched clips from YouTube that they'd retrieved from links on this dude's blog: Petrenko family footage from a different directorial viewpoint than Pete's work, including shots of a family dinner that proved only half the Petrenko family had truly disgusting table manners. While the agent took notes, Pete and I named the cousins we'd fingered earlier in Pete's footage. A couple other videos showed family business activities in action.

The agent said, "There's a message in all this. We just haven't been able to decode it. We've called in experts from the private sector."

"It's an homage to Nicolas Winding Refn, don't you think?" Pete mused. "The nature of the violence. The camera angles. I don't think there's a coded message. Except maybe the traditional one."

"What's that?" the agent asked.

"'Fuck with me, I'll fuck you up,'" Pete said.

At that point, we'd given my agent friend all we had. Except he held out his hand as we prepared to depart. Pete reluctantly handed over his laptop.

129. Sam Looks at Pictures

"LET'S WRAP IT FOR tonight," Quinn said. It was already after four in the morning. I was still used to those kinds of hours, but fatigue was showing on everyone else, except Natalia Dragon.

Yet the day wasn't over. Evan stopped Stephen at the door. "Can you bring Ms. Byron downtown? We have more evidence we'd like her to review."

Stephen was negotiating for a time later in the day.

"Can we just do it now?" I said.

§

In a better lit conference room in the Federal building than where they'd questioned me the day before, with more comfortable chairs, Evan Mulasky set photos before me, all action shots, no mug shots.

"Do you recognized any of these people?"

"Yes!" Relieved that everyone wasn't a ghost, I pointed to one. "That's Alec Ramsey. Or at least, he said he was."

Evan said. "What about this one?"

"Wait," I said. "Are you going to tell me who it is?"

"We believe that it's Olekzandr Petrenko of the Petrenko crime family. Now this person."

He pointed to the blue guy I'd last seen in the trunk of the Challenger. In the picture he appeared in a tuxedo, lifting one of those demi-flutes for the bad champagne you get at a reception, offering a toast. The long-haired wedding singer on the stage behind him stared at the camera.

These were Pete's pictures.

I was stumped for what to say next. In another picture, the same gentleman who toted a dirty pillowcase on the early morning ferry ride with me and then appeared in the Challenger's trunk lifted his flute of bubbly while a shaved-and-groomed version of Danny,

Matt's hostage, was being punched in the shoulder by the blue guy I'd found on the dock. Maybe I imagined it, but the photograph caught Danny's face in a frozen half-smile, like someone who had been bullied since first leaving home for kindergarten.

Not liking that I found myself in Matt's business without guidance, I pointed to Danny. "This person was visiting at Matt Owens's house and left with Tom Tremain. This person," I pointed to the champagne tooter, "was on the ferry to Limberlost on Christmas morning. He wasn't so well dressed then. Perhaps the owner at Café D might recognize him." I pointed to Maybe-Andrij. "This looks like the person we found dead on Limberlost Christmas day."

"Are you sure?" Evan asked.

"No. I only saw that body for a moment and—" Blue Guy One. Blue Guy Two. "He was tied and wrapped in plastic like the body in the freezer at Soul Meets Body. Did Fake Alec Ramsey kill them both?"

"We don't think the killings are related," Evan said.

"The bodies were both bound in the same way."

"We have evidence—" Evan began.

"Phffttt!" I said, quoting Natalia. "You made up a lot of things about me without evidence."

"We have *good* evidence," Evan paused to emphasize, "that this man and another body found in a state park are part of inter-gang violence." He pointed to the guy who provided ballast in the trunk of my car. "They aren't ethnic Russian. If there's any relationship, we believe it's because the same Russians who pursued you were taking out their competitors."

"Well, that's a relief," I said.

§

Not much relief at all.

When we all stepped onto the street, even Agent Mulasky felt friendly toward me. I was sure we weren't near our last conversation. He dropped me back at Quinn's office.

As he departed, I stood alone on Terry Avenue North. It was warmer, only just at freezing point, after five days in the teens and twenties. The snow would start to melt soon, leaving the Greater Puget Sound Area to navigate through a giant mud slushy. People would rescue their abandoned cars and restock food and T.P. from the supermarkets. Tomorrow would be just another work day.

Dawn wanted to break. The mercury vapor street lights cast sepia shadows. I peered up and down the street, not able to peak around any corners, hoping not to see White Knights waiting for me. Nothing seemed out of place. Similar to Christmas Eve dawn except for the snow. Maria had flipped on the neon at Soul Meets Body. I waved to her, but she was busy with her first customer, who stood staring out the window while she pulled espresso. She held up his coffee cup. He fetched what she offered and returned with it to the window: a blond fellow in a dark wool coat like men wear in London. I placed bets with myself: an Oxford maths graduate, interviewing in South Lake Union for a Big Data job. Private companies have to fish far and wide, since NSA picks up most of the math PhD geniuses from U.S. universities.

A black Jeep Cherokee pulled up to the curb. I hesitated on the top step until I recognized the driver.

How long would I be looking over my shoulder?

5

Harley and Roz drove me back to Limberlost Island. At that point, there was nowhere else to go.

"Where's Matt? Please tell me Pippi is OK," I said.

"She's fine," Roz said. "She's visiting her Aunt Isabella in New York. I'm joining her tomorrow."

"Good," I said. "Tom Tremain was right to insist. Is Matt OK?"

"See," Roslyn said to Harley. She was really happy, for some reason. "Sam proved my point herself."

"What point?" I asked. "That I still get everyone else in trouble?"

"You got caught behind an FBI mistake," Harley said. "None of us ever thought otherwise."

"Then what's Roz's point?"

"She says you're in love all over again," Harley said.

"I was never in love," I said.

"Oh?" Roslyn said. "Will it be more than ten years this time before you get over it?"

"I've got a lot of other stuff on my mind right now," I said. "I'm not thinking about love."

"Really? That's why Matt was the first person you asked about?"

"Why didn't he come?" I said aloud what had been nagging me.

"Matt had a deposition date in Oakland yesterday," Harley said. "Pete picked him up at SeaTac. They should be back later today."

"Matt's not ticked off at me?"

"Why would he be?" Harley was puzzled.

"Because he got thrown in jail when the FBI came for me. Is he ticked off?"

"That I'm not sure about," Harley said as he drove up the ramp to the Limberlost ferry. "You'll have to ask him."

130. Nicky Watches the Detectives

SAMSARA BYRON STOOD ON the curb looking around, and then got into the backseat of a black SUV.

Earlier, when that crowd of people left Quinn's office, everyone was laughing. That meant most things had been set right in her world. From his viewpoint in the café window, Nicky surveyed the frozen, nearly deserted streets. No sign of any White Knights.

Nicky shifted in his seat. He picked up the cheap cell phone from the café table, guessed at the number, and sent a text.

Unidentified> You lose zandr. They just shut every door. Bet white knights want their $$$ bak.

Zandr> shut up niky. U know they can trace everything.

Unidentified> Except me. Bye zandr.

The café had switched to Espresso Vivace—beans, signage, branding on the cups. No more Caffé Vita. Nicky wondered if she would approve.

How long would he have to keep looking out for her? Might there still be an opportunity to serve as her hero? Or were the White Knights now interested only in finding his cousin Zandr?

Epilogue

131. Sam and the Way We Live Now

MATT USED THE INSURANCE PAYOUT from his accident to get a really well-made glass eye. If you don't know Matt, it probably looks normal. However, you can read the expression on only one half of his face. The way I read it, Matt's face says he loves me in equal parts with how much he loves Pippi.

Insurance payouts are due on my house and car. Quinn and Natalia triangulated my cell phone data from Christmas Eve, to map the exact position of all those abortive calls and texts, and the insurance company accepted that as proof that I didn't set my own house on fire—oh that, and a note from the FBI.

Mrs. Waddington and Tom Tremain helped convince my insurers that I didn't blow up my own car. In fact, her watchfulness gave Tom and the state police enough information about the White Knights' other SUV that the vehicle and driver were seized at SeaTac rental check-in. Mrs. Waddington saw it all, because she took pictures to document the inconvenience she had endured from "that oaf," by whom she meant Uncle Bob, who traipsed through her yard all of Boxing Day.

In December I had a modest personal fortune, which grew considerably when stock prices rose over the holiday. Although most of my liquid assets disappeared on Christmas Eve, my attorney made my credit card companies and FDIC-insured banks eat their losses, since not one of them put up a red flag while my accounts were being raided by Fake Alec Ramsey. Thankfully the FBI placed that credit flag on Boxing Day, even if it was for the wrong reasons.

The last trace anyone could make of Nicky Peterson was a B&E on Limberlost on Christmas night. No fingerprints. A giant phone bill to somewhere in Transfu— oh, never mind. Pippi makes me pay up if I use words like that. Let's just say, "To an untraceable eastern European endpoint." There was also a huge pay-per-view charge on Christmas night:

> *North by Northwest*
> *Crimes and Misdemeanors*
> *Marathon Man*
> *The Mysterious Death of Nina Chereau*

Obviously it was Nicky, since he's a big film buff.

The feds are still looking for Nicky and Fake Alec Ramsey to understand their roles in that national security incident. Matt says they are part of that crime family, but both disappeared. Pete says he's working on finding them—from what evidence, I do not know.

Pete says that we should hope that Alec and the bad guys come back for me. "That way, the good guys can grab them."

I don't agree, since I find myself looking twice whenever a car turns into the driveway off Lost Point Road. My attorney argued for federal protection, since I'm a crime victim in danger. The FBI agreed to electronic tracking plus computer access to all my activities for thirty-six months. I'm not sure whether I like that. The tracking device is just an electronic leash, which obscures the tattoo on my ankle, which is one of my favorites. At least I get my own key, so I don't have to wear it in the shower or when I'm in bed, if I'm not sleeping alone.

Gerard invited me to his wedding (he's marrying his director of marketing), but I declined because of deadlines at work. I'm no longer being harassed with his stalking messages, though Gerard claims he is not now and has never been my BlueHatLvr. We never really talked in the past, so I'll have to take his word for it, since it's too late to start a conversation now.

Aunt Lucky's doctor says her debilitation is temporary, though her shaking seems worse on cold, wet days. Myself, I only shake when I drink too much coffee. I live at Aunt Lucky's house, commuting by ferry to work at Quinn's shop in South Lake Union. But most nights I sleep with Matt. Among other things that feel nice, that feels safer. My own house in Seattle, after the repairs, is rented for a year to a friend from Virginia who took a job with one of the local Dark Lords of Big Data. After Pippi finishes the next school year, we can practice making life-changing decisions about urban versus exurban living. Right now the mutual decisions that Matt and I make are more like: "What do you want for dinner tonight?" "I dunno. What do you want?" Since we are each used to going it alone, those kinds of decisions are enough challenge for now.

To give back to the community, as Roz says all privileged adults owe, I tutor math at the high school. I'm betting myself that my kids can beat last year's averaged PSAT scores by at least five points. When her school ends in the afternoon, Pippi comes across the street to meet me at the high school and does her homework while I'm tutoring. Then we drink coffee and cocoa at Yuri's while waiting for Matt to come home.

I've learned my lesson:

> 1) My family—which includes the Owenses, based on performance and how often I eat breakfast at their house— does not present a knee-high speed bump between me and the life I want. I now think of them more as a vert ramp.

> 2) Trash the hubris. (Thanks, Natalia, for clarifying.)

Otherwise, the earth is still round. Its rotation gives the illusion that the sun still rises in the east. With spring coming, the Supreme Master occasionally lifts the dimmer switch behind the grey scrim across Seattle skies.

Last week I got a postcard from Uncle Bob, with excuses for not returning the Challenger. He and Huck are in the Sierra Nevada hills, working to rebuild their capital. Which means, alas, they are back in the weed business, but as members of the working class, rather than entrepreneurs. He promised the return of my Challenger by next Christmas. I look forward to that return more than the Saturn return Huck described in the hand-drawn horoscope he sent on my birthday, along with a note: "Mars is leaving Aquarius. Your urn of bad luck will be emptied with the spring rains."

I hope Uncle Bob makes sure Huck takes his meds. I don't like to think of Huck in a strange town, wheezing over some hippie asthma remedy.

132. Matt Finds His Rhythm

THE FERRY HORN BLASTED as it pulled away from the Limberlost terminal.

"That porn farm video!"

Since I started law school at the UW, I catch the ferry early each morning with Sam and ride into Seattle. At that moment, she stood over me with two cups of canteen-service coffee, so excited that she sloshed her boots. Everyone in the first-level gallery turned to see who disturbed their morning commute by shouting *Porn farm video!*

"What, Sam?"

"The video Pete made with you in Transfu—somewhere. The Ukraine? Where were you? Where was that server farm?"

"I was in Palo Alto getting married. Number two. The worst."

"Oh, I thought it was one of those post-Soviet porn operations."

"It was. Pete edited two clips together to prove—"

"Geezus pieces. Maybe that was Nicky." She sat down beside me and sipped her coffee. "Though I remember thinking the guy was Russian—you know, really Slavic looking. Do you have that video? Where did Pete post it?"

"He pulled it from his website. It was only on his laptop."

"Let's call him now and—oh." She looked out the ferry's clouded window at the grey dawn, drumming her fingers on the ledge. "It was on the last laptop Pete lost, huh?"

"We can ask the next time he Skypes to let us know where he is."

That ferry ride at dawn should give us time to talk, since we are still more kinesthetic than verbal at night, but it's hard to do heart-to-heart at dawn. Besides, she's still obsessed about finding Fake Alec Ramsey and her friend Nicky, so we have conversations like this over sudden epiphanies that might lead to answers. Often we spend time on the ferry's wireless searching for clues, and she tutors me on computer forensics. Sam has a wild idea that forensics would be a good direction for me. "We can be partners," she says.

Riding home alone on the ferry in the late afternoon, I try to get the better part of my law-school homework done. I'm thinking more federal prosecutor than forensics technologies.

Later that morning, I texted my federal friend, the one who seized Pete's laptop, to query whether Pete's data was still under analysis because we might have more insights. Sam and I share almost everything, but not quite all yet. I didn't think it appropriate to share that weak hope.

Everything isn't about that dysfunctional Christmas. First and best, I have a normal, everyday life, with school and work and Pippi. And normal nights: I sleep with a woman who knows who I really am, and seems to like it OK.

Sam proposed some excitement (she needs that more than I do) when Yuri leased the former VFW hall from Lucinda, who had picked it up in a distressed divorce sale. He found the old Drift On Inn neon sign in the café store room, so he reopened the VFW as a lounge, where he serves burgers and beer, plus chardonnay in-a-box for off-islanders and newcomers who need to drink wine when they go out. He gave Sam's Grandma Flo a job as hostess, which keeps both her and Lucinda out of the casinos most nights.

When Yuri opened the inn, Sam pushed me to start a band again, and Yuri lets us rehearse in the hall weekend mornings in exchange for performing one night a week. Eliot's boyfriend (that's another story) plays bass and Josh Parks plays drums, minimally better than the worst drummer in rock and roll (that would be Pete, who's still looking for Petrenko cousins in eastern Europe). Sam plays lead on most songs, since she's the better guitarist. I'm on rhythm and share vocals. About once a month we gig in bars in Silverdale and Bremerton, sometimes as far as Port Townsend. It's a good time. We only make enough cash to pay for gas, but I don't need the money. Which feels good to say.

We play golden-oldie skate-punk and hard-core emo covers at the all-new Drift On Inn every Thursday night. We call ourselves the Lost Point Posse. Come out and see us when you get the chance.

It's on the left after the first light when you drive off the Seattle-Limberlost Island ferry.

133. Nicky Switches Lanes

Nick's American Business 301: Urban Magic Realism
Entry #33: Persuasion – July 4, 12:00 EDT

Apologies for the gap—a personal longueur forced the interruption, giving you the opportunity for lengthy personal studies, eh?

Shooting from New York now, truly indie. I'm exploring Magic Realism, no more film noir. After all, there's no film anymore, right? We're all digital, all the time.

My role model is John Fredericks, who just won best animated feature at Seattle International Film Festival for <u>Monkey King: Journey to the West</u>. My homage to him, while I learn everything I can from what he's pioneered, is Persuasion [working title]. <u>Check out the director's cut.</u>

Nick's Fan Forum | Permanent Link | 4 comments

welcome back!
AuteurGrrrl | Homepage | 4.4 - 1:15 pm |
Nicky, we missed you so! Don't just disappear like that again

Cultural cooptation
BruceRulz | 4.4 - 2:07 pm |
The way Fredericks mixes Asian myth, manga and surrealism—he's really just ripping off other cultures like any other capitalist.

Hardware?
ponyboy | Homepage | 4.4 - 2:11 pm |
What are you shooting with these days, Nicky? I learn the most if I try things out with the same setup. Tell all: model, settings, how you configure the environment.

Persuasion = Sunset Boulevard on meth

JustMike | 4.4 - 2:12 pm |

You just need a body floating in a swimming pool at the beginning and then again at the end.

END — PLAY AGAIN?
⏮ ◀ | ▶ ⏭

About the Author

ANNIE PEARSON lives and writes in Seattle. In addition to the *Rain City Incidents* series, she also writes the *Accidental Heretics* adventure series (as E.A. Stewart).

The *Rain City Incidents* series focuses on life in contemporary Seattle, among people whose work drives their hearts' desires, often in conflict with other love affairs.

Annie Pearson posts about writing and eclectic project planning at www.anniepearson.com.

From Jūgum Press

RAIN CITY INCIDENTS SERIES by Annie Pearson
When bad things happen to quirky people under grey skies

Artemis in the Desert
Eliot Arden, a Seattle artisan, and Sean Frederick Wentworth, the steampunk manga artist, undertake the same motorcycle journey they traveled ten years before. But this time, dreams and desires might just heat up like red slickrock in the sun. Or is that fire sparked by a 900cc bike sliding sideways down a backcountry highway?

Nine Volt Heart
He said, "I love you." She said, "You don't even know the real me." He said, "Great title for a song. Key of G? Can we try close harmony?" Jason, the singer-songwriter, and Susi, a music teacher, meet by accident in Seattle. Secrets, songs, and stalkers quickly entwine their lives in unpredictable ways.

ACCIDENTAL HERETICS SERIES by E.A. Stewart
Lost in the Languedoc Crusade

Bone-mend and Salt (Book 1)
Fight or beg for mercy when enemies turn an unjust war against you? Three ruined crusaders battle conspiracy and disaster while trapped in the new war against the Cathar heresy. Swords and grit must defend against deceit.

Trebuchets in the Garden (Book 2)
How do you prepare for the dawn of the Inquisition? Three embattled crusaders seek justice and respite amidst terror, siege, and conspiracy—as zealots prepare to ignite the next heretics' pyre.

ECLECTIC FICTION

Bad Reputation by Ajax Bell
A close-up portrait of pre-AIDS Seattle that illuminates dark corners, where homeless kids cluster for safety near the revitalized Pike Place Market. *Bad Reputation* contrasts the deeply personal need for friendship with the universal dilemma: people aren't always what they seem.

www.jugumpress.net